Ann Packer [illegible] and three novels, including t[illegible] *n Clausen's Pier*, which recei[illegible] ong many other prizes and h[illegible] *The New Yorker* and in the O[illegible] r work has been translated int[illegible] ne lives between New York, the Bay Area and Maine. Her latest novel, *Some Bright Nowhere*, is published by 4th Estate.

Praise for *The Children's Crusade*:

'Packer's portrayal of one family's breakdown is tragic and utterly engrossing' *O, The Oprah Magazine*

'What sets this novel apart from [Packer's] previous work . . . is how deeply and intimately her big, plot-rich canvas captures the Blair clan's collective and individual yearnings and disappointments . . . Packer's golden touch makes us care that much more deeply for this memorable tribe' *Elle*

'Bursting with poignancy . . . the novel's most refreshing quality is its treatment of Silicon Valley, where the evolution of an essential modern setting is revealed through its reverberations' *New Yorker*

'A big, heavily plotted family saga to dive into and savour: deftly written, at times funny, and always psychologically astute' *NPR*

'Packer is an expert American realist at every level, from the interior monologue to the bird's-eye view' *Vulture*

'Absorbing . . . celebrates family even as it catalogues its damages' *People Magazine*

'Compelling . . . a complex, textured tapestry . . . a gift to the reader' *Boston Globe*

'A superb storyteller . . . Packer's dissection of domestic life reminds me of her elders in the field Anne Tyler and Louise Erdrich . . . I've rarely read a novel so astute about the jumble of love and respect, rivalry and envy, empathy and scorn that makes up family dynamics' *San Francisco Chronicle*

'Psychologically astute . . . this is a novel with something to teach about forgiving the people we love' *Newsday*

'Do our childhood experiences determine our destinies? In shimmering prose and with exceptional wisdom, Ann Packer examines the life of a California family, laying bare the relationships between brother and sister, parent and child, while at the same time revealing the ways in which the past casts both shadow and light on the present . . . a provocative, dazzling novel from a world-class fiction writer' Christina Baker Kline, author of *The Exiles*

'A coming-of-age tale of family as well as an American pastoral; the language is beautiful, painterly, even as it shows us how much of our adult identity has been fully formed in childhood. Ann Packer's eye for detail, her genius at evoking an era with such faithfulness, and her mastery of story make us identify with and deeply care for her characters' Abraham Verghese, author of *The Covenant of Water*

'Packer flawlessly executes the most daring, difficult and exhilarating feat in the novelist's repertoire: to recreate the history of an era and a place through the history of one family, finding intimacy in the sweep of time and import in the nuance of everyday life, pulling it off with mastery, authority and all the passionate artistry that lovers of her work have come to expect' Michael Chabon, author of *The Amazing Adventures of Kavalier & Clay*

'Tender, absorbing . . . Packer has great compassion for her characters, with their ancient injuries, their blundering desires. The way she tangles their perspectives perfectly, painfully captures the tumult of selves within a family' Catherine Newman, in *More*

ALSO BY ANN PACKER:

Some Bright Nowhere

Swim Back to Me

Songs Without Words

The Dive from Clausen's Pier

Mendocino and Other Stories

THE CHILDREN'S CRUSADE

ANN PACKER

4th ESTATE • *London*

4th Estate
An imprint of HarperCollins*Publishers*
1 London Bridge Street
London SE1 9GF

www.4thestate.co.uk

HarperCollins*Publishers*
Macken House, 39/40 Mayor Street Upper,
Dublin 1, D01 C9W8, Ireland

First published in Great Britain in 2026 by 4th Estate
First published in the US in 2015 by Scribner
This 4th Estate paperback published in 2026

1

A catalogue record for this book is available from the British Library

ISBN 978-0-00-873507-4

Set in Adobe Garamond Pro

Printed and bound in the UK [using 100% renewable electricity at CPI Group (UK) Ltd]

FSC
www.fsc.org
MIX
Paper | Supporting responsible forestry
FSC® C013604

To Jane

CONTENTS

THE CHILDREN'S CRUSADE

1

CALIFORNIA LIVE OAK

Bill Blair received his discharge from the navy on a September morning in 1954. He'd served on hospital ships off Inchon and Pusan, Korea, for two years and then completed his service at the Oak Knoll Naval Hospital, a cluster of wooden barracks on a grassy hillside in Oakland, California.

On the afternoon of his discharge, he borrowed a convertible and headed across the Bay Bridge, an unplanned adventure that seemed like just the ticket for a fellow with some time on his hands. The sky was the same lovely shade of blue as the hyacinths in the bridal bouquet at his sister's wedding four months earlier. He'd gotten a weekend's leave and made it home to Michigan in time for a pre-wedding family breakfast at which his years of service were so celebrated that the very thing he'd sought from the trip, a return to the life he'd known before open wounds and gangrenous limbs and amputations, slipped finally and irrevocably out of his grasp. Outside the church, he stood with his parents in his dress blues and felt as lonely as he ever had in his life.

He'd first seen San Francisco from the deck of the U.S.S. *Haven* under a sky choked with clouds. Now, as he drove, he found himself drawn less to the bright downtown than to the low-lying hills beyond it, beribboned with candy-colored houses. He stayed on the highway, heading for the next set of hills, and soon he was moving alongside the pale bay, approaching the airport. Seagulls swooped out of the sky, tiny icons of the aircraft landing on the glittering tarmac. This was the first convertible he'd ever driven, and despite all his time at sea he'd never had quite such a confrontation with the wind. His face was pummeled, his hair blown flatter than the bunk of an enlisted man. Up ahead of him, on the prow of the car, the noble brave Pontiac bore down on the unknown with an attitude of calm determination.

Leaving the bay shore, Bill meandered for a mile or two until he found the King's Highway, or so it would be called if the name were rendered in English—this he knew from the bits of Spanish he'd picked up in Oakland. El Camino Real. This king's highway boasted car lots and supermarkets, nothing to fill Bill's heart, but every so often a vista opened and included the sudden rise of yet more hills, some thickly forested, others the color of hay bales in autumn. He pointed the chrome Indian westward and drove through neighborhoods of brand-new houses that seemed like decoys for something marvelous he would discover soon.

Twisting past a golf course, he entered a grove of pines. Narrow roads split off and disappeared around curves and up hills. On an impulse he followed one of these, winding among low-hanging branches with leaves like tiny silver spears. When he slowed down, a smell of earth and bark came to him, and overlaying that something pleasantly medicinal, the inside of a pharmacy staffed by wood creatures. The road leveled off, and a path beckoned him to leave the car and make his way to a clearing where a magnificent oak tree stood guard.

He was the grandson of a farmer on his mother's side and a doctor on his father's, both third-generation Michiganders. As a boy, he'd expected a life like that of his father, the doctor's son, who'd gone to work at a local bank and was now president and chairman of the board, a man who dressed in a suit and tie every day and had the house painted biannually because it was important to keep up appearances. Bill's mother was an exemplary housekeeper, using vinegar to make the windows sparkle and bleach to keep the bedsheets bright on the line. Known locally as the gal whose one visit to Chicago had left her half-blind after a small rock kicked up by a streetcar struck her in the eye, she had a glass eyeball with a blue iris two or three shades lighter than her true eye color, an asymmetry that made her shy with strangers and unassailable to her children. Bill had grown up believing virtue was a ticket to contentment, but the war had exploded that notion, and he needed something to replace it.

The oak was the most splendid tree he'd ever seen, its gnarled branches snaking every which way. He would learn later that it was a California live oak, species *Quercus agrifolia,* or sharp-leaved oak, and the ground beneath it was carpeted with curled, brittle leaves and peculiar elongated acorns. An idea had been forming during his last months of service that his skills and training could be adapted toward a type of medicine that might, over time, supplant his memories of men blown open with bodies that wouldn't be subjected to such violence: the bodies of children. He would have to do a second residency in pediatrics, but he did not mind the idea of deferring his work life for a few more years. A period of preparation more or less equal to the number of months he'd given the navy might in some way cancel that experience and return him to the confidence and optimism he'd felt on the day he received his sheepskin from the University of Michigan Medical School, the best he could hope for now that his family had mistaken him for a hero. He surveyed the land in front of him and slipped into a reverie in which he was surrounded by children, dozens of them, darting between trees, throwing balls, jumping in leaf piles, calling "olly olly oxen free"—more children than he could father himself but not nearly as many as he could help.

With the assistance of a gift from his father, he put a down payment on the 3.1 acres surrounding the oak tree against a total purchase price that would be laughable a few decades later, when the value of the land had increased by a factor of three hundred. He had no funds left to build anything on the property, and for the next couple of years he saw it only rarely, when he could steal time from the eighteen-hour days and eighty-hour weeks at UCSF, where he was learning the intricacies of health and illness in the young. He lived in a furnished apartment on Frederick Street, where he did little other than sleep the sleep of the exhausted.

From his paternal grandfather he had inherited a 1935 Hamilton Seckron dual-dial doctor's watch. Throughout the war he'd used the second hand to measure the pulse of the injured men he treated, and the habit had stayed with him, so that when the watch stopped working during rounds one morning, he found time the very next day to take it to be repaired.

Reliable Clock and Watch was on Cole Street, a cramped shop with a battered swing counter dividing the entry area from the cash register and the workbench, each of which was occupied: the bench by a bespectacled balding man wearing a blue butcher's apron over a white shirt and tie; and the counter by a slender, gawky girl with messy dark hair and a cameo pin fastened to her blouse.

The girl was Penny Greenway, and the man was her uncle, a bachelor who'd invited his sister's daughter to come from her home in Sacramento to work for him in exchange for room and board and twenty-five dollars a week. Penny had been with him for six months, and along with a little bookkeeping and a few rudimentary dishes to serve him for dinner, she'd learned that time was not just a property of physics but also a receptacle for loneliness.

Initially, she had been somewhat reluctant to accept his offer. He was kind, but through her childhood he'd barely spoken to her, and in fact never spoke much to anyone when he came to visit, only sitting after dinner with her parents and nodding when her mother told him news about people they'd known long before. Penny had had no plans, though, and no beaux, and she viewed his invitation as a solution to the problem that was her life. Desperate to leave home, she said yes with the false certainty that he couldn't be as taciturn as he seemed.

Bill had the air of a hurried businessman, and she was surprised when he went to the trouble of explaining that he was a doctor and needed the second hand for his work. He smiled and waited while she peered at the face of the watch, and she was struck by the way his hurry seemed to vanish, replaced by a kind, keen patience. Her uncle came forward from the repair bench and looked the watch over, frowning in his characteristic way, and she felt an urge to reassure the man that his watch would be right as rain again. Instead, she pulled out a ticket and asked him for his address, and she blushed when he said he lived just around the corner, in an apartment upstairs from the coffee shop where she took her break every afternoon. He said his clothes smelled of hamburger grease but the rent was cheap and he hadn't cooked a meal in over a year.

A few days later, they ran into each other at the coffee shop. "Now we'll see each other all the time," he said as he held the door for her, and she said, "Though until you have your watch back it'll be hard to measure." It took him a moment to react, and she liked the way his plain brown eyes narrowed briefly and then widened again as he smiled.

He came back to the shop the following week. Strapping on his repaired watch, he beamed at the steady spinning of the second hand and said, "Well done," but in a voice so soft she couldn't tell if he was speaking to himself or her. She was tongue-tied and wished she could think of another joke.

"She's partial to pie," her uncle said, coming forward from his bench and using his soft red cloth to wipe oil from his thickened fingertips. He looked at Bill and said, "You can take her for thirty minutes."

Embarrassed, Penny stood still until her uncle gave her a push toward the closet. She pulled her coat from its hook and was about to put it on when Bill took it from her and held it behind her for her arms to find.

"Do you want pie?" he said when they were on the sidewalk.

She shook her head.

"Coffee?"

She looked up and found his eyes focused on hers, gentle and wary. "Let's go this way," she said, and they turned away from the coffee shop and walked two blocks without talking, Bill making sure he didn't outpace her. He was perplexed by what had occurred back at the shop and even more so by his cooperation with it, when he had charts to update from morning rounds and clinic starting in an hour. Yet, seeing how her hair drifted in front of her face, he imagined pushing it back with his fingers.

They came to the corner of Stanyan and Parnassus, where cars raced by in both directions.

"I like pie," she said, "but I can't bake one."

"'Billy Boy'?" he said with a smile, and she had an idea, brief but intense, that he'd come into the shop only to court her.

Up until this point she had lived mostly inside herself, with the world of other people a destination more attractive in the abstract than in reality. At school she had limited herself to one friend at a time, switching every few years. Her classmates viewed her as studious because they had no other way to think about a girl who said little but was well mannered enough to blend in. In fact, she was indifferent to her schoolwork and earned mediocre grades.

She had never liked a boy, and the kisses she'd seen on movie screens suggested the whole business would require more hot breath than she could tolerate. In her experience, men smelled like soap in the morning and it went downhill from there. Her uncle smelled worse than her father, probably because of the cigars he smoked after dinner. Every night he sat in the parlor that looked onto Taraval Street and smoked his cigar and listened to polka music on the hi-fi. He kept time on the arm of his chair, boom-duh-duh, boom-duh-duh, drumming with his palm until Penny had to leave the room so she wouldn't scream. She wondered what it would be like to have Bill Blair sitting in the chair instead. She imagined he would have a lot of interesting things to say.

"Have you been across the Golden Gate Bridge?" she asked him.

"Across it, no. I've been under it. I'd like to go across it someday. I'd like to *walk* across it. Would you?"

She'd been thinking of a ride in a handsome car, with herself wearing new lipstick, but she nodded enthusiastically and said, "Yes, that's my *dream*!"

He smiled and put his hand behind her elbow, signaling that they should cross the street. He liked the way she held her head, cocked slightly to the side. She was dark, whereas his mother and sister were fair.

Bill's first experience with a woman had taken place at a whorehouse in Yokosuka, a ten-minute visit that had given him all the satisfaction of a trapped burp finally making its way up his esophagus and out of his mouth. He'd never gone back, despite the ribbing he got from the other men, who seemed to view the availability of the "hostesses," as they were sometimes called, as the equivalent of a mandate. Since moving to San Francisco, he had taken out four or five nurses, but in each there had been something missing, a quality resembling hunger, though he could not have identified it that way. Even so, he might have continued with any one of them had she pursued him, but he was so reserved that they were all a little relieved when they didn't hear from him again.

His celibacy bothered him no more than the occasional desire he felt for a better dinner than he could get at the coffee shop downstairs. He knew he would have a home someday in which he would enjoy good, nourishing meals, and in the same way he knew there would be a woman to share his bed once the grueling work of his residency was behind him.

Within weeks of meeting her he began to wonder if this woman might be Penny. She had a yearning attitude toward life that struck him as sweet and answerable, and she was lovely to kiss, the way her eyelashes felt against his jaw once their mouths had parted. "There now," he often said at such moments, and she laughed in a way that seemed to appreciate rather than object to his diffidence.

She begged him for stories of his boyhood, and when his birthday came around, ten months after they met, she presented him with a collage she'd made from photographs she secretly requested from his mother. "But how did you think to write to her?" he asked. "And how did you find the address?" She said being happy gave her good ideas. For her part, his mother had been delighted by the young lady's request and, a few weeks later, emboldened by hope, she decided to send him a snapshot of herself as a young woman holding him as an infant. It was 1928, and he was wearing a long lace dress. "Father was so very proud," she wrote on the back of the photo, the closest she could come to suggesting that Bill get down to the business of starting his own family. His sister had been married three years by then and was still childless, and their mother had begun to despair of having grandchildren.

Penny was an only child who for company during her school years had drawn pictures of the children she expected to bear. On the day Bill proposed to her, she handed him a portfolio containing a sampling of these sketches, and he was moved and intrigued by her having chosen to include two boys and one girl rather than the one of each most people would have selected. "Three, then?" he said, and she said, "Yes, don't you think?"

They were married at a small ceremony in Sacramento and received her parents' friends' good wishes at a late-morning reception where coffee was served from a large silver urn. Bill's side was represented only by a colleague from the hospital; his parents and sister had never flown, and he had convinced them to forgo the long, tiring trip in favor of a more leisurely visit that he and Penny would make to Michigan. He believed he was looking out for them, and perhaps he was, but it also suited him to take Penny as his wife without his family's witness, though he would have denied this had anyone suggested it.

Penny's head fit perfectly into the hollow of his shoulder, and they spent their first year together in a state of deep contentment. At the end of the day, when he came in from work and found her in the kitchen with a cookbook open and a smudge of flour on her jaw, he was tempted to set aside his trust in science and believe, if only for the moment, that it was fate that had led him on the long road from Michigan to Korea to this woman. Every night she sat with him while he bathed, often leaning over the side of the tub and scrubbing his shoulders with a sudsy washcloth. If he leaned back against the porcelain, she sometimes abandoned the washcloth and reached into the water to stroke him. This thrilled him, but his greatest pleasure came when, at the peak moment of his attentions in bed, she threw her head back and sighed. Matrimony, he began to think, was a cure for an illness he hadn't known he had.

As for Penny, it seemed to her that the formlessness of her life until now had been a kind of prepayment for the many perfections of her husband: the perfection of his good black hair, the perfection of his even temperament, the perfection of his voice on the telephone consulting about an ill child. "I know it's frightening," he said into the phone one night as she lay next to him in bed, "but I'm going to tell you how to bring the fever down now, all right? The baby will be fine, and you'll feel better, too." Once the call was finished, he pulled Penny back into his arms, and while he murmured apologies for the interruption and moved his lips and tongue down her neck, she decided it was the last part of what he'd said to the worried mother—"and you'll feel better, too"—that made him such a good, kind man.

Only one thing troubled her, but it sometimes troubled her a great deal: she didn't always know what he was thinking. Often, almost daily, she would say, "Me for your thoughts"—me, since she was Penny. And he would say, "Oh, just daydreaming" or "Oh, my thoughts aren't worth near that much."

He liked to be outdoors when he had free time, but San Francisco was mostly too cold for that, so they began Sunday trips to visit his property in Portola Valley. He bought a used car with a mammoth front seat, and one day when the ground under the oak tree was too damp for their usual picnic, they sat in the car and ate Penny's deviled eggs, and then Bill stretched out with his head and shoulders against the passenger door and arranged her on top of him, half sitting and half lying. He kissed her, and she felt the change beginning between his legs. She pressed against him, and he patted his hip pocket, where he kept his wallet, and said, "I don't have a rubber."

"I should hope not," she said in the arch, slightly flirtatious voice she sometimes adopted, a voice he didn't like and she didn't hear. "Why would you carry one of those around?"

He kissed her again while trying to sit up a bit to change the way their bodies were meeting.

"Let's start a baby," she said. "Right here. Right now."

He smiled, but a sadness tracked across his face, and it seemed to her that he disappeared for a moment. She said, "Bill, what is it?"

He shook his head. He was ready for children, but not if he and his wife differed in something as important as how they might each view this moment. If he continued today, they would give up rubbers until there was an infant in the house, but they would never know which ejaculation had released the one successful sperm. She—he saw this whole—would want to believe conception had taken place here, now, on this cool, damp afternoon when the oak leaves were at their softest and she was wearing her lucky cameo pin on her collar. He didn't think he would be able to tolerate that.

She loomed over him, hands on his chest, her pelvis moving against his. "Won't we live here with him?" she said. "With all of them?"

He looked past her head, through the windshield with its edges cloudy from released breath. The land he'd bought all that time ago had lost something. It no longer seemed quite so splendid, and he knew the change had come about when he started bringing her with him to see it. This was not knowledge he could accept, and to make it go away he kissed her. She pressed again, and he made a decision that necessitated a rearrangement of clothing and resulted in the start of something new, whether in their minds or in her body only time would tell.

2

THE PARTY

The children got up early and gathered in the kitchen. Their mother was still in bed and their father was already gone, rounding at the hospital so he could get to his clinic and be home by midafternoon. At ten, Robert was the oldest, a serious-looking boy with straight dark hair and a habit of blinking two or three times before he spoke. Rebecca was two years younger and the only girl. Ryan was six and James was three.

The kitchen had the tranquility of early morning, the counters and stovetop gleaming from the wipe-down they'd received the night before. Penny Blair was a dogged if uneven housekeeper, and the chrome sink fixtures shone while streaks of day-old juice created a sticky archipelago on the floor.

Robert brought out cereal and bowls and told the others to eat quickly. James was allergic to milk, so Rebecca poured orange juice on his cornflakes, and the four of them spooned up their breakfast without talking. At dinnertime they had set places at the table—Robert and Rebecca on one side, Ryan and James on the other, and their mother and father at the ends—but when they were alone they sat anywhere, including the places usually occupied by their parents. Without being obvious about it, Robert generally tried for his father's chair, and that was where he sat this morning as he finished his cereal.

"Hurry up, you guys," he said, carrying his bowl to the sink and turning on the water so hard that it hit the inside of his bowl and splashed his face. This was an insult to his dignity, but it was possible the other children hadn't seen, so he didn't dry off, though he hated the idea of cereal water on his eyelid.

"Don't put it in the dishwasher," Rebecca said. "Wash it and put it away."

"I was there," he said. "I have ears."

The night before, the family had talked about how the children could help their mother get ready for their annual summer party. Robert and Rebecca wanted to do more than just leave the kitchen clean after breakfast and keep James busy, and their mother had said there would be all kinds of ways to help: mushroom caps to stuff with bread crumbs and parsley, carrots to scrape for the crudités platter, soft cheese to roll in chopped nuts. And dozens of cookies to bake. "We'll have an assembly line," she said. "A cookie factory."

"Doesn't that sound like fun?" their father said. "I wish I could help with that. I'll be the iceman, though. I'll bring home lots of ice."

Drying his cereal bowl and putting it away, Robert went to the sliding glass door. From where he stood he could see the backyard, a small square of lawn bordered by the beds of flowers his father cared for with the attentive nurturing Robert had heard him recommend to the parents of newborn babies. The property was on a hill, with a shallow upward climb out the eastern windows and a steep descent to the west. Beyond the house and the driveway and the groomed backyard, the land was crowded with oak trees and bay laurel, eucalyptus and manzanita. In summertime, the clear areas were hot and dry, but in the areas of heavy growth the earth seemed damp until June or later, and the fallen leaves made a soft blanket on the ground.

The house was low and spread out, with doors and windows that slid open and a roof with deep eaves to protect against the afternoon sun. Portola Valley was known for its rustic quality, and like most of the houses in the neighborhood, the Blairs' was painted shades of tan and brown that blended with the bark of the trees and the dusty gold of the hills. Bill often told the children that he'd bought the land on a whim, precisely because of how rural the area still was, long after the last of the ranches and orchards that once spread from the bay to the mountains had been replaced by shopping centers and crowded subdivisions. He was not a man given to whims, and they viewed the story as central to their family's creation myth, though they wouldn't have those words for it until many years had passed and Rebecca had begun to collect terms and phrases that helped her explain people to themselves.

At the moment, she was at the table, finishing her cereal. She liked the kitchen in the morning, before her mother was up, and if she'd been alone she would have lingered, but she didn't want to get stuck with all the cleanup. She had read in a book of her mother's that women should make sure their daughters didn't internalize the idea that the kitchen was their domain, and since she couldn't really count on her mother to make sure of this, she was trying to make sure of it herself. She had a very large vocabulary for an eight-year-old, but she hadn't known that "domain" meant "place" rather than "job," and Robert had laughed at her when she announced at dinner one evening that she was going to get a summer domain when she was sixteen because she wanted to save up to buy a microscope.

Her mother's door was closed, and Rebecca tiptoed past it to her own room. On the bedside table was a stack of library books: *All-of-a-Kind Family, More All-of-a-Kind Family,* and *All-of-a-Kind Family Downtown,* the first three in a series of books she loved, about a family of five girls growing up in New York in the olden days. Rebecca had withdrawn them yesterday, for the fourth or fifth time. She wasn't sure she would read them, but it was nice to have them again. At bedtime her father had noticed the books and said, "Ah, Rebecca. You've been having sister wishes again, haven't you? Let's get you a friend over this weekend, shall we?" Sometimes he knew what she wanted even before she did.

She kicked off her shoes and lay down. Staring at the ceiling, she had the thought she always had when she lay on her bed after breakfast, which was that sleep was a very strange thing because you had no control over when you did it. Also: when you went to sleep you forgot who you were—really, you forgot everything—but when you woke up you remembered what you'd been thinking and doing just before you dropped off. It was like taking the needle off a record, waiting ten hours, and then putting it back down in the same groove as before. Another strange thing about sleep was that sometimes you thought you were awake but then you woke up, which proved you hadn't been awake after all. The night before, she had dreamed about the party—she realized this as she lay looking at her ceiling. She had dreamed that the party was the way it always was but without any lights. All the grown-ups were standing around the living room with their cocktails and talking as if it were normal that they couldn't really see each other. Rebecca and Robert were watching them from the kitchen and saying to each other, "Dahlink, pass me my drink because I can't see it. Dahlink, I'm blind but I don't care." Remembering this made Rebecca sit up. Another thing she couldn't control was whether or not Robert would be in her dreams. Sometimes, falling asleep, she would issue a statement—*You can come tonight* or *Tonight you have to stay out*—but he did whatever he wanted.

James and Ryan were still at the table, James because he was playing with his food and Ryan because he was the slowest eater. His father said he had his own clock—meaning he didn't feel time in the same way the other children did—and though Ryan knew what his father meant, he wondered what it would be like to carry around an actual clock, invisible to everyone else, ticking in his hands. He didn't really remember last year's party. "Is it the one with all the food and all the people?" he'd asked the night before, and his father had placed his palm on Ryan's head and smiled.

James spooned sugar into the mush of cereal and juice in his bowl. "I see, I see, I see," he sang; or maybe it was "Icy, icy, icy."

"What do you see, James?" Ryan said. His badger was on the table near his elbow, and he thought they'd been apart long enough and tucked the animal under his arm.

"Goin' for the salt now," James said, unscrewing the top of the saltshaker and trying to pour some into his spoon. It came out fast and spilled into his bowl. "Goin' for the pepper now," he crowed.

Robert came over and grabbed his hand. "James, no."

Ryan made big eyes and covered his mouth to show James that he shouldn't be scared of Robert.

"Nye-nee," James said happily.

"Nye-nee" was as close as James could get to "Ryan," and Ryan smiled. "You want to come with me?" he said. "Come with Nye-nee?"

James launched himself from his chair. He was big and clumsy, prone to spectacular tumbles—loud wailing, tears and mucus everywhere, blood on his knees. This morning his feet landed flat on the linoleum. "Go with Nye-nee!" he said.

Robert watched his brothers head off. This moment alone in the kitchen was rare and not to be wasted. He knew he should clean up, but on a shelf next to the refrigerator a jar of coins waited for him. He scooped out a handful and slid them into his pocket. He was quite certain his father wouldn't mind if he knew why Robert was taking the coins, which was so he could practice the magic tricks he'd been teaching himself since summer began.

"I'm telling."

He turned and there was Rebecca, standing in the doorway. He said, "I don't know what you're talking about."

"Yes, you do."

"What then?"

Just a day earlier Rebecca had overheard her father telling her mother that this minor stealing of Robert's was just a phase, some need to approach the line between good and bad, and "not an occasion to humiliate the boy." Rebecca thought wrong was wrong, but because it was the day of the party she decided to let it go.

"We should clean up," she said.

"Then let's clean up."

Once they were finished, she went outside to see what needed to be done. The house had its morning look, closed and dark. She had never thought about the house's color until the day in first grade when she saw a house that was violet. Now she knew houses could be any surprising color you could come up with—turquoise, buttercup yellow—and she thought the dull, plain surface of her house demonstrated a failure of imagination. She kept this to herself, though, because of how much her father loved the house and how much she loved her father.

Robert wondered when his mother would get up. With nothing else to do, he sat at the piano and looked at his sheet music. He hadn't practiced in weeks and was in a state of conflict about the whole matter. When school started up again he would be in the fifth grade, the age at which Mrs. Bostock, his piano teacher, made you start playing in recitals. This wouldn't be so bad except she wanted the students to memorize their pieces, and Robert was sure he wouldn't be able to do that. The obvious solution was to begin campaigning to quit piano well in advance of an actual recital setting up residence in his worries, but the problem was that he was pretty good at piano, and it wasn't just his father who said so—Mrs.

Bostock did, too, and so did Mr. Gleason, his fourth-grade teacher. "Very agile" was what Mrs. Bostock said, while Mr. Gleason demonstrated his approval by sometimes calling on Robert—but never anyone else—to accompany the class when they sang rounds on Fridays.

Robert realized that once again he was acting as if Mr. Gleason were still his teacher. He was not and never would be again. He was by far the best teacher Robert had ever had, and when Robert thought about a new set of kids sitting at the desks in Room 9 come September, his stomach began to hurt. His stomach hadn't hurt in a few weeks, not since the Fourth of July, when his father had brought him home from the club while everyone else ate hot dogs and played capture the flag.

He left the piano and lay on the couch. His stomach really hurt, and his father wouldn't be home for hours. There was a chance the milk had turned, though if that were the case then the other children would start feeling sick soon, too. He reached over to the coffee table and picked up his mother's abalone shell from the beach at Sea Ranch. People used it as an ashtray, and it smelled like cigarettes, or actually more like after-cigarettes, which was a dirtier, nastier smell. At the party there would be a little smoking and a lot of drinking. He enjoyed watching adults, and never more than when they were tipsy. He thought they were very, very funny, with their loud voices and sudden, jerky movements. At last year's party, his father's friend Marvin Miller had gotten so loud that his father had left the party to take him home, and the next day he'd told Robert that for some adults, alcohol could be like candy in that it tasted really good but you could go overboard and then not feel well.

Robert returned the shell to the table and concentrated on his stomach. His father said not to think about whatever hurt, but Robert couldn't help it. On the Fourth of July, lying on the couch while his father sat beside him and stroked his head, Robert noticed that the pain in his stomach had gone away, and he told his father it was good he'd been concentrating on it because otherwise he might not have realized he was feeling better.

He sat up slowly. In the bedroom hallway his brothers were being rather loud, and he went to investigate. When he was Ryan's age, he'd read chapter books and ridden a two-wheeler, but Ryan could do neither. Maybe worse, Ryan cried whenever he was taken to the barber, so his hair was almost as long as a girl's.

"You guys are being really loud," Robert said.

"We're playing track meet," Ryan said. "Want to play with us?"

Track meet was a game they'd invented early in the summer, following a trip to an actual track meet at Stanford. Robert said he was busy and disappeared into his room, and Ryan shrugged at James and returned his attention to his next event, which was long jump. He took a run and a leap and then at the last minute tucked into a somersault that delivered him to the floor right in front of his mother's closed door. This hurt his shoulder and his ear, and he made his badger give them both a nuzzle. Badger had been a present to Ryan from James, on the day James was born; James had given Robert a play bow-and-arrow set and Rebecca a book of paper dolls. Ryan wasn't sure why James hadn't given their parents anything. Their mother would have wanted a present, he felt sure.

He half pushed and half slid closer to her room. His feet needed somewhere to go, and they landed against the door. From there, it was possible to tap his toes without making any noise. He tapped out "Baa Baa Black Sheep," using the big toe of his left foot for a few words, and then the big toe of his right foot, and back and forth. "Have you any wool," he sang softly, and for the rest of the song he patted his badger once for every toe tap.

He heard his mother on the other side of the door, saying, "Oh, how can it be so late?"

She didn't sound upset, so he got to his knees and turned the knob slowly.

"Who is it?"

He pushed the door open just a little and hoped she would somehow know it was him.

But the next thing he heard was the sound of the bathroom door closing, and he realized she wasn't coming to see him after all. The water went on, and he got to his feet and entered the room, which was dark and musty and smelled like bed. On his father's side, the blankets were straight and so was the pillow, but his mother's side was like a nest, and he got in and covered himself, head and all. The toilet flushed, and he hugged his badger, bringing his knees up to his chest so that he would look like a pillow under the covers. She would be very surprised to see him. She might even want to get back in with him. Sometimes when they were alone, she pulled him onto her lap and said he was supposed to be her baby.

The bathroom door opened, and he tried not to breathe so the surprise would take a little longer. He heard a drawer open and close. "Look at you," she said, and he felt himself smile. But nothing happened, and in a moment she said it again, a little differently: "Why, look at you!" He hadn't heard her steps, so she must still be at her dresser. Then, again: "Look at you! Penny Blair, aren't you a sight for sore eyes?" Then her voice went very low, and she said something almost like a hum: "Mmmmm." It went up and down as if she were tasting a pretend cookie he'd offered her.

"Mom?" This was Robert, from outside the open door. "Who are you talking to?"

Something clicked onto the dresser top, and it occurred to Ryan that she'd been brushing her hair. He brought Badger to his mouth and let his lips brush Badger's fur.

"No one," his mother said. "Where's James?" This was the

moment when she would say, in a loud happy voice, "And where's Ryan?" Ryan was so sure of this he needed to pee. But she didn't say anything more, and when someone spoke it was Robert.

"I took his diaper off. It was soaked."

"Well, I don't want him running around naked, I've got way too much to do today. You'll have to get him dressed." And then Ryan heard her steps and knew she'd left the room.

The door creaked a little more. "Good hiding place," Robert said.

Ryan pulled the covers from his head and looked at his brother.

Robert was wearing his fake nice face. "What? It is." He crossed the room and opened the curtains. The room appeared, the teak bed and dressers, the huge picture of their land as it had been before the house was built. It was a painting that almost looked like a photograph, painted by an artist hired by their father a long time ago. This artist was extremely good at trees. He wasn't as good at colors—the greens were gray greens and the browns were gray browns, and the sky was a whiter blue than in real life. But the tree trunks, the branches, the leaves—these were perfect. Sometimes, when their father had gone into the bedroom to change, one or another of the children would track him down and find him sitting on the end of the bed, just looking at the painting.

Robert stared at Ryan, lying there with his dumb badger. It took everything he had to say, "You can come help me with James if you want. You can do his shirt." He had his hands on his hips, and his cheeks were red.

"Does your stomach hurt?" Ryan said.

"Not very much. Does yours?"

"No."

They went to find James, who was, predictably enough, standing on the counter in the children's bathroom peeing into the sink.

"James, no!" Robert said.

James turned to face the older boys and sprayed them both—Robert on the neck and Ryan in the hair.

"James, no!" they both said.

Laughing, dribbling pee, James swiveled around and got down on his knees and felt with his feet for the closed toilet cover. He took off running. He had white-blond hair and a pudgy pink behind, and thighs that were as big around as Ryan's.

"James," Robert yelled, and halfway down the hallway James stopped and turned. His face wild with glee, he began to run back, and Robert planted himself so James had no choice but to run into the room he and Ryan shared. "Block the door," Robert shouted.

Ryan darted into the doorway. James was jumping on the bed now, and Robert pushed past Ryan into the room and tried to kick the door closed, almost hitting Ryan in the process.

"James," Robert said, "stop jumping! We're going to help Mommy, but you need to get dressed first." His voice was gruff, and James jumped faster, his hair flapping against his ears.

"James," Ryan said in a sweet voice. He moved to the bed and held out his hands. "Come to Nye-nee."

"James!" Robert said, and then, softer, "Remember the cookie factory?"

James turned his back on his brothers and jumped, and the bed creaked, and through the window he saw Rebecca standing outside under the oak tree, balancing on one foot with the other held way behind her, toes pointed, arms up over her head as if she were going to dive.

"Beck," he cried.

"Beck will play with you," Robert said, "but first you need to get dressed." He lunged at James, and Ryan grabbed an arm, and together they got James flat on the bed.

"Here," Ryan said, "you can hold Badger," but James rolled to his side and grabbed his own stuffed animal, a small brown-and-white dog that he had more or less abandoned, though Ryan put it on James's bed whenever he found it lying on the floor or in the closet.

"Are you going to take care of Dog today?" Ryan said. "You can find him a new collar, or we could make one."

"Get clothes," Robert said, "I'll hold him," and though Ryan knew that there was no need, that James would be still now, he went to the dresser while Robert kept his hands on James's shoulders.

They called Rebecca to come inside. In the kitchen, they told their mother they were ready to help, but she was busy chopping nuts and sent them away. A little later they tried again, but she was busy washing parsley and sent them away. They waited half an hour and tried again, then twenty more minutes and tried again.

"I'm sorry," she said at last. "I have way too much work to stop and show you how to help. Go play, all right?"

The children left the kitchen, the three R's downcast while James dashed ahead of them with a three-year-old's talent for easily abandoning dubious goals. "Chase me," he called, but when he arrived at his room and turned around, his siblings were taking their time, too frustrated for their usual indulgence.

Back in the kitchen, Penny *was* sorry—she knew she was disappointing them—but she really did have too much to do to be able to stop and explain the little jobs they could manage. She hadn't been thinking straight at dinner last night, agreeing to let them help. Bill had encouraged them, and she'd gotten swept up in their excitement, which generally seemed manageable when he was around and overwhelming when he wasn't. There was so much to do today, she needed to just put her head down and work. And the truth was she wanted to do it herself.

The other truth was she didn't want to do it at all. She was plagued by conundrums like this. A few days earlier she'd seen a picture in a magazine of a smiling woman wearing a little white apron decorated with the same red roosters as the ones on her own dish towels. Oh, how Penny hated that woman! And oh, how she wanted to be her! Even more, she wanted to be a woman she'd seen in another magazine, dressed in a sleeveless black dress and holding a martini. She'd cut out both pictures and taped them into a notebook where she kept articles she clipped from the newspaper about, as the headlines put it, "the social scene." When Bill asked why she clipped these articles, she shrugged and turned her back on him, a gesture she'd inaugurated early in their marriage that was as unsuccessful now as it always had been. Rather than make him try harder, it made him give up.

All morning, the children sensed their mother's tension and were tense themselves. They tried to play Sorry, but James refused to follow the rules and hopped his yellow piece around willy-nilly, jumping over the other pieces or knocking them off the board. They tried to play Tinker Toys, but James kept initiating duels with the wooden sticks.

Toward noon they went outside and sat under the oak tree. They figured she'd be getting to the cookies soon. The older two sent Ryan to check, and he came back and said yes, she had the big bowl out. They went around the back of the house so she wouldn't see them through the kitchen window, then stopped before they reached the sliding door. The sun was high, and there was no shade. They began to sweat. They heard the clack of one pan of cookies going into the oven, followed by the rattling of another as she began to drop balls of dough onto it. Robert and Rebecca exchanged a nod, and the four of them stormed in.

"Now we can help, right?"

"Can we roll the dough?"

"We'll wash our hands. James, come on, we need to wash our hands."

"We roll it in little balls, right?"

"Can we have one bite of dough? Just one small bite?"

"No," Penny said. "I'm sorry, no. I have too much to do."

"But it's the cookies!"

"What did I say?"

At the sound of her raised voice the children fell silent. Worse, they fell away from one another; in spirit they did. Each was alone and disappointed. Robert thought that if it weren't for the younger boys, he'd be allowed to help. Rebecca thought the same. They both believed themselves to possess special maturity.

They watched. She ripped pieces of dough from the giant hunk in her bowl, rolled them between her palms until they were smooth and slick, and plunked them haphazardly on cookie sheets. Rip, roll, plunk; rip, roll, plunk. Rebecca thought it would make more sense to set them in straight lines—she thought you could get more on each sheet that way—but she didn't say so.

Then a faint smell of smoke came from the oven. "Oh, no!" Penny cried, yanking open the door and grabbing a pot holder. From where they stood, the children could see that the first batch of cookies was burned. Not black, but a fairly dark brown. "Damn it!" Penny shouted as she yanked the pan from the oven and dropped it on the stovetop. "Damn it all!"

Their father didn't like the word "damn," so naturally each of the children thought of him: Robert remembered the stomachache he had to report, Rebecca recalled her father's promise to help her invite a friend to come play, Ryan thought of the praise he'd received from his father on the care he was giving Badger, and James simply wailed the two syllables that formed the heart of his emotional life: "Dada."

"Of course!" Penny exclaimed. "Who else? All of you, out! Now!" And then—regretful and reaching for kindness but ending up with its poor relation, charity—she took her spatula, freed the cookies from the pan, and said, "Here, take these. They won't be terrible. Just take them and go."

Robert gathered the burned cookies in a paper towel and led the way to the front door. Rebecca's hair hung in front of her shoulders in two long, thin braids, and for some reason he thought of how he used to sit on her—she would be lying on her stomach—and hold the braids like reins, nudging her sides with his knees and yelling, "Go, horsie."

They sat together under the oak tree, James settling with his legs in their customary W, a contortionist with dirty knees. Ryan reached for one of the cookies and took a nibble. "It's not bad. It kind of tastes like toast."

"I don't want a burned cookie," Rebecca said. She hesitated and then grabbed one and threw it into the bushes. This made Robert mad, the fact that she'd thought of it first, and he threw one cookie after another down the long driveway, leaving only a few for his younger brothers. He kicked the cookies into the bushes, then continued down the hill, the driveway twisting near the end so that when he reached the road, the house was no longer visible. For something to do, he opened the mailbox, but of course it was empty; it was far too early for the mail. He felt faintly ridiculous even though no one could see him. Toward the end of the school year, when Mr. Gleason ignored the breaking of small rules, Robert had left the room while everyone was supposed to stay seated and work on math problems, and he'd gone into the cloakroom (his cover story being that he'd left his eraser in his jacket pocket) and quickly transferred the contents of his lunch box into Valerie Pinckney's lunch box and vice versa. Then, at lunch, he had watched with increasing dismay as she proceeded to eat his ham sandwich and savor his brownie without so much as a tiny wrinkle of confusion disturbing her pretty face. He felt the same kind of silly now as he had then.

He started the climb back to the house, but instead of continuing up the driveway he veered to the left, down what his father called the spur. A narrower branch of the driveway, the spur sloped through a dense cover of trees and stopped at a storage shed that was several years older than the house and had been built by Robert's father on a month of Sundays when Robert was a baby. "A month of Sundays" was just an expression, but as a very young child Robert had imagined a special month that was all Sundays, an anomaly of the calendar not unlike the one every fourth year that gave February twenty-nine days. Robert had imagined that he and his mother had come, too, on the special Sundays of that special month, perhaps sitting on a blanket while his father worked, and he'd been very disappointed to learn, from a passing remark of his mother's, that they'd been left at home in San Francisco.

The shed was small, about eight by ten feet, a rough wooden structure with a door held closed by a padlock. Inside was a set of patio furniture his mother no longer liked and a rowboat not quite old enough to have lost all its blue paint. The boat was an impulse purchase of his father's, bought in a junk shop because it reminded him of a boat he'd used as a boy, on a pond in Michigan.

The key to the padlock was kept in a drawer in the kitchen, but all at once Robert remembered there was a spare key hidden in a gap between the foundation and the base of one of the walls. He knew this with the strange conviction one has about things learned in dreams: it was absolute fact shrouded in mystery. How did he know it? Why would there be a key hidden in such an unlikely place? He had no idea.

But he wanted to see the rowboat. They'd never once used it, not in two years. "Someday," was his father's insufficient answer to the question of when they might put it in water. Crouching at the door, Robert felt with his fingers for a gap between the foundation and the wall. Nothing. He slid his fingers sideways. Still nothing. It was a little creepy, not knowing what might be lurking there, what soft bug or moldy leaf, so he changed his mind about the whole thing and headed up to the house.

His brothers and sister had disappeared, and he lay down under the oak tree. There were so many branches it was like being in a room. Robert remembered Mr. Gleason showing the class slides of his trip to France, where he'd been inside a church that didn't have normal walls or a ceiling but instead a vast network of oak beams like an overturned sailing ship with its framing exposed. Mr. Gleason had brought out a box of balsa wood sticks and some glue, and they'd had a lesson on engineering. He was the only teacher who used science in English lessons and social studies in math lessons and made it so you didn't even notice you were learning. A great example was the way he took a unit on the human body and ended up teaching the class a history lesson about "the four humors," which was basically a big mistake doctors had made about how the body worked. In ancient Greece and Rome, doctors thought the body was filled with four substances—black bile, yellow bile, phlegm, and blood—and that all diseases resulted from having an imbalance of the humors.

Robert told his father about the humors, partly to show him how smart Mr. Gleason was and partly to make sure he knew about them, and his father said that even though the theory was long discredited, it wasn't as outlandish as most people thought, because when blood was drawn and left to sit in a transparent container such as a glass vial, you ended up with four different layers, from a dark clot at the bottom to a yellow serum at the top. It was easy to understand how, in very early medicine, the observation of those layers might have given rise to all kinds of speculation and theorizing. He asked Robert if Mr. Gleason had shared with the class the idea that each humor was associated with a certain type of personality—black bile with the melancholic type, yellow bile with the choleric type, blood with the sanguine, and phlegm with the phlegmatic, a word that made Robert snort with laughter until he realized his father wasn't kidding and it was a real word. It meant rational, calm, unemotional. Choleric meant angry or bad-tempered. Sanguine meant courageous and hopeful, and melancholic meant sad. "I guess I'm sanguine," Robert's father had said in answer to Robert's question, "though your mother might say I'm phlegmatic." Robert found it interesting that there seemed to be two good types and two bad types, and his father was both of the good types while his mother—well, at least sometimes she was both of the bad.

"What is Rebecca?" he said, avoiding the question he really wanted to ask.

"Oh, Rebecca is sanguine," his father said. "She is definitely sanguine."

Lying under the tree, Robert squeezed his eyes shut as tightly as he could, and when he opened them bright spots fluttered in his vision. He waited for the world to become normal again. Above the branches of the oak tree, the sky was a harsh, crystalline blue. He thought it was probably about one o'clock, and then he remembered his watch, a gift from his father for his tenth birthday—a special gift for him because he was the oldest. It was a gift his father had received from his own grandfather, and his mother's reaction had been confusing, almost as if she thought his father should have given the watch to her.

It was in Robert's desk. He entered the house through the laundry room and slipped into his room unnoticed. He fastened the leather strap around his wrist, though it was too big on even the tightest hole. It was only 12:20. Hours more until his father would be home.

Through the window he saw Rebecca dragging a wooden bench away from the garage, and his anger at her intensified. He'd forgotten that they always put the wooden bench outside the kitchen so people would have a place to set an empty glass or plate if they happened to step outside for a little air. Now she would get all the credit. It was possible she'd even been assigned the job by their mother, and he couldn't decide if that would make it better or worse.

Out under the hot sun, Rebecca dragged the bench and rested, dragged it and rested. In fact, she'd had the idea on her own, and it was turning out to be not such a good one. The bench was incredibly heavy. She heard the phone ring in the house, and as she listened to the muffled sound of her mother's voice she realized it was her father calling. Though she couldn't hear words, she knew her mother was complaining about being home alone with the children and the party preparations, and Rebecca could almost fill in the gaps in her mother's speech with the sound of her father's calm, reassuring voice. "Your dad is like a mom," one of Rebecca's friends said once on a Saturday when her father was home with a houseful of kids while her mother was out shopping. Robert had a friend over that day, too, and their father helped them make Popsicles with lemonade and made sure everyone got a turn with Rebecca's new pogo stick.

Ryan found his mother alone at the kitchen table, thumb and forefinger pinching the handle on a coffee cup. She had her back to the door, and he was very quiet as he approached her. He stopped just behind her chair and waited. Then he moved forward and made his badger approach her for a big surprise kiss.

"Oh, good grief," she cried, scraping the chair away from the table and waving her hands near her face. "What are you doing?"

He brought the badger back to his chest.

"Ryan, what? What?"

"Hi," he said.

"Oh, I see," she said. "Hi. Hi!" She leaned toward him and grinned a horrible jack-o'-lantern grin. "My God, this day. Where have you been? Where are the rest of them? Your father has a meningitis case. He's hours behind schedule."

She pushed her hair away from her face, and Ryan thought about how sometimes he did that for her: if they were sitting together on the couch he might get on his knees and turn his fingers into a comb and do her hair. She liked a lot of combing when he did that. More combing than tying, though he'd recently learned how to tighten a rubber band on something—twist, wrap, twist, wrap—and he had made her some good ponytails. Her hair was dark brown—the same color as Robert's, a little darker than Rebecca's—and wavy.

She took Badger and made him kiss Ryan. "It's okay, baby," she said. "I'm sorry." She held Badger near his eyes. "He's thirsty. He'll drink those tears. Are *you* thirsty, baby?" She increased Badger's pressure on Ryan's face, and he understood that he should hold Badger steady while she got him some water. She returned to the table, pulled him onto her lap, and held the glass while he drank. Badger listened to Ryan's heartbeat and said it sounded very good and healthy.

"I'm sorry about before," she said, "with the cookies. We'll make some together another time, okay? Chocolate chip—you don't even like this kind very much." She was about to ask him not to tell Bill how she'd yelled, but Bill had told her she shouldn't do that kind of thing. And with four kids, he was bound to find out anyway.

She pushed away from the table. "How's the children's bathroom?"

Ryan thought of James peeing into the sink. "Okay," he said, meaning *I want to protect you,* and not understanding, as he would in a few years, that there were times to postpone bad news and times to hurry it, and this was a time to hurry it.

"Where is everyone?" she said. "What's James doing?"

Ryan found James and took him outside. The lawn had been freshly mowed, and Ryan took off his shoes and wiggled his toes in the grass. The blades tickled his feet, and he thought of barefoot time at his school, which started with sitting and ended with dancing. He took hold of James's hands and swayed back and forth, but James got excited and began running in circles, fast and then faster.

"We all fall *down,*" James shouted, and he pulled Ryan to the grass, where they lay together in a heap, panting. James's face was pink and sweaty, his hair stuck to his head in damp strands. Suddenly his smile disappeared, and he stared at Ryan with giant, wounded eyes. "We fall down!" he said mournfully. "When is Dada?"

"Dada will come home, James. We didn't hurt ourselves."

Tears spilled from James's eyes.

"You want Mama?"

"Dada takin' me on my twike," James said. "Down the hill."

Their father taught them to ride their bicycles on the driveway, up by the house where it was flat, but to really practice you had to go down to the village, or even to Menlo Park.

"My wed twike," James added.

"What's your favorite color?" Ryan said.

"Wed!"

"What color are your shoes?"

James waved a foot in Ryan's face. "Wed!"

"That's right," Ryan said. "You like red the best. And I like blue the best." But as soon as he said this, he thought of the other colors, the green of the grass today, and the white of his milk, and the dark orange he'd chosen for his new blanket. All the colors together helped each other be the best. He lay back on the grass. He would never say that grayish brown was his favorite color, but that was Badger's color and it was the right one for Badger.

High in the sky, the sun shone down on them. It shone on the roof of the house, heating the kitchen even hotter than the oven had. But it didn't shine on the shed.

Robert had gone down there again. He had decided that the table part of the old patio furniture set might be very helpful and that it would be fun to surprise his father by getting it out of the shed and bringing it up to the house. His father and his mother. She wouldn't mind—she might even appreciate it—because it was only the cushions of the furniture set that she didn't like.

He'd looked in the kitchen but couldn't find the key. And he still couldn't find it on the foundation. He felt all along the front, crawling on all fours, bits of leaves and dirt embedding themselves in his hands and knees. Nothing. He heard the sound of his father's car laboring up the steep part of the road and turning in to the driveway, and he ran up the spur waving just as the car, a four-year-old white Plymouth Valiant, roared past him. ("More my style," his father had said when he bought the car, "than the Barracuda.")

"Dad!" Robert yelled, and through the back window he saw his father's head tilt up—a look into the rearview mirror—and the brake lights flashed red.

Robert ran. The car door swung open, and his father stepped out and gave Robert a giant wave. "Welcoming committee," he called. He brought his palm to the back of his neck, a customary gesture that accentuated how tall and skinny he was, elbow triangling away from his head like the point of a signal flag.

"How'd you get here so early?" Robert said as he reached the car. He was panting lightly. "What time is it?" Asking the question, he realized he was no longer wearing his watch.

"Well, there's a complicated answer to that," his father said.

Robert's heart pounded, his absent watch leading the assault but followed closely by the uphill run and a fear, materializing by the moment, that his father would be going out again. "You haven't gone to the clinic yet?"

"I've been, but I have to go back. There are four patients left from this morning and six more when we reopen."

Robert thought he'd left the watch in his room—he must have—but he needed to get back to the house and check. "But why?"

"I had an emergency."

The word "emergency" was familiar enough—it was an everyday word—but with his own emergency developing Robert let a small whimper escape, and his father squatted so he was looking up into Robert's eyes.

"It's okay, son," he said. "We have an infant with meningitis. It's serious, but we're treating him with antibiotics and I'm optimistic."

"What about us?" Robert cried, and he was so ashamed that he took off down the hill again, knowing he was humiliating himself further but unable to stop.

Bill drove the rest of the way up to the house. The three other children crowded around him as soon as he was out of the car, James hugging his leg, Ryan leaning against his hip, Rebecca resting her head on his stomach. Usually when he came home they were inside, and they tackled him on the entry hall floor and worked him over as if he were a giant slab of clay. Greeting him outside, they settled for extra volume.

"Do you need help with the ice, Dad?" Rebecca said. "I moved the bench, I put it by the kitchen. That's right, isn't it, Dad? Isn't that what we do?"

"Yes, it is, Rebeck," he said, "but I don't have the ice yet. I'm going to see if your mother needs any help."

The children followed him to the bedroom hallway, where Ryan smelled Lysol and remembered the lie he'd told his mother about the bathroom.

And there she was, hair covered by a shower cap, a giant sponge in one yellow-gloved hand.

"Oh, dear," their father said.

She scowled. "You can say that again!"

"We're closed for lunch. Thought I'd see what I could do for half an hour. Chopping? Mopping?"

"Hoppin'!" James shouted, and he marched his feet up and down.

"James," Bill said, and he reached down and lifted James in his arms.

"Get them some lunch, would you?" Penny said irritably. "Someone peed in here!"

Bill carried James to the kitchen with Rebecca and Ryan following. "I suppose," he said, "it might be better not to ask who peed in the bathroom."

It took Rebecca a moment to get it, but then she burst out laughing. How dare someone *pee* in the *bathroom*! Ryan laughed, too, unconvincingly. She wished Robert were there, because he would have been cracking up, and the two of them might have started knocking into each other and ended up on the floor laughing their heads off.

"It was James," Ryan said.

"James!" their father said. "Lunchtime!"

Mornings when he wasn't at the hospital, he did assembly-line lunch making, bread in pairs, slap on a slice of meat, slap on a slice of cheese, swipe on the mayo, and the children lined up to receive the sandwiches and wrapped them up themselves, in waxed paper he'd previously torn from the roll, each piece coming off with a satisfying rip against the tiny metal teeth of the box.

Now they all dove in. He found paper plates, and they took their food outside and crowded onto the bench, their father in the middle, Rebecca on one side, Ryan on the other, and James standing facing his father with his plate on his father's lap.

"Where's Robert?" Ryan said.

"I'm sure he's working," their father said, and this seemed right.

Rebecca finished quickly and went back inside. This made room for Ryan's badger to take a seat on the bench. "James was going to play with his dog today," Ryan said, and James looked up at their father with peanut butter ringing his lips.

"I'm goin' on my twike," he said. "Down the hill."

"Ah, James," their father said. "Your trike."

Ryan stopped eating. He had a feeling he knew what was going to happen.

"Down the hill," James said again.

"Oh, dear," their father said, smiling sadly at James. "That will have to wait for another day."

Ryan recovered Badger and took his paper plate into the house. James's screams were not as hard to hear when he was on the other side of a door, even a screen door. Leaving the kitchen, he heard his mother in her bedroom, and he crept past her open door to his room. There was James's dog, on the floor again. He set his badger on his bed and put the two of them face-to-face. "Dog," said the badger. "Badger," said the dog. "Mmm mmm mmmm," they said to each other, kissing. Ryan felt sorry for Dog, but he couldn't take care of him and do a good job with Badger. He needed to find a way to help James take care of Dog. Ever since Dog's collar got lost, James had ignored him. He wondered if Rebecca might have a ribbon that would be a good collar. Ryan sat on his bed, bringing both animals onto his lap. He held their paws together, and they swayed the way he and James had earlier, back and forth, back and forth. He held their bodies together, and they danced.

Back outside, James was on the ground having a tantrum. He hit his fists against the concrete and pounded his feet, and Bill watched him.

"James," Bill said.

James looked up. "My twike," he whimpered, getting to his knees.

"Oh, I know," Bill said. "I know. Now can you stand up?"

James stood.

"We'll go another time. All right?"

James nodded, using his palm to wipe the tears from his face.

Bill lifted him onto his lap, facing the grass, and began bouncing him, ba-bump, ba-bump, ba-bump. He said:

James James
Morrison Morrison
Weatherby George Dupree
Took great
Care of his Mother,
Though he was only three.
James James
Said to his Mother,
"Mother," he said, said he;
"You must never go down
to the end of the town
if you don't go down with me."

"You must never go down," James said.

"You must never go down," his father said, "to the end of the town *if you don't go down with me*." On the final "me" he gave James an extra bump, and James slid off his lap and ran onto the grass, where he sped around in circles until he fell, dizzy, onto the ground.

"To work," Bill said, getting to his feet.

• • •

All afternoon the children avoided their mother: moving from room to room, or from indoors to outdoors, a step or two ahead of her. They joined together occasionally, all except Robert, but they didn't gather again until their father returned. By then it was late afternoon; when they stood on the driveway, their shadows stretched from their feet nearly to the house. Robert's stomach hurt most when he stood up straight, so he walked bent over at the waist, hobbling like an old man. Their father had eight bags of ice, and they each took one from the trunk of his car and carried it to the deep freeze in the garage—each except James, who ran from one sibling to another, touching the bags of ice and yipping with something that wasn't quite shock and wasn't quite laughter.

"I think baths might be in order," their father said. "Or showers, as the case may be," he added, giving Robert a look that acknowledged his seniority.

Normally this would have pleased Robert, but he was too worried to smile or even nod. The others dashed toward the laundry room door, conscious of an earlier dictum of their mother's that they avoid the other entrances to the house for the rest of the afternoon, since she had "done" them already and didn't want to have to "do" them again. Robert trudged after them.

His watch was gone. He had been everywhere, retraced every step from his room to the piano to the spur; he had searched and searched, bent over examining every inch of the house and every inch of the ground. And now he was bent over again, not searching but shuffling in pain.

In his room, he looked in his desk again, just in case he was wrong in remembering that he had already looked there, but to no avail. With no choice but to search outside a fourth time, he left his room and headed back to the laundry room, almost literally bumping into his father as he came in.

"Line for the tub?" his father said.

"What?"

"There's hot water to go around. I'll bathe James and call you when we're finished."

"Okay."

With Robert gone, Bill took a deep breath and let it out slowly. It was 4:55 and the party started at 6:00. Early in the summer he'd suggested they have the party on a Saturday this year, so he could help more, but Penny had insisted that it was a weekday kind of party—that a Saturday party was a different sort of thing and would change the guests' expectations and her ability to deliver.

He found the children's bathroom door closed and tapped at it. "Is that you in there, Rebeck?"

"Dad, can you come in?"

He opened the door and poked his head in. Rebecca was in the tub, slouched so that the ends of her braids skimmed the water. With her left forefinger she was stroking her right palm, which was a little red and raw from her work with the bench.

"Can you pass me the good-smelling soap?" she said.

Penny had cleaned, leaving the countertop sparkling and fresh hand towels on the rack, but there was no soap in sight.

"I'm not sure where . . ."

"Maybe the medicine cabinet?"

He opened the cabinet only to have three bars of soap and a glass bottle of cough medicine come tumbling out.

"Oh, oops, whoops," he said, slapping at the soaps but slowing the bottle enough that it landed gently and didn't break. "Now which of these is the good-smelling one?"

Rebecca grinned.

"Ah, you want me to smell them." He brought a plain white bar to his nose, then a yellow bar of Dial, and then a pink bar that smelled of strawberries and chemicals.

"Don't mistake it for an ice cream," he said, handing her the pink one.

She watched him from under her dark eyebrows and brought the bar close to her lips.

"How was your day?" he said, easing himself onto the closed toilet seat.

She dipped the soap in the water and rubbed it between her palms. She thought of telling him about not getting to help, but she didn't want to make him sad. She rubbed the soap harder, but it didn't get sudsy; there was only a little foam, large-bubbled and unsatisfying. She was a bit sorry she'd asked for the strawberry, which wouldn't be the most mature thing for her to smell like. She didn't like it when adults spoke to her as if she were a little girl. Or a little *girl*—she hated it when people were talking to the boys and then changed their voices when they started talking to her. She brought one foot up out of the water and rubbed it with the soap.

"Hot," she said at last.

"A hot day. That could be a good day, I suppose."

"It wasn't."

"You aren't a heat-loving girl."

"I'm a comfort-loving girl," she said, "who *tolerates* heat."

"Rebeck, it's good to be home." Leaning against the toilet tank, Bill felt the hours of work drain from his body.

"How many people are coming?" Rebecca asked, setting the soap in the soap holder.

"Looks like about sixty."

"Good thing it won't rain!"

"That's right."

"No, that's what you always say! You say, 'Good thing it won't rain,' and Mom says, 'You don't know it won't,' and you say it's never rained in late July since you came to California."

"I believe you," he said with a smile. "You are one of the most reliable people I know."

Rebecca looked away. "Dad?"

"Sweetie?"

"I tried to keep James occupied."

He smiled. "Of course you did. I would never have thought otherwise."

Ryan had tried, too, and he was trying again, lying with James on their bedroom floor, playing animals. He had a number of props for this, and he'd brought them out of the closet: old washcloths for blankets, a collection of bottle caps that Badger and Dog could use when they were ready to eat.

"Dog sayin' arf arf arf," James cried, making his dog lunge at Ryan's badger.

"No, James," Ryan said. "Dog is gentle. You love him, right?"

James didn't answer.

"Maybe we should give him a bath before the party. Then he can put his new collar on." Ryan went to the closet for a shallow plastic basin. "Let's give them a bath together." He set the basin between them and walked Badger over to it. "One, two, three," he said, and he jumped Badger into the imaginary water, where Badger bounced up and down, splashing vigorously. "Alley-oop," Ryan said, and he jumped Dog in, too. "Look, they're splashing."

"Alley-oop," James said. "Alley-oop, *alley-oop,* ALLEY-OOP!" He scrambled onto his bed and jumped, shouting, "NO MORE MONKEYS JUMPIN' ON THE BED."

Their father appeared in the doorway. He had the rumpled look of late evening, his tie pulled loose, shirtsleeves rolled. "Time for your bath now, James," he said quietly, and James slid off the bed and ran to him.

In her room Rebecca considered what to wear. Her colorful dresses were on one side of her closet and her plain dresses were on the other, and though she loved getting a bright new dress like the purple-striped one she'd picked out a couple weeks earlier, she generally ended up with something darker and less adorned. She had a navy dress with a small white collar that she had worn at least once a week this school year, and she was reaching for it when she saw, hanging way off to the side, a sleeveless white dress decorated with yellow daffodils, not just printed on the material but embroidered with bright yellow embroidery floss, the effect being of real flowers floating over a white background. Her Michigan grandmother had made it for her and sent it in a box with small floral sachets tucked between the folds of tissue paper. She had never worn it for fear of ruining it, and she was relieved, as she pulled it over her head, that it still fit, though it pulled slightly across her shoulders and was shorter than most of her other dresses. She found some white socks with yellow edges, sat on the bed, and pulled them onto her clean feet, carefully folding them down so they were cuffed identically. She strapped on her black patent-leather Mary Janes and stood before the mirror. She was satisfied with the way she looked—satisfied was the happiest you ought to be about how you looked; she had read that somewhere—though her hair, in the day's braids, wasn't quite as partyish as the rest of her. In fact, they were yesterday's braids. She needed her mother's help to redo them, though, and at this point, with the party starting in under an hour, Rebecca didn't want to bother her.

She pulled the elastics off the tips of the braids and combed her fingers through her hair. When she was finished, it fell in sharp zigzags halfway to her elbows, and tears pricked at her eyes. She should have washed it. She really should have washed it, but it was far too late now—James was in the tub, with Ryan and Robert yet to go—and even if she had time she wouldn't take a second bath just for her hair.

Or would she? She was caught in the middle, with the right but difficult thing off to one side and the wrong but easy thing off to the other, and she imagined the bathtub empty right now, available, and herself carefully taking off the dress, and removing the shoes and spotless socks, and putting her robe on, and going back down the hall to the bathroom—and she couldn't say for sure that she would do it, which made her imagine shaking a finger at herself, a picture that came to her so frequently it might as well have been a scene captured by her father's camera and put in one of the family photo albums. Except it wasn't a real picture: it was the Rebecca of the moment, in this case wearing the daffodil dress, shaking her finger at another Rebecca, usually a younger, smaller Rebecca, standing with her head down.

"Carry on," her father sometimes said when one or another of the children was stuck in a bad situation. He didn't say it in a mean way; it was more: *I know this is hard, I'm sorry it's so hard, there are various things you could do, you could sit down and cry, or you could try to carry on. Can you carry on? I have a feeling you'll be able to carry on.*

Rebecca ran her brush through her hair, and that helped—the kinked strands blended together, and it looked a little less messy. She decided it would have to do. She left her room and headed for the kitchen, pausing when she saw that her mother's door was ajar. She stood outside the door, listening. Water running, drawers opening: there was none of that.

Just then James came running out of the bedroom hallway in clean clothes. Her father followed, and when he saw Rebecca he stopped and smiled. "You look lovely," he said, and a flood of warmth rose into Rebecca's face.

"I forgot to wash my hair."

"I'd never have known. To me you look perfect."

"Let me see," her mother called from the bedroom, and then she pulled open the door as if she'd been standing right there all along.

But she hadn't. She'd been sitting on her bed gathering strength for the final push. She had cooked and cleaned, but the last part, getting herself ready, was the hardest. With the house and the food, she simply followed a plan that was the same from party to party, year to year. But when it came to herself, to her hair and makeup, her clothes and shoes, she was not so easily satisfied. Yes, she was a doctor's wife and a mother of four, a suburban matron to the core of her being. But she wanted, just once a year, to look like someone important. The women she saw photographed at galas—they had something that went beyond a fashionable hairstyle or an expensive couture gown. It was an air of not doubting their right to be photographed, an air of having. As the daughter of a hardware store owner, Penny had never enjoyed anything like the advantages these women probably took for granted.

"Look at you," she said to Rebecca.

Rebecca looked up at her father. When he was around she understood her mother better, or at least found it easier to know what to expect. She waited for him to say something that would make her mother go further, tell Rebecca how she liked the dress.

But Penny said nothing, and Bill hesitated and then said he was making progress on getting the children bathed. Cutting her losses, Rebecca reached for James's hand and led him to the kitchen. Trays of hors d'oeuvres lay everywhere: on the stove, the countertops, the table, even the top of the refrigerator. "That's a ton of food," she said, more to herself than to James. "She did a lot of work."

In the master bedroom, Penny was telling Bill the same thing.

She wasn't complaining, but she wanted him to be aware of her work so that he would feel honor-bound to do his, which wasn't simply the shaking of hands and the fixing of drinks—it was much more than that.

"I *am* glad to see them," he said. "Or I will be."

"But I want you to *act* glad. Enthusiastic." "Spirited" was another word. She wanted him to be spirited in the way he greeted the guests and even more spirited in the way he moved from group to group and joked with the men and teased or complimented the women.

"I'll try," he said mildly.

"Why can't you say you *will*?"

"Because I tried last year." And the year before that, he thought but didn't say. "I may not have it in me."

She was at her dresser with her back to him, holding her hair on top of her head with one hand and using the other to pull tendrils loose in front of her ears. He could see her face reflected in the mirror, the way she turned her head slightly and cast her eyes sideways to look at her profile.

He said, "Is there anything else I can do?"

Dropping her hair, she found his eyes in the mirror and looked at him. She couldn't say she wanted him to cross the room and turn her around to face him and then to hold her close. He couldn't say he knew this but had Ryan to move along and himself to get ready—that even if he couldn't transform himself as fully as she wanted, he needed to wash up and change. And so they held each other's gaze for another moment until Penny—who of the two of them had more to lose—broke the look and opened a drawer in search of bobby pins. And with that, Bill returned to the children's bathroom.

Rebecca and James were still in the kitchen. The cheese rolls were as tasty as she remembered from last year, and the cookies were mostly just the right light brown color, and the highball glasses were ready on one tray while the old-fashioned glasses were ready on another, but something was off.

"Where's Robert?" she said. "Where is he and where has he been?"

James went to the sliding door. "Outside."

And sure enough, just out of view, Robert was sitting on the bench, where so many hours ago they'd all had lunch. But no: Robert hadn't been with them. Except for in the garage, at the freezer, she had barely seen him all afternoon.

He looked up at them.

"What are you doing?" she said.

"Go away."

"Robert."

"Go away!"

Robert could be like this, and she shrugged and went to check on Ryan. The bathroom was empty, and his door was closed.

"Ryan," she said, knocking.

"Where's James?" he called.

She opened the door and found Ryan sitting cross-legged on the rug, naked. She said, "Aren't you getting dressed?"

He was holding his badger upright, while James's dog lay on its side, somehow looking perkier than usual. "Where's James?" he said again. "I thought he was going to take Dog to the party."

"Ryan," she said. "He might not want to."

"Well, I thought he was." Ryan went to his dresser. He didn't put the badger down as he pulled on underpants and shorts and a clean shirt. "Why are you so dressed up?"

"I'm not."

Robert would have argued, but Ryan just picked up the dog and set it on James's bed.

"Maybe he'll come back for it," she said.

"Maybe," Ryan said sadly.

They went to the living room and sat on the couch. The door to their parents' bedroom was closed, but they could hear James on the other side of it, jabbering to their father. The abalone shell was on the coffee table, and Rebecca leaned forward and looked at it. She said, "Not as many people smoke these days, but the ones who do smoke more."

She and Ryan were sitting side by side when Robert came in from the kitchen, looking bedraggled and forlorn. He said, "What are you guys doing?"

"We're ready," Rebecca said.

"For the party," Ryan added. He held up his badger and waved him back and forth. "Badger's ready, too."

Robert was tired and angry. His knees were dirty, and his eyes were red. He looked at Ryan and said, "Your badger makes me sick."

"Robert!" Rebecca gasped.

The injury Ryan felt was enormous, and he reacted in stages: first not moving, then a hot feeling in his stomach, and finally an acute and terrible worry for Badger's feelings. He bent his head and whispered some consoling words into Badger's ear.

"You're six," Robert said to him.

"And you're mean," Rebecca said, jumping to her feet. "And you aren't even ready."

Robert stood in front of the coffee table. "Who cares about a stupid party? What's that dress, anyway?"

They stared at each other. Rebecca, in the ten minutes that had elapsed since her mother had neither complimented nor ignored the daffodil dress, had arrived at a feeling of deep humiliation in regard to what she was wearing. This was the kind of humiliation that poses as insolence, however, and she planted her hands on her hips and stuck out her chin. "Grandma Blair made it for me," she said. "As something special."

Robert sank deeper into despair. The watch he'd lost had originally been owned by Great-grandpa Blair, which made it far more special than the dress, since Great-grandpa Blair was dead. But how special was a watch when it was gone?

"I've never worn it before," Rebecca said. "It still smells like Grandma's bedroom. Remember how I got to sleep with her when we visited?"

"You know that tree house thing?" Robert snapped. "It's going to be just for the boys. That's what Dad said."

"I don't believe you."

"He did," Robert said, but thinking of the tree house made him sink lower. When his father first mentioned the idea of building a tree house, he said they'd get some redwood and make it sturdy enough to withstand rain and time, a combination of words that had prompted Robert to try to come up with a haiku, as Mr. Gleason sometimes assigned the class during the last minutes before lunch. Mr. Gleason would write two words on the board, always one-syllable words, and say, "All right, class, fifteen more syllables. Go." And they would write as fast as they could, the object being speed rather than elegance, for which Robert loved him all the more.

> Rain in the winter
> Hot all the time in summer
> Spring and fall have both

Robert was pleased with himself for thinking so fast, and he recited the poem to his father and the other children, earning a smile from his father, a laugh from Ryan, and a long, curious look from Rebecca, who then said, speaking slowly, "In time all the world dangles like an ornament swaying in the rain," and with his hands clenched into fists, Robert pressed his fingertips to his palms one by one, counting off her syllables, though he'd known as soon as she opened her mouth that she would outdo him.

He turned his back on Rebecca and Ryan and looked out the window. How long ago it seemed that they'd sat under the oak tree with the burned cookies. How long ago since he'd thought about Mr. Gleason and the four humors! If Rebecca was sanguine, then what was he? What was he?

"Robert," she said, "why are you so mad?"

"I'm not."

"Or sad."

He turned around and gave her a mournful look. "I can't find—"

"What?"

He couldn't admit it. It was too terrible. Once he'd said the words out loud he would have to tell his father. "The key to the shed," he finished.

"Why do you want the key to the shed?"

"I think we need that table up here. The table from the old patio furniture."

"What for?"

"For people to put things on outside the kitchen."

Rebecca was about to say they had the bench for that, but she stopped herself. "It's in a drawer in the kitchen. The key."

"It's not."

"That's where it always is."

"It isn't there. But there's supposed to be an extra one hidden on the foundation, and I can't find it."

"The foundation of the shed? You mean the concrete?"

"Yeah."

"Well, let's go look. Ryan and I will help you." She crossed the living room and in one leap took the two steps up to the main level. From there she strode to the front door. "Come on."

She skipped down the front steps to the driveway, Ryan following behind her and Robert a few long paces behind him, and James, alerted somehow that the older children were on the move, bringing up the rear.

Robert picked up his pace, wanting to be in the lead if they were going at all. The pain in his stomach was sharper now, a knife slicing into his belly each time his feet struck the ground.

"Wait," James cried. Excited, he began to run, and he hit something with his toe and was on the ground before he even knew he was falling. He screamed a scream from his store of special-occasion screams, giant and piercing, and immediately Ryan turned and ran back up the driveway.

"James!"

"Dada," James wailed, pushing up onto his knees, his chin scraped raw and the heels of his hands bleeding. "Dada!"

"Shhh," Ryan said, crouching at his brother's side. "It's okay, it's okay. Should I go get Dog? He'll kiss you."

"Want Dada!"

"Should I get Dog *and* Dada?"

Robert and Rebecca were nearly at the spur, and they carefully avoided looking at each other so they wouldn't have to acknowledge that they should go help Ryan. It was gloomy under the trees this late in the afternoon. At the shed they squatted and felt along the foundation for a gap where the key might be, probing with their fingers and then, when they came up empty, lowering their heads to the ground and peering sideways. They went around a second time on their hands and knees. At last they stood. Rebecca had gotten dirty again, her forearms and her shins in particular, but she'd tried to be careful with her dress, and she was relieved to see that aside from one streak of dirt at the bottom, it was clean. At least the front was. She twisted to look at the back and saw that one of the daffodils had snagged on something. The formerly pristine flower had turned into a mess of broken threads. "Oh, no," she cried.

Robert stared at the dress, and his eyes welled with tears. "You think that's bad."

He told her about his lost watch, and they sat side by side in front of the shed, and because he was crying so hard Rebecca didn't cry at all. She patted his shoulder a few times and waited. At last she wrapped her arm around him in an imitation of what their father would do if someone were upset. "Carry on," she whispered.

He looked into her face. "I hate this party!"

"Me, too."

Off in the distance, a dog began to bark. It was the six o'clock bark—the bark of their neighbor Mr. Pope arriving home from work. The Popes' dog alerted the neighborhood to every move his owners made, and on days when there was no barking it was assumed that the Popes were all home sick.

"It's starting right now," Rebecca said. "And we're filthy."

They climbed to the top of the driveway, where there was already an unfamiliar car parked behind the Valiant, and circled the house to the laundry room. Rebecca turned on the water in the soaking sink. "Here," she said, reaching into a basket of towels and holding a washcloth under the stream. She found a bar of soap, rough and harsh-smelling, and rubbed it against the cloth until it was soapy.

Robert took off his shirt and washed his face, his chest, his arms. He got out of his shorts and underpants, turned around for modesty, and washed his privates and then his legs. "How am I going to do my feet?" he said, and she looked around, uncertain.

"Climb up here," she said, patting the washing machine, and she had him sit with his feet dangling in the sink and washed them for him, which reminded her of something, maybe a book.

"What about you?" he said. "You're dirty, too."

She unzipped her dress and took her turn. When she was done with her body, she turned the water hotter and stuck her head under the faucet. She sloshed water through her hair and used the bar to soap it up. After she dried off she looked at her dress long enough to determine that she couldn't put it back on.

They heard party noises through the closed laundry room door.

"I know," she said, and she opened a cabinet and found a box marked "Too small." With younger brothers, Robert's clothes never made it into this box, but some of Rebecca's clothes could pass for something a boy would wear, and, giggling a little, they both pulled on checked shorts so tight they looked like underwear and T-shirts that exposed their belly buttons.

She held her finger to her lips and reached for the doorknob.

"You should see your hair," he said.

She didn't care. If satisfied was the best you could feel about how you looked, then dissatisfied was the worst, not nearly as bad as upset or embarrassed. She had squeezed as much water from her hair as she could, but already the shoulders of her shirt were soaked through, and she knew there'd be a huge wet spot on her back.

She opened the door. The party voices swelled, and she gave Robert a shrug.

He followed her up the hall. They'd decided he should wait until tomorrow to tell their father about the watch, and his stomachache had changed from the knife-stab type to the empty type. He was hungry, and he realized he'd never had lunch.

Standing in the living room were a dozen adults: holding drinks, talking, and laughing, already seeming to fill the space despite the fact that eventually there would be several dozen more of them crowding the room and spilling onto the patio. Their mother was there, too, wearing a black dress and black high heels, her hair in a twist on top of her head. For decoration, she had added a fake red rose. "Kids!" she called. "It's the party! Come say hello! You can help me entertain!"

They recognized her elation and kept going, both of them aware that they were disappointing her. In the kitchen Robert pulled the plastic off a tray of cheese logs and stuffed three into his mouth. Rebecca poured them each a glass of juice and said, "What do you think happened to Ryan and James?"

Robert went to the sliding door. Outside, their father sat on the grass with the two younger boys, cradling James on his lap while Ryan leaned against him and rested his hand on his leg. Their father was in the clothes he'd worn all day, though his tie was missing and the top buttons of his shirt were undone. He looked up at Robert and Rebecca and smiled. "There you are," he said. "Now we're all together."

"Except Mom," Ryan said.

"Well, that's true, but you know how she feels about the party. I think she's where she wants to be right now."

James's face was smeared with tears and dirt, but there were Band-Aids on his knees and he was quiet, his thumb in his mouth and the side of his face pressed to his father's chest. Robert and Rebecca sat down.

"Quite a day," their father said.

Ryan lifted his badger. "Badger is feeling better."

"That is one good thing."

"And Dog is," Ryan said. "Wait, James, where is he? You just had him."

"Dad," Rebecca said, "Robert had a good idea." She explained about the old patio table in the shed and how it would have been good to have it at the house for the party. "We should remember for next year."

"That is a good idea," Bill said. "But I wonder what became of the key."

"The keys," she said. "We couldn't find either of them."

"There's only one that I know of. In the junk drawer in the kitchen. If it's gone we may have to cut the padlock."

Robert had been silent until now. "No, Dad," he said, "there's supposed to be a key down there, remember?" He described his search, the careful way he, and then he and Rebecca, had crawled around the shed, feeling every inch of the way for the gap between the foundation and the wall.

"I'm confounded," Bill said. "I just don't have any recollection of that."

"It's there, Dad. It's supposed to be. On the foundation."

"On the foundation," Bill said, something tickling at his memory, a June day in 1961 that began with the infant Robert standing on his father's thighs, pushing downward with his soft wedge feet as Bill held him under the arms, his small body rigid with excitement. Or so it had struck Bill, who departed reluctantly, leaving the baby and his mother to wait for him while he drove to the Portola Valley property and poured the foundation for the shed. In the hardening concrete he scratched a capital R, and then, for no good reason, a second R and a third.

"Maybe so," he said, "but I think that's something to solve some other day. I have some hosting to do and I suspect I'd better change my clothes."

"*There* he is," Ryan said, reaching behind Bill and retrieving James's dog. "Here, James, don't forget to hold him."

James held out his arms for Dog. "He got a new collar," he said proudly.

"He certainly did," Bill said, lifting James from his lap and setting him on the grass. "I guess you loaned it to him, did you, Rob?"

"I borrowed it," Ryan said.

Around Dog's neck was Robert's watch, and Robert put his face in his hands and began to cry again. This time he didn't feel so bad. It was a free, easy kind of cry, gentle as a stream. Bill watched his oldest, puzzled by the tears but aware that he needed to get into the house. He stood still for another moment and then told the children he'd see them inside. Halfway to the door, he turned and looked at them. Rebecca wondered if he was going to ask what had happened to her dress, but instead he came back and lifted James in his arms. "James James Morrison Morrison," he murmured, and he pressed his lips to James's silky hair.

3

ROBERT

When I was in medical school, much was made of the need for compassion, and we talked about it as if it could be learned, like the names of the cranial nerves or the ability to detect pneumonia on exam. This made sense to me at first. My father—the doctor I knew best—was full of compassion, not just for the children he treated but for everyone: their parents, his own children, a stranger at the side of a highway waiting for a tow truck. At last I had to recognize that he hadn't picked it up in class, and I was afraid I'd never measure up.

But I needn't have worried. As it turned out, I pity the sick; I feel for them. In my group internal medicine practice, I'm the doctor new patients request most frequently (a statistic I did not seek out; such is the state of managed care that gathering data like these has become an integral part of our operation). According to our scheduling staff, people are always calling and saying, "I saw Dr. Blair when my regular doctor was out, and I want to switch" or "I've heard Dr. Blair really *cares.*"

And yet. How do you care without feeling each grim diagnosis, each death, as a drop of grief making its way through your bloodstream? How do you *continue* to care?

For two decades I was all kindness and concern, and then suddenly, as I hit my mid-forties, I wasn't. I dawdled over charts in my office while the sickest of my patients waited for me; I postponed phone calls to deliver bad news for hours or even days, berating myself the longer I waited but unable to pick up the phone. I didn't know what was wrong. I felt I had lost my feelings. A broken heart can masquerade as a cold one.

At home, I avoided my wife and our two boys. I thought I was very, very tired, and I took naps before dinner, after weekend breakfasts, on holiday afternoons. I used my fatigue to justify all kinds of low behavior. I snapped, I growled, I sank into silence. The boys fought over which of them had caused my bad moods. "You yelled and woke him up!" "Well, you didn't try your cauliflower!" Jen scowled at me when they weren't looking, but after a few months, when nothing had changed, she slipped a mask over her expressive features and presented me with a single multipurpose half-smile. "Daddy isn't going with us this time," she would say to the boys without asking me. It was true. Daddy wasn't really going anywhere.

This might have gone on indefinitely had James not shown up unexpectedly. He was living in Eugene, Oregon, the only one of us not to settle on the Peninsula—though the truth was, he hadn't *settled* anywhere. After dropping out of college—just seven months shy of getting his degree, which was so typical—he began drifting from one job to another, one life to another; and now, at thirty-eight, if he wasn't actually drifting, he was nevertheless living what seemed to the rest of us to be a pretty unstable life.

He arrived on a Friday night, knocking on Rebecca's door without advance notice or explanation, and within days he'd established a kind of pattern, dropping by my house every second or third evening for dinner, or at eight in the morning so he could "keep the boys company at breakfast," his term of art for freeloading.

But I'm getting ahead of myself. That first Sunday, Rebecca and her husband had us all over for brunch: me, Jen, and our boys; Ryan and his wife and daughter; and of course James. The house was on a shady street in north Palo Alto, all unfinished concrete walls and steel railings, the yard full of river stones and carefully managed wild grasses. Jen said the house was as elegant and severe as Rebecca herself, not exactly a compliment but I knew what she meant.

James came to the door in his boxers that morning, unshaved, hair matted. "What?" he said as I looked him over. "I'm not ready."

I gave this the response it deserved.

The boys pushed past me to their uncle, and he held out his palm so they could give him some skin. No matter how long it had been since they'd last seen him, they were always ready for some James-style fun, and he always delivered. It was easy enough for him, I suppose; he was still a child himself.

Rebecca and Walt were in the kitchen setting out fruit and bagels. The boys went for a pink bakery box, Jen poured herself coffee, and I shook hands with Walt because we always shook hands, even if it had been only a day or two since we'd seen each other. James followed behind us and helped himself to a slice of cantaloupe. I tried to get a notion from Rebecca of how things were going with him, but she stayed busy with the fruit, fanning melon slices, mounding strawberries. As I watched, she took a step back, tilted her head to the side, and then stepped forward again and made a micro-adjustment to the grapes. She readily admitted to being a perfectionist, but, also being a psychiatrist, she couched it in the lingo of her profession and referred to it as a characteristic defense. At our father's funeral, a few years earlier, his sister Irene had made a point of telling Rebecca how sad he'd been that he never had the chance to walk his one daughter down the aisle, and Rebecca said, "Oh, Aunt Irene, I think he felt worse about not getting to be a pallbearer at your funeral." Irene laughed, but Rebecca told me later that she'd felt terrible, having allowed those words to escape from her careful mouth.

Licking his fingers, James leaned against the refrigerator door, all six-four of him. He had a way of being in a room that was at once provisional and accusatory. He might leave at any minute, but until then everyone should back the fuck off. His naked chest was smooth, almost hairless, his body joining in the argument that he shouldn't be held to the standards of adulthood yet.

The doorbell rang, and Ryan and Marielle came in with loads of fresh flowers, the kind of disruption that can take a minute if everyone already present is engaged in conversation or ten if they are desperate for distraction. It took us ten.

At last the hubbub died down, and Marielle looked around and said, "This is so nice." She was from Montreal, one of those angular French brunettes with no belly fat and intensely muscular lower legs. She'd come to California on a vacation with three girlfriends and met Ryan at a sandwich shop in Palo Alto. They had the kind of effortless-seeming relationship that you assume belies great effort, except theirs didn't. "We just click," Ryan always said, and for those of us who found the human conversation to have its difficulties, this was annoying and enviable and also somehow consoling—it could happen, it wasn't impossible; it had happened to Ryan, who deserved it if anyone did.

Ryan nodded eagerly in response to his wife's comment. "It is nice, it's really nice, I wish we could do this more often, all of us getting together." He looked at James. "So how's it going, J? How long can you stay?"

James smirked and stared at his hands, examining his nails, the backs of his fingers. He looked up and said, "Dunno, *Ry*."

I saw, or thought I saw, a flicker of hurt cross Ryan's face.

"Yeah," I said to James, "talk to us. We're all dying to know what's up."

James looked at his hands again, perhaps this time in contemplation of using them as fists. Even if he wasn't going to strike me, it was obvious that he was pissed off.

"I'm making eggs," Rebecca said. "When everyone's ready. James, do you want to get dressed?"

For a moment it seemed he might refuse, but he gave her an easy smile and left the room. He had been the most ingenuous child, a sweet enthusiast for any promising plan. In the late nineties, during a stint in Boulder, he'd come up with an idea for a new business and presented it to me over dinner as if I were an investor, complete with spreadsheets and projections and a firm handshake. I was in Denver for a conference, though I probably wouldn't have gone if it hadn't meant a chance to check up on him. Basically, the idea was AAA for bicycles: he was going to pass around flyers with his name and phone number, and if you had bike trouble "anytime or anywhere," he'd show up and service your ride on the spot. It wasn't a terrible plan, though he didn't seem to understand that AAA succeeded by charging its customers in advance, insurance-style. We sat in an overpriced steak house near my hotel and he talked his idea up until I took out my checkbook and gave him three thousand dollars to get started. "It's an investment," he said, and for purposes of face-saving I didn't argue. I debated whether or not to tell Jen and finally knocked the amount down to five hundred so I could maintain the idea that I didn't keep secrets from her—just details.

He came back in a wrinkled T-shirt and jeans and over Rebecca's eggs proceeded to entertain the kids with stories from the Blair family almanac. My boys liked hearing about the time I went looking for a lost tennis ball and instead came face-to-face with a skunk. But what, they asked James, did our dad *do* while Penny went to get the tomato juice? Where did he *wait*? How bad did he *smell*? They wanted to know how many cans of tomato juice I'd bathed in and what had happened to the juice afterward.

Ryan's daughter was only four, too young to believe in a childhood for her father. The story James told failed to engage her, and he fell silent and began poking through his eggs as if there might be something valuable hidden in them. "So what should we talk about?" he said at last, looking around the table. "Robert's misery?"

Ryan's eyes widened. Marielle licked the corners of her mouth. My boys stared at their plates, and Jen put a steady bead on me. I could feel Rebecca's medical interest stir from deep within its weekend resting place.

"You people," James said, "are so dishonest. Wishing doesn't make it so, remember? I don't think I've heard one real thing from any of you since I got here. It's all 'how nice,' 'how nice.' You guys are so corrupt."

Rebecca was motionless, the only sign of distress a twitch below her left eye. She had our father's strong nose and our mother's narrow chin. She was sometimes called handsome, which Jen said was worse than nothing as compliments went, but I saw beauty in her: in the straightness of her back and in her heavily lashed gray eyes.

"It's okay, James," Ryan said. "We know things might be complicated."

"That's it?" James said. "Can you go further, Ry? One little step? What 'things' might be complicated? And who is 'we'? You and your lovely French lady, or you and your esteemed older siblings, Dr. and Dr. Blair?"

I was experiencing a kind of basement-level rage overlaid by a number of competing urges—to say something funny, to say something lacerating, to pretend nothing had happened, to leave the table. Perhaps because none of these was within my reach, I said, inflecting it into a question, "'Wishing doesn't make it so'?" though I knew the answer. Our mother had been famous among us for her pointed and yet strikingly unhelpful proverbs. I think she believed such comments fulfilled her maternal duties, for she rarely had anything to add in the way of empathy or even consolation.

"Penny," Rebecca said.

"I know."

"Well," Ryan said. "So anyway—"

James set his fork down with a clank. "You want to know why I'm here, don't you? You think there has to be a reason, like I'm in trouble, I'm broke again. God forbid I just wanted to come home. And no, Rebecca, I'm not projecting."

I'd felt Jen watching me since James's comment about my misery, and now I looked at her, wondering if I'd receive censure or forgiveness. Instead, she gave me one of her loveliest and most encouraging smiles, and my lachrymal glands lurched into action.

Ryan was speaking, but I hadn't heard a word. ". . . take some time," he was saying, "and create some space . . ." and I was off again, because Jen's sympathetic look had gotten me thinking that James might have helped me, saying what he'd said—that I might, if I were very careful, find a way to use it to my advantage.

Immediately, I felt the kind of shame I associated with my father, with whom—or with whose image—I had created a tightly constructed system of self-esteem manipulation, a habit pointed out to me and elaborated by Rebecca, bless her analytical heart. It was as if I had a flow chart in my head that began with any action I performed, any comment I uttered, any thought I had, and from which there extended two arrows, one toward my father's approval and the other pointing definitively in the opposite direction. From each of these, of course, there was only one way to go: toward peace in the first instance and self-loathing in the second. On occasion I would stop to consider—would he truly have objected to this idea, that choice?—but for the most part life, my life, divided neatly into the good and the bad. And this was bad. He would have argued vigorously that milking one person's offensive comment for emotional credit from another person was a shabby show, as he liked to say.

Ah, but I could get so much from Jen if I played it right: patience, succor, forgiveness, *relief from chores*—the husbandly things having to do with fence posts and torn screens and constantly running toilets that a handyman could knock off in minutes but that the men of my social class felt they needed to do themselves, however awkwardly, and if they could do it, why couldn't I? I was the grandson of a hardware store owner, for God's sake! This was my hang-up, not Jen's—she would have been delighted if I'd hired someone to fix the little things I diligently postponed week after week.

"More eggs, anyone?" Rebecca said.

After brunch James invited himself over. He claimed he wanted to play with the boys, but I suspected his true motive was to make sure he'd get the opportunity to add insult to injury. At the car he took the shotgun seat without so much as a glance at Jen—a move that pleased me, perversely enough, since it gave me further reason to be angry at him—and as I drove he jiggled one leg at warp speed while holding the rest of his body in an attitude of exaggerated relaxation.

The boys had earned an hour of DVDs, and James dug through our overstocked library until he found an old Smurf disc he had sent them for Christmas a couple of years earlier. He settled on the couch and began a disquisition that was surely not intended for his nephews, ages eight and five. "This whole show," he said, "is an argument in favor of socialism. The Smurfs are basically a workers' collective."

I had decided, doubtless with my father's imagined eye fastened tight on me, that rather than try to get sympathy from Jen I should face one of the annoying fix-it jobs I'd been postponing, the longest-standing of which involved the latch on the gate to our side yard, which hadn't worked properly for months.

My untrained eye had diagnosed the latch problem as secondary to the gate coming loose from its hinges, so my first task was to make a study of the gate/stucco exterior wall/hinge complex to determine whether fixing the hinge would require that I drill into the stucco, a business that was beyond the scope of my interest. As fate would have it, the gate was just outside the master bedroom, and before I could get to work, Jen appeared on the other side of the window, cranked it open a few inches, and asked me if I was okay.

I'm sure there are loaded questions in every marriage, and "Are you okay?" was one of the big ones in ours. "Are you okay?" meaning *Are you mad at me?* "Are you okay?" meaning *Why are you mad at me?* "Are you okay?" meaning *I thought you were going to fix the gate . . . take the boys . . . come to bed . . .* And "Are you okay?" meaning *I love you, I'm worried, please talk to me.*

"What do you mean?" I said, stalling.

"Well, at brunch," she said. "James."

I gave the gate a swing before I answered, its long, shrill creak making me think the whole problem might be solved with a simple squirt of WD-40, though I knew even as I thought this that it was ridiculous. Turning back to Jen, I countered with a question of my own: "Am I okay *about what James said,* or am I okay *given that he said it?*"

She shook her head sadly. "Oh, babe."

I walked a few paces, then turned back. James and the boys had the TV turned up so high that I could almost figure out what bit of Beethoven was playing as background to the little blues, as the Smurfs were known in our family. "You know what gets me?" I said to Jen. "They have no idea . . ." I let the sentence trail off and took a step back. I could see Jen's silhouette on the other side of the screen, but the angled window was catching a lot of sun and it was almost possible to pretend she wasn't there. This was an October day, clear blue, and I was leaning against a fence I owned, looking at a house I owned, contemplating a gate I owned, and the world seemed a dismal and unforgiving place.

"What?" Jen said. She stepped closer to the screen, and now I could see her square shoulders and her smooth, straight hair. "Who is 'they'?"

"Rebecca," I said. "And Ryan and James."

"Your family," she said.

"Right."

In residency we used to say the last hour of call was as long as all the previous hours combined, and we compared notes on the physical sensations of exhaustion: the heavy limbs, the watery eyes, the sour taste in your mouth no matter how much you brushed your teeth, the faint hum emanating from your own head. Worst for me was the crawling skin, what a friend of mine called "the furs" because to him it was as if you were beginning to sprout hair. I felt it just below my eyes and on my forearms: a sensation not unlike what toast might feel, if toast were sentient, when it was spread with butter.

That evening I forced myself to read three chapters of a Hardy Boys adventure to the boys. It was dark by the time I'd finished, and the boys were close to sleep: Sammy, the older, in his bed, since we were in his room, while Luke lay on Sammy's floor in his beloved junior sleeping bag and made his body as floppy as possible so I would give up on trying to move him and leave him there for the night.

What followed was like that last hour of call, with its abrupt onset of deferred suffering. I stood in the kitchen boiling water for tea and remembered my final patient Friday afternoon, a twenty-eight-year-old man complaining of fatigue and occasional fever. On exam, he had swollen lymph nodes in his neck (but no sore throat), and his abdomen was normal. I assumed a virus, and after the usual rote and unhelpful recommendations (time, rest), we spent a few minutes talking about his work, which had always fascinated me: he assisted the pastry chef at a trendy restaurant in San Francisco. He told me that in the next year or so we'd be seeing a revival of verticality in desserts and described a mousse/cake concoction topped by a six-inch shard of hazelnut brittle, upright and thin as a knife blade.

Now, as I pictured him on the exam table, I noticed in memory what I'd failed to see in the moment: that as he talked, he was running his fingernails up and down his forearms, scratching. I was stricken. Fatigue, fever, swollen lymph nodes, itchy skin: had I thought of lymphoma, much less sent him for labs? I had not. I felt so terrible I had to sit down. What earthly good was I to anyone if I could not pay attention to what was right in front of me? What else had I missed on Friday, or last week, or last month?

Then I remembered something else, not worse but more embarrassing. As I sat in my office late Friday afternoon, getting ready to leave for the weekend, I phoned the restaurant where this patient worked on the off chance that they might have a free table for Saturday night. And when I learned they were fully booked, I very nearly called my patient to see if he could help.

Asking a favor of a patient. *Thinking* about asking a favor of a patient. My father, that holy ghost, intruded yet again. Though he never would have said so to them, he was troubled by the stories his colleagues in adult medicine told him about receiving gifts from patients—bottles of Scotch, theater tickets, seats at sporting events. These were offerings, he thought, to the part of the doctor who was, in the patient's estimation, God, and they expressed the patient's belief not just in the doctor's omnipotence but also in the notion that this was a capricious and demanding god whose favors would not be bestowed equally. If the gifts were not bribes, they were at the very least plaintive cries for attention, and by accepting them the doctors entered into, participated in, essentially encouraged the patients' beliefs. As a pediatrician, my father was given finger paintings and clay pencil holders and could not tell their creators that it would be wrong for him to accept them, but he always studied the parents to make sure they weren't too invested in the giving of the gift, since if there was any apotheosizing going on he wanted to head it off at the first opportunity. In this way he was ahead of his time, trying to throw off the mantle of the all-powerful wizard while most physicians enjoyed the warmth and grandeur of the garment.

My father never would have considered asking a favor of his patients' parents. He never would have missed an obvious sign like urgent scratching. He never would have allowed himself a slump of several months' duration during which he failed his patients, his wife, his children.

Our kitchen faced southwest, allowing, in daylight, a view of some of the trees on my family's land; Jen and I had bought a house not far from the one where I'd grown up. Now, in the dark, I could make out nothing of my childhood home, but I peered through the window anyway. I wished I could see not the old place itself but my life in it—the life of the younger Robert, possessed of a little of the competence of the oldest child and a lot of the grandiosity. How satisfying it had been for me that my father had made me the general contractor of table setting, responsible for getting the subs to do the work but not having to touch utensils or place mats myself. This was a neat trick on his part, since getting kids to set the table is a far greater chore than setting it. (Jen and I had learned this conclusively thanks to a brief experiment we conducted in transferring various responsibilities onto our kids' shoulders by allowing "natural consequences" to develop when said responsibilities were shirked. A woman in Jen's moms' group swore by this method, but at our house the kids won easily, pushing aside their dirty breakfast dishes to sit at the unset table and go at their dinners with their bare hands because all the utensils were still encrusted with food and lying on the previous day's unwashed plates. "You have to give it some time," Jen's friend said, but we caved after a few days.)

I'd brought home straight A's, and though my father refused to praise us for good report cards, saying instead that what mattered to him was that we worked hard, I believed that in the deeper regions of his mind, my academic accomplishments burned like the eternal flame of the Olympics torch.

Then there was the power I enjoyed in the matter of my siblings' self-esteem. I was a pretty nice older brother, but I always knew this was a choice, an act of generosity I could reverse at any time, and with my brothers especially I refined a narrow-eyed tilt of the head that offered a reminder of my gifts in the area of sly undermining should I in any way be provoked.

Rebecca presented a more complicated challenge, since she was as unflappable as our father and, I knew, quite a bit smarter than I. My best ammunition with her was indifference, which I never actually felt but simulated fairly well until she was in high school with me and began making friends with some of my friends, at which point I had to feign unthreatened friendliness lest someone get a whiff of the true terror I felt that she would surpass me.

After brunch that morning, Rebecca had pulled me aside and said meaningfully, and no doubt apropos of James's comment about my misery, that I could talk to her anytime, which until this moment in my kitchen I had managed to find for the most part sweet rather than enraging. Now, with the world outside my window narrowed to a house where I once was happy—or if not happy at least somewhat unaware of my true, wretched character—I felt the full humiliation of the morning reach deeper into my being. James's word struck me as both accurate and inadequate. Reading to the boys earlier, I had deliberately made my voice into a monotone at the moment when Frank and Joe first saw the peregrine falcon they would use to aid their investigation. I was hoping the kids might be only half listening and that we could therefore avoid a three- or four-minute discussion of whether or not it was really possible to train a bird to intercept a message and instead finish the nightly session as soon as possible.

And now I remembered something Jen had said about some other failure of a father: that it wasn't the kids she worried about, it was the man himself, that he'd be hit by regret for all he'd missed. Which brought me again to my father. On the day he held his first grandchild—Sammy, born during a rainstorm that flooded the hospital parking lot and broke branches off trees—he claimed he had only one piece of advice for us, the novice and nervous parents: "Enjoy him."

Had I? Had I enjoyed my children?

If I hadn't, then the question of which of my parents I more resembled—settled and obvious for my entire life—was all at once open and terrifying. Penny may have enjoyed motherhood when she was very new to it; she may even have enjoyed me and Rebecca when there were just the two of us, and Ryan because of his nature. But generally? As a retrospective assessment? Nuh-uh, as my kids liked to say.

This onslaught of self-torment took approximately two minutes. I turned the water off, grabbed my car keys, and told Jen that I was going out.

"Where?" she said. "Why? You look terrible."

"Only because I am."

"Robert, please."

We stared at each other for a long moment. She was sitting cross-legged on our bed, surrounded by pieces of paper printed with the words "A Night to Remember, December 2, 2006" in maybe a dozen different fonts. A lawyer by training, Jen was "home with the kids," a detour I had feared would make her bored and resentful, but she was at least as busy now as she had been while she was working, and her current project organizing a fund-raiser for the boys' school required as much time and energy as preparing for a complicated litigation.

She straightened her legs and reached for her feet, her forefingers grazing the teardrop spaces between her big toes and the toes next to them. In better times I might have found this erotic, but we were in a lull, or rather I was—with "lull" being a euphemism for the most pitiful kind of sexual problem—and in any case I had something else on my mind.

She sighed. "Where are you going?"

"The old place. I won't be long."

The actual property was half a mile away as the crow flies, but the route meandered down one long hill and up another, in the process winding past oak trees and toyon shrubs and hulking modernist mansions. The night was clear and chilly, and as I rounded one curve I saw a deer vanishing into the woods, all spindly hind legs and arcing motion, maybe two seconds ahead of what would have been a grisly car crash.

There was a fork just past the mailbox, with Ryan's small cottage down to the left and the main house up to the right. I rolled down the window and listened. Cars on the freeway, so far away they sounded like the inside of a seashell. We'd spread my father's ashes on a night like this, the four of us passing the urn, scooping, tossing. "Should we say something?" Ryan said, and Rebecca said, "If we want to," and then we didn't. James had arrived from South America too late to say goodbye, and he bore this burden in uncharacteristic silence.

The house was now occupied by a Silicon Valley CEO who'd coveted the place so much that he'd agreed to rent in the hope that, despite what my siblings and I said, we might someday sell it to him. Putting up with Ryan on the property was part of the agreement, and so far they'd coexisted peacefully.

I should have driven down to Ryan's place, but instead I headed up the driveway. It was a little before nine and all the lights were on. I got out of the car and closed the door softly. I had no subterfuge in mind but no desire to be discovered, either. The CEO had two daughters, and through an open window came the sound of one of them practicing the flute.

The front door was flanked by narrow floor-to-ceiling windows. When the doorbell rang, we kids plastered our faces to the glass of the left-hand window—always the left, never the right—and as I climbed the steps I had a powerful wish to summon those four figures.

I sat in front of the door and drew my knees to my chest. If my patient had lymphoma, I would be lost. A three-day delay on a CBC would mean nothing for his prognosis, but my carelessness would haunt my practice and turn me into a nervous, sweating mess. This—the image of myself in an exam room, trembling in fear of my own fallibility—made me bow my head, and when I looked up again one of the daughters was standing in front of me.

"Excuse me," I said, hurrying to my feet, though since I was on the downslope to fifty this was no longer something I could accomplish with any speed. "I don't want to bother anyone."

She was twelve or thirteen, blond, and terribly thin, though prepubescent enough that I didn't immediately worry for her health. I recalled her mother's absurdly long, slender legs and figured it was genetic.

"I don't mind," she said. "But I need my envelope." She pointed at the door, and I saw that I'd been leaning against a manila envelope with "Susanna" written on it.

"Oh, sorry," I said, retrieving it and handing it to her. "Are you Susanna? I'm Robert. I used to live here."

"Ryan used to live here."

"Ryan is my brother."

She gave me a look that conveyed a good deal of doubt. "I babysit for his daughter."

"Katya," I said. "My niece. Actually, I was just leaving."

"Obviously not."

Somewhere deep in my mind I understood that this was a cheeky and therefore amusing remark, but I couldn't even smile. "Well," I said. "That's the kind of thing people say. I *am* just leaving, how's that?"

"I still have to tell."

There was nothing to do but knock on the door and explain myself to her parents. The CEO greeted me with a surplus of pleasantries and, sweeping his arm to the side, welcomed me into my house. We stopped short of descending into the sunken living room, and while I grappled with the dissonance of his furniture and art—tasteful enough, but not my family's—he dismissed my apologies and told Susanna that this was Dr. Blair, the owner, and why didn't she go get her mother?

"What were you doing out there, anyway?" he called after her disappearing figure. "And how'd you get there?"

She'd gone out the laundry room door, of course. My father had always called this "taking the perimeter."

The CEO's wife came in trailed by both daughters, the smaller an even thinner and blonder replica of her sister. "Laurel," she said when I asked her name, and her mother sighed and said to the child, a little sharply, "Honey, we've talked about this." And then, to me:

"Her name is Daphne." At which point the child put her palm against her mother's hip and pushed ever so slightly, and the CEO and his wife exchanged a look.

We passed an awkward five minutes talking about our summers, or theirs, anyway, which had consisted of trips to Greece, Montana, and the country club, while mine had been a matter of living inside a fugue state and waiting for the trust bestowed on me by patients and family to wither away. "Oh, you know," I said when questioned. "Low-key stuff. Barbecues and picnics."

Back in the car, I headed to Ryan's via the downhill spur, which simply stopped, with no turning area; you had to back up to get out. I parked behind the Jetta that he and Marielle somehow, improbably, shared. Their house—bungalow, cottage, hut, shack—had started life as a storage shed, and though now twice its original size it still had a probationary look.

"We were just talking about you," Marielle said, opening the door. "This second."

Ryan stood behind her. "Robert, what's the matter?"

I let them bring me inside, into the room that served as living room, dining room, kitchen, and bedroom. Katya had a tiny space to herself, and its closed door confirmed that she was in bed, hopefully asleep—a state for which I suddenly yearned.

"Why were you talking about me?" I said as Ryan produced a pitcher of ice water and Marielle hurried to clear a chair of unfolded laundry. They sat side by side on the love seat, a piece of furniture with a name in perfect harmony with its function in that room: Ryan put his arm around Marielle, and she idly laid her hand in his lap, as if it—the lap, the body—were her own.

They began to speak, interrupting or helping each other as they went, their voices a duet of kind concern.

"Just hoping that doof didn't bug you today."

"We know you love him."

"We all love him."

"Though he sometimes makes himself hard to love."

"He's going through something."

"He's not quite himself."

"Were you hurt? We really hope you weren't hurt."

"It was just James."

"Just James being James."

"But more so."

"*Were* you hurt?"

Abruptly they both stopped talking, and I said, "Not at all," convincing no one.

The cottage had unfinished plywood walls and a kitchen area so small and rudimentary that they had to balance a cutting board over the sink to create a workspace. They slept on a Murphy bed that they had to rearrange the furniture to unfold, and they ate off folding TV trays acquired at a yard sale.

Marielle filled one of our mother's hand-thrown ceramic mugs. "Here," she said, and I brought the water to my lips and remembered how much I'd always hated my mother's mugs, the walls of which were so thick it was like having some kind of dental instrument in your mouth while trying to drink.

The two of them watched me, Ryan in faded blue jeans so patched, with squares cut from old flowered dresses of Marielle's, that they seemed less a pair of pants than a piece of folk art. His hair was long, pulled back in a ponytail. He was a teacher at Sand Hill Day School, which happened to be his alma mater, and the director had requested that he maintain his current style when one day he happened to comment that he was considering a haircut. Marielle had a wide, heart-shaped face and a friendly gap between her front teeth, and she wore her hair cut very short, like Jean Seberg in *Breathless*.

"I just stopped in on the CEO," I said. "They spent two weeks in Europe this summer. I'm thinking we should raise their rent."

"They're nice folks," Ryan said. "Very sweet kids."

"Or maybe we should kick them out, do a little upgrade, and then we could *really* raise the rent, like maybe double it."

"Does Jen know where you are?"

This question, innocent and doubtless well meaning, drove another stake into my perforated heart. I was a cause. For the first time I wondered what James had said to Rebecca when he got back there. And how had he gotten back there? All I could remember was his boisterous goodbye to the boys, and the grimace he gave me as he walked out the front door.

I said, "What the fuck is he *doing* here?"

Ryan and Marielle exchanged a glance. "Visiting us?" Ryan said. "He loves us, you know."

"Yeah, which is why he lives five hundred miles away. Something's up, mark my words."

"Robert," Ryan began, "these last few months—"

I cut him off. "You have no idea how hard it is to treat old people. It's one thing after another, the hypertension, the bone weakness, the intestinal distress, the TIAs . . . and each time they come in with a new complaint, they express all this consternation, as if it isn't the best-case scenario that their bodies are giving out. I want to tell them, Either you're declining or you're already dead. I mean, I don't *want* to want to . . . I actually want to keep them in the dark, which, you know, I despise about myself. The dishonesty. My God, James was right. My entire life is a deception. Dad never had to go through this. He had CF, muscular dystrophy, childhood cancers, but that was the exception, not the rule. No wonder he was always in such a fucking good mood. He got to *heal* his patients."

"This is about Dad?" Ryan said.

"There is no 'this,'" I said. "Relax."

Marielle turned to Ryan and said, "Did you just hear Katya?" and in a moment she was slipping through the door, leaving her husband to deal with his brother.

"Rob," Ryan said. "Have you thought of taking some time off? We could stay with the boys, you and Jen could go away."

He was so kind I couldn't stand it, and I pushed myself up from the chair. I knew what it was to be James, the temptation to burn bridges nearly overwhelming.

Ryan followed me to the door. "I'm going to call Jen," he said as I headed toward my car, and while he might have meant he wanted to give her the same suggestion he'd given me—that the two of us should go away and he and Marielle would babysit—I took it as a threat and gave him the finger as I unlocked my car.

I should have gone home, but I drove back up to the big house. Maybe half an hour had gone by; there were fewer windows lit. I returned to the front door and sat down. In under ten hours I had to be at work, where I would see something in the neighborhood of twenty-five patients. And I needed to wade through the stack of applications we'd received for the position of office manager, a task better suited to an office manager, but ours had fractured her elbow ice-skating and decided, since she couldn't work anyway, that she would take a year to reassess her priorities.

Why had I gone on and on with Ryan about treating the elderly? What monstrousness I'd introduced into that little house, visions of illness and coldness combined. I wondered how he and Marielle were restoring peace. Maybe they were just sitting on the love seat together again, drinking from those terrible mugs. Our mother had favored earthy colors for her pottery, glazes that fired to glossy shades of tan and brown. Surveying the fruits of her labor one day when he was thirteen or fourteen, James had pointed out that she'd gone to a lot of trouble to produce a bunch of stuff that looked like shellacked shit.

I got up and brushed off the seat of my pants. The temperature had dropped a good ten degrees since I'd left home, and I took the steps down to the driveway two at a time. I had a jacket in the trunk of my car, and I got it out as quietly as I could, carefully lowering the trunk lid until, with an inch to go, I pressed it closed.

Above me, another light in the house went off. I imagined the CEO and his wife getting ready for bed. By now Jen would be worried, though more so if Ryan had called, or less? She and I had spent a week in the house once, early in our marriage, when my father was away visiting my errant mother in Taos and wanted someone to water the plants and fill the bird feeder. Jen assumed we'd take the master bedroom, but it was too weird for me, so we slept in Rebecca's room, where there was a double bed. Thinking about this now—the strange nights in Rebecca's old bed, being wakened over and over by the creaking trees outside the uncurtained window—I was angry that the CEO could feel comfortable in, could view as his own, a bedroom I'd considered off-limits.

We hadn't had any rain yet, and dry leaves crunched under my feet as I moved to the edge of the driveway and found the trail that would take me to the low edge of our property, the site of our tree house. I'd navigated this trail hundreds of times—dark or day, it didn't matter—and I wanted to believe I had the muscle memory to stride down it without a thought, but some unease overcame me and I went slowly, using my toes to explore the terrain of each step before committing my entire foot. Just before the trail gave out there was a steep pitch downward, and I was so dismayed by my hesitation that I took the last ten yards at a jog and then had to stop short so I wouldn't snag myself on the rusty barbed wire fence dividing our property from the neighbors'.

Our father had nailed short boards into the trunk of the tree, for a ladder up to the fort, and I tested them to see if they were holding. They were. The fort itself was about ten feet off the ground, and when I looked up I was a boy again, not sure I could manage the climb yet determined not to let either of my brothers see my hesitation or beat me to it.

But the boards were thin. I set the outside of my right foot across the top of the lowest board, launched myself upward, and then had to wrap my arms around the tree to keep from falling back. I knew that to truly climb I had to lead with my hands, but I couldn't remember how our fingers had gotten any purchase on the boards above us.

I had never brought Sammy and Luke here. I'd thought of it but had decided to wait until they were older. I recalled how I'd sped through the Hardy boys earlier, turning the pages so I could get away, and a sob heaved out of me. Those boys, with their dirty necks: they were everything to me. Sammy, whose idea of heaven was being allowed to jump on our little backyard trampoline unsupervised. The trampoline was only a foot off the ground, but his point of reference was firmly rooted in the past, when he was a toddler and it had been a little dangerous, and so there he was, eight years old, exultant as a skydiver. Luke was five but in some ways more grown-up than Sammy. When I dropped him at a playdate he said, "Thanks for the ride, Dad," breezy as a teenager. He thought kissing was for babies, so we kissed him only when he was asleep.

I felt another sob trying to break through and gritted my teeth. I reached with my hand, but the board above my head was far too thin to grasp. I let go of the trunk for an instant and clapped my arms around it again, higher.

Slowly, clumsily, I hauled myself up. My father had done this at my age, and with such a combination of grace and good humor. I remembered when we were building the fort, how he made it both extraordinary—that we were, with our hands, bringing this structure into being—and also an everyday accomplishment, the kind of thing we could count on pulling off, if we worked hard, for the rest of our lives.

I sat in the fort brushing wood debris from my chest and legs, then plucked a leaf from a nearby bay laurel for a dose of the medicinal smell. My father knew just how to sit up here with us: authoritative, benevolent, self-effacing. He was the opposite of the kind of father who makes his children into his own personal fan club—like my neighbor Jack Stillman, who I once heard say to his daughter, "Kelly, what's the only major sport your star athlete of a dad has never played?" At which point Kelly, apparently the fan in charge of trivia, said, "Hockey!"

I couldn't recall my father complaining—ever. His burden was the burden of loneliness, his marriage having given him a houseful of people but no one his own age to talk to. His conversations with my mother revolved around whatever had taken hold of her mind most recently, whatever it was she wanted, and while on occasion she may have sat still as he presented a thought, a feeling, a dilemma, she was not genuinely interested in him. In truth, they seemed closest when she was ill and he was more doctor than husband. How all of this didn't sap something essential from him, I don't know. Perhaps it did. Perhaps, with his wife's love, he would have been even more than he was.

When he said good night to me, he always sat on the edge of my bed. He stroked my face, and his fingers smelled of the peppermint antacids he chewed after meals. He said he loved me. He said the oak tree would stand guard all night, and that a new day was scheduled to arrive first thing in the morning. Sometimes, to delay his departure, I asked about his day, what patients he'd seen, how sick they were; I would want to know if any of them had barfed on him, and he would say no, but come to think of it there had been a Charles on the ceiling (an upchuck). He never talked about the actual children he treated. This was long before HIPAA; he simply didn't think it was right. And I think he knew it would make me jealous. His close friend and colleague Marvin Miller sometimes used phrases like "my boys and girls." My father said "my patients."

His family had not owned a car until he was ten years old. This was fantastic to me—he might as well have said they lived in a cave. The strangest thing about it was that they hadn't needed one. They lived in a small town. They walked everywhere. And yet the first time I went there—on a visit we all took in the summer of 1969—it wasn't the size of the place, the four short blocks that encompassed the downtown, that amazed me. It was the humidity. I didn't see how he could have told us about his early life without mentioning it. Every moment coated your skin; to go from air-conditioned car to air-conditioned restaurant was to traverse a tiny hell. On our first afternoon in town, when it was 95 degrees out with 88 percent humidity, we knocked on the door of his childhood home, and the current owners invited us to come in and look around. The relief from the heat was minor, and there was an unpleasant cooked-meat smell. I wondered how you went about visiting people you didn't know, but our father was very good at this kind of interaction, and after a compliment and an anecdote he beckoned us to the dark, narrow passageway that ran from the entry hall to the kitchen. "Come stand here, children," he said. "Do you feel that little breeze? This is where I played on days like this." And we stood in the passageway, the six of us making quite a crowd, and I thought that my father's ability to make the best of a situation was something I would acquire one day, like underarm hair or a deeper voice.

California enchanted him. He loved the dry air and the gold

hills, the particular dust-and-tree-bark scent of our land. Long after everyone was gone—we kids and our mother—he stayed in the house, expanding his territory into the empty rooms so that, at the time of his death, he was using my bedroom for the TV, Rebecca's for a guest room, and the one shared by Ryan and James for a snug library lined with bookcases, in the center of which sat a leather armchair and a lamp. When he had us all to dinner, he set the table with linens and the silver candlesticks our mother had rejected as too conservative and, with an unnecessary apology, served us undercooked broccoli and bland meat loaf procured at the prepared-foods department of the local supermarket.

A few months after his seventy-fourth birthday, he had a bout of pneumonia that put him in the hospital for several days, and not long after that he suffered a stroke that was mild enough to leave him with deficits in no area other than confidence, though there it affected him deeply. He seemed to age overnight, to begin refusing invitations, pleading fatigue when we urged him to accompany us on weekend trips, even visits to the city. Then, on December 27, 2003, after two days of constipation, vomiting, and intense abdominal pain, he drove himself to the ER, not wanting to bother us for something that might turn out to be a simple case of overeating at Christmas dinner. This was not the problem. We were called in, and within an hour he was referred to surgery for an intestinal blockage, apologizing to us as they wheeled him away for being a burden yet again.

He had a laparoscopic colectomy with so much colon removed he was given a colostomy that was likely to be permanent. Four days later, with his pain manageable, I wanted him discharged; I thought he'd be better off at home with twenty-four-hour nursing and a bottle of antibacterial soap at the front door than in the breeding ground of infection known as the Stanford Hospital. Rebecca disagreed, and we argued about it in the corridor outside his room.

She had to go see a patient, and I sat with my father again. For an hour or so he'd been saying he felt dizzy, and he shivered once or twice. He was too tired to talk, and I cast about in my mind for something he might enjoy hearing, settling on a year-old story about Sammy that I'd probably already told him.

At four, Sammy had loved nothing better than the vast backyard of his preschool, where he and a few other little boys played with an abundant assortment of plastic trucks, sometimes zooming them around on the concrete patio, other times flooding parts of the yard to create appropriate terrain for the bulldozers and backhoes. All of this took place under the kind and watchful eye of a teacher named Gary, a huge linebacker of a guy with thick black sideburns. If the kids needed help diverting a stream of water through the giant sandbox, Gary would show them how to dig a trench to create a new riverbed. When it was time to clean up at the end of the morning, Gary would hold open the plastic storage bin where the trucks were kept overnight while the boys brought the vehicles over and, according to their personalities, placed, dropped, or threw them in. One morning Jen arrived in time for the last few minutes of play, and she watched as Gary and Sammy created a racetrack for two fire trucks, filling a dip with enough water to guarantee a big splashing finish. When it was time to go, Sammy waited for Gary's hug before letting Jen take his hand. On the way to the car, he said, in his high, squeaky voice, "It might be good to be a teacher." Jen asked why, and he said, "Because then you would have a really big sand area in your backyard."

My father smiled. Age had given him pouches under his eyes and a gravelly voice. "I can just hear him," he said. "Sammy."

I said, "He thought the teacher lived at the school."

"It's all right, honey," he said. "We don't have to talk."

He closed his eyes and after a short while seemed to drift off, his lips parting enough for a bead of drool to edge out of the corner of his mouth. His colostomy bag was covered by his sheet, but I could see its outline and wondered for the hundredth time if he would be able to bear it. He'd been accepting, or maybe fatalistic. "Not ideal," was how he'd termed it, "but better than the alternative."

"I'm cold," he said, startling to alertness, and I found a blanket and tucked it around him, noticing as I worked that there was a film of sweat on his forehead.

"Dad?"

He shook his head, and a shudder grabbed him, violent as a seizure. His forehead was hot. I grabbed his wrist, felt his pulse galloping, and hurried to the nurses' station. When I got back, his respirations seemed faster. I counted breaths as the nurse pulled the blood pressure cuff up his thin, naked-looking arm. In old age, men become hairy as apes or smooth as children, and my father was firmly in the second category, though on his head his once-black hair had turned cloud-white but thinned only a little.

His temperature was 103, BP 70 over 40, respirations 24 per minute.

"He has an infection," I said, and the nurse said she would page the doctor. "*I'll* place the order," I said, and then I turned from her and put my face in my hands. "I'm sorry," I said. "Thank you for your help. Thank you."

When she was gone I leaned close to my father. "It's okay," I said.

"Lock the front door," he whispered.

Half an hour later he was in the ICU, and Rebecca and Ryan were on their way.

With sepsis, toxins swarm the body, launching a series of inflammatory responses that can be fatal in combination, especially in the elderly. His BP did not respond to the initial bolus of fluids, and soon he was receiving norepinephrine along with the broad-spectrum antibiotic the attending had ordered right away.

He lasted until daybreak, unconscious. For most of that time, except when the staff was working on him, I rested my hand on his leg: a weight to keep him down with us, the living. Rebecca and Ryan each held a foot. We were gowned, of course, and masked and gloved. I kept thinking it would scare him to see us that way, unless he could somehow find it funny. He'd been a great fan of Halloween, corralling us on the weekend before the holiday to drive to a farm south of San Jose to pick our own pumpkins. As I looked at my brother and sister with their voluminous robes and white muzzles and bright blue hands, I thought we could pass for aliens from a benign sci-fi movie, no blood and guts, just strange-looking creatures with fluid pooling in front of their eyes.

4

THE CRUSADE

James started kindergarten on the hottest September day in recorded history. At seven-thirty in the morning it was already 92 degrees outside. “I stay inside when it’s hot,” he said at breakfast, attempting to bolster the case he’d been making for several days, that he shouldn’t go to school this year after all. At bedtime the night before, his father had told him that on his own first day of school, back in 1934, he had been so reluctant that his sister had been forced to take him by the hand and pull him along. The heels of his new shoes were worn down, he’d dragged his feet so hard. James usually liked stories about his father’s childhood mistakes, but this one didn’t help.

His teacher, a Miss McKinley, was new to the school. When the bell rang, she waved off the mothers and invited her charges to sit cross-legged at the front of the room, on a large square of indoor/outdoor carpeting strewn with paper cutouts of the letters of the alphabet. James sat on the letter F and felt it crinkle under his bottom. He stood up, sat down, and felt it crinkle again. He got to his feet and said in a loud voice, “My fuh is wrinkling.”

The teacher’s back was turned, and she didn’t respond.

“Teacher! My fuh is wrinkled!”

The other boys and girls were sitting with their hands in their laps, as the teacher had asked. She turned and looked down at James.

He had a paper name tag hanging from a piece of yarn around his neck, and she peered at it and said, "James, that is not a fuh, that is an eff. And we're big boys and girls now. We stay seated until we are told we may get up." Then she smiled a dazzling smile, her teeth bright as Chiclets, and in that instant he fell in love.

At home that evening, all four Blair children were hot and tired. Their father had made his special first-day-of-school dinner, barbecued spare ribs and corn on the cob, but the children only poked at their food. At her end of the table, their mother gazed off into the distance and took occasional sips of her iced tea.

"I guess," their father said, "we may have some spare ribs this evening."

"Ha," Rebecca said. "I get it."

Robert got it, too, but he wasn't going to say so and be second. Instead, he drained his lemonade and said, "I'm not that hungry, but I'm incredibly thirsty."

Rebecca gave him a long look.

"What?"

"Let's hope you're not dehydrated."

"Why would I be dehydrated?"

"You've probably been sweating a lot from the heat."

Bill pressed his napkin to his lips. He'd been on call the night before, and a febrile infant had necessitated a trip to the hospital. He was very tired, no longer able to recover from sleep deprivation as easily as he had in the past.

He said, "Do you children know how to tell if you're dehydrated?"

They were silent for a moment. "Your urine is very concentrated," Rebecca said decisively. "It's dark yellow."

"Look, here's a trick." He held out his arm and pinched the skin on the back of his hand. "If your skin holds the pinch, you need fluids."

All four children pinched themselves and then repeated the test to be sure.

"I'm not dehydrated," Rebecca said.

"I'm not, either," Ryan said.

"We're all healthy," their father said. "Hot but healthy. Now, I want to hear about school. How was the first day?"

At the sound of this question, their mother returned her attention to the table. "Heaven," she said. Their father held her gaze, unblinking and keeping everything in reserve. She glanced at him and then looked away.

Robert and Rebecca were accustomed to this kind of muted confrontation and coped by briefly suspending their feelings, as if feelings were objects unruled by gravity, capable of floating in the air until they were claimed again. James was not yet aware of his parents' difficulties. It was hardest for Ryan.

"Dad," he said.

"Yes, Ryan?"

"I didn't have school. I don't start till next week."

"I know that, honey. I should have said I wanted to hear about school or not-school, as the case may be."

"I think it's funny," Rebecca said, "when you say 'as the case may be.' Because 'case,' get it? You're a doctor, you have cases."

"So do lawyers," Robert said.

"I have patients," Bill said. "I try not to think of them as cases."

Penny looked at her husband, sitting at the opposite end of the table so straight and tall. This kind of comment generally annoyed her: Bill the paragon, Bill the saint. But because the day *had* been heaven, her objection occurred at a lower register than usual and faded away. Since James's birth she'd been overwhelmed by the children—by James, really—but today had been lovely, and once Ryan started back to school, her time would be her own. She was almost forty, ready to start a new chapter of her life. During the family's recent week at Sea Ranch she'd gathered dozens of shells from the beach and was planning to decorate something with them. And she had a new five-pound bag of clay and some colored wax for making sand candles. She could hardly wait to get started.

"James," Bill said. "You first. How was it?"

Bill and James had already had two or three brief but charged conversations about James's morning, during which Bill had gotten bursts of story, but it was his practice to make sure everyone had a few uninterrupted minutes at the dinner table, to talk about the day or anything else, and he waited for James to begin.

"Her name," James said, "is Miss McKinley."

Robert snorted and then tried to cover it up with a cough. He wasn't worried about James's feelings so much as his own reputation as a teenager, which he was half a year away from becoming. A teenager would have better things to do than make fun of his little brother. His little five-year-old kindergarten brother. He had to remember who he really was.

"You liked her," Bill said.

"My letter wrinkled," James said. "I sat on it and it wrinkled. I got a eff."

"*An* eff," Robert said. "And I highly doubt you got a grade for your first day of kindergarten."

"No," James said, "eff like A, B, C, D, E, F, G—" He began singing the alphabet song.

"Okay, okay," Robert said. "We get it."

"Let's let James finish," Bill said.

"I painted at the easel," James said. "I went on the slide and got burned."

"I'll bet that metal slide was hot," Bill said.

"We had juice," James said. "One cup. Miss McKinley said there was water if we wanted more."

"Is she nice?" Ryan asked, wanting for his brother all the sweetness of his own school life.

James had been holding a spare rib, and he set it down. His hands were covered with barbecue sauce, and he flung them wide and said, "She is my queen."

Rebecca was directly across from him, and she looked down at her plate and bit the inside of her lip to keep from laughing. She could feel Robert next to her, revving, and she bit harder. The urge to giggle overcame the tiny pain, and heat flooded her face. Moisture formed on her upper lip and forehead. If her shoulders started shaking, all would be lost. She pressed her thighs together, afraid she'd wet her pants. And slowly, gradually, the laugh subsided. She wiped the sweat from her face. She had won, but just barely.

"I'm hot," James said, sticking out his lower lip.

"It is very hot," Bill said.

In fact, it was 101 degrees outside, at six o'clock. The kitchen felt like the desert at noon, an expression the children had learned from their maternal grandfather. The living room was even hotter, with its windows that faced the setting sun.

James pushed his plate away. "I'm done." He got down from his chair and went to his father, cupping his hands around Bill's ear and whispering something.

"Fuh is the sound it makes," Bill said, "but eff is what it's called. Just like muh is the sound made by the letter emm."

"And wuh is the sound made by the letter double you!" James cried with the excessive enthusiasm he often used in moments of confusion.

"Like that," Bill said. "You've got it."

James returned to his chair.

"James," Penny exclaimed. "Look what you did!"

Everyone looked. Bill's shirt was stained with barbecue sauce, paw prints on the white. There was sauce on his face, too. "No harm," he said, dabbing at his shirt with his napkin. "It's an old one."

"Easy for you to say," Penny said. "You don't have to wash it."

"I mean it's about worn out. I should get some new ones. *Please* don't worry about it right now," he added as she pushed away from the table.

"I'm getting more iced tea." But as she went to the refrigerator, she fumed. There were times when he reminded her of someone, though she couldn't figure out whom—it was someone she'd never actually known. Someone unbending. Though that wasn't exactly it. He was too bending, really, folding over on himself like the rubbery green Gumby figures the children collected. Head to his toes and then spring right back as if nothing had ever happened. It was possible to provoke him, but she never knew what would and what wouldn't. When provoked, he turned pink and went silent. She also never knew, in advance, how she would feel about it. Sometimes she hated it. She wanted to throw herself at his feet.

Bill looked around the table at the children. "Let's see, where were we? Ryan?"

Ryan hesitated. He didn't want to start if his mother was upset. He also wasn't sure what to say because his day had been very strange, entirely different from any day he could remember. His school was on a different schedule from the public school, so he was accustomed to being home on some days when Robert and Rebecca were not, but he had never been home without James. It had been only two and a half hours, but it had seemed far longer. Like a day in a book—a child in a faraway land. He tried out most of his favorite places to sit, and then he drew for a while, and then he went outside and walked around the house with his hand out, his fingertips brushing against the wood all the way around. After that, it felt good to soak his hand in cold water. Just before it was time to get James, his mother brought out some old photo albums, and they sat together and paged through them, his mother pointing at his face each time it appeared. "There you are," she said. "And there you are. And there you are." At the end of one album was a picture of James holding Dog very tightly, his eyes squeezed shut, and his mother said, "Was that real love, do you think?" And Ryan didn't respond because the answer—that it was real but not wide and deep, like his love for Badger—seemed disloyal.

His mother returned to the dinner table, and he told the family about coloring a picture of the sky. He had taken great care with it, and it was beautifully, unvaryingly blue—a giant piece of paper, almost as big as a pillowcase, all blue. He had used his characteristic soft, light strokes, and as he fetched the picture and held it up for everyone to see, he realized he had made a window to hang above his bed. When he went to sleep at night, it would be like looking at the daytime sky.

For her turn, Rebecca named the girls who were in her class, starting with her three best friends, going down the list through the girls she liked and the girls she didn't mind, and finishing with the two girls who bothered her, Leanne Mack and Edith Ketler, the one who smelled bad and the other who was as big as a teenager.

"Why don't you like Leanne and Edith?" Robert said.

"It's not that I don't like them," Rebecca said. "I just don't know them that well." This made her uncomfortable, and she hurried on to the desk she'd been assigned (second row, far left) and the number of pencils she'd been given for her pencil tray (three) and the games she'd played at recess (foursquare and then Chinese jump rope, which she had gotten really bad at over the summer). Finally she spent a couple of minutes talking about her teacher, Mrs. House, and saved the best detail till last: her daughter was a pediatrician!

"Well, I'll be," Bill said.

"Why shouldn't she be a pediatrician?" Penny said.

"She should be. By all means."

"You mean she shouldn't not be," Rebecca said.

"Yes, that's what I mean." Bill kept his eyes off Penny, who seemed cross about something. He turned to Robert. "And the first day of seventh grade?"

Robert should have been ready to launch, but he was annoyed that Rebecca's teacher's daughter was a pediatrician: now Rebecca would have something extra with their father for a whole year. "It was boring."

"Really?" Bill said. "A new school boring? There must have been something of interest. Something new, something different."

Robert glanced at Rebecca. "Well, I change classes now. I have seven teachers."

"And I have one!" James shouted.

"James, it's not your turn," Robert snapped. "Not that I have anything else to say. Forget it, I'm done."

"Oh, my goodness," Bill said. "I believe we have met our match in this heat. What say we go out for ice cream?"

The three younger children clamored their approval, leaping to take their plates to the sink, asserting their choice of flavor as if only one of them could have any one type of ice cream. After a moment Robert followed, silently so no one would think he was finished being mad.

Penny waited to see if anyone wanted her to go. She thought she'd say yes, but only if someone asked. She looked from child to child, settling at last on Ryan, who was likeliest to care. Did Bill care? Why didn't he ask? She imagined the two of them walking hand in hand from the car to the ice cream parlor, the children either so far up ahead or so quiet that it would be possible to pretend she and her husband were alone together. She couldn't remember the last time that had happened, and it wouldn't happen if she went along for ice cream, not even for a few moments, and it probably wouldn't happen in bed tonight, either—they'd be alone together but they probably wouldn't touch; they didn't much these days. She remembered being five years old, eight, ten, and her mother telling her not to cut off her nose to spite her face, and she thought all she needed was one smile, from any one of them; and then, somehow, they were all on the move, and Bill was giving her a look that said he'd expected her to stay behind, to opt out, to *fail as a mother*—and they were at the front door without her.

Down the hill, down the winding road. They passed their neighbors' mailboxes, painted tin boxes attached to wooden posts; they went by the fruit and vegetable stand at Webb Ranch, with its crates of melons and tomatoes shaded by a corrugated roof. Each summer the Blairs marked the passage of time by the berries at Webb: first strawberries, which lasted all season; then raspberries, blackberries, and loganberries; and finally boysenberries, which Bill said were the sweetest of all and which he dipped in sugar and let dry overnight, making them almost as good as candy.

At the ice cream parlor they slid into a booth, Bill on one side between the two younger boys while Robert and Rebecca settled as far apart as they could on the opposite bench, Rebecca unclear why they were fighting and Robert no longer angry at her but upset about his father's comment at dinner. If Robert thought his new school was boring, it was boring, period. He didn't appreciate being corrected. His father had no idea what it was like plodding from one strange classroom to another on the hottest first day of school imaginable. And trying to learn each teacher's name, and looking around for a familiar face in each class, just one, and discovering on two separate occasions, in science and German, that he didn't know a single other person in the room.

They had bowls and cones and sundaes, according to appetite and drip tolerance. Outside again, they found the evening even hotter, if that was possible. "We'll walk around the block, shall we?" Bill said, and the children were too hot to decide if this would make things better or worse. James dropped to his knees after a few steps, and his father carried him piggyback the rest of the way. People they passed on the sidewalk smiled at the sight of them. "The Pied Piper," said an old man, and Bill whistled a quick tune and kept walking.

"Why didn't Mom come?" Ryan said as they approached the car.

"I think she was tired," Bill said.

"I'm tired," James grumbled.

Bill settled James on the front seat, and the others sat in back, Rebecca in the middle. The sun had disappeared; the sky was the color of a glass of water into which you'd dipped a calligraphy pen.

"Why *didn't* Mom come?" Ryan said again, but softly, so that only Rebecca heard him. "Because she was mad?"

"Because she didn't feel like it," Rebecca whispered, but she knew this was only half the story. She felt guilty that she hadn't urged her mother to join them, and in that moment she began to hatch a plan.

The next day was much cooler, and after school she gathered her brothers under the oak tree and told them what was on her mind. "We have to think of things to do," she said, "that Mom will want to do with us."

"You mean like go out for ice cream?" Ryan said.

"I mean like *not* go out for ice cream. Like something else."

Robert had had a much better second day, in fact a pretty good second day, with a great lunch period playing kickball with some other seventh-graders who didn't think that just because you were in junior high you had to act so big all of a sudden. "I have an idea," he said.

"What?" Ryan said.

"We'll go on a crusade."

Rebecca liked it instantly. It had just the kind of purposeful sound she loved, the real, official sound of a job, instead of the kind of soft, ill-formed half-intention that so often led nowhere.

"We have to brainstorm," she said. "Hang on." She ran for the house and returned to the boys with a clipboard and pen.

"We could buy her some colored pencils," Ryan said.

"No," Robert said, "that's the opposite of what we should do."

"We're brainstorming," Rebecca said. "We're going to write down every idea." She wrote "Colored pencils" on the notepad and looked up again.

"Miss McKinley showed us the crayons today," James said. "And the scissors and glue. And they go back where they came from." He'd had a wonderful morning, three special talks with Miss McKinley by himself, near her desk. "Oh, James," she had said at the beginning of the third talk, and he had said, "Oh, Miss McKinley," right back at her, and she had smiled her big white smile, extra wide that time.

"When my school starts," Ryan said, "I'm going to have Dixon and Julia for my teachers." At his school, the classes weren't as separate as they were at the public school, and when he said he was going to have Dixon and Julia, what he meant was that he was especially looking forward to seeing them again, Dixon because he was always ready to sit on the floor with the students and help them do their work, and Julia because she had the softest hair. Sand Hill Day was for creative children, and Ryan felt bad for his siblings that they didn't get to go there with him. Especially James—he had hoped James would join him there, so it would be two and two.

"We have one thing," Rebecca said. "We should have five by now."

"How about a nature walk," Robert said, and she wrote that down.

"A trip!" she said. It had been four years since the family had gone to Michigan, and though they'd gone somewhere every summer since then—Disneyland and Yosemite and places like that—they hadn't been on an airplane in all that time.

"We just went on one," Robert said, referring to the week they'd spent at Sea Ranch.

"Somewhere far away," Rebecca said. "Anyway, I'm writing it down."

"Mommy doesn't like the tree house," James said.

"No, that's right, James," Ryan said. "We're thinking about what she *does* like."

"She likes the party again now. Why did we almost not have the party this year?"

"She was tired of it," Rebecca reminded him.

"But then she found the Chinese caterer," Ryan added.

"This is boring," James said, getting to his feet. "I'm going to the tree house."

"Not by yourself, James," Robert said, but James took off anyway, and via a quick look Robert and Rebecca decided he could go alone this time. The trail to the tree house was easy to follow and steep in only a couple of places.

"I think New York City," Rebecca said.

"Too far away for a weekend," Robert said.

"For Christmas."

"But that's Christmas. I want to be home for Christmas."

"Where's your spirit of adventure?" She was not happy that there were only three items on the list, so she wrote "Trip" and then, below it, "New York City," feeling a small pang that she was counting them as two separate things when they really weren't.

"The Golden Gate Bridge," Ryan said, and both Robert and Rebecca beamed at him, an occurrence that was rare and special: both of them smiling at him at once. He felt a shiver across his shoulders.

"Brilliant," Rebecca said, writing it down. Their mother liked going across the Golden Gate Bridge, and since you had to do something once you were on the other side, they sometimes went to Muir Beach, which was small and sheltered in a way the beaches closer to home weren't.

"Sacramento?" Ryan said.

The older children shook their heads. Sacramento was where their grandparents lived, and they went there a few times a year, their mother always moody on the way home, saying things like "She's so fussy" or "He can't see an inch in front of his nose."

"Not the zoo," Rebecca said, and the boys didn't even bother nodding.

"If it weren't for James," Robert said, "we could say a restaurant."

"He might be better now," Rebecca said, but she didn't write it down.

Ryan said, "James should come back." When neither of his older siblings responded, he got to his feet and went over to the top of the trail and called, "James!"

Behind him, Robert and Rebecca exchanged a nervous look.

"James!" Ryan shouted again.

"I think Carmel," Robert said, and Rebecca wrote that down deliberately, adding "Monterey?" beneath it.

"That's good enough," Robert said. "We're just brainstorming today."

"I guess."

Over at the top of the trail, Ryan glanced back at them with a doubtful expression. His straw-colored hair hung in wavy strands almost to his shoulders.

"He can't climb up to the tree house by himself," Robert said, "so it's not a big deal."

Rebecca headed for Ryan. "Let's go down."

She led the way. There were bees everywhere at this time of year, so she slowed each time she crossed a patch of sunlight. She had been stung when she was five years old, and she still remembered the ice her father had held against her ankle, so cold she couldn't bear it but so necessary just moments after he'd withdrawn it.

"Here I am!"

James was on the trail below her in his shirt and shoes, his pants nowhere to be seen. His legs were tan from the midthigh down and pale pink where he'd been covered all summer by shorts.

"What happened to your pants?"

"I didn't need them anymore."

"James, what did you do?" Exasperated, she brushed past him. "James took off his pants," she called over her shoulder.

Ryan saw James standing in front of him, half-naked.

"I didn't climb up to the tree house," James said.

"Good boy."

"What the hell?" Robert said.

"I didn't climb up to the tree house," James said again, but with less certainty this time, recognizing that Robert's praise was unlikely.

Rebecca returned with James's discarded clothes. "He wet his pants. And left them there. James, what were you thinking, leaving them? Well, let's go up. You can't put these back on."

He started scratching an hour later. He was in clean shorts, sitting on the floor of his and Ryan's room playing with a small car. Ryan lay on his bed. Robert would have told James to stop, but

Ryan didn't think it was all that important. The back was worse than the front, and James was mostly scratching the front.

"Stop scratching," Ryan said five minutes later, by which point James had been going at it so vigorously that Ryan had started feeling a little strange in his own parts.

"I itch," James cried.

Ryan found his mother in the mud pantry, knotting string for a wall hanging. The room was a tiny closet-size space off the kitchen, so named because it had begun life in Bill's mind as a mudroom, done time on their architect's drafting table as a pantry, and ended up a battleground for the ongoing fight between Penny's crafts and an assortment of household items, some edible and some not.

"How's my boy?" she said. Her hair hung in a single thick braid down her back; she almost never wore it loose anymore. "Not so hot today, is it?"

"Not nearly."

"Want to check?"

The thermometer hung just outside the kitchen. It was green and white and said "Texaco" on it—they'd gotten it for free at a gas station. Eighty-one degrees, he told her.

"Positively bearable," she said with a smile.

"I'm ready for my school."

"I'll bet you are, baby. Next week."

He wondered what she'd do once he was gone. Today, with James away all morning again, she had taken him to the grocery store and then the two of them had spent an hour doing watercolors. When it was time to go get James, she kissed the top of his head and said, "That was nice."

There was a wail from the bedroom hallway, and Ryan went to see what was going on. Rebecca and James were outside the children's bathroom, James with his shorts off and Rebecca squatting in front of him. When she heard Ryan, she turned and mouthed the words *Oh, no.*

James had a rash; that was all anyone could say until their father got home. Penny applied calamine lotion and gave him cold compresses, and he lay crying and scratching on his bed while she phoned the clinic once to report the problem and once more to tell her husband to hurry. It was on his penis and bottom and thighs: tiny, angry-looking red dots.

Bill got home a little before six and said the words everyone was fearing: poison oak. The older children put together the story. Down at the tree house, having wet himself, James sat down to unbuckle and remove his shoes, stood up to pull off his wet pants, sat again bare-bottomed to put his shoes back on, and finally stood and headed up the hill. For the rest of his life he would associate the terrible days of his poison oak with the letter F, never realizing it was the down, up, down, up—sit, stand, sit, stand; the same motions as on his first day with Miss McKinley—that linked them in his mind. Effing poison oak, he always said when he told the story, avoiding an actual "fucking" as if he were decorous rather than gripped by a buried memory.

Oh, but he was miserable that evening. His father gave him Benadryl, bathed him in cool water, tried to distract him with games and stories. At dusk he was put to bed and whimpered for an hour or longer, falling asleep just long enough to allow Ryan to drop off and then waking with his hand already at work, scratching. This cycle was repeated twice. Bill didn't prescribe for his children, an ironclad rule he was never so tempted to break as on this occasion. Instead, he put James in the car and drove him to the nearby home of his colleague Marvin Miller, who had a much more relaxed attitude about doctors treating family members and who therefore would have allowed a little irritation to show at being awakened if he hadn't been so indebted to Bill. It was nearly midnight, and his wife was sleeping; his children were away at college. "I'm afraid," he said, "that you'll have to go to the hospital—" At the last minute he left off the word "anyway," realizing it contained a rebuke for the middle-of-the-night consultation.

Bill rubbed his hand over his face. Of course he would; there was nowhere else to get prednisone at this hour. Back in the car, James wailed and subsided into sobs and wailed again. Bill carried him into the ER and explained the situation, feeling a pang of guilt as he exercised his doctor's *droit du seigneur* and followed the attending to an exam room while a little boy lay curled on the floor with obvious abdominal pain and a young man held a bloody cloth to his eye. Bill could hear the cries and groans of an adult, and he thought there was no mistaking the sound of a man with a gunshot wound. The first time he saw such a man, on the U.S.S. *Consolation* in Inchon Harbor, he was so flooded by adrenaline he nearly vomited.

It was almost three a.m. when he and James got home. He didn't want to disturb his wife or Ryan, so he went into the living room with James, who was so worn out that he fell asleep right away, curled at one end of the couch, his first dose of prednisone just reaching his bloodstream. Bill lay with his head at the opposite end and waited for relief.

The living room windows were uncurtained, four floor-to-ceiling panes that were almost as wide as they were tall. Plus the couch was too soft, so Bill rolled from side to side, clamping a throw pillow to his face as the room grew bright. Ryan, as usual the first one up, saw his father and James on the couch and got a blanket to cover them, stretching it from James's chin to his father's and then sitting carefully next to his father's hip.

"Are you asleep?" he whispered.

"Not really," his father murmured from under the pillow.

"Is James better?"

"He will be. Let's try not to wake him up."

Ryan stayed at his father's side. He felt bad that he hadn't stopped James from going down the trail alone, and also that he hadn't tried harder to stop James from scratching, since scratching might have spread the rash. James would not be able to go back to kindergarten today, which Ryan imagined would make him very sad.

In a little while, his father took the pillow from his face and brought one long arm out from under the blankets to pat Ryan's knee. He sat up and yawned.

Ryan gestured for his father to follow him to the kitchen, and slowly, careful not to disturb James, Bill got to his feet. He stood still for a moment watching Ryan, halfway there and so confident of his father that he didn't look back to make sure he was coming. Ryan was Bill's most trusting child. He was small for eight and delicately featured; with his long hair he was often mistaken for a girl. Bill loved the way young children's faces didn't betray gender; how, if it weren't for hair and clothing, you wouldn't know. The point when it became obvious varied from child to child. Sometimes, encountering a patient for the first time, he would try to imagine away the sundress or crew cut, to see the face as simply a face, partly for fun and partly as a clue to the likely timing of puberty. Robert's biceps and quadriceps were just beginning to swell. Rebecca with a haircut could still be a boy. Of Bill's four children, only James's gender had seemed obvious from the day he began to crawl, if not earlier.

Ryan was obvious about his inner life; his eyes mapped his emotions perfectly. He was a dreamy boy given to long periods of contentment, disturbed every now and then by a very adult sadness. In the kitchen he told his father that he had gone to the top of the trail and then stopped.

"Honey," his father said, "you are not responsible for James. And listen. When you make a mistake, you grow. The next time around, you know better. James is five now. Do you think he'll ever sit in poison oak again?"

Ryan brought his fingertips to his lips to cover the beginnings of a smile.

"Oh, dear," his father said. "I see your point."

"I'll remind him," Ryan said. "But Dad?"

"Yes?"

Ryan had planned to mention how sad James was going to be about missing school, but instead he said, "Are you very tired?"

"I am," his father said. "But 'very' isn't so terribly much, is it? Is 'very' more than 'really'?"

"It's not *more* more," Ryan said. "But it's more serious."

His father smiled. "Do you know who we sound like?"

Ryan shook his head.

"Rebecca."

The idea that he sounded like Rebecca made Ryan happy. If Rebecca had been a boy, she would have been the one person in the world, aside from Ryan's father, whom he'd most want to resemble. He knew it should have been Robert.

"James has to stay home today," he said.

"Yes, I suppose he does."

"Does Mom know?"

"Not yet, Ry."

"Do you want me to tell her for you?"

"Oh, Ryan." His father squatted so they were eye to eye. "You don't need to worry about that, okay?"

"I'm not," Ryan said, but he resolved that once Robert and Rebecca were at school, he and James would do some more brainstorming on things that might interest their mother.

James was too unhappy, though. The day passed with Ryan trailing after their mother as she ministered to James in small, intense bursts—icy washcloths, Popsicles, brief bouts of reading aloud. As suddenly, she disappeared, and the two boys lay on their beds, James woozy with antihistamines but unable to sleep.

When Robert and Rebecca got home, Ryan brought up the list, but Robert was in a dark mood and Rebecca had her first homework of the year and wanted to get started right away.

James recovered and returned to school, where Miss McKinley led the boys and girls in a song to welcome him back. They stood in rows on the indoor/outdoor carpeting, and James, sitting on a small painted chair at the front of the room, hoped there might be a place for him once he was no longer special. Ryan returned to Sand Hill Day with such joy that his father—who entertained the occasional doubt about the wisdom of sending his middle son to private school when the others seemed fine where they were—resolved to banish his doubts for the rest of Ryan's elementary education.

It had been his idea. Three years earlier Ryan had started at the same school as his older siblings, but by November he had disappeared inside a boy who resembled Ryan superficially but lacked Ryan's spirit, his soul, his essence—that quality of sweet, lively tenderness that Bill had never seen in another human being. The new Ryan even moved differently, without the old Ryan's bashful grace. Penny, at that time busy chasing the toddler James around the house, was concerned about having to drive to two different schools, but Bill cajoled her into giving it a try, and once Ryan had switched, she found that the extra driving helped fill up the long hours she now spent alone with James.

At Sand Hill Day the children were divided into groups not according to age or interests or abilities but almost at random, because one of the founding principles of the school was the idea that everyone should learn how to get along with everyone else. The makeup of the groups changed every few months, on a timetable that was also almost random; a teacher or two might raise the possibility at a staff meeting, discussion would ensue, and as likely as not a reshuffling would take place in the next week or so.

That early fall, Ryan was in Mountain—the other groups at that point being Ocean, River, Desert, and Valley—but soon the groups were adjusted and he was in Marigold. On his first morning in the new circle, he looked around at the other children and thought that the trick to finding something his mother would like to do with the family might be less a matter of thinking up the right thing than of finding a different way for the family to be organized. Now the breakdown was according to age: his father and mother, Robert and Rebecca, himself and James. But what if that changed? If his mother were paired with someone else, mightn't she want to join in? The problem was that his father and mother were too different. Just the day before, his father had suggested a drive to the boardwalk at Santa Cruz as if that were something his mother would want to do. But she didn't like cotton candy and she didn't like rides. And she didn't like the drive! Of course she wouldn't want to go to Santa Cruz.

Ryan thought that of everyone in the family, he would be the best match for her, but he wasn't sure who should pair with their father, Robert or Rebecca. He considered asking them, but whoever didn't would have to be with James, and he didn't like to think about neither of them wanting that.

He decided not to mention it. The point was not the small parts but the bigger whole. He was in Marigold—not Zinnia or Sunflower—but he and everyone else at his school were all part of Sand Hill Day.

Just before dinner one day, he asked Rebecca what had happened to the crusade. They were in her room, Ryan sitting on the floor while she played "We Have No Secrets" from her Carly Simon album over and over again, lifting the needle and repositioning it at the beginning of the song before the final chords had faded.

"We can still have it," she said. She had thought of the crusade herself, on and off, but doubted that any of the items on the list were likely to succeed, so she'd let it drop. The piece of paper was in her desk drawer, in a folder on which she'd written "Our Crusade" in her best cursive.

"When?" Ryan said.

"It's not something you really do. I mean, it has to be subtle. She can't know."

"But don't we want her to—"

"We want her to want to." She was about to lift the needle off the record but stopped and said, "That could almost be a palindrome! We want her to . . . want her . . . her want . . ."

"What?"

"It would be like 'Able was I ere I saw Elba,' but with words, not letters. A something-else-drome."

"I don't know where James is," Ryan said, getting to his feet. He didn't like palindromes and things like that, and he started for the door.

"You don't have to go. I'll let you choose the next song. You want 'You're So Vain'?"

"She says 'vine.'"

Rebecca nodded eagerly and sang, "You're so *vine.* I'll bet you think this song is about you, you're so VINE." She was all set to play it, but Ryan slipped out the door, and she knew she'd lost him for the afternoon. Softer now, she took up the song again: "You had one eye in the mirror as you watched yourself guffaw." It was actually "gavotte," but she had thought it was "guffaw" at first and liked to sing it that way.

There was a mirror on the inside of her closet door. She had some Magic Markers on her desk, and she clutched a handful and sang into them, watching herself dip and sway. She tried to look like a star, but she wasn't very convincing. She was extremely ordinary, if "ordinary" could even have a modifier like "extremely." In her class, she was the exact middle in height, the exact middle in weight, and the exact middle in hair color if you put blond on one end and black on the other. The only thing she wasn't the middle of was grades. Mrs. House posted points every Friday, and Rebecca was routinely at the top. She didn't like the postings and felt sorry for the people at the bottom, Leanne Mack and Rodney Deetjen. Rodney was a mean boy, and "Rodney" was a terrible name, which made it doubly bad that Rebecca once mentioned it as one of the R names James could adopt when he turned eighteen if he was still upset about being the only non-R among the kids. "*Rodney?*" Robert had said, and she'd started giggling, and all of a sudden James was crying. She hadn't known it would upset him. That wasn't quite true, but the small part of her that had known it might upset him belonged to the small part of her that wasn't very kind, and she tried to make it go away.

Leanne was another story—not mean but pitiful. Her smell wasn't body odor but more a bean-soup smell, as if she kept all her clothes in the kitchen and her mother made the same thing for dinner every night. She couldn't spell, and Rebecca wasn't absolutely sure she could read. And she went to a different room for math, a small room off the library where she and a few kids from other grades met with a "specialist." Rebecca was used to thinking of specialists as certain kinds of doctors, like cancer doctors or heart doctors, and whenever she pictured the kids sitting in that little room she pictured someone in a white coat with them.

Rebecca worked hard not to be mean to Leanne, always letting her go through the door first if they got there at the same time, passing up easy opportunities to trip her, which somehow presented themselves all the time and were seized eagerly by the other girls. Rebecca couldn't believe how immature they were. They giggled in class when Leanne couldn't answer a question, and they made a big show of stepping away from her if she got too close.

For a while it had been enough for Rebecca to keep herself neutral, in between kind and unkind, but lately the dividing line seemed to have moved, and neutrality began to seem malicious.

And then today. After school Leanne was walking by herself as always, and Rebecca, a few feet behind her in the company of two friends, noticed a tear in her top—the sleeve was pulling away from the back, revealing an oval of Leanne's pale, plump shoulder. Rebecca's friends noticed at the same moment and began giggling.

"Nice shirt," Marie said.

"I think her mom made it," Debbie said.

"You guys," Rebecca said. "Don't."

Debbie gave her an impatient look. They had been best friends for four years, ever since the first day of first grade, but lately Debbie seemed more attracted to Marie, who had a capacity for frenzy that Rebecca lacked. Rebecca missed Debbie but also felt relieved—of the pressure to get wound up.

"Anyway, her mom didn't make it," Marie said. "She's crazy."

"You don't know that," Rebecca said.

"I do. She's mental. My mom told me."

"Wait a sec," Debbie said, crouching to tie her shoe, and Marie waited, and Rebecca kept walking, pretending she hadn't heard. Some boys were riding their bicycles on the playground, which wasn't allowed on school days, and suddenly they rode directly across Leanne's path, cutting so close she had to stop short to avoid a collision. Rebecca looked at Leanne, standing there in her torn plaid top, wearing kneesocks that didn't quite match: both white but one cabled and a couple inches shorter than the other. Leanne's shoulders sagged, and she bowed her head. Then she glanced back, and Rebecca felt pinned by her hurt, watchful eyes.

At dinner Rebecca used her talking time to tell her family that she was planning to do her fifth-grade science experiment on the electrical charge in fruits and vegetables. She said she was going to need to buy an amp meter and a pair of probes, but she was really thinking about Leanne, and she decided to ask her father what she should do.

But he was busy—getting James ready for bed and then helping Robert with his math. Rebecca didn't feel like listening to music, and she was ahead in her schoolwork, so there was no homework for her to do. She went off in search of Ryan and found him in the mud pantry with their mother, looking at a cigar box Penny had decorated with shells from the beach at Sea Ranch.

"Rebecca, look," Ryan said. "Isn't it pretty?"

It was pretty, and she said so. "Come on. Let's do something."

"Stay," Penny said. "I've got a lot more shells. You guys can each make one if you want."

"Why would we need three?" Rebecca said.

"Very funny. You might enjoy it."

"I think I'll read instead."

Penny looked at Ryan. "Will *you* stay?"

Ryan said he would, and as Rebecca walked away Penny wished for a moment that her one daughter were more like her. Then again, she hadn't been much like her mother. As a child, Penny had pretended sometimes that she was a changeling whose real parents were English nobility. She thought Royal Doulton was the name of a family rather than a china, and in school, when her teacher wasn't looking, she practiced writing "Penny Doulton" in fancy handwriting on the flyleaf of her grammar book. She wanted to be royalty and was wounded when she heard her mother criticizing a neighbor for putting on airs.

"Look at these," she said to Ryan, pulling out a bucket of shells. "Aren't they nice?"

Ryan leaned close. "They still smell like the ocean."

They knelt together and Ryan poked through the shells. Penny loved the colors at Sea Ranch, the smoky gray-brown of the houses and the straw of the summer grasses. The ocean green and black. On a walk one afternoon she had come upon an older man near the edge of the cliffs, sitting on a folding chair in front of an easel. He was holding a palette with dabs of color on it, painting a picture of the sea and the sky. She stopped and watched and they began to talk. "How did you learn to paint?" she asked him, and he smiled and said, "I haven't yet." She puzzled over that for days afterward, wondering what he'd meant.

"Where are the cigar boxes?" Ryan said.

"I don't have any more right now, but you start by laying the shells on the counter anyway. Choose some, I'll show you. You can try out different arrangements if you don't like the first one."

"But I would like it if I did it."

"Half the fun is trying a lot of different possibilities. You'll see."

Ryan picked out a dozen shells and set them on the counter in three rows of four. He couldn't help noticing that they were all about the same brown and all had about the same white speckles. He didn't want to hurt her feelings, so he moved them around and then moved them around again.

"Look," she said. "See how the darker one looks good in the corner?" She slid one of the shells out of the middle row and repositioned it. "Then you probably want the next darkest one down near the opposite corner."

"Not *in* the opposite corner?"

"No, near is better, see? I'll get some more cigar boxes tomorrow."

"I'll *smoke* some cigars tomorrow!"

There was James, wearing his red cowboy pajamas and a maniac smile. Exultant over his escape from bed, he leaped into the air, reaching for the lintel though it was several feet above his head. "I'll go with you, okay? To the cigar store, right? Can I get Red Hots? Can we go out for lunch, too?" Then, diving for the shells: "What're these? Are these from Sea Ranch? Remember the kelp? Pee-you!"

"James," Penny said, "you were supposed to be in bed half an hour ago."

"I was, but I got back up! See, here I am!"

"No," Penny said. "No and no."

"Did you have trouble falling asleep?" Ryan suggested.

"Yeah, I had trouble falling asleep. I couldn't fall asleep, it was too hard!"

"Get up from there," Penny said, trying to lift him by his arm. "Oh, for heaven's sake."

"James, come on," Ryan said. "I'll take him."

"Have Rebecca sit with him. You come back."

Ignoring both of them, James poked through the shells. He'd helped his mother collect them, and he wondered if any of the shells in the bucket were ones he'd found. He'd had the best time at Sea Ranch, where every morning his father took him out to stomp the trails that crisscrossed the meadows so they'd still be there next summer.

"Maybe Dog can help you sleep," Ryan said.

"Dog's a frog," James said. "Dog's *dead*."

Dog had been on a shelf below the window for weeks, and it upset Ryan that James thought of him as dead rather than resting or waiting. Ryan remembered the day in September when his mother pointed out the picture of James holding Dog with his eyes squeezed shut, and he thought James really did love Dog but needed to be reminded.

At last James let Ryan take his hand. Ryan passed him on to Rebecca, and Rebecca got him a glass of water and followed him into his and Ryan's room.

"I'm not tired," he said.

"You will be."

"I'll never be tired again. I'm wide-awake man! Are you sleeping here? Where's Ryan going to sleep?"

Finally he gave up and got into bed. Not trusting him to stay there, Rebecca sat at Ryan's desk. Down the hall, her father was helping Robert, and she heard him say, very clearly, "I think they're both important—the concepts and the practice." This meant they were having yet another conversation about how Robert liked to solve problems before taking the time to understand them. Their father always said he sympathized with this because of his work: when he saw a child in terrible pain, or feverish and limp, he wanted to relieve the child's misery immediately, but he couldn't do that until he figured out what was going on. A high fever could mean a number of different things, so you had to go through the differential diagnosis. Then you came up with a treatment plan. Dx before Tx.

James sighed and rolled over, and Rebecca reached for Ryan's badger. The fur was worn away in places, and she recalled a conversation between her father and the mother of one of Ryan's friends. This woman said she was worried because her younger son had worn a hole straight through his security blanket from rubbing the same spot over and over, and Rebecca's father told her not to worry. He said, "I always tell parents, just be glad he has so much love in him."

Ryan had a lot of love in him; Rebecca knew this in her bones.

And she wasn't sure if she did or not. She had other things, like maturity and common sense, but she felt she wasn't quite as lovable as Ryan. Which, she understood, was not the same thing as having or not having love inside herself, though it was close. Being lovable versus being lov*ing*. She thought again of Leanne Mack and decided that she really didn't need to consult her father.

This marked the beginning of a new phase for Rebecca. She began bringing girls like Leanne Mack home from school, inviting them for Saturdays, even sleepovers. The first time, Leanne sat on Rebecca's bed and Rebecca stood at the record player and played different songs from *No Secrets,* always lifting the needle when a song finished and holding it above the record so she could tell Leanne what she liked about it without ruining the next song with talk. Leanne had never heard of Carly Simon and admitted to not having a record player, though when Rebecca tried to find out if that meant Leanne didn't have one in her room or in her house, Leanne's disjointed reply told Rebecca she should drop it.

After they had listened to all the songs Rebecca liked, Leanne accepted the album cover from Rebecca and made a comment that Rebecca would remember for years. "Do you think those are peas?" Leanne said, giggling as she looked at Carly Simon's chest. The simple fact was that Carly Simon wasn't wearing a bra and her nipples were sticking out. Rebecca had discovered recently that her own nipples felt good when she touched them; the lighter the touch, the better the feeling, especially if she went around in circles. Leanne's comment was very immature and Rebecca had to try a lot harder to give her the benefit of the doubt.

That wasn't quite it, though. She wasn't just trying to give Leanne the benefit of the doubt; she was trying to give her whatever the opposite of doubt was. Faith, said the antonym dictionary, but that didn't sound right to Rebecca, as if Leanne were God or a religion. "Hope" and "charity" were words that went with "faith," and they were more like what Rebecca was trying to give. She was trying to give Leanne a friend, which was strange, because if asked she would never describe Leanne as *her* friend. There was a difference.

She invited Edith Ketler over, too. Edith had woman-size bosoms and obviously wore a bra; you could see the indentation of the straps on her shoulders and across her back. She didn't look at the picture of Carly Simon at all. When she slept over she put on her nightgown in Rebecca's closet, but it was thin and clingy and Rebecca could see the exact shape and size of her bosoms, which were even more huge and hanging than Rebecca expected. Rebecca's mother's bosoms were small, and she began to wonder what that might mean about the future of her own body. She was curious about her future in general and sometimes thought about how every single step she took sealed off a hundred or a thousand other steps she no longer had the option of taking. Ryan disagreed and showed her, with wet footprints on her bedroom carpet, how you could step backward into your own footprints and return without a trace to the place you'd begun.

Ryan was a mama's boy—so Robert said to Rebecca. In Robert's view it went along with Ryan going to Sand Hill Day and augured nothing good for his future. Robert, as of March a bona fide teenager who managed to find something sarcastic to say at any and every juncture, thought Ryan needed a good kick in the pants.

"Don't hold Mom's hand," Robert said. "You're nine. And don't hold James's hand, either, he doesn't need it anymore. You can put your hands in your pockets if you need something to do with them. See, look, my hands are in my pockets and I'm just walking. I'm strolling."

The family was on its way to a recital in Atherton. They had to park almost a block away and proceed one by one up the shoulder of the road, crowding to the side when a car zoomed past. Hundred-year-old shade trees filtered the sunlight, and through gaps in walls and hedges they glimpsed neat beds of daylilies planted in front of mansions.

Halfway there, Penny said she had to return to the car for something. She got the keys from Bill and headed back.

"Come along," he said to the children. "We'll get seats."

The daughter of one of his colleagues was an aspiring cellist, and her grandmother was hosting this special afternoon performance. She was to be accompanied on the piano by a prodigy Robert knew slightly from his days as a piano student, and this was one of the reasons he felt grumpy. Another was that he was dressed in a stiff blue shirt with fold marks from the cardboard. His brothers wore identical shirts, Ryan's big in the shoulders with cuffs nearly covering his hands, and James's a little small, which their mother had pointed out only as they were getting into the car. Their father, who had bought the shirts late the afternoon before, smiled grimly but didn't comment, and Robert had almost wished he'd just snap a response at her. He wondered if she ever felt that way herself.

"Why," Robert said, "do you need good seats at a recital? It's not like you need to see."

"He didn't say good seats," Rebecca said. "He just said seats. But it does matter where you sit at a recital, especially at someone's house. The acoustics may not be that great."

"The *acoustics* may not be that *great,*" Robert muttered, but when his father raised his eyebrows he feigned a look of distraction.

Harold Lawson stood on the gravel drive in front of the house. His wife was from an old Atherton family with roots in early San

Francisco banking, and the house was an imposing stone structure with three floors and a five-car garage. Harold had come to the Peninsula from a small town in eastern Washington, and to Bill he was a kindred spirit, modest and reserved, markedly different from both the California natives and the East Coast transplants.

"Dr. Blair," he said, shaking Bill's hand. "What a fine-looking family."

"How are the jitters?" Bill said.

"Janet is fine. My wife is a wreck."

"Like any good mother under the circumstances. Children, do you remember Dr. Lawson?"

Dr. Lawson had taken care of each of them on occasion—sent James for an X-ray, swabbed Rebecca's throat. He was tremendously tall, and Robert had always been a little afraid of him.

"Young man," Dr. Lawson said to him.

Robert offered Dr. Lawson his hand, and Dr. Lawson registered a flicker of surprise and possibly amusement before extending his own hand and giving Robert's a hearty shake.

Ryan looked up at their father. "I'll just wait out here for Mom."

"No, let's go in," their father said. "She'll be along."

The front door opened into a large entry hall that was full of people, maybe thirty altogether. A young woman approached them, wearing a jumpsuit patterned with green and blue chevrons. She handed each of them a mimeographed program. "The recital will be in there," she said, indicating a pair of closed double doors. "We'll open up in just a few minutes. For now we're asking everyone to wait in the foy-yay."

She moved on to another family, and Rebecca said, to no one in particular, "I thought it was 'foyer.'" She looked up at her father. "Isn't it 'foyer'?"

"Well, we knew what she meant."

"But which is it?"

"It depends where you live, Rebeck. In France it would be 'foy-yay.'"

"So here it's 'foyer'?"

"Rebecca," Robert said. "You're being a nitpicker."

"I'm being meticulous."

"Same diff."

"No, it's not. In fact, the diff between 'nitpicker' and 'meticulous' is bigger than the diff between 'foy-yay' and 'foyer.'"

"Oh, my God," Robert said. "I'm going to kill myself."

"Now you're being melodramatic."

Robert walked away. He hadn't wanted to come, and even his trump card—the fact that he was thirteen—hadn't made a bit of difference. He saw that there were no other teenage boys, which was partly a relief (no one to see him here) and partly a confirmation that attending a cello recital on a Sunday afternoon was not an appropriate thing for him to be doing. What would his friends say if they could see him? The fact that he didn't really have friends anymore made the question all the more painful. It seemed junior high meant you needed four or five people to be able to do anything, and otherwise everyone stayed home. He'd been invited to go bowling by a guy in his German class, and then on the evening before the guy called and said there weren't enough people so he was canceling. Robert couldn't remember the last time he'd been to anyone's house just to play, though obviously they wouldn't call it that.

He returned to his family in time to hear James say, with a familiar edge to his voice, "Where's Mommy? When are we going to sit down?"

"James," their father said in a low voice. "It won't be too much longer, honey. Can you be patient?"

"No. I want to sit *down,*" James said loudly, and he plunked himself down in the middle of the rug.

"James, get up!" Rebecca said.

"Daddy," he wailed, and people near them began edging away.

"Never mind," Rebecca said, "I'll take him outside," and she grabbed James's hand and motioned for her brothers to go with her. Ryan followed easily, but Robert delayed long enough to calculate the costs and benefits of complying, ultimately deciding that getting out of the crowded room more than outweighed the loss of status he'd suffer by doing as Rebecca wished.

Dr. Lawson was still in front of the house, talking to a stocky white-haired man the children recognized as their father's doctor, the existence of whom they found both preposterous and consoling.

Pulling free of Rebecca's hand, James headed for a flowerpot, which he dragged over to a low stone wall and used as a stepping stone. Once he was on the wall, he held his arms out, lifted one foot, and began to hop. After advancing no more than a yard, he paused with his foot in the air and dipped sideways in what was obviously a bogus move meant to suggest he'd nearly lost his balance. Then he continued forward.

The other children watched him. More guests arrived, walking up the long driveway in couples and families.

Ryan said, "I just don't know where Mom is."

"You should spend less time thinking about Mom," Robert exclaimed, "and more time—" He was going to say "more time working on your fielding" but stopped himself. That spring Ryan had gotten involved in Little League for the first time, and he was the only boy on his team who had never played before. On afternoons when Ryan had practice, Robert tried to assess his skills. It wasn't that Robert thought Ryan should be as good as he'd been, but he ought to take it more seriously if he was going to bother doing it at all. Robert's father had asked him to be careful of Ryan's feelings, though, so he didn't finish the thought.

"You guys?" Ryan said. "Why did we stop our crusade? I think we still need it."

"Not this again," Robert said. "It was a bullshit idea then and it's a bullshit idea now."

"Don't say that!" Rebecca exclaimed. "Just because you're a quitter doesn't mean we are. And it doesn't mean it's impossible. Maybe we're not going to have a crusade, but that doesn't mean we can't do something."

"Why can't we have a crusade?" Ryan said.

"It was just a word."

"But it was a thing."

"It can still be a thing," Rebecca said, turning away so she could focus. She had thought about the crusade many times since the start of school, but lately it had slipped her mind. This made her feel guilty. But what was there her mother might want to do? Nothing. All she was interested in was some craft or other.

"Uh-oh," Ryan said.

James had reached the far end of the wall and was using his belly to ease his way to the ground. Now his shirtfront was streaked with dirt, and he brushed at it with both hands, succeeding only in spreading the dirt around.

"He's like Pig-Pen," Robert said.

"He's young," Ryan offered.

"No, it's true, he is like Pig-Pen," Rebecca said, and that seemed to decide it.

Robert went back into the house and saw his father talking to a few other men. He squeezed past small knots of adults and arrived in time to hear his father say, "He's working very hard," and though Robert knew it was unlikely, he hoped his father was talking about him. He *was* working very hard; he needed to get home to rewrite an essay that was due the next morning. He had a sound thesis, but he'd been too literal when it came to "Tell 'em what you're gonna tell 'em, tell 'em, then tell 'em what you told 'em." He thought he ought to use his thesaurus to change some of the words.

"And doing brilliantly," said a man with thinning red-blond hair and a bushy mustache.

"I wouldn't say *brilliantly,*" said a man Robert thought he recognized. "I'd say he's doing well."

If this was the person Robert thought it was, his name was John Mallon and he was an orthopod, a word Rebecca found hilarious because it sounded like some kind of prehistoric creature that walked on all fours. Either that or a robot. But orthopedics interested Robert. Lately he'd been thinking that if he became a doctor he might want to be an orthopedist, a doctor of muscles and bones, since that seemed a much cleaner business than most other specialties.

Robert's father saw him and said, "Gentlemen, I'd like to introduce my oldest. Robert, these are Doctors Mallon, Burke, and Friedlander."

One by one the men offered Robert their hands, and he felt a blast of righteousness. Dr. Lawson had viewed him as a child, but that didn't mean everyone would.

Dr. Mallon asked where he was in school, and Dr. Burke asked if he was dissecting earthworms in science class. "Quite a business, dissection," Dr. Burke went on without waiting for an answer. "Earthworms, frogs. The world inside."

"Nothing can prepare you for opening up a human body," said Dr. Friedlander, who wore aviator sunglasses even though he was indoors. "Not an earthworm, not any other animal."

Dr. Mallon tsked.

"You disagree?" Dr. Friedlander said.

"Alas," Dr. Mallon said, "I fear we are not so far from our predecessors as all that."

There was a brief silence. Robert had found Dr. Mallon's "I wouldn't say *brilliantly*" a little obnoxious, and now he saw that Dr. Mallon was possibly an obnoxious person.

"I don't mean anatomically," Dr. Friedlander said. "I mean what it feels like. Another human being. Are you thinking about medicine, son?"

Robert said he was, but he wasn't sure what kind.

"That's okay," Dr. Friedlander said. "You've got plenty of time."

"If you ever want to talk about orthopedics," Dr. Mallon said, putting a palm to his chest.

"I don't think it would be orthopedics," Robert said quickly. "Or gastroenterology."

All the men laughed except Robert's father. Dr. Burke said, "A GI doc I know married a gal who's an OB/GYN. Tells me, 'We've got both holes covered.'"

"Gentlemen," Robert's father said. "Excuse us." And he put a hand on Robert's shoulder and guided him away.

"Dad," Robert said when they were clear of the crowd. "I'm thirteen. I got it."

"I know you got it," his father said. "But that doesn't mean I liked it."

Robert thought his father was a bit of a prude, but he didn't mind being taken from the conversation. In the matter of sex, and especially the female body, and most especially the lower half of the female body, he was allowing himself a kind of Indian summer of disinterest, set off by some diagrams at his father's clinic that he'd spied one Sunday afternoon. While his father was busy, Robert had wandered into an empty exam room and found a booklet—or not exactly found it, since he'd seen it a few times without having had the opportunity to take a good look—and he spent a few minutes flipping back and forth between the page about male reproductive organs and the page about female reproductive organs, the complementary nature of which had left him uneasy.

"So, no orthopedics?" his father said now. "I remember teaching you the bones when you were, oh, just a little fellow. Five or six. You really enjoyed learning. I think you still do."

"Can I see your wrist?" Robert said.

His father pulled back his cuff and held out his arm. Robert put his forefinger on the knobby protrusion on the outside of the wrist and said, "That's your ulnar styloid process."

"Why ulnar?"

"It's at the end of the ulna. Can I try the carpals?"

His father put his hand on the crown of Robert's head. "You can try anything, Robby. You can do anything." As he spoke, his face changed around the eyes and mouth, as if love lived in particular regions of the skin, and Robert felt his own face grow warm.

"Scaphoid," he said. "Lunate. Pisiform."

His father shook his head. "You missed one."

"I thought I knew them!"

"No reason you should. There are twenty-seven bones in the hand alone."

"But I—"

"Remember the mnemonic?"

A mnemonic was a mental cheat sheet; Robert's favorite had always been Kids Prefer Cheese Over Fried Green Spinach—Kingdom, Phylum, Class, Order, Family, Genus, Species. He tried to remember the one for the carpal bones. It was something a little naughty. Then he got it: She Looks Too Pretty, Try To Catch Her. He had left out a T. He said, "Scaphoid, lunate, triquetrum, pisiform." He paused to think. "Trapezoid, trapezium, capitate, hamate."

"That's all eight of them."

"But in the right order?"

"Very close. Trapezium comes before trapezoid, but what mnemonic could remind you of that?"

"Actually, there are three Ts," Robert said. "Triquetrum."

"So there are."

"Like there are three Rs in our family. What would be a mnemonic for us?"

"I would never need a mnemonic for you," his father said, but then he smiled.

"What?"

"I thought, 'Run, Run, Run, Jump.' And speak of the devil."

Ryan and James arrived, slightly breathless, James leading the way and moving so fast that when he flung his arms around his father, his father had to take a step back for balance. "When's it going to be over?" James cried. "Mommy still isn't here."

Robert went back outside and saw Rebecca talking to a strange-looking little girl, something not quite right about her head or her body, either her head was too big or her body was too small.

"Have you seen Mom?" Robert asked Rebecca.

"I'm kind of talking."

"Sorry, but have you?"

"This is my brother," Rebecca said to the girl. "Robert, the oldest. Remember I told you I have three brothers?"

The girl nodded but didn't speak, and now Robert really looked at her. She was a head shorter than Rebecca, but her body seemed like that of an even younger child, her skin a damp ivory.

"Cassie is ten," Rebecca said to Robert. "Like me for one more week."

"Hi," Robert said, toward but not exactly to the girl. "You still haven't said if you've seen Mom."

"I haven't." Rebecca glared at him and turned back to the girl. "Do you want to go in with me? I'm taking Cassie in," she told Robert, and she put her hand behind Cassie's elbow as if to help her, though Robert couldn't tell if Cassie needed it or not.

Rebecca wasn't absolutely sure herself, but she thought it better to err on the side of too much help than too little. It was tricky, though. She'd seen Cassie standing alone on the driveway looking very sad, and she'd gone right over and then realized she couldn't say what she was thinking. *What's the matter? How can I help you?* But she also couldn't just say hi as if it hadn't occurred to her that something might be a little bit wrong. She had settled on a generic "Hi, my name is Rebecca," but delivered in a voice that offered solace or sympathy or whatever might be required.

Cassie had gotten separated from her mother, but Rebecca thought that was only part of it, and that Cassie was sad not because she was alone but because her odd appearance meant people were reluctant to approach her.

Rebecca looked around the entry hall until she saw her father. She guided Cassie through the crowd and asked him to help. He crouched so his head was level with Cassie's and told her his name, saying she might have noticed that he was on the tall side, which was useful if you wanted to see over people's heads in a crowded room. He asked Cassie to describe her mother, and after each thing Cassie said, he nodded and repeated it back to her with a question tacked on at the end. "Brown hair? How long?" "Glasses? Are they wire-rimmed?" It was such a leisurely conversation that Rebecca began to get impatient. She thought her father could get Cassie to her mother faster, but he just moseyed along, and in a little while she noticed Cassie looked less sad.

"I think I see her over there," he said. "Does she smile a lot? And tap her lips?" He brought two fingers to his own mouth.

Cassie nodded happily.

"There you go, Rebecca," her father said, putting a hand between

Rebecca's shoulder blades. "Your path is behind the man with the white hair, around the family of redheads, and along that wall where the painting of the horse is. And she's just below the horse's front legs."

Robert was still outside. Earlier, he'd noticed a large sculpture at the far end of the flagstone terrace, and he went to investigate. It was solid black and not in the shape of anything he could recognize, unless it was a large egg with the insides missing and the shell pulled away in irregular shards. He imagined climbing into it and looking out at all the guests as if he were a monkey in a cage.

The woman in the patterned jumpsuit came over. "Do you like it?" she said. "It's bronze—my grandmother commissioned it. You can touch it if you want."

Robert didn't like it but didn't want to be rude. He touched it and found it surprisingly cold. He wondered if it was difficult to carve bronze. Back in fourth grade, Mr. Gleason had told the class that it took Michelangelo over two years to carve the *David,* but it was marble and probably the hardest material to carve.

"I guess you'd start with a chisel," Robert said.

"Bronze is cast," she said. "Melted and poured. We went to the foundry and watched. They heat the bronze to two thousand degrees and then pour it into a ceramic mold."

He was embarrassed and said quickly, "I guess you'd need a pot holder for that," and now she smiled.

"Is your family inside waiting? If we don't let people sit down soon there's going to be a riot. A very polite riot—instead of tear gas people would spray perfume, and they'd hit each other with fountain pens. Your father is handsome," she added.

"My father?"

"He looks like a movie star."

"No, he doesn't."

"Okay, have it your way. He doesn't."

"Actually, I have to find my mother," he said, and he took off at a quick walk that became a trot when he had some distance from her. He found it weird that she'd commented on his father's looks and even weirder that she thought he looked like a movie star. His father was ordinary-looking, with extra-long earlobes and hands that bulged with blue veins at the end of the day.

Dr. Lawson and a couple of guests lingered at the front door, but the driveway was deserted. Robert decided he'd intercept his mother to make sure she saw the bronze on her way in. He wanted to ask if she'd ever been to a foundry. She took her clay pieces to a store with a kiln and then went back a few days later to pick them up, and he thought she might enjoy a visit to a foundry, where you could see the action. In fact, this could be it, the very thing that would bring her back to the family or take the rest of them to her. The crusade had been his idea in the first place, and now he'd come up with the perfect solution.

He made his way out to the street and turned toward where they'd parked. He walked past other parked cars, past other houses, farther than he'd remembered coming, far enough that he reached a corner and had to cross the street. Yet they hadn't crossed a street, had they? He wondered if he'd somehow gone the wrong way. He stood at an intersection with a high boxwood hedge on one corner and a row of palm trees on another, and he understood that his mother had taken the car and left them.

Dr. Mallon gave the Blairs a ride home. They sat quietly on the leather seats of his shiny black BMW and felt, each of them, a separate and private shame. Only James was spared, because he was so young, but even he knew not to talk and instead sat in the backseat between his brothers and kept as still as he could. Rebecca was squished with her father into the front passenger seat. She knew she should keep things in perspective—she didn't have it nearly as bad as Cassie—and she wished she could be as calming as her father.

Her mother was walled off: she was inside a large circle of fence, a corral, and Rebecca moved across the landscape and made her small and then smaller.

Robert was furious and Ryan was heartbroken. As the car moved along the leafy lanes of Atherton, they stayed angled toward their respective windows and thought about what it would be like to see her at home.

For that's where she was. Bill had ascertained this—he had telephoned, and she had answered. She had "changed her mind." Bill hadn't known what to do but convey this to the children, and so he simply told them, straight out. She changed her mind. They accepted this as the incomplete story it was and asked no questions, but when he offered them the option of staying for the recital, they said no in a single voice.

Enraged though he was, Robert imagined a great act of forgiveness. He would find her, in the mud pantry or the kitchen or her bedroom, and he would describe the sculpture. He would explain that bronze was cast, that you melted it to 2000 degrees and then poured it into a ceramic mold, and he would give her time to picture this and then unfurl his great idea, his invitation.

Or else he wouldn't. He had already learned that his plans collapsed sometimes, and he was familiar with the dismay of realizing he'd done exactly what he'd decided not to do, or not done what he'd set out to do. At home, in just a little while, he would pardon her and ennoble himself with the gift, to the entire family, of a brilliant, restorative scheme. Or he would sulk. It was no use deciding now, it would go how it would go.

Ryan drew his knees to his chest and wrapped his arms around his legs. He rested his head against the car door and knew he would cry when he saw her. He didn't fight the knowledge, just as at home he wouldn't fight the tears. After some time had passed, he would sit near her on the couch. This was less a plan than a prophecy. He attached a near-magical power to the simple act of sitting near another person on a couch and would continue to do so for the rest of his life.

"Dad," Rebecca whispered, twisting around so she could look up into her father's eyes.

"Rebeck?"

"Do you think she has a condition?"

"Your mother?"

"Cassie, Dad. My friend."

"I don't know, honey. I suspect she might."

"But do you think she'll be okay?"

Bill felt Rebecca's shoulder digging into his upper arm. He would have liked to wrap her in a hug, but the constraint of John Mallon's leather bucket seats and the sadness emanating from the backseat left him unable to move.

"Do you, Dad?"

"You have a wise heart, Rebecca. And a kind heart. You'll never want for friends."

The station wagon was in the driveway, at an angle to the steps and several yards short of its usual place next to the Valiant: less parked than abandoned. John Mallon stopped but didn't cut the engine. It was rare for him to do anyone a favor, and he found himself overtaken by a powerful feeling that he mistook for concern for the Blair children when in fact it was a desire to be extravagantly thanked. What he received of gratitude was heartfelt but inevitably truncated, and twelve years later, as an attending at UCSF, he would take a powerful dislike to a serious dark-haired medical student named Robert Blair and seek to make the young man's orthopedics rotation as difficult as possible, without ever becoming aware of the connection.

James was the first out of the car. Unencumbered by so much as a tiny layer of propriety, he scrambled over Robert and was up the steps and banging on the front door before the others had set both feet on the ground. He pounded with the flat of his hand and then turned the knob and was inside. "Mommy," he shouted. "Mommeeeeeee!"

The house was empty: the kitchen and mud pantry as they'd been before the recital, the living room sunny and quiet, his parents' bedroom darkened by the drawn curtains and betraying an indentation on the bedspread but no human form anywhere. Their bathroom—empty, too.

"Mommy," he shouted as he barreled down the bedroom hallway, past the children's bathroom, and into the laundry room. By then the others had come inside, and James rejoined them at the front door and waited while they saw for themselves.

"Where is she?" Rebecca said. She was the only one who could make it a question and not merely a lament. "Where on earth is she?"

"I think I might know," their father said. He glanced through the window next to the door—reflexively verifying that John Mallon had departed—and then led the way down the driveway with the children trailing behind and to his sides like the wake of a motorboat, until he reached the spur that led to the storage shed.

And there she was, standing with her hands on her hips, twenty or thirty yards away. She was facing the shed and didn't turn around, though she must have heard them; she must have heard John Mallon's car, for that matter. She'd changed into blue jeans and a plaid shirt, and her hair in its single braid hung down her back.

"Penny," he called.

She turned.

"What—" he began, but he found he couldn't put into a meaningful group of words the hurt he felt on behalf of his children. He couldn't speak, and so he held his arms out wide in a gesture that could have indicated confusion and could possibly have indicated forgiveness but that Penny took to be a reference to Jesus on the cross.

And so she laughed.

"Mom," Ryan whimpered.

"Why is she laughing?" Rebecca asked.

"She's happy we found her," Robert said, going for sarcasm but landing considerably short of his target.

"There's my mommy!" James shouted.

He ran down the spur, and the other children followed, and Bill watched them crowd around her: Ryan crying, Robert tapping her shoulder intently. Only Rebecca remained at a slight remove, but even she seemed primed for engagement: head tilted to the side, her trademark announcement that she was thinking hard and would soon have something to say.

Bill saw that the children were defining the moment as a rescue operation rather than the act of capture it actually was.

Penny watched him approach, each step a concession she knew he didn't want to make. He was obviously angry, and she wished she had it in her to apologize, but she was too caught up in the thing that had drawn her away from the recital in the first place: her realization that the path to happiness she'd thought she might never find was an actual path that lay a mere hundred yards from her house.

The shed was going to be her salvation.

"Don't say anything," she said when he reached her and the children. "Don't say anything. I shouldn't have left and I'm sorry, but did you know there are many kinds of emergencies? Children, did you? There are all the normal kinds of emergency, the medical kinds, but an idea can be an emergency, too. You can have an idea that is so important, you have to act on it or you'll . . . you'll die. Not really, but the part of you that thought of it and that was so excited—that part will die just a little bit. And that's your soul, children. That's the creative, beautiful, mysterious thing we all have inside of us, and if it doesn't get what it wants, if it doesn't get air, it begins to shrivel. What good would I be to you if I began to shrivel? I have to keep myself alive so I can help you live. It's not just doctors who do that."

"Mom, what is it?" Ryan said. He wanted to put his hands on her face, to smooth her eyebrows. "What's your idea?"

"*I* have an idea," Robert said.

"And I have a hammer!" James exclaimed.

"Shut up, James," Robert said, stomping his foot.

"I hammer in the morning! I hammer in the evening! I hammer in the afternoon! I hammer at night!"

"James," Ryan said. "That's not how it goes."

"I always wonder about that song," Rebecca said. "Why is it 'I'd hammer out danger' and then 'I'd hammer out love between my brothers and my sisters'? Danger is bad, so you're hammering it out, right? But then why do you want to hammer out love?"

"I have something to say," Penny cried.

"Oh, goodness," Bill said. "Let's all take a deep breath."

"It's not *a medical emergency,*" Penny said. "We don't need *deep breaths!*"

"But you said ideas need air," Rebecca said.

"*No!*" Penny cried. "*Please!*"

She hadn't wanted it to be like this: she had wanted everyone to admire her idea, to see how it would help her and thereby help them all. But it had gone very quickly from promising to muddled, like so many other moments of family life. She said, "This is what I can't take, this is what I can't stand!"

Everyone fell silent. Bill put his hand to his mouth, as if her words had not yet been uttered and he might prevent them by suggestion; but they were far from speaking with a single voice. At times he viewed himself as a kind of diplomat/translator for her and the children, and after she said something hostile or confusing he tried to convert it into a sweeter, clearer statement. But he was dry now.

"I need a place," she said. "For my supplies, my arts and crafts. For me. And we've got this shed down here going to waste. I mean, why do we have a rowboat? Why don't we have a kiln?"

Robert had been holding back, reserving his beautiful foundry trip for just the right moment, and now he saw it sailing past, departing without him. "But wait," he said. "There was this sculpture—"

"And if we're going to clear it out and make windows," his mother continued, with a glance in his direction that seemed to convey censure, forgiveness, and apology all at once, "we might as well go the extra step and make it a little bigger, since there's plenty of level ground off to the side here. And we could put in a small bathroom just to save me time, so I wouldn't have to go up and down to the house all day. Just a toilet and a sink. I'd need a sink anyway, so really the only extra would be the toilet. You can spare me a toilet, can't you, Bill?"

All this time, the children had thought she was speaking to all of them, but now they understood it was only their father she was addressing. She wanted something from him.

"Mom," Ryan said. "You aren't moving down here, are you?"

"No, of course not," Bill said. "Of course she isn't."

5

REBECCA

People have always asked how it was for me, being the only girl in a family of boys, but I never felt we were a family of boys. We didn't have the kind of household in which the brothers set the tone with roughhousing and smelly socks, and my brothers didn't gang up on me or put slugs in my bed, which happened regularly at my friend Joyce's house, where there were only two boys and a far warmer and more watchful mother to boot. My brothers shared a room at Sea Ranch, where we spent a week each summer, but even there I was never the odd one out. In fact, Ryan and I were particularly close during those vacations. Arriving late on a Friday evening, after a four-hour drive that always seemed even longer, we'd grab flashlights and make our way across the meadow to the cliffs overlooking the ocean. We'd stand close together under the thick stars and listen to the waves pounding the rocks. This was the Pacific as wild beast, and we loved it. We loved the harsh air and the glints of moonlight far out on the water. If we weren't too cold or tired, we would hike to the piece of driftwood someone had set like a bench overlooking the scrap of beach where we would have our salty lunches the next day. "We're back!" we would yell at the ocean. "We're back!"

Unless James came with us. He sometimes tagged along, and when that happened I kept my eyes on his every move. I was terrified he would fall off the cliff. "I think part of you wished he would fall," my first therapist said in response to this, and I suppose it's an indication of how primed I was for psychology that I didn't spend a lot of time arguing with her. Maybe she was right: it was possible that my maternal feelings toward James began as a reaction formation against an unconscious hatred of him.

Now he was back, and though I was forty-three and he was thirty-eight, I felt it all start up again. I wanted him to get to bed at a reasonable hour; I wanted him to tell me whether or not he'd be home for dinner. Mostly I held my tongue, but one evening I knocked on the guest room door and asked if he had any laundry he wanted me to do.

"You're kidding," he said with a smirk.

"I wasn't."

"What are we going to do with you?"

"What are we going to do with *you*?" I said, and a shadow crossed his face, reminding me of how defensive he'd been about having shown up unexpectedly. "I'm sorry," I said. "I'll leave you be."

"No, hang on a sec." He was sitting cross-legged on the bed, computer open in his lap. "Come in."

Already the room felt less like my guest room than his bedroom. This was not so much a matter of his dirty clothes in puddles on the floor as a feeling I noticed in myself, of nervous restlessness, as I stood there looking at him.

He said, "I've been wanting to ask you something, pick the famous steel-trap brain. I hitchhiked back from Rob's yesterday, and I—"

"Wait, you hitchhiked?"

"Yes, I hitchhiked. What's so terrible? It's two people, one has a car and one doesn't. Kind of a win-win, right? But no. Don't hitchhike, the driver may be a serial killer. Or the hitchhiker may be a serial killer. Someone's going to be a serial killer."

"James."

"No, it's like how people don't let their kids play outside anymore. The paranoia. This woman I know—" Abruptly, he lowered the cover of his laptop and very deliberately set it off to the side.

"This woman you know?"

"Never mind. I hitchhiked, and the guy who picked me up was going to the hospital, so I got out there and walked the rest of the way. But here's the thing: seeing the hospital reminded me of this memory. And I can't make sense of it or even be sure it's real or—" He paused and stared at me. "God, please don't go all shrinky on me, okay? I don't want to hear how whatever I think I'm remembering *signifies something* whether it happened or not. I want to know, was I ever alone in the hospital?"

I was wondering about this woman he knew, so it took me a moment to respond. "I don't think so."

"I have this memory of walking down a hospital corridor by myself. And I looked through an open door and saw an old man with a huge stomach like a pregnant woman."

This was our father: what James might have done with the information that our father's abdomen was distended when he was admitted to the hospital just before he died. James wasn't there, so he could only invent the scene, and distort it. A hypothesis, anyway, if a very shrinky one.

"Dad wouldn't have taken us on rounds, would he?" James continued. "And I wandered away?"

"Never. But if he had, you wouldn't have seen an old man. We'd have been on the pediatric ward."

"It's really bugging me. I want to go up there," he added, and for a moment I thought he meant the pediatric ward, though it no longer existed; now there was an entire children's hospital. "To the house, I mean."

"You miss it."

He shrugged.

"It's a loss. I miss it, too."

"So where's that husband of yours, anyway?"

"Work."

"The honeymoon's over?"

Walt and I had been married for only a year, but we'd never had a honeymoon of the kind James apparently imagined, spending every possible minute together. For most of our careers we'd both believed that a serious relationship would hamper us professionally, and when we met and began dating we were amused to discover we were both inventing busy calendars to protect our weeknights for work. Early on, we decided that Monday and Tuesday evenings would be spent separately unless arranged otherwise in advance, and this seemed at least partially responsible for how happy we were together.

"He's a nice guy," James said. "I'm glad I finally met him." Quickly, he picked up his laptop, hit a key several times, and pressed the cover closed again.

I said, "Honey, what's going on?"

He froze and then began nodding and snapping his fingers R&B-style, singing, "What's goin' on? What's goin' on?"

"James, please. Tell me with the crap cut?"

This was something our father had said when the teenage James, caught one night coming into the house around three a.m., said he'd heard something in the yard as he was going to bed, had stepped outside to investigate, and had fallen asleep on the ground. It usually got a smile out of James, but not this time.

"James?"

"Nothing's going on." He looked away and pinched the bridge of his nose. "Things are weird in Eugene, okay?"

Since 1989, when he left school for good, James had lived in so many places even I couldn't remember them all. He'd moved from Santa Cruz to Tucson to Boulder to Portland to Arcata. He'd spent over a year wandering around South America. He'd odd-jobbed, dishwashed, house-sat; he'd done carpentry and lawn maintenance and telemarketing. He'd driven a cab from midnight to eight a.m. and worked at a bakery from four a.m. till noon. He was itinerant, peripatetic; our father always said he was a seeker who was seeking the identity of his own grail. The stability of his life in Eugene had seemed too good to be true; perhaps it had been.

"Oh, James," I said.

"'Oh, James,'" he repeated bitterly. "'Oh, James.' That's the Blair family mantra, isn't it? 'What will we do about James?' It's like 'How do you solve a problem like Maria?' How *did* they solve a problem like Maria? There she is, Julie Andrews, running through the alpine meadows, just so difficult. What do they do? They make her a governess. Sorry to disappoint you, Rebecca, or do you think maybe *I* should become a governess? I'd like to go to bed now if you don't mind."

"Of course," I said, taking a step toward the door. I wanted to add that I was available anytime he felt like talking, but I didn't want to crowd him.

"I know," he said as if I'd spoken. "Thank you."

I returned to my office and began writing up notes from the day's sessions. I saw anywhere from a quarter to a third of my patients at the hospital, children who had cancers or autoimmune diseases and were too sick to come to my office. My first patient of the day had been one of these, a boy who was gravely ill with leukemia. He was eleven, and I'd been treating him for three years, the longest I'd treated any critically ill child. He had gone through hell several times. He hadn't left the hospital in over four months, and lately it seemed he wouldn't be able to go home for even a final brief visit.

That morning, near the end of our time together, I asked him a question, and he said with the impish quality he still sometimes displayed, "Rebecca, Rebecca, Rebecca. No more questions. It's time to say good boy." He looked embarrassed and said quickly, "Goodbye. I meant goodbye." But "good boy" stayed with me, and now I thought of how important the word "good" had been to us in the conversations we'd had. Packard was a good hospital, and his oncologist was a good doctor, and his parents were good people. That was always the word: and it could mean anything from mediocre (we used it forgivingly in that case) to excellent (when we used it almost superstitiously, as if to say anything more would be to invite trouble).

He was a good boy. Thinking about him, I did what I always did when I was on the verge of being overcome by grief about a patient, though perhaps in this instance I was also influenced by having heard James's memory of being in the hospital: I remembered a moment from my early childhood. Or rather, I remembered my memory of the moment, because after so long that's what memory is: the replaying of filmstrip that's slightly warped from having gone through the projector so many times. I'll never know what actually happened and what distortions I added.

It was a Saturday, and we were going somewhere as a family. This was before James was born. Our father needed to look in on a patient, so we stopped at the hospital and he left the three of us kids to wait with our mother in the cafeteria. I didn't want to sit down, so I stood at her elbow and watched while she drank coffee and the boys drank milk. There was a terrible weight to the place, a heaviness in the way people held themselves, in the way they lifted their skimpy sandwiches to their mouths. Some were in wheelchairs. Others were terrified or grief-stricken, but I didn't understand: at such a young age I had no knowledge of illness and no awareness that people suffered because they loved. Despite having a doctor for a father, I didn't really know what hospitals were for, why some people were sick enough to need them and others weren't. In my family, sick meant it hurt to swallow; it meant aching arms and legs and sleeping during the day.

I told my mother I wanted to leave, and she said we couldn't leave, but if I promised to be quiet I could go over to the window. On the other side of the glass people were moving quickly: doctors in white coats, nurses in caps, regular people in regular clothes. They were alone or in pairs, talking or not. I didn't know why or how, but I knew they were different from the people in the cafeteria. And to get closer to them, all I had to do was be quiet.

Was this the moment when the seeds of my vocation were planted? I've always thought so. I wanted to be on the other side of the window, away from the sick and the worried. And to get there, I should cease talking. I should listen.

Heavy, James would say. Maybe Robert and Ryan would, too. Walt would nod politely and perhaps ask a question, but his only comment would be something like "Huh" or "Interesting." He's a scientist, and for him the mind and its mysteries don't hold a candle to the brain.

Though now that I think about it: doesn't the brain hold a candle to the mind? Isn't that what neuroscience wants it to do—illuminate? This is the kind of idea I would have taken to my father, whose interest in psychology had bloomed as I hit my stride. We handed dense books back and forth long after he'd retired and up until the end of his life. Freud, Klein, Winnicott—especially Winnicott. There was one paper, "The Capacity to Be Alone," that he asked me to photocopy for him—poignantly, I thought, given his life at that point. In those years I finished work early on Friday afternoons, and I'd go up to the house, where we'd sit and talk until I felt he should, for the sake of his health, get up and move around. "Well, Rebecca," he'd say, "this has been very interesting, thanks for stopping by," as if it were an occasional rather than a weekly occurrence. He didn't want me to think he depended on it.

"Oh, hallelujah," James said when I got home the next afternoon, early because of a cancellation. "I'm bored out of my mind. What say we drive up to Skyline? Bet you haven't been there in a while."

"Actually, I have. Walt and I hike a lot."

"Walt and you *hike* a lot?"

"You didn't think I was capable of surprising you?"

The October sun hung above the hilltops as we headed west. We took Sand Hill Road up past the turnoff for the freeway, with the mile-long tan barracks of the Stanford Linear Accelerator Center off to our left, visible and then invisible behind all the new construction. We passed the fenced-off entrance to Searsville Lake, where we'd swum as children. Soon we were on the winding road to the ridgetop dividing the valley from the Pacific Ocean.

The forest was dense, and I pushed my sunglasses to the top of my head. Every quarter mile or so we passed a small turnoff marked only by a cluster of mailboxes. When we were children, these roads led mostly to undeveloped land, to the occasional cabin. Now they were as likely to lead to locked gates protecting the estates of venture capitalists and billionaire patent holders.

"I know," James said after we'd been climbing for a few minutes, "let's go find Neil Young's ranch."

"What, and knock on the door?"

"I was thinking a love note in the mailbox. Ryan would."

Redwood trees soared all around us, making the sky very small. At the intersection of Woodside Road, Skyline, and La Honda, there was a restaurant that was jammed on weekends, but today there were just a few cars and motorcycles and maybe half a dozen bicycles.

I looked at James, with his hollowed-out face and ropy arms. Tell me, I wanted to say. Tell me about Eugene and why things are weird there. Instead I said, "Let's go in and have a beer."

"I've never had a beer with you in my life. Jeez, Rebecca, hiking and beer, what's next?"

We sat on the deck with foamy amber pints. Six or seven cyclists coasted to the bike rack and dismounted. They wore tight black shorts and brightly colored shirts festooned with giant logos. James and I talked for a while about the kids; he'd gone to Katya's preschool at circle time that morning, to be her show-and-tell.

"Do you even like beer?" he said abruptly.

"Not much."

"So you're what? Trying to make me feel better?"

"I wish I could. I'm hoping you'll feel safe telling me what's going on."

He looked away; he was having none of it. "Hey, it's Google," he said, pointing over my shoulder.

I saw a small blue car with a Google logo on its side and a camera mounted to its roof.

"I've never seen that before, have you? That must be how they do the maps. Which— Wow, I didn't even think of this. I'll bet Neil Young's ranch is on Google Maps. What's to stop someone from looking it up?"

"Conscience?"

"Ha. You're obviously not going to finish that, are you, so let's get out of here."

I asked for the check, and while I waited he strolled over to the colorfully dressed cyclists and began chatting with them, bending over to look more closely at the bicycles. Heading down the mountain a little later, we were silent for so long that I turned on the radio. He reached over and turned it off.

"If you won't help me find Neil Young can we at least stop at the house?"

"Our house?"

"Of course our house."

"People live there."

"Ryan said they won't mind."

"We can't just barge in on them. It's almost dinnertime."

"So they'll probably be home. Please, I really feel like I need to see it. For my, you know, *psychological well-being*."

I smiled, and he smiled, too, but only for a moment.

"I'm serious, Rebecca. It's something I need to do."

It was dusk when we arrived. Robert had been the point person in our dealings with the tenants, and I'd only ever met the husband—and him just a couple of times, when I was on my way to see Ryan and he was on his way down the driveway in his black Ferrari. His name was Lewis Vincent, and he was home alone and seemed to relish the intrusion, offering us glasses of wine and then beckoning us to see his "brand-new toy." A muscle-bound five-eight, he was the kind of man who'd transformed a slightly awkward body into an asset—or this was my thought as we followed him to the garage.

"Wow," James said.

In place of our father's tools and workbench there were now three floor-to-ceiling steel cabinets with glass fronts, revealing shelving for hundreds of bottles of wine.

"Temperature-controlled, of course," Lewis said with a grin. "The installation guys just left. That's why I'm home—normally I'm at work till seven or later. Isn't it beautiful? I've got my work cut out for me, though, moving bottles from the house. I have at least a couple hundred in various cabinets and closets."

"Want a hand getting started?" James said.

Lewis looked surprised. "I couldn't ask you to do that."

"You didn't, I offered. That's what I do."

Lewis said something about how he hadn't gotten where he was in life by saying no to people who wanted to help him, and he led the way back, talking about his plan to invest in a winery someday or maybe spend a month in Napa learning how to make the stuff himself. I was only half listening, wondering instead at James saying "That's what I do" and thinking there was something different about him, though I couldn't put my finger on what it was.

In the kitchen he told me to leave without him—"I can always hitchhike"—but I figured I'd help, and I listened while he and Lewis spent a few minutes talking about the best way to move the wine: packed into roll-aboard suitcases with towels, placed upright in cardboard boxes, or simply carried in our hands. By now James was calling Lewis "Vince," which seemed to amuse Lewis, even please him. It reminded me of James's charisma, his way of tunneling through diffidence or reserve, even through indifference, to create a quick if impermanent rapport with a stranger. His talent for this had begun to reveal itself toward the end of his teenage years, as he gained impulse control and recognized the usefulness of being liked.

Hands for now, they decided. We went into the mud pantry, where three or four dozen bottles were stored, in racks jammed into cabinets and on a freestanding shelf unit that had been wedged behind the door. Lewis's wife and daughters were out, and as we gathered bottles he began talking about the younger girl's unhappiness with her new school, to which she'd been admitted a week after the year got under way, and what did I think of that, moving a child under those circumstances, was it okay?

I said, "It sounds like you're worried about her."

"Einstein," James said. "That's what we call her at home."

Lewis glanced at James curiously. To me James seemed distracted, the comment delivered almost automatically, and I imagined myself explaining to Lewis that James didn't mean anything by it, he was just discharging excess energy.

"Is there research on that?" Lewis asked me. "Changing schools? This is your field, right, aren't you a child therapist? She's eight, if that matters."

"I don't know of any research."

"She also has trouble falling asleep at night—but I guess that's not so unusual." He hesitated. "Is it?"

I smiled noncommittally, and he let the subject drop as we took our first load of bottles to the garage. At first I was afraid James would drop one, but with his big hands and long arms he was able to carry eight at a time.

After depositing a load of bottles I asked if I could use the bathroom, and Lewis and James were gone when I returned. It was nearly six, dusk; I'd told a colleague I'd be free for a phone conversation at six-thirty.

I thought about carrying some more bottles to the garage, but once I begin to think about being late it's as if it's already happened. I didn't want to delay our departure by the few extra minutes it would take me to make another trip, given that they'd likely be back in a moment or two. Then a few more minutes went by, and I regretted that I hadn't gone because I'd spent at least as long standing there waiting for them as a trip to and from the garage would have taken me.

At last I set off, and it turned out they'd stopped working and were standing there talking.

"Rebecca," James said, "you just missed it. Vince was telling me about the amazing ideas he has for the property. Tell her," he said to Lewis. "Beck, you've got to hear this."

"Actually, I've got to get going."

"It won't take a minute. Then we'll go, I promise."

Lewis was obviously uncomfortable; Robert had told him we had no interest in selling the house. But he began to talk, and as he went along his voice picked up speed and he grew animated. He described the multilevel house he envisioned, probably six or seven thousand square feet; and the series of terraces that could be created once the woods were cleared; and what could go on the top terrace (a swimming pool), and the next terrace (a tennis court), and the third (a guesthouse), which he was thinking could have a separate driveway. "I don't know," he said as he finished. "It's just fun to think about."

I glanced at my watch; it was six-fifteen. "I've got a call scheduled," I said, and we exchanged thank-yous and shook hands, and James and I headed for my car, James whispering "Shh-shh-shh" as we hurried along.

"What?" I said in a low voice.

"Wait till we get going."

He stayed silent until we'd closed the car doors. Then he gave me a mischievous smile and said, "One way to think about it? The more detailed his vision, the more he'll pay to realize it."

"James," I said. "We're not selling, remember?" Then suddenly I was afraid. "Wait—how did it come up?"

He smiled. "I brought it up. Told him things have changed." He fastened his seat belt with a hard click. "I'm crossing over," he added. "Hello, dark side."

Ryan once had a dream in which the house hadn't been built. He stood under the oak tree, surrounded by other trees and shrubs, and felt utterly bewildered. At last he realized he was in our father's painting of the land before the ground was broken. He knew this because the colors he saw were muted: they were the painting's colors, based on the true colors of nature but lightened and grayed.

He had this dream at a low point in his life, after his heart had been broken for the first time. We were both in college. He told me about it on a weekend afternoon, the two of us side by side on lawn chairs in the backyard. When he finished describing the dream, he closed his eyes and held out his hand, and I took it. We sat like that for several minutes. It was the first time I'd sat holding anyone's hand in . . . well, perhaps in my life. Of course I'd walked while holding hands any number of times, when I was very little and one of my parents was escorting me or when I was older and escorting Ryan or James. But to sit holding hands: this was new for me. Finally, Ryan gave my hand a squeeze and dropped it. Then he said, almost as an afterthought, that in the dream the rest of us weren't there with him, but he knew we were coming. He was alone but not lonely.

The night James said he wanted to sell the house, I dreamed Ryan's dream. I was alone under the oak tree and also inside the painting, surrounded by a version of our land that had been bled of its true colors. In my dream, the family was there, too, standing among the shrubs, leaning against trees I'd never seen in real life because they'd been removed to make room for the house. I could see them—my father, my mother, all three of my brothers—but I couldn't reach them. I was lonely but not alone.

I woke from this dream at 4:28 a.m. Emotions in dreams can build to a pitch they may not reach in waking time because of our defenses, and I was suffused with feeling. I wasn't just lonely, I was bereft. I was desolate. Walt was asleep beside me, and I moved closer to him, put my arm around his waist, and waited for equilibrium.

My father's painting had been the subject of much discussion after he died. Having decided unanimously that we didn't want to sell the house, we may have needed a point of contention or even just deliberation; in any case, we debated endlessly over who should get the painting. Realistically, only Robert or I could take it—only we had room—but it seemed important that we go through some kind of process that allowed Ryan and James an equal and valid claim. Then one day all three boys came to me as a group—I didn't think this had ever happened before, for any reason—and told me they'd decided I should have it. Maybe this story invalidates the idea that I was never the only girl in a family of boys, but I see it more as the exception that proves the rule.

The house, the painting, the dream: I feared I wouldn't be able to get back to sleep. Hello, dark side. James had been referring to the terms of our father's estate plan. He'd been referring to Penny.

She first went to Taos in 1988, for a weeklong workshop on the found object in art, or The Found Object in Art, as my brothers and I somehow termed it, using emphasis and enunciation to capitalize the initial letters. A few years later she announced that she was going to spend the entire month of June there, and the following year it was the entire summer. Our father reported these plans with careful neutrality, and I let (or made) myself believe he was pleased with them, happy to have the house to himself for a while. I was busy with my residency and didn't think about it very much.

At the end of the summer, she called and told him she'd found a room to rent in a tiny adobe house and wanted a year to figure out if she could support herself selling her art. She asked him for $2,000 a month and said that if by the end of twelve months she had not earned $24,000, she would give up and come home.

When he told me about this he tried to maintain his previous detachment, but I could tell he was flummoxed. "She needs to give it a whirl," he said more than once, and it was his repetition of that exact phrase as much as anything else that clued me in to his anxiety. It was as if he'd memorized a line, the better not to say what he was really thinking. And "whirl": the word seemed important. I suspected he was worried that the disturbed air might reach California and unbalance him.

Incredibly, she succeeded. By the end of the first year she had sold several dozen pieces, had rented space in a shared studio, and had broken even. And though he visited her a few times, and though she stayed at the Portola Valley house on the rare occasions when she came to California, they never lived together again.

When he turned seventy, he began to think about the house and what would happen if he died with his current will in effect. Despite California's community property laws, he held the title to the house as his separate property, a state of affairs that had arisen from the fact that he'd owned the land before his marriage. From time to time he'd told Penny they could get a lawyer to do the legal work necessary to change this, but she never seemed to care and it never happened. In the original will, drafted when we were children, she was to receive half his estate while my brothers and I would split the other half. Thirty-odd years later he still wanted her to have half, but he knew she was itching to buy a place in Taos and was afraid she would force a sale of the house in order to cash out. He wanted us kids to be able to hold on to the place for as long as we all wanted. In the end, his lawyer set up a plan that left the house in trust to the five of us with the provision that it couldn't be sold without the consent of Penny and at least one of the children.

And after his death she *did* want to sell; it was only because of the trust that we were able to hold on to the property. We were united in our desire to keep it, but we had our separate rationalizations. Robert said he might buy out the rest of us someday and live there, even though his current house was larger and more up-to-date, with a fabulous kitchen that his wife had designed. I was concerned about Ryan, who depended on the shed as a home for himself and his family. Ryan wanted to keep the house so Sammy, Luke, and Katya would know the place where we'd all grown up. And James wanted to thwart Penny. If I'd had to list us in order of how likely we were to break rank—to go to the "dark side"—James would have been last.

It took me a long time to get back to sleep, and I was tired and groggy all the next day, slow with my patients and spent by the time I got home. James was out somewhere, and Walt made dinner for the two of us. I was in bed by nine, and when he woke me at dawn the next morning and suggested we go for a hike, I nearly said no. But I knew I'd be glad if I went. I had wondered if being married would change my medical practice, and it had: thanks to Walt, I'd become the kind of psychiatrist who recommends outdoor exercise to her patients.

The county park was deserted and green, with a dirt road that quickly ascended to a network of trails winding through the trees. When our trail narrowed, Walt took the lead. He was fifty-nine, but his shoulders were bowed after several decades at the microscope and the computer, and he liked to use a walking stick because of an old knee injury, so he appeared older—though not yet an "older adult," as the saying goes, the noun apparently added for dignity to make up for the potentially damning adjective. (In that way, "older adult" reminded me of "gay American," and both seemed to be opposites of phrases like "vagina area," in which the potentially offending noun is neutralized by conversion into an adjective.) Still, watching him up ahead of me, I felt acutely aware of the sixteen-year difference in our ages.

"Sorry about last night," I said. "All that stuff with my brothers." Over the course of half a dozen phone calls, Robert and Ryan and I had spent at least an hour talking about James wanting to sell the house. "Is James driving you crazy?"

"I enjoy him," Walt said with a smile. "I don't think he's as much of a puzzle to me as he is to you."

"He's not as much of a puzzle? Or you're less preoccupied with trying to figure it out?"

"Is a puzzle still a puzzle if no one wants to solve it?"

I loved Walt's shy playfulness. It was among the first things I noticed about him. His serious, professorial demeanor belied a sweet, merry core. We met at a lecture on the neurobiology of depression; he was an immunologist, and when I asked what had brought him to the event, he said he thought depression could be viewed as an autoimmune disease, in which the mind produced antibodies against the self. "Oh, I like that," I said, and he said, "I was hoping you would." This was before my father's death, but not enough before that I ever introduced them. It's possible that, had my father lived, I wouldn't have allowed myself to get close to Walt. Regardless, the timing of our meeting denied all three of us whatever might have come of the two of them getting to know each other.

"The thing about selling," I said, "is that it's so final."

Walt chuckled. "I suppose you could always buy it back someday."

"No, we either keep it or we sell and it's over."

He didn't respond. We were navigating a place where erupting tree roots had created a staircase effect, and I wondered if he was having trouble with the terrain. Then he said, "What if *we* bought it?"

"The house? We don't want to buy it. I love our house."

"We don't want to buy it or we don't want to live there?"

"Why buy it if we don't want to live there?"

"Why *own* it if we don't want to live there?"

"I own twelve and a half percent. We can't live in twelve and a half percent of a house."

"That's very literal-minded of you."

"Of course."

"Rebecca?"

"Mmm?"

"I'd live there if you wanted."

In response I reached up and touched his back, and he kissed me and pulled me close. My nose was inches from his neck, and I smelled his somewhat odd, idiosyncratic smell, which reminded me of baked squash. At first, when we started getting physically intimate, I had found the smell unpleasant and wondered if it might make the relationship impossible for me. I'd had several lovers though nothing serious, and already I knew this was different. But how could I be with someone whose native smell bothered me? And how could I let something so minor get in the way? Up until that point I'd treated a number of lonely, isolated people whose presenting complaint was that they were single but who then revealed themselves to be unable to get beyond small objections to the people they met. I'd had patients who couldn't stand a new partner's laugh or extremely heavy eyebrows. I never failed to interpret a conflict, often regarding how torn my patient felt about the prospect of actually getting what he or she wanted. Walt's smell made me reconsider. I began to think more about chemistry—not "chemistry" but actual chemistry. I read about attraction and smell and came across a fascinating study in which it was found that women who were given samples of the body odor of a variety of men rated as most appealing the smells of the men who were genetically most different from them—those who would help them reproduce most successfully. Was my reaction to Walt's smell an indication that we might not be a good match reproductively? We weren't going to reproduce, so what did it matter? I worked hard to get over my revulsion, and over time, perhaps because of my work and perhaps because Walt in love smelled different from Walt alone, I felt less revulsion, and then no revulsion, more an awareness that I could, most of the time, keep neutral.

Walt released me and smiled mildly. "So you don't want to be queen of the manse?"

I shook my head and we started hiking again. I could live in that house only as one of the selves I'd already been: the self-contained little girl, the preternaturally calm adolescent.

He said, "Tell me again what Ryan said?"

"'Whether it happens now or not,'" I quoted, "'the question will keep coming up until it does happen.'"

"He's right, you know."

"I know."

James was still asleep when we got home. Walt and I showered and dressed and went our separate ways, but it was a lovely start to the day, and when we met again in the kitchen at dusk I thanked him for having woken me. Now James was out. We made dinner together and settled in front of the TV to watch DVDs of some TED talks. We had two by colleagues of Walt's and a third by a child advocacy expert whose work focused on immigrant children in border states. A couple days earlier, James had teased us about our taste. "And now I'm joining Rebecca Blair and Walt Newhall for a little light entertainment about the neuroplasticity of the brain."

The phone rang and I saw from the caller ID that it was Lewis Vincent. I answered, thinking he must be calling about his conversation with James, but he said he and his wife wanted to talk to me about their daughter.

"I'm sorry, but I don't treat acquaintances or their children. I'd be happy to give you a referral."

"No, no, she doesn't need therapy. Lisa and I just want to get your perspective."

"I understand. But I've found that even a single consultation changes a social relationship."

"We don't have a social relationship, we have a business relationship."

I kept silent.

"Really? You won't meet with us once and give us your expertise? *Sell* us your expertise?"

"I have a lot of very experienced colleagues. I'd be happy to give you a name. It was nice seeing you the other day. How's the wine migration going?"

"I'm getting a couple of guys in to do it. They're selling me their expertise. Ha, I'm kidding. That was a joke."

After we hung up I returned to the couch, and a moment later James came in, smiling as he saw us in front of the TV and saying, "Don't tell me you're watching this trash again. So how are you guys? I just spent a few hours with Rob. The two of us are talking about funding research on the mood disorders of middle-aged primary care physicians."

I suppressed a smile. "Did Jen cook?"

"She threw something together. An Indian lamb dish with homemade naan in the wood-fired oven and chutney from mangoes she grew."

"I don't think you can grow mangoes here."

"Metaphorically. She grew them metaphorically. I think she grew the onions literally."

"How are the boys?"

"I like the boys. I am very much in favor of the boys."

"That's a strange way to put it."

"I'm in favor of children. What did Dad always say? Children deserve care. I'm down with that."

"You're in a funny mood."

"I'm not high."

"I didn't think you were high."

"I haven't partaken in like five years, in case you care. Isn't this so reminiscent, though? I walk in late, and my adult keepers are sitting up watching TV? And I have to persuade them that I'm not drunk or stoned?"

"Your adult keepers."

"You and Dad. Ryan and Dad. It was never Robert and Dad—I don't think my delinquency really took root until he was gone. Robert," he added, "is a tad angry about the prospect of selling the house. Are you? I don't think Ryan is. I saw him today, too."

"I'm not sure yet, James," I said, though on some level I was. "It's so laden."

"Laden," he said. "Laden. That's a strange word if you think about it. It means loaded, right? Or overloaded? But it sounds like the past tense of 'lade.' Is there a word 'lade'? I remember I used to say 'boughten.' 'I wish I'd "boughten" that Matchbox car.' 'You could've "boughten" it for me.'" He shrugged. "Don't you like the idea of Vince and his wife building a monstrosity, though? I think whatever gets built there has to be completely different. I don't want to recognize it. I'd like to see a god-awful Mediterranean villa with a red tile roof."

"You've really decided," I said.

"I'm not sure yet, Rebecca. It's so laden."

He said good night and headed off to the guest room, and Walt and I decided to go to bed as well. We went downstairs to the ground-level master suite, almost a thousand square feet dedicated to private space, an architectural possibility only when there aren't and won't be children. From the sitting area, sliding doors opened onto a beautifully landscaped yard full of native plants, and we finished the evening by turning on the outside lights and enjoying the view as if we were tiny creatures looking into a terrarium.

• • •

One thing I believed about myself for a long time was that I would go as far as I could academically. I got both a BA and a BS in college, I completed a master's in psychology while working toward my MD, I did a fellowship in child and adolescent psychiatry once I'd finished my residency. I began my private practice assuming I'd spend three or four years establishing myself and then begin training to become a psychoanalyst. But I didn't—not after three or four years and not after eight or ten, either. I saw friends enter into and benefit from analytic training, and I was hovering on the threshold: already reading deeply in the literature, my practice analytically oriented. My resistance seemed to focus, at least superficially, on the indeterminate length of the training. I consulted a former therapist, wanting help with figuring it out, and she related my anxiety to my childhood experience with James: I signed up to watch out for him without knowing I'd end up holding the job for life. "Maybe," I said, but it didn't sound right.

Then, as my father began to fail, I reconsidered. My objections disintegrated; I developed an itch. I began a five-day-a-week training analysis (with one of the few Palo Alto psychiatrists I didn't already know), started my coursework, and at the ripe old age of forty-two reentered supervision. A little over a year later, I had two adult cases in supervision and had recently begun supervision on a child case, a four-year-old girl named Alissa whom I was seeing four times a week.

She was my first session the next morning. Initially referred to treatment for an eating disorder, Alissa ate only certain foods—certain white foods—but unlike most such children, she frequently refused food altogether. She declared certain days "yes" days and other days "no" days and announced over breakfast each morning which kind of day it would be. On "yes" days she ate jicama for breakfast and for lunch and dinner some combination of bread, pasta, rice, and potatoes; on "no" days she consumed only coconut water. She weighed twenty-eight pounds.

Not surprisingly, most of our play centered around eating. I had bought a bin full of plastic foods—hamburgers the size of egg yolks, apples the size of walnuts. We fed these items to a group of dolls. Beforehand, we "washed" the food in cups of water we'd tinted with drops of white paint. By this point in the treatment it had become clear that white meant clean and stood in contrast to brown, which meant dirty. Food itself stood in contrast to feces. In eating nothing but rice and potatoes, Alissa was doing her best to avoid eating poop. And in skipping food a few times a week, she was doing the only thing she could think of to avoid producing it.

The play area in my office looked out onto the parking lot, and toward the end of the session I happened to glance down and see a woman stepping out of a sleek silver sedan. She had blond hair to her shoulders and was dressed in a light blue polo shirt and what appeared to be a pair of jodhpurs tucked into riding boots.

Alissa sensed the drift of my attention and threw her doll to the floor. "She's finished."

"And maybe a little angry."

"No!"

Anger was a dangerous substance in Alissa's family. Her parents, when I first met with them, spent a lot of time preemptively disavowing any so-called negative feelings toward their daughter. "You probably think we're furious at her," the father declared, "but we're not."

"What does she feel?" I asked Alissa about the doll.

"Hungry, but she's not going to eat anymore."

"Hungry and angry almost sound the same."

"I didn't want you to tell me that again!" With that, Alissa lay on her side and drew her knees to her chest. She wore a short turquoise dress, and her folded legs looked like kindling.

"You're curled in a ball. Maybe that will protect you from my words."

"It's not a ball, it's a shell."

"Shells protect the soft creature inside."

"Kari is a soft creature."

Kari was the baby sister whose birth had accelerated Alissa's eating issues and begun the yearlong health concerns that had led her to my office. When I fetched Alissa from the waiting room, Kari was always in their mother's arms, while Alissa sat by herself on the floor.

"Is Kari protected?"

"That's stupid. She's a baby. Of course she is."

"What about you?"

"I'm making a wall at home." She unfolded herself and got onto her knees. "It's going to be really high."

"What will be outside the wall?"

"There is no outside. It's all inside."

"I see. What's inside?"

"It's not what, it's who. Everyone but you."

The session was just about over, and I told her it was time to put the toys away. After, I walked her back to the waiting room. Her mother was where we'd left her, with Kari still in her arms but asleep now, her head thrown back and one hand draped over her forehead like an actress overdoing a sickbed scene. I remembered Robert once arranging the sleeping baby Sammy to look like an old man clutching his stomach after a heavy meal, and how this prompted our father to say mildly that one of the hardest parts of being a parent was boredom, the difficulty of waiting for your child to reach the next phase of development.

The blonde from the parking lot was in the waiting room, too, and when she saw me she got to her feet. "Dr. Blair?"

"Yes, just a moment," I said, and I crouched down to say goodbye to Alissa. It was Friday, so I wouldn't see her for a few days.

"I changed my mind," Alissa said. "You can be on our side of the wall."

"You wanted to make sure to say that."

"I had to." With that she bolted for the door, and her mother stood up and trailed after her, trying simultaneously to smile at me, adjust her diaper bag on her shoulder, and support the sleeping baby in her arms.

The blonde watched her go and said, "God, I'm so glad to be past that. The *stuff.* You seriously *don't* know how you're going to manage."

I looked harder and realized she was Lewis Vincent's wife. I'd never met her, but I'd seen photos of her in the house when I was there with James, including a few in which she was dressed as she was now, in riding clothes.

"I'm Lisa Jansen," she said, holding out her hand. "I got your name from a friend and was going to call you, but I happened to be in the building this morning, and as I was leaving I saw your name on the directory and figured, Hey, I'll just pop in and see if she's there." She hesitated. "Oh, God, you're going to want to know my friend's name! I'm such a space cadet, can you believe I don't remember? She's not really a friend, I just met her. I'm sure we will be friends, I can always tell. But in our conversation, our short conversation, she mentioned that she'd heard really good things about you. And I just wanted to talk to you maybe once about my daughter."

Lisa had woven a far more tangled web than was needed to obscure the fact that she was married to the person to whom I'd already said no. I should have been more careful, but I needed to get to my notes about the session with Alissa, especially important because of the supervision.

"Ms. Jansen," I said. "I think there may be some confusion. *I'm* confused."

Her face filled with color. "Actually, maybe I should just call you—I'm late for a riding lesson, anyway." And she lunged for the door.

I returned to my desk and wrote up my notes, but the strange intrusion and my clumsy reaction hung over me for the rest of the morning, and I realized I was blaming James because he was behind the chain of events that had led Lisa to my office. I was glad I was seeing my own analyst in a few hours. How would she have handled Lisa? I was making her into an authority, as I so often did. "We never get over it," she said to me during one of our first sessions together. "What's that?" I said, and she said, "Having started out as children."

I woke into what I knew immediately was the middle of the night. This time there was no dream in the background, no intense emotion to metabolize.

Then I heard James's voice. Our house had an acoustical oddity that funneled kitchen sounds into our walk-in closet, and after a moment there was no mistaking the fact that James was upstairs talking to someone. I strained and at last heard a second, fainter voice—a woman's.

I put on my robe and made my way to the bottom of the stairs. I hit the light switch that would illuminate not just the stairway but also the main hall light upstairs, which James would see from the kitchen. By the time I got there, he was alone at the counter, his chin resting in his hand.

I said, "That's so strange, I could have sworn I heard voices."

"Maybe you did."

His cell phone, which I hadn't previously noticed, began to buzz, and he reached for it, pressed a button that silenced it, and began composing a text. I saw that his laptop was also in arm's reach, its lid closed.

"Hang on," he said, "or better yet, go back to bed."

"Who were you talking to?"

He stared at the screen, texted, stared some more. Then he looked up and said, "Want to meet someone?" He opened the computer, waited a few seconds, and it began to chirp. "Come say hello," he said to me. "I want you to meet Celia."

She was his girlfriend: his paramour, he said, almost without irony. I *had* heard him talking to someone—she'd been sitting at her computer up in Eugene, and they'd been video-chatting. She had shoulder-length brown hair and big dark eyes.

She held her hand up and waved it back and forth, tiny waves like the trembling of a dial on a scale settling back to zero. She said, "I've heard so much about you. It's really nice to meet you, but I wish I didn't look so disheveled."

We chatted a little—it had been raining for weeks in Eugene; no, it was still dry in the Bay Area—and then James said it was time to stop.

I told her it was nice to meet her. James waited until I was downstairs before he spoke again. I used the bathroom and drank a glass of water, and by the time I was back in bed the house was silent.

He was in love. That's what he told me the next morning—he'd never felt this way before, not with anyone. He said he was glad I'd come upstairs and interrupted them; it had made for an awkward introduction, but now that I knew about her, now that I'd met her, he was realizing he'd needed exactly this, to talk about it with me.

As he spoke, I felt myself fill with hope. During all his years of wandering he'd been a drifter of the heart as well: a serial bigamist, he sometimes joked. There had been nothing lasting, nothing that required having his house key copied or buying an extra toothbrush to leave in a woman's bathroom. Was it possible he was truly settling, had truly settled, into a satisfying relationship? Maybe at last . . .

He told me about her gentleness, how he was only now realizing how often and unfortunately he'd been drawn to sharp women. Celia was soft, she was softness personified. She listened with so much empathy. And she was smart, the kind of person who makes a seemingly random observation that you don't fully consider until days later, when it comes back to you with the force of a self-evident truth.

She was from Los Angeles, an only child. She'd gone to Eugene for school, back in the nineties. She was, he said, a good person; it seemed very important to him that I understand this.

Something wasn't making sense, and at last I recognized what it was. "Why didn't you mention her earlier?" I felt a pang of worry, remembering our conversation in the guest room and how he'd said things were weird in Eugene.

He hesitated, looked away. Cleared his throat. Said, "There are some issues." And then, "She's married." And then, "Actually, it's more than that."

"There aren't *children*?"

"There are."

I had a somatic response before I'd even registered the emotional one. My heart raced and I began to sweat lightly. My body was in fight-or-flight mode, but my mind lagged behind, unable to do much more than recognize the hazy outlines of various unhappy thoughts and feelings as they assembled on the horizon.

We were both silent. He shrugged elaborately and said, as if the issue were why I hadn't figured out the situation rather than its heartbreak, "I mentioned her to you the other night in the context of overprotective parents."

And it came back to me: *It's like how people don't let their kids play outside anymore. The paranoia. This woman I know—*

"Her husband knows, though," I said. "And they're separated."

"No."

"James, my God. This is very serious."

We were in the kitchen, sitting opposite each other at the table. It was a Saturday, but Walt wasn't home; he'd gone into work for a few hours. James said, "You've got to be fucking kidding me. Really, it's serious? You think I don't know that? Why do you think I'm here when the woman I love is five hundred miles away? We're figuring things out."

"Of course," I said. "Of course you are."

"It's a really hard situation."

"Wait," I said. "Are you thinking if we sell the property you'll use your share of the proceeds so the two of you can . . . set up house together or something?"

"Asked Rebecca, making a huge leap."

I stood up and crossed the room. I faced him again. "How many?"

"Two."

"Gender?"

"Both boys."

"Like Sammy and Luke."

"Like Sammy and Luke. She hasn't decided," he added.

"Whether or not to leave him."

He nodded.

"Oh, I get it," I said. "The self-evident truth. You want her to make a declaration of independence."

• • •

Among my patients, I'd seen three women with children go all the way from an unhappy marriage to a divorce, and of the three it was the one who'd had another man waiting who'd had the hardest time. She'd been in treatment for a couple of years before she met her lover, unhappy in her marriage, unable to enjoy her children, and then she encountered this man at a party, fell into an idealizing affair, and her depression lifted. She mistook her rapture for a guarantee of a beautiful future life, believing that as long as she made sure to put her foot down firmly on each stepping stone in the path before her—the mediation stepping stone, the careful coparenting stepping stone, the family therapy stepping stone—then all would be well.

She didn't count on how her guilt would knock her over at every step. Insidiously, by preventing her from enjoying anything. She didn't like the party her friends threw for her first post-separation birthday; she hated the apartment she rented for herself and her children.

Her mood worsened and gave way to major depression. She started Zoloft, got a little better, got worse again. Eventually her lover broke it off with her, saying he wanted light in his life and her heart had become too heavy. She was devastated and suffered acutely, lost weight and couldn't sleep, but it was only after all of this—after she had, in effect, paid—that she began to report she was feeling better.

I wondered about Celia. What breaking her marriage would mean to her. And what it would mean to James. And what it would mean to their relationship.

On Sunday my brothers and I arranged to meet at a café in Palo Alto to discuss selling the house. By then James had told Robert and

Ryan about Celia, and when Robert wasn't there at the appointed time I wondered if he was registering a protest about James's relationship. He was outraged and had told me so at length on the phone the night before.

Ryan, on the other hand, was overjoyed. "I'm so happy for you," he said to James. "So happy. I know there are things to work out, but it's amazing that you finally found her. I mean, I don't believe in *the* right person, but I knew you'd find *a* right person. And she sounds so good for you."

James looked around and lowered his voice. "It may be weird of me to say this, but the sex is like nothing I've ever experienced before. It's astounding."

"One of the best kinds," Ryan said with a smile.

"I'd have thought *the* best."

"Well, there's also sacred."

"Yeah, I guess. Which is proof enough—I'd never have let you get away with that in the past. Believe it or not, I was about to say 'she completes me.'"

"Do you have a picture?"

James opened his wallet and pulled out a photo that appeared to have been edited hastily with a pair of dull scissors. Celia was in a brightly lit outdoor place, smiling. She looked, in comparison to the video image, peaceful. On her right, a child's hand reached up and grasped the hem of her shirt. On her left was the outer eighth of a man's body. Both had been cut out of the picture. Her hair was much shorter than it was now, a no-nonsense crop with bangs that covered her forehead, which in my memory had been furrowed.

"She's pretty," Ryan said. "I like her shoulders."

"Right?" James exclaimed.

At that moment, Robert rapped on the outside of the café window as he hurried by.

"Here we go," James muttered.

The bell over the door jingled, and Robert squeezed between the crowded tables to reach us. He plunked into the chair next to mine and said, "Halloween errands, sorry."

"Such a busy bee," James said.

"What?" Robert said with a glare. "Better change your tune if you're going to shack up with someone who has kids. This is the kind of thing you have to do all the time."

"Maybe it's the kind of thing I like to do."

"Yeah, trying to find a giant remote-control spider two days before Halloween is so much fun."

"We're glad you're here," Ryan said, reaching over and giving Robert's arm a pat. "It's totally hectic out there today. I passed a costume place and it was jammed. What are the boys going as?"

Robert rolled his eyes. "Jen had this great plan to get empty ice cream tubs at Baskin-Robbins and decorate them to look like jars of peanut butter and jelly. Which the boys would then wear. But I'm sorry to say they're going in store-bought X-Men costumes."

"Guys," I said, leaning forward. "Should we get started? I think we've all had individual conversations with James and each other, but it would be good to talk it through as a group. As a foursome instead of several twosomes."

We all looked at James, and he shrugged. "I'm not sure there's anything to talk about. I need the dough. I'm sorry."

Robert looked incredulous. "Wait, now it's definite?"

"Yeah."

James had not told me this. Obviously he hadn't told Robert, either.

"Jeez, spring it on us why don't you," Robert said.

"Let's ask Rebecca if she thinks you're upset about *how* I told you."

"I'll make you a loan if you're so broke! Or I'll just buy your share. Obviously I can't buy the whole house at this point or I'd do that."

"We're talking probably three million," James said. "Which is close to four hundred thousand for each of us. Do you have four hundred thousand dollars?"

"I don't think three million."

"The land *alone* is worth almost that much."

"It would have to be, the house is a teardown."

The waitress was coming our way, and I caught her eye and shook my head slightly. The café was new but stood on the site of an old-fashioned coffee shop our father had liked. On weekend mornings he often took one or two of us out to do an errand, and as often as not we'd end up swinging by afterward and sitting at the counter for grilled cheese sandwiches. I wondered if the boys thought of this every time they came here, as I did.

Robert leaned toward James and said, "I can't believe you'd do this."

"Whatever, I'm a home-wrecker, I'm a terrible person."

Robert rolled his eyes. "That's a whole other issue. Which— Don't get me started. You're being, at the very least, incredibly reckless. What I meant was I can't believe you'd do something that benefits Penny."

"I'm not that small-minded."

"You're exactly that small-minded. 'I don't really care, but I'll stick with you guys just to fuck her up.'"

"I didn't say that."

"You did. On January 16, 2004. At the kitchen table at Dad's, after the ashes."

"What'd you do, take notes?"

"In fact, yes."

"Unbelievable." James looked at Ryan and me. "Can't you just see him? Sitting in his car afterward, writing it all down?"

"Let's order," Ryan said. "Can we order? I'm really hungry."

"When," Robert said, "are you going to call her?"

James looked astonished. "Me?"

"Who else?"

"I don't want to call her."

"Minor stumbling block!" Robert said with a triumphant smile, but his face fell when he saw that neither Ryan nor I was with him. "She has to be told," he said. "Technically, she has to be *asked*."

With a questioning look on his face, James turned to me.

"The terms of the trust," I explained.

"When was the last time you talked to her?" Robert asked him.

"None of your business."

"I can't figure out if that means it's longer ago than I'd have thought or shorter."

"Guys," I said, leaning forward. "It's a complicated situation with a lot of history. Maybe we should—"

James waved me off and looked at Robert. "It was your wedding if you really care so much."

Robert's eyes widened, and Ryan and I exchanged a look: Robert and Jen had gotten married in 1995, eleven years earlier.

"That's ridiculous," Robert said.

Ryan reached over and touched James's elbow. "It's actually impossible, J. You saw her at our wedding, and that was way after Robert and Jen's."

"Doesn't mean I talked to her."

Robert rolled his eyes. "Oh, come on, you talked to her."

"I didn't. And I haven't seen her since then."

"What about when we cleared out the house?" Robert said. "Remember she found all those horrible ceramic platters in the garage from the summer parties? And she wanted us each to take one?"

"And we had that whole conversation," I said, "about whether the last party was in '80 or '81."

"It was '80," Robert said.

"It was '81. It was the summer after my senior year of high school."

"It couldn't have been '81, that was my first summer in Michigan."

"You came home in August—we waited and had it then. We went through this exact conversation in the garage with Penny. Anyway, James didn't come down when we did the clearing out." I'd offered to buy him a ticket, but he said no, he was just getting settled in Eugene, and in any case he didn't particularly want to hang with Penny. I said something about how if we took away the word "with" maybe he'd be interested, and he said, amiably enough, "Fuck you, Rebecca."

"Bottom line," Ryan said, "it's been a long time." He caught the waitress's eye, and she came over and took our order, and for a little while we talked about other things. Then, during a lull, Robert turned to James and said, "I guess the only hope for the house is you decide it would look too much like forgiveness."

"Please," James said. "It's not like I'm walking around feeling like my mother abused me."

"As long as it wasn't"—Robert lifted his hands and made quick curling motions with his index and middle fingers—"abuse."

"What are you even talking about?"

"Well, how about your little dog for one?"

James broke into a laugh. "Are you kidding? Do you really think I'm losing sleep over that? If that's how you operate, maybe you should see someone. Rebecca, don't you think he should see someone?"

Robert smirked. "You're the one who hasn't spoken to his mother in eleven years."

"Hey," James said. "Time got away from me."

• • •

The view from the house had changed over the decades, from a green and brown valley to "a bowl of mansions," as Sammy once said. Our closest neighbors had sold their three acres in 1999, at the peak of the dot-com bubble, and had, according to rumor, used the proceeds to buy both a house in the French countryside and an apartment in San Francisco, an expensive Russian Hill penthouse. The new owners had torn the old place down and built a blinding white cube of a house that flashed at us through the trees. "But look at this," our father had said when it became clear the new structure had permanently altered our view. "Sit on the lowest step here and lean back, and you can pretend they aren't even there."

That's what Ryan and James wanted to do. After lunch James and I had given Ryan a ride home, and now, as we walked up the driveway, the boys were insisting that the Vincents might not even notice us and wouldn't mind if they did.

The silver car wasn't there, only Lewis's Ferrari. The house was decorated for Halloween, with a skeleton tacked to the front door, six pumpkins of varying sizes arranged on the steps, and stretchy spiderweb stuff covering the bushes. As one we sat on the lowest step, me between the boys. Leaning back, all we could see was green and gold, the trees and the hills, and the giant blue dome overhead.

"Here we are," Ryan said. He had so much to lose, the only one among us who'd never really lived anywhere else. He felt me looking at him and smiled.

A car engine became audible, and a moment later the silver car came into view with Lewis driving. He lowered the window. "Great to see you," he called.

I got to my feet, and Ryan and James stood, too. Lisa was next to Lewis, and I wondered if she'd told him about coming to my office. I hoped it wouldn't be awkward for her to see me.

There were two girls in back, and I turned to Ryan. "What are their names?"

"Susanna and Daphne. They're very sweet kids."

Grinning broadly, Lewis joined us. As we took turns shaking hands with him, I saw that Lisa was still in the car, staring straight ahead.

The girls had run to Ryan. He put an arm around each of them and smoothed their hair. Susanna appeared to be about thirteen, while Daphne, I remembered from my conversation with Lewis, was eight.

The passenger door flew open and Lisa burst out of the car, a flurry of hair and arms and shopping bags. "Daphne," she called, "come get your things," and she held up a Neiman Marcus shopping bag until the younger girl pulled away from Ryan and returned to the far side of the car.

"Daphne got things?" Ryan said to Susanna in a quiet voice.

"It's totally ridiculous. She's in third grade and she got *two* cashmere sweaters."

"Life is so unfair," Ryan said, and the two of them exchanged a smile that suggested the statement had gotten a fair amount of play between them in the past.

"Is Katya at her playdate?" Susanna said.

"Probably on the way home by now."

"I got her a cupcake. With a candy pumpkin on top. Is that okay?"

"For sure. I hope you got one, too."

Susanna smiled. She had the watchful, cautious look of certain firstborns. She held her shoulders high, and the space between the bottoms of her jeans and the tops of her shoes suggested a recent growth spurt.

Lewis was telling James that if we were serious it would take him no time at all to have his Realtor draw up an offer. Lisa was still on the far side of the car, and I began to think she might stay there until we left, to avoid me. I was about to make an excuse when she mobilized, gathering the shopping bags and striding purposefully in our direction.

"You're Ryan's sister, aren't you?" she said, handing her bags to Susanna so she could shake my hand. "I can't believe we've never met. It's Rebecca, right? I'm Lisa."

So she hadn't told Lewis . . . and she wanted me to pretend we hadn't met.

"Honey," she said to Lewis, "why aren't you inviting them in for something to drink? I think we could even sit outside. I can't believe it's almost November—global warming, right? Girls, if it's locked, set the bags down and come get the keys!" This last she shouted at the girls, who'd taken the bags up to the door. She dropped her voice and said, "I feel like I have to explain *everything*. The other day we stopped for gas and they wanted Life Savers, so I sent them inside with some money and they came back out and said, 'There's no one there, what do we do?' So I go back in with them, and the cashier is right there stocking a shelf! I tell them, 'You say, "Excuse me, I'd like to buy this."' Didn't occur to them!"

"And it doesn't occur to us how much we're going to have to teach them," Ryan said, but she didn't seem to take this in.

I said we needed to leave, and as we walked away James said, "Maybe it's the house," and Ryan said, "She's not that bad," and James said, "You knew what I meant, which kind of proves she is. Don't you think, Rebecca?" He was saying he thought Lisa was like Penny, but to me she seemed less a beleaguered mother than an actress playing a beleaguered mother and trying to enlist her children to play opposite her. Penny was truly beleaguered—a woman not cut out for the job of raising four children.

At home, James and I sat at the kitchen table and read the Sunday paper, but soon we were talking about Celia again, James brightening and obviously happy that his secret was out. He made another reference to their sexual compatibility, and I thought of the moment in the café when he used the word "astounding." I kept thinking about it through the afternoon and evening, and by bedtime I was feeling stirred up. I imagined Walt would be surprised; we'd had sex the night before and usually went a few days in between. I must have communicated something to him, though, because as soon as we got into bed, he reached for me. Our hands and mouths moved. We sped up. We took turns coaxing each other to the brink and backing off. At last I pulled him on top of me and brought him over the line, and for a little while he rested and nearly slept. Then: "Your turn," he murmured, and he reached again. There was pure sensation for a while, but then I realized I was picturing an old stone house at dusk, set far back in a snowy field, a two-story house with light shining from the windows. What was this place? The closer I got, the closer I got. But then I was so far along that there was no more thinking, and the image dissolved as I came.

Tuesday was Halloween, and my practice was full of masked and costumed children, along with a fifty-four-year-old man who arrived in plaid Bermuda shorts and a garishly flowered Hawaiian shirt and began weeping about twenty minutes into the session because he'd meant the outfit as a Halloween joke and, by not commenting on it, I'd implied I thought it was something he might actually wear. The session took an interesting turn after that, and we arrived at some rich material, but he was a fairly new patient and I was a bit flummoxed, and afterward I spent some extra time on my notes so I could bring the case to a class I was taking on analytic beginnings.

Late in the afternoon I made a trip to the hospital to see my eleven-year-old leukemia patient, who'd been asleep when I got to his room last time. He was sitting up in bed with his mother at his side, and I sat with them for a while, the mother wearing a different kind of mask, one I saw too often: the forced smile below the hollow eyes.

Sammy and Luke had begged James to go trick-or-treating with them and spend the night, so Walt and I had the house to ourselves for the first time in almost two weeks. We set a basket of candy outside the front door and settled on the couch in the living room. I'd had special lights installed before hanging the picture of the land, and at night, when it was dark out and the lamps were off, the painting had a dreamlike quality.

"It's funny," Walt said, "that it was your father's painting when your mother was the artist."

"He commissioned it. Before they even broke ground on the house. Before she was an artist."

"What was she before she was an artist?"

"A wife and mother. To her dismay. I was thinking about this the other day. Maybe she liked it at first, but it wasn't enough for her."

"It wasn't enough or she got sick of it?"

"It's probably not either/or. When I was four or five we sometimes played hide-and-seek with her, and she laughed and laughed. But she could also be really grumpy and put upon. She would say, 'The house isn't going to clean itself!' which for some reason Robert and I found very funny. Once time he said, 'Maybe the kitchen can clean the living room since it has running water,' and she got really angry at him. I guess she thought he was making fun of her. My father loved the house, which somehow made it worse. God, he loved it."

Walt took my hand. "How are you holding up?"

"I'm fine. Ryan seems fine. Robert seems to be carrying the upset for all of us."

Walt reached for my face and began to kiss me. Next thing I knew, the heel of his hand was brushing my nipple. The couch was deep and soft, and gradually we moved from upright to reclining. "Three times in four days?" I said, and he said, "I'm not sixty yet." I suggested we go downstairs, but he kept touching and kissing, and I considered the cushions and wondered how much longer I would or could continue without asking him to pause so I could grab the throw draped over the back of the couch and arrange it beneath us to protect the cushions. Ah, Rebecca, I thought, you are such a wildcat. In the end it was Walt who paused for the throw, and then it all went very fast, and the last thing I thought was not that we should be careful or that I was always careful; it was that the stone house had come into view again, old stone in a snowy field with light shining from the windows.

James seemed hyped up when I got home the next afternoon, and I wondered if it was the weather—it had been raining all day and he'd been inside for hours. Then again, it might have been the fact that he'd spent the previous evening with Robert, who I was certain had not been easy company. He'd left me two voice mails that morning, one complaining about the prospect of James forcing a sale of the house and the other complaining about the prospect of James ruining the lives of two children.

"Vince wanted me to stop by the house," James said as I took off my coat. "Can I borrow your car?"

"Why did he want you to stop by?"

"Well, it was more like I wanted to and he said okay. Give me your keys."

"You can't barge in again, James."

"I'm thirty-eight, Rebecca, it's not up to you. May I borrow your car?"

I ended up driving him, the phrase "damage control" in my mind though I didn't know what damage I was anticipating. Lewis's car wasn't there, just Lisa's. It was raining hard now, and we hurried up the steps. Daphne opened the front door, and I realized that I hadn't noticed how much she resembled her mother: less in her facial features or in the shape of her body than in her quickly moving eyes. Her thin blond hair hung past her shoulders, and she wore a T-shirt with sequined lips on the front.

Lisa came in from the kitchen. On Sunday she'd looked put together in the way of many mothers on the Peninsula, who wore the same kinds of jeans as their teenage daughters but with four-inch heels and thousand-dollar silk blouses. Today she was dressed in yoga clothes, her hair in a ponytail, and she was obviously irritated.

"Here you are, as promised. Lewis is running late. I'm not sure exactly what you wanted to do, but I'm elbow-deep in getting dinner ready, so if you don't mind, I'll just let you wander."

"Mom, you're not," Daphne said.

"Not what?"

"Getting dinner ready."

Lisa whirled around and went back to the kitchen.

"Awk-ward," James said under his breath.

I wanted to ask what he'd expected, but Daphne was right there. "What did you want to see?" I said.

"Nothing in particular."

"I can show you my room," Daphne said. "It used to be Ryan's."

"And mine," James told her.

"You shared a room?"

"Yes, in the old days people weren't very nice to children."

The two of them set off, and I stood still for a moment, wondering what would be the least intrusive thing for me to do. I settled on taking a few steps toward the living room but not going down into it.

It had been a while since I'd been in the house, and I thought of my father—not the aging solitary figure I'd last loved but the father of my childhood. He'd commanded this house: like a ship captain, like a battalion leader whose mandate was not just victory but also, and more significantly, the well-being of his troops. He led us morally, empathically. He would be dismayed by the idea of James disturbing the lives of two children. Was I dismayed? I was trying not to be. I was trying to think interpretively. James couldn't risk true intimacy, so he chose a woman who wasn't really available. James couldn't allow himself the pleasure of a happy relationship, so he was going to mitigate it with the pain of gratifying Penny. James couldn't get past the suffering he'd experienced as a child, so he felt compelled to create similar distress in others.

He returned, followed by Daphne. Looking at her slight frame and darting eyes, I recalled that she had trouble with sleeping and school and wondered what her parents' other concerns were.

"Everyone," she was saying to James, "has one special thing that they're great at. My dad is great at business. My mom is great at riding horses. My sister is great at playing the flute."

"I know what you're great at," he said.

"No, you don't. There's nothing to know."

"You're great at being Daphne."

"No, I'm not," she said. "Anyway, my name is Laurel."

She went into the living room and made her way to an end table on the far side of the couch. It was a boxy wooden table with heavy legs and a low shelf four inches off the floor. On top of the table was an unusual lamp, a perforated metal tower about two feet tall, and at first I thought she was going to turn it on. Instead she squatted, ducked her head, and climbed onto the shelf. This left her crouching inside the table, though "crouching" might not be the right word, given that it implies some kind of action, and once Daphne was situated the table did all the work of holding her in place. Her body filled the space, the back of her head and the upper part of her spine flat up against the underside of the tabletop. Her knees were bent so tightly you couldn't have slid a coin between her calves and her thighs, which left her buttocks about an inch off the shelf, with no support.

James and I exchanged a look. *Do something,* his expression seemed to say.

"She's in a tight spot," I murmured.

"Literally."

"I meant literally."

Daphne wrapped her arms around her lower legs. From the kitchen came the sound of running water, and I wondered if this was a common late-afternoon scenario, Lisa in the kitchen and Daphne in the table. She was obviously accustomed to being there.

James cleared his throat and took a few steps in her direction. "Daphne, you should come out of there."

Huddled in her ball, she shook her head and clutched her legs even tighter.

"Should I go get your mom? Do you need help?"

When she didn't respond, he hesitated for a moment and then headed to the kitchen.

"You like to be called Laurel?" I said, approaching her.

"Daphne is a stupid name. And it *means* Laurel, so I'm changing my name when I turn eighteen."

"How is it stupid?"

"Daffy, daffy, daffy."

"Is that what people say?"

"None of your business."

"That's true. What's it like in there? You had to make yourself very small to fit."

"I'm the exact same size I always have been."

"Daphne!" Lisa said, coming out of the kitchen. "We talked about this." She avoided looking at me as she made her way to the table. "Now," she added as she held out her hand.

Daphne reached out and slapped it.

"Daphne!"

"I'm a scorpion," Daphne said. "That's what scorpions do."

"You may not hit."

"That's what scorpions *do*."

Lisa turned away from Daphne and sighed. Then she looked at me and James and said, "What do you people want? Why are you here? Sell us the house or don't, but please, please decide."

We were silent in the car, rain pouring over us as we made our way back to Palo Alto. I knew James was uncomfortable, but I also knew that if I said anything about what had just happened, he'd take it as a rebuke. Walt was working late, and the prospect of spending several hours alone with James seemed overwhelming. I told him I had a dinner meeting, dropped him at the house, and returned to my office. I lay on the couch, which gave me a view I never had from my desk or from the chair where I sat during sessions with adults: of a wire sculpture of Penny's. Made of copper, it was abstract but looked from certain angles like a crouching lion and from others like a seascape.

I'd last spoken to her during the summer. She sounded as she usually did, joyful and slightly harried, which I chalked up to maternal awkwardness: if she acted rushed or distracted, she could end the call abruptly if she didn't like the way it was going. We exchanged news and then, toward the end of the conversation, she asked about James—for the first time in a long time. She said, "Tell him I'm glad to hear he's doing well." I hadn't conveyed the message, and as I lay there in my office I wondered what would happen if I did so now, if it would help him get over his block against calling her so we could move forward on the house.

But I didn't want to move forward on the house—did I?

I wanted the uncertainty to be over, for the next phase of my life to start.

Then all at once I pictured the house again: not the Portola Valley house but the one I'd been imagining lately: the stone house in the snowy field. It was in England, I suddenly knew. Some romanticized Christmastime England. And I thought of Edward Beale, who apparently had been in the back of my mind for several days.

Edward was an Englishman I'd met halfway through my residency at Stanford; he was doing a fellowship in neuromuscular medicine. Until then, I'd had only one real boyfriend, during medical school, but we were both so busy it lasted just three or four months. Edward was my lover for over a year. He had thinning sandy hair and a divot below his left eye where he'd been cut by a sharp rock in a fall when he was twelve. When we could get time off, we went on car trips to the coast—Half Moon Bay if we had only an afternoon, West Marin, Big Sur. "Staggering," he always murmured as we looked at the ocean, in a mild tone that stood in marked contrast to the wildly enthusiastic yelling that Ryan and I had done all those years earlier at Sea Ranch.

With his fellowship coming to an end, Edward applied for positions up and down the West Coast and was choosing between the University of Washington and USC when he received a phone call from home with the news that his brother was losing muscle tone in his right leg, likely the first signs of Charcot-Marie-Tooth disease, a hereditary neuromuscular illness suffered by Edward's grandfather as well. It was in order to learn about the inexorable march of weakness, numbness, and pain that had laid waste to his grandfather's body that Edward had chosen neurology in the first place.

Within a few weeks Edward decided to decline both positions and go home. We'd spoken of the easy flights from San Francisco to Los Angeles or Portland and how his move would not have to end our relationship, but in some way I was relieved by his decision. We'd been very compatible sexually, but now, with an end in sight, it got more intense. Mornings when we'd slept together I woke him with oral sex, and after an evening out I often reached for him while he was still behind the wheel of the car. On our last coastal trip, we had sex in the restroom of a filling station where we stopped for gas before starting the drive home. The restroom was the single-occupancy kind for which there's a key on a giant ring hanging at the cash register. I bought a bottle of water and took the key. Edward was at the pump. I held up the key for him to see and then went around the side of the building and let myself in. He knocked on the door a few minutes later and then pressed me against the concrete wall as if we were characters in a movie performing the kind of urgent upright copulation that looks painful if not impossible. Turns out it's neither.

"Have you invited Rebecca to visit you in England?" my father asked Edward.

This was maybe five days before Edward was to leave. We were with my parents at a stuffy Italian restaurant in Menlo Park, a relic of times gone by complete with a coat check at the door and starched white linens on the tables. For the occasion my father and Edward wore neckties, but this was just before the summer Penny spent in Taos, and she was in her high artist phase, wearing her daily uniform of dusty, irregularly washed blue jeans and a waffle-weave shirt the color of oatmeal.

From another person my father's question might have seemed

pushy, or at least a little presumptuous, but from my father it had the feel of the gentle relationship advice that it was: he liked Edward and was sorry he was leaving.

"That would be lovely," Edward said.

"Just think," my father said to me. "You could see Big Ben."

"And Buckingham Palace. And the Tower of London."

My father smiled and recited: "'They're changing the guard at Buckingham Palace. Christopher Robin went down with Alice.'"

I smiled, too. "Ryan always liked that one."

"But the minute I started it," my father said, "James would beg me to do 'James, James, Morrison, Morrison.'"

"And what James wanted—" Penny said.

"Don't!" my father snapped, more anger in his voice than I could remember hearing in a long time.

She stared at the backs of her hands and then reached for her glass and dunked her fingers in the water. She swirled them around and shook them off. "No finger bowls," she said defiantly. Then she dried her hands on her napkin and left it crumpled on the table, streaked with gray.

No one spoke. My father had bowed his head. At last he looked up and said, "I'm sorry"—but to the table, not to her.

After dinner Edward and I headed for his apartment. It was May and the daytime temperature had been close to eighty, but the evening was chilly and I wrapped my jacket tight. We didn't say much until we were inside again.

"That must have been uncomfortable for you," I said. "Sorry about that."

"Not at all. It sounded like an old argument."

"They don't really argue. It's more like they disagree."

"About?"

"Everything."

We were, by then, undressing in his bedroom, I on one side of the bed and he on the other. We seemed to have made an unspoken, mutual decision to go straight to bed.

"Do you ever think of them having sex?" he said, taking off his underwear and approaching me. He had the beginning of an erection, and I got on my tiptoes and squeezed him between my legs.

"They don't anymore."

"You sound very certain."

"Shhh," I said, and he walked me backward to the bed. His apartment was a second-story unit with a bedroom that looked over the top of a fence into a bedroom in another building. We had noticed that the inhabitant of this other apartment frequently stood at his window looking out, and he was there now. "The curtain," I said.

Edward glanced over his shoulder. "Imagine he's you and we're your parents."

"I'd rather not, but what choice do I have now?"

"I saw my parents once."

"That could be an invention, you know. Rather than a memory. They're very common, they're called primal scene fantasies."

"Shut up."

"The curtain."

He dropped to the floor and crawled to the window, where he got hold of the curtain and pulled it closed. "What if you're wrong?" he said, returning to my side. "About your parents. Perhaps they have an ongoing secret sexual life."

"I really don't think so."

"All right, they don't. You're the only one in your family to do this. And," he added, "it has to be said that you quite enjoy it."

After that we stopped talking. It was only at times like this that the idea of losing him made me unhappy, and usually the feeling vanished within an hour or so. It was particularly intense that night, though, the dread of loss, and when we were finished and lying limp in each other's arms, I thought maybe I *would* fly over for Christmas. I knew Edward had grown up in a postwar housing development, a sort of British Levittown, but as I drifted toward sleep I imagined instead a picturesque village of the kind seen on *Masterpiece Theatre* and how it would be to arrive after dark and get out of a taxi in front of a glowing stone house set back in a snowy field. How inside that house I would find him again, my partner in astounding sex.

6

THE STUDIO

Robert was seventeen. He was five-eleven and weighed 132 pounds, and for an entire school year, on even the warmest days, he wore long-sleeved shirts so no one could see his puny biceps. He met Gina at debate club, but he saw her before he met her and he liked her before he knew her. She had pale skin and severe freckles, and she carried her books in a worn leather briefcase instead of the usual backpack.

An only child who came from a broken home—though she preferred "shattered" and said so to any and all—she accepted his attentions so blithely, it was as if he were trying to return a dropped pencil, not go out with her.

From the beginning she enjoyed dinners with his family. Dr. Blair, with his poignant gray hair and frequent throat-clearing, struck her as the most polite person she had ever met. Her own father was perennially late and sloppily dressed and had not mastered the routine apology, a skill he needed all the time. The month she spent with him in San Diego each summer was like a sentence for a crime she couldn't remember committing. Dinners with Robert's family—school-night dinners, which had the delightful feel of a last run-through before opening night, everyone hurrying to deliver their lines—were to Gina a perfect antidote to the time spent with her father: a reward for a success she couldn't remember achieving.

This was in 1978. Robert was a senior, and by November he was spending part of each evening working on his college applications. He wanted to go to the University of Michigan, as his father had, but his grades and SATs made everyone think he should try for an Ivy. Gina was a junior, but she seemed to understand. She sat on his bed and did her homework while he rolled onto the platen of his typewriter forms bearing the crests of Harvard and Yale. "Make a typo," she said. "Or you could write the world's shortest essay. 'Why do you want to go to Harvard?' 'I just do.'"

Robert enjoyed her flippancy but wondered at her nonchalance over the fact that he would be leaving. Best-case scenario, they had ten more months—if they lasted.

Their relationship had begun when they were jointly assigned the task of putting up recruiting signs for the debate club, which had, the previous June, seen two-thirds of its members graduate. Within several days they had sped through the stages of holding hands and walking arm in arm, but they slowed down on the stretch from first base to second, a deceleration that Robert had decided was his choice, reflecting a gentlemanly restraint, and therefore not just acceptable but honorable. Still, he had a goal in mind, the shedding of his virginity sometime before his eighteenth birthday in March, or by graduation at the latest, and he worried that her apparent indifference to their impending separation meant she had decided against crossing that final frontier with him.

James was ten and large for his age. He was attracted to Gina in the way a dog is attracted to and quickly overtaxes the patience of a friendly new human. When she came through the front door he ran to greet her and, lacking any real conversation, reported to her in excruciating detail the games he'd played during recess and lunch on each of the days since he'd last seen her.

"James never leaves us alone," Robert said to his father early one morning when the two of them were up before the rest of the family.

"Never?" his father said.

"He bothers Gina. He makes eyes at her, I'm serious."

"Does Gina complain?"

"No, but she doesn't like it."

"Has she said so?"

Robert had hoped to elicit a different reaction from his father, and he changed the subject. He said, "I'm going to talk to Mr. Verhoeven after school today." Mr. Verhoeven was the honors physics teacher, a thin, bespectacled man with a wing of white hair over each ear. He had given Robert an A+ on the most recent test, but had written—somewhat ominously, in Robert's view—"See me if you want" on the test paper, below the grade. Robert had agonized for a couple of days but had finally decided, thanks in part to Gina's input, that the A+ probably meant Mr. Verhoeven wanted to encourage him. "He wants to recommend you for Harvard" was what Gina actually said.

"James is young," his father said, not taking the bait.

"He's ten."

"I mean he's young for his age. Development is very individual. He's big, so people expect a lot of him."

"You mean I do."

"No, honey, that's not what I'm saying. He's your brother and that colors how you see him. If he were someone else's brother, or a neighbor, I think you would react differently to him."

"He wouldn't be in my house bugging my girlfriend."

"It's you he's bugging."

"He lies down in my doorway! And then won't move!"

"And to think he used to save that for Rebecca."

Robert had forgotten this: James lying in Rebecca's doorway

after dinner, and how she called Ryan to bring her glasses of water or sharpened pencils so she could avoid stepping over James and thereby gratifying him.

"You know what I'm going to say?"

"It's important to treat little kids well."

His father smiled. "Children deserve care."

Robert thought there was something unfair about this, because what was he but a child who deserved his father's care? Also, his father used to say it wasn't Robert's job to take care of his siblings, which was a nice idea but hardly true in real life. Robert had been watching out for all of them, especially James, forever.

"You're shipping out soon," his father said.

"So I should be more tolerant."

"No, I was just thinking how much I'll miss you."

As November progressed, Robert began to talk about inviting Gina to go on the family's annual Thanksgiving trip to Sacramento. He imagined walking with her around his grandparents' neighborhood and perhaps stopping at the local elementary school to make out. The family car held only six people, though, and his mother raised the question of what Gina's mother would do without her. She also pointed out that there would be nowhere for Gina to sleep, given how tight it always was with just the family.

So Robert was out of luck. When they arrived on Wednesday evening, he greeted his grandparents with an obvious lack of enthusiasm and then spent the next two hours trying to make up for it by playing cards with his grandfather and brothers. John Greenway had congestive heart failure and pretty much lived in a chair in the front room. He was supposed to wear special socks to improve the blood flow in his swollen ankles and feet, but he claimed they were too stretched out and did him no good anymore. He wore plain black socks instead, and corduroy slippers both indoors and out.

Sometimes he was so tired that he had one of the boys play his hand for him; he would have his proxy set his cards in a rack only he and the proxy could see, and he would whisper instructions while the other two boys hummed so they couldn't hear. James loved this, and when it was time to hum he got to his feet and marched in place and did a fair imitation of a kazoo. His once silky white-blond hair had darkened gradually; it was nearly black now and growing thicker and coarser. He was taller than Ryan. Ryan watched him march and hum and thought there was a good chance that James's voice would start to change before he reached junior high.

Ryan had skipped junior high. Sand Hill Day had turned into a K through 8, with Ryan and the other five kids his age forming the pioneer class, and he was going straight to high school when he left. Wednesday night, once the cardplaying was over and he was in bed, he realized that when he got back to school on Monday he'd have only six more months at the school he loved.

Thanksgiving dinner took place at two o'clock in the afternoon and involved moving Grandpa Greenway from the front room to the dining room, where custom required that he relieve the turkey of its meat with a carving knife that once belonged to his grandfather. He could neither stand up for ten minutes nor relinquish the duty, so Bill put the bird on a rolling cocktail cart and pushed it to the old man's chair. Ryan remembered being in a store with his grandfather when he was seven or eight and how his grandfather spent a long time looking at an electric carving knife and then said, as he led Ryan away, "That would be giving in."

Penny sat next to her father but returned to the kitchen, where her mother was transferring peas to a serving bowl. At seventy-six, Audrey Greenway was as shrunken as her husband was puffy, and her hands were knobby with arthritis. She had been cooking for a day and a half and was pleased with the way everything had come out, the stuffing just how her grandchildren liked it, the sweet potatoes mashed for her husband.

"Coming, coming," she said to Penny. "This is the last thing."

"Mom, Dad shouldn't be trying to carve. Bill should be doing it."

"Oh, I don't know. What's the harm?"

Penny had hoped her mother would recognize and appreciate her concern for her father, and there was a slight edge to her voice as she said, "He could have a heart attack."

"He's probably going to have a heart attack."

"Not today! How can you be so blasé?"

"Penny, please. Try to relax."

"I can't believe *you're* telling *me* to relax."

Audrey raised her eyebrows briefly, a tactic Penny knew from early childhood, when it had had the power to silence her. Audrey had married and borne Penny late in life, and Penny sometimes thought her whole existence would have been different if she'd had a younger mother.

"Go on," Audrey said. "I'm right behind you."

Penny returned to the table, but she felt chastised. She listened to the holiday talk: the children telling their grandparents what they were doing in school; Bill asking his usual questions about his in-laws' lives, remembering, as he always did, to inquire especially about Audrey's work at the horticulture club and how John's hardware store was doing under the new ownership. Penny stayed quiet and felt expendable, also familiar from childhood.

After dinner, the children lounged in the front room and watched through the windows as the afternoon light failed. It was fully dark before long, and they were lethargic from the food yet at the same time restless.

"I'm going to call Gina," Robert announced, but then he didn't move, which peeved Rebecca since he had taken the only comfortable chair not occupied by their grandfather, leaving the rest of them to make do with the couch and folding chairs.

"Go if you're going," she said.

Robert frowned. "What is that? God."

"Don't say 'God.'" Rebecca took a quick look around, but her grandmother was out of the room and her grandfather was asleep in his chair.

"What are you talking about?" Robert said. "I can if I want to."

Their father sat on a folding chair, holding open a section of newspaper that Robert knew, from having checked the date earlier in the day, was over a week old. He said to Robert, "But do you want to?"

Robert felt his face grow warm. He knew it was a trick question but didn't know in which direction the trick would go. "What do you mean?"

"I mean if it would make someone else unhappy. It's your choice, but—" Bill let his voice trail off and looked at Robert.

"I said it once," Robert said.

"It's okay," Bill said gently. "I think you understand now."

"Understand what?" Penny called from the dining room. She had found a measure of solace in a junk drawer from the garage that she'd brought inside to see if it contained anything interesting, but she was still out of sorts. "How can you expect them to understand?"

"I'm sorry?" Bill said.

She came to the arch between the front room and the dining room. She'd pulled her braid over her shoulder, and it hung like a pull-cord down the front of her shirt. She was thin, but time had softened her face, making her look younger than her forty-four years, which in turn made her hands—roughened and crisscrossed with cuts, the nails permanently split and discolored—appear to have been borrowed from a woman who'd spent her life cleaning other people's houses. She said, "We've never educated them about religion, so how can they understand?"

Bill cleared his throat. "I just meant Robert might choose his words differently here. I was saying I thought he understood it's a choice." He glanced at Robert and smiled slightly. "As I think he does."

At this, Grandpa Greenway startled awake and said, "Now then, now then." He shifted in his chair and moved his hands to his lap. They looked like baseball gloves: big shapeless paws with fingers like sausages and no definition at the knuckles. For dinner he'd worn a camel sport coat, but he'd traded it for a golf cardigan, and he fumbled for a moment with the buttons, then gave up. He said, "Who's hungry? James, are you hungry?"

James looked to his father to see if this was a joke. His father was smiling but looking at Robert, so James couldn't be sure the smile meant he should laugh.

"James," Grandma Greenway called from the kitchen. "There's more pie."

Ryan nudged James. He wanted James to wriggle around and maybe laugh a little and then go into the kitchen. That's what he would have done—not for pie but to make both grandparents happy. In the kitchen, his grandmother would put her finger to her lips and then get out a plate and a knife and noisily draw the knife across the plate. Then he would open the silverware drawer and rustle around in the forks and perhaps, if he felt like it, smack his lips together a few times.

Bill said a walk might be a good idea, and the children—including Robert, who had forgotten entirely that he wanted to call Gina—jumped to their feet and found their jackets. Penny stayed behind, her interest in the junk drawer sharpening into excitement, followed by a vision of nuts and bolts and washers stacked together so they looked like trees, then laid out—maybe in an old metal cake pan—

to resemble a forest. Or maybe her father's old tools themselves—screwdrivers and wrenches and pliers—could be made to look like trees, shrubs, flowers, and could populate a metal garden. Her father might even get a kick out of it. She remembered going to the store with him on the occasional Sunday, when he was closed for business, and how she walked up and down the empty aisles while he sat in his office and went over the books. Her favorite was the electrical aisle, with its spools of wire and cartons of lightbulbs. She was fascinated by lightbulbs, how delicate and shatterable they were. At home she always begged to be the one to replace a burned-out bulb, a task her father carefully supervised, his finger at the switch so they could test the new bulb as soon as she'd finished screwing it into the socket.

He was just sitting there in his chair, staring off into space. "Dad," she said, but quietly, and he didn't hear her.

She laid two metal spacers at right angles and thought of Jesus on the cross, then of Bill reprimanding Robert for saying "God." Long ago, his efforts to please her parents had delighted her, but when she tried to thank him he brushed it off, as if insulted by the idea that he might have behaved otherwise.

The God thing didn't come up again until the next day, when the three younger children were alone in the front room. Robert and their father had gone to buy their grandparents a Christmas tree, their mother and grandmother were grocery shopping, and their grandfather was resting in his room.

"I don't get it," Ryan said. "We say 'God' all the time."

"But we shouldn't here," Rebecca said. "Grandma and Grandpa believe."

"Since when?"

"Since always. It's not that big a deal. I just thought Robert should be more careful." She felt a little guilty about scolding Robert for saying something they all said all the time, but Robert wasn't present for her to make it up to him. "You can if you want," she told Ryan. "Believe, I mean."

She had, back when she was eleven or twelve—or had tried to, praying on her knees beside her bed several nights running. She'd stopped when she found herself squinching her eyes shut as hard as she could and clasping her hands together as tightly as she could—as if the activation of small muscles could speed things along.

"I might want to someday," Ryan said.

Rebecca and Ryan were on the couch, each reclining against an arm, while James sat on the floor in front of the TV. He had the volume low, as he'd been instructed for his grandfather's rest. Flipping the channel whenever an ad came on, he was listening to his brother and sister with more interest than he generally felt. Life for James revolved around the difficulty and necessity of making changes to his mental or physical state, or both: to get from sitting to running, from reading to listening, required an effort akin to that of a traveler who must repack his suitcase and change countries every day or so.

"What's pantheism?" Ryan said. "Is that where you believe in nature?"

Rebecca said, "It means you believe God is everywhere, God is in all things. 'Pan' is all, 'theism' is belief. 'Pandemonium' is all devils. 'Pan-American' is all Americas."

"Pan American is an airplane," James said.

"Dad went to church when he was little," Rebecca went on. "So did Mom. Religion was a much bigger deal back then."

Ryan knew all about his father's churchgoing because his father told stories about spit-shining his shoes and how important it was in those days for children to "mind" their parents, especially at church, which was an occasion for solemnity above all. Ryan remembered a story in which his father had gotten the giggles in church and literally gnawed open his knuckle, he was trying so hard not to laugh.

Ryan had wanted to know what was so funny, but his father couldn't remember. What made his father's face change was when Ryan asked why *their* family didn't go to church. His father's cheeks seemed to droop, and the area above his upper lip grew dark. "I guess I lost my religion," he said after some time had gone by. "Where?" Ryan said, and his father said, "Korea, son." Ryan stayed quiet after that; all the children knew their father didn't like to talk about the war.

"I've never been on an airplane," James said now, looking at Rebecca and Ryan.

"That's not true," Rebecca said. "We went to Michigan when you were a baby."

"That doesn't count, I don't remember it. Why is it so hot in here? When's everyone coming back?"

"Not for a while. And Grandpa needs it like this." Rebecca turned to Ryan. "Did you do the Greek myths at your school? Oh, yeah, I remember, you were each a god. You wanted to be Apollo but you were the ocean one, what's his name, Poseidon."

"I had a blue cape."

"I'd be Hera but she married her brother."

"I used to want to marry you."

Rebecca knew this but wished Ryan hadn't said it. What was going to happen to him next year when he joined her at Woodside High School and saw what life was really like? Someone who would say something like that didn't have the skin for high school; she wasn't sure he had the skin to walk around in the world.

She said she needed to do homework and left the boys by themselves. As the only girl she had a tiny room all to herself—the boys slept in the front room, Ryan and James on the foldout couch and Robert on a cot. She climbed onto her bed and leaned against the pillows. The difference between religions seemed less important than the difference between religion and its absence. Belief would drape itself over everything else in your mind. She imagined Ryan taking refuge in religion as a way to limit the social options of high school—he'd be in an even smaller group than Robert's tiny world of debaters. And it would separate him from the family. What would her father say? She couldn't imagine his reaction.

Ryan's hair reached his shoulders, and his eyes were deeply, startlingly blue. He could go longer without something to occupy him than anyone else she knew. When he was younger, about nine or ten, their mother had told him one day with some irritation that idle hands were the devil's tools, and he was so hurt that he went to bed in the middle of the afternoon. Rebecca tried to console him, but it wasn't easy to console someone who wasn't crying or even talking—who was just lying there. She lay with him, face-to-face. And—this came to her from nowhere—she had her period; she recalled the thick cottony wad between her legs and the sudden gush of blood that meant she should go to the bathroom and change pads soon. That meant she'd been at least twelve, so Ryan would have been at least ten. How strange that Ryan at ten had been that much smaller, that much more fragile, than James was now; and also that much more perceptive.

The TV blared, and Rebecca jumped off the bed and raced for the front room. There was James, standing on the couch with his arms in the air as if he were about to conduct an orchestra. "James," she cried, hurrying to turn off the TV. "Stop it! We leave you for one minute!"

"Arghh-grrrr-gahhhh," James cried, and he lunged at Rebecca, screaming, fists flying. He was a torrent of noise and motion, his feet, his arms, his legs: all flailing.

"James!" she shrieked.

Ryan ran in from the kitchen and threw himself between them.

"James," Rebecca screamed again, because now James was hitting Ryan. "James, stop it."

Ryan lay on the carpet with his forearms in front of his face. "No, no, no, no, no," James cried as he kept hitting.

"James!" Rebecca said. "Stop! Grandpa's resting!"

Abruptly James stopped hitting Ryan and dove to the carpet, where he rolled from side to side and sobbed. "No, no, no, no, no," he cried again.

"James," Ryan said. He knelt next to his brother. He'd been struck once on his face, above the eye, but it stung only a little and his arms were fine. "Baby honey," he murmured to James. "Honey boy."

James curled up on his side. His face was streaked with tears, his mouth contorted into a deep, open-lipped frown that revealed the tops of his lower teeth. He made a high-pitched keening noise.

"James," Ryan said. "Come on, let's do something. Let's play Yahtzee."

James looked at Rebecca and hissed.

"How about just you and me? Rebecca was doing homework anyway."

Rebecca returned to her room. All was quiet in the house, but she couldn't imagine that her grandfather had stayed asleep. She was worried about her grandfather, mostly because she thought her father was worried about him: he'd been watching her grandfather closely ever since they arrived.

She wasn't exactly babysitting, but she felt responsible for the noise, and as this feeling grew, she began to wish she hadn't reacted so dramatically. She should have spoken gently in the first place, and if James had gotten upset anyway, she should have soothed him instead of provoking him further.

She heard the TV go on again, softly. From the sound—a serious, droning voice—it seemed the news was on. She returned to the front room. The boys sat cross-legged on the floor watching. On the screen, a newscaster sat at his desk, behind him a light blue map of South America with a small finger near the top highlighted in black. Immediately Rebecca knew what this was—the country of Guyana. Hundreds of Americans had died there over the previous weekend, a mass suicide. She didn't want either of her brothers to watch, though they knew about it—everyone did. It had started when Congressman Leo Ryan, who represented the district north of Portola Valley, went to investigate a cult.

"Officials say the original figure of four hundred nine is far lower than the actual number of dead," said the announcer. "Reports today suggest the death toll could be as high as seven or eight hundred."

All three of them watched the screen. The picture switched to a black-and-white photo of the cult leader, wearing a cleric's collar under a sport jacket.

"He looks like Dad," James said.

Rebecca was appalled but kept her voice steady. "James, he does not."

"In the newspaper picture."

She knew the picture he meant: years ago their father had been photographed at a local elementary school on career day, giving a group of students a chance to take turns with his stethoscope. Normally he looked nothing like Jim Jones, but in that one picture—in his mouth and perhaps a little in his shiny black hair—she had to admit there was a real resemblance.

Now it was back to the map, this time a close-up of the country of Guyana with a dot for Jonestown and another for Georgetown, the capital.

"The kids took it first," Ryan said. "Then the parents."

"It had to be that way," Rebecca said. "If the parents drank theirs first and the kids decided not to drink it, what would they do? Where would they go? Who would help them? The parents were protecting their kids by having them go first." At school she'd heard teachers discussing it, and this was what one of them had said. She hadn't asked her father for his opinion. At home on the night they found out he said, "Some things are just too horrible to contemplate."

"Is Grandpa awake?" Ryan said.

"He's still resting. We should turn this off."

James said, "Jim Jones was lucky he found Jonestown to live in."

Rebecca and Ryan exchanged a look.

"He didn't find it, he founded it," Rebecca said.

"He named it after himself," Ryan said.

The map disappeared and was replaced by a different photograph, this one a high aerial shot of a field that appeared to be strewn with garbage, only Rebecca knew it wasn't garbage. She stepped past the boys and turned off the TV.

"Hey, we were watching that," James said.

"Is anyone thirsty? I want something to drink."

"Kool-Aid?" James said with a smirk.

"James," Ryan said.

"Hey," James said, scrambling to his feet. "Congressman *Ryan*. Get it? You were shot, Ryan. Pow-pow-blam!" On "blam" James raised his hands to mimic holding a rifle and took aim at Ryan.

"James," Rebecca said. She understood that she had a chance to do better than before, and not just to keep from disturbing their grandfather. She wanted to do better because it would be better. She said, "I want you to put the gun down now, James."

This caught James's attention. He kept his right hand near his face, his left arm fully extended with the fingers of his left hand curled.

"It'll be okay," she said, "if you put it down now."

James didn't know if he was excited or scared. He brought his eye closer to the scope and said, "Are you talking to me?"

She held her hands out, palms up. "I'm not armed," she said. "You're in control."

"Are you talking to me? Are you talking to me?"

"Why is he saying that?" Ryan said.

"It's a line from a movie," Rebecca said. "*Taxi Driver*. James, you didn't see that, did you?"

James was confused. He felt like he might do something.

"Put your hands out," Rebecca told Ryan. "Show him you aren't armed."

Ryan extended his hands, and then slowly, watching each other, they both raised their hands over their heads.

"What do you want to do now?" she asked James. "It's up to you."

James held a serious look and then burst out laughing. "I got you guys!" he crowed.

Rebecca said, "Shhh, quietly." Then: "You sure did."

"That was funny," he said. "What was in the Kool-Aid, anyway? What flavor was it?"

"Some kind of poison," Rebecca said.

"Why didn't they just pretend to drink it? You could hold your cup to your mouth"—he pantomimed this, tipping his head back—"and then you could just act poisoned." He bent over and staggered around, then made a strangled noise and collapsed to the carpet. As a final touch, he stuck out his tongue and rolled his eyes back in his head.

Ryan had had enough. He went into the bathroom and locked the door. His head hurt, and he sat on the edge of the tub and tried to forget James and his pretend rifle. He tried to banish the image of the dead people on the grass. Why were they all lying facedown? Had they lain that way as soon as they'd drunk the poison, so they'd be in orderly rows when their bodies were found? Or had someone moved them—and if so, who would have done that? Would the last person have stood at the end of the last row, drunk his poison, and then gotten down on the ground to die?

He turned on the bathwater. Leaving his clothes on the floor, he lowered himself into the tub and lay back until the ends of his hair got wet. At Sand Hill Day, snacks and meals were served to the youngest children first, which meant that Ryan, now one of the oldest, sometimes waited five or ten minutes for a sandwich or a cup of juice. He wondered what he would do if, standing at the end of the line, he watched as his schoolmates fell to the floor and died, one after another. Would he stay and have the juice, too? His closest friend at school was a girl named Sierra, a tall green-eyed beauty with a blond waterfall of hair that reached her waist. Most days Ryan brushed her hair for her, and then she brushed his, and afterward they pulled the hairs from the brush—hers pale, his sandy—and stuffed the mass of them into a pillow they were making together. This had started over a year earlier, and the pillow was nearly full. "Ryan, come on," she said each morning when she saw him. He always went. If she wanted to drink the juice and said "Ryan, come on," he would drink it, too. Tears ran down his cheeks and dropped into the bathwater. No one else in his family would do this—only he. This knowledge made him yearn for his parents and for the house in Portola Valley. They had another day and a half in Sacramento, though, and his shoulders began to shake.

Someone knocked at the door. "Ryan?" It was Rebecca. "Are you in there?"

"Yes." He slid down lower and let the water cover his face, then sat up and reached for the soap. "I'm almost done."

"Are you taking a bath?"

"I'm almost done," he repeated.

He soaped his body, slowing as he approached his penis and at the last moment choosing to go around it. If he got into rubbing it, he might forget what he'd been feeling, the sadness and terror, and it seemed important that he remember them.

Because he slept in the front room, his suitcase and all of his clothes were in his parents' bedroom. He wrapped himself in a towel and went down the hall. His grandfather's door was still closed, and Ryan closed his parents' door. Their bed here was very small, much smaller than the one they had at home.

He dressed and went into the kitchen. James sat at the table in front of a huge piece of crumpled tinfoil, inside of which was the leftover turkey, which he was browsing for bits of skin. "Want some?" he asked Ryan.

Ryan shook his head and sat opposite James. After a moment he reached over and helped himself to a piece of white meat.

"Sorry," James said.

"What for?"

"Because I shot you."

The house began to fill again. Grandpa Greenway returned to the front room, and Rebecca sat on the couch with a book. Bill and Robert arrived home just ahead of Penny and her mother.

In the garage looking for the Christmas-tree stand, Robert noticed a stack of games and puzzles, at the top of which was a plain white box labeled "Your Jigsaw Puzzle—1,000 Pieces Guaranteed." Once the tree was up in the front room, he and Rebecca cleared the dining room table and got to work. The subject of the puzzle was a mystery as there was no picture on the box, but they both thought a thousand-piece puzzle was as good a way as any to while away the hours.

Penny walked past them late in the afternoon, took a look at the box, and said, "Oh, no. Not that."

"What?"

"Nothing. You'll see."

The border came together slowly, the colors of the puzzle pieces varying only in their shade of gray. The inside took even longer and was far enough from finished at bedtime that Robert was tempted to break apart what they'd done and put the pieces back in the box so they wouldn't have to continue in the morning. He didn't suggest it, though. Rebecca would never quit.

He got into bed, his brothers on the couch nearby, and realized he hadn't called Gina. Partly it was because they'd never talked long-distance before. They didn't talk on the phone much at all, and when they did it was because she'd called him; after several minutes, fearing he was boring her, he'd say, "I should get going." This was an improvement on their first few phone conversations, which he'd cut short by saying, "I'm going to go now." He might have gone on that way forever had she not pointed out that in putting it that way, he essentially left her no option but to say, "Okay, bye." When he asked her to elaborate, she said, "If you say 'I *should* go now' instead of 'I'm *going to* go now' then I can say 'Really?' or 'Wait, I want to tell you one more thing' or even just 'Oh, okay' and then maybe we'd get a few more minutes out of it." It was this last—her assumption that they both wanted to get a few more minutes out of it—that cemented his adoration of her.

"Why are we still here?" he asked Rebecca as they worked on the puzzle the next morning. "Why do we stay till Sunday every year? I have a lot of homework."

"I brought mine with me."

"Well, so did I, but I don't have a private room."

"Unlike some people," she said, and they both smiled and then smiled again at the unexpected camaraderie. "Do you miss Gina?" she said, and he nodded.

It was almost noon, and the house was quiet. Bill had gone out, Ryan and James were playing cards with their grandfather, and Penny was in her parents' bedroom with her mother, the two of them ostensibly folding laundry together but in fact covering, in hushed voices, the same conversational territory they'd covered while grocery shopping the day before.

"Those kids need you in the house when they get home from school."

"They're fine. They're learning how to be independent."

"You should be there when they walk in."

"They know where I am. They can always come down."

Audrey shook her head and set a folded white undershirt on a pile of folded white undershirts and then pressed the entire stack flat, as she did each time she added to it. Penny understood that her mother's point of view came from an earlier era, but she couldn't get over the inherent unfairness of being judged by the mother of a single child: a docile girl.

As opposed to a pack of kids led by a brilliant and demanding boy, complicated by a headstrong girl with no gift at all for the arts, softened and therefore confounded by a meek and dreamy boy, and finally overwhelmed by a miniature wild man.

"Do they?" her mother said.

"What?"

"Go down to your studio."

"Ryan sometimes does," Penny said, thinking of a day when Ryan's school was dismissed early and he spent the afternoon in the studio with her, making coil pots with leftover bits of clay. She'd had several bowls ready for glazing, and the two of them had fun using squeeze bottles to squirt spirals and zigzags of glaze on the bowls.

"What about James?" her mother said.

"No, thank goodness."

"Penny, honestly."

"Oh, he's fine. He's doing a lot better in school this year. I've only gotten one phone call."

"I wasn't going to tell you this," her mother said, "but Dad heard an awful commotion yesterday afternoon. It got him out of bed and all the way to the door—he was afraid he'd have to go in and break it up. James yelling and screaming and from the sound of it punching, too."

"Really?" Penny said. "He doesn't—"

"Penny, that boy needs more discipline. Bill can't see past his healthy body, so it's going to have to be you."

"What can I do?"

"The carrot and the stick, Penny, the carrot and the stick."

"We don't strike our children!" Penny spoke as if from outrage, but she felt something closer to satisfaction at her mother's apparent agreement with her on the subject of spanking. It wasn't that Penny advocated anything like hard hitting, but she did think a light swat on the behind could be useful to get a child's attention. Bill absolutely disagreed, and he made her feel bad by calling it "corporal punishment." He had no idea what it was like at the end of a long afternoon to cope with a child who was cranky and determined to misbehave. Though to be fair to herself, she hadn't swatted James in years. He was too big, for one thing.

She said something about making lunch and left her mother with the laundry. In the dining room, the puzzle was coming in mostly from the top right, where an indistinct tree was taking shape; and the bottom left, where a banister held a shrub at bay. Within an hour or two, the subject of the photo would be revealed, and she would have to endure the sight of herself being the person she had only barely escaped being.

"You're still sitting here?" she said to Robert and Rebecca. "Don't you want to do something constructive?"

"How much more constructive can you get," Robert said, "than putting together a jigsaw puzzle?"

"Where's your father?" she said, but she didn't wait for a reply and wandered down the hall to the small room she and Bill were sharing. She knew where he was; she'd asked the kids in order to raise the question in their minds, since she wanted them to recognize that even he needed a break sometimes.

He'd gone to the pharmacy to get new compression stockings for her father. Penny believed there was more he could do for her father, but he was walking the line between physician and son-in-law as carefully as ever, saying he was a *pediatrician*—as if he'd never treated old men with heart disease, which he'd done constantly at the Oakland Naval Hospital, where veterans of World War I had made up a good portion of the patient population.

"Penny," her mother said, knocking on the open door. "I think you should take the kids downtown. When was the last time they saw the state capitol? You could go out to lunch."

"Has it changed? Anyway, they're busy."

"Ryan and James might want to go."

"Bill can take them when he gets back."

"While you do what?"

"Mom, I'm a visitor. Pretend I'm a real guest, how about? I'm forty-four. I run a household. Do my kids seem undernourished? Are their clothes torn?"

Audrey had noticed that Ryan looked quite shabby, his corduroys worn thin over the thighs and frayed at the hem. Probably they had belonged to Robert first—maybe James, too. She imagined taking Ryan downtown herself and buying him some new clothes. Of the four, he was the one most likely to enjoy such an outing. But she didn't much like going downtown these days. If she could get Penny and the older children out of the house, she'd take Ryan into the kitchen with her and teach him how to make angel food cake, which, she remembered from previous visits, he loved.

"Oh, Penny, never mind," she said. "Never mind."

She made her way to the kitchen with a glance into the front room to make sure her husband was okay. Describing the uproar he'd overheard during his rest the day before, he'd said of James, "That little son of a bitch will get things done in life if no one kills him first." He had begun using profanity freely in the last few years, which concerned her nearly as much as his health.

While Robert and Rebecca worked on the puzzle and Ryan and James played cards with their grandfather and Penny and her mother bickered in one room after another, Bill bypassed the Payless and went to the family-owned drugstore he'd first frequented in 1957, when Penny brought him to meet her parents and twisted her ankle climbing down from the train. Her parents had been waiting at the station, and after the four of them drove to the house and he got Penny settled in the front room with her leg up and ice on her ankle, he borrowed the car and set off in search of some Tylenol, which at that time was being marketed just for children and was absent from most home medicine cabinets.

The store was called Haskell's, and it reminded him of the drugstore of his Michigan childhood, with its soda fountain on one wall and its pharmacy opposite and between them shelf after shelf of motley household goods. He found the health aids aisle and located men's compression stockings in a size large. He bought three pairs, remembering how long they took to drip-dry between washings.

Back at his in laws', he entered the house just as Robert and Rebecca put the final pieces into the puzzle and called for everyone to admire it. "Look, it's Jim Jones!" James cried, and Bill was startled by a hugely enlarged black-and-white photograph of himself and Penny and the children sitting in front of his childhood home. Years earlier, his in-laws had ordered the puzzle as a gift; he'd forgotten it existed.

"Shhhh," Rebecca said to James, "I told you, don't say that."

"Dad," James said, "look, you're Jim Jones, you're Jim Jones! See, you look like him, look at this! I was a baby, see, Mom's holding me. This is us in Michigan. Did you kidnap us all and take us to *Billtown*? What kind of Kool-Aid did they have? How could a baby drink it, did the parents put it in their bottles? 'Waaah, Mama, waah, waah, give me my baba!'"

Everyone was silent, staring at James. Rebecca wanted to roll time back thirty seconds so she could solve the situation instead of making it worse. Robert felt a pang of pleasure at having his worst thoughts about James confirmed. Ryan slipped away and closed himself in the bathroom again.

Bill took a step closer to James. "How do I look like him?"

James looked up. He couldn't see any of Jim Jones in his actual father. "I don't know."

"It would be Blairtown," Robert said. "Not Billtown. It's Jonestown, not Jimtown."

"What would happen in Billtown?" their father said, ignoring Robert.

"You would be the Bill of Billtown!" James said, but everything had changed and he felt like someone who was huffing and puffing and suddenly realized there was no house to blow down. "Billtown, USA!" he cried for good measure. He climbed onto one of the chairs and shouted, "Subjects! Welcome to Jamestown!"

"James," Penny cried, "get down from there this instant! Why are we all standing here? Dad, this will wear you out. James, I mean it, now."

"Come down, son," Bill said, and he held out a hand for James.

He took his youngest son outside. They had an easy kinship outdoors, and they began walking without the need to say anything right away. At home, they alone still went to the tree house, and as often as not it was Bill who suggested they climb up and see how the platform was holding. When it needed repair, James carried the toolbox down from the garage and tapped the nails his father held. "What if I hit your fingers?" he asked, and Bill said he didn't think that would happen because James was so careful. It was a calculated risk that paid off; lately, when there was hammering to be done, James held the nail and the hammer.

"Tell me about Jim Jones," Bill said.

James felt the cool November air on his bare arms; the sky was a mottled gray. He didn't want to talk about Jim Jones—he'd said the only thing he had to say, and now that he was with his dad and could look at his face, he knew even that one thing had been wrong.

"He wasn't very smart," he said.

"In that . . ."

"He killed himself, too. So he didn't get to keep the money after all."

"The money?"

"Everyone gave him all their money just so they could go with him. Then he made them live in shacks."

"I wonder about that. 'Made them.' How do you suppose he did that?"

James was tired of the conversation. Thanksgiving night the family had come this same way, and he wondered when they'd pass the house with the giant turkey in the front yard. "Where's the turkey house?" he said. "We should've seen it by now."

His father said, "Maybe the turkey only comes out on Thanksgiving."

"Dad, stop. I'm not a baby. People put it up, it's a decoration."

Bill put his hand on his son's head. "Let's keep going, maybe we'll see it. I need to stretch my legs."

"I need to stretch my whole body," James said, and he jumped as high as he could, extending his arms over his head, and then did it again after he landed. "Imagine if you could swim through air," he said, circling his arms one after the other. "I'm swimming," he said. "Dad, swim with me!"

Bill circled one arm and then the other and tried kicking his feet behind him. "Not much of a swimmer."

"Race me," James said, and he took off with his arms flying—a flailing four-limbed creature ungoverned by pattern unless you knew where to look. When he got to the corner, he turned around. "Dad, do it!" he called, and Bill cycled his arms as he jogged—halfway on board, which he knew would satisfy his son.

They walked for another twenty minutes. Bill didn't bring up Jim Jones again. He'd heard that syringes were used to get the cyanide-laced Kool-Aid into the babies' mouths, and he cringed to think they must have used the same technique he taught parents whose infants required liquid analgesics: squeezing and pulling forward on the cheeks to create a dam against backflow. His nurse, Dorie, a grandmother, had wept when she learned there'd been a nurse in Jonestown handing children cups of poison.

His father-in-law was resting when they got back to the house. James joined the other children in the kitchen, where their grandmother was serving turkey sandwiches, and Bill headed for the bathroom only to have Penny walk in behind him, saying, "James is out of control. I hope you gave him a good talking-to."

Bill paused, his back to her though he could see her in the mirror over the sink. She wore a necklace of clay beads she'd made herself, and a scowl on her face. He said, "You didn't like him standing on the chair?"

"And yelling! Did you? Why do I have to be the one to object?"

Over the years, as things had gotten worse at home, Penny had become more and more particular about the children's conduct when they visited her parents. It would have made sense to Bill if she'd been that way from the beginning, but when Robert and Rebecca were small she'd actually encouraged what she called "free expression" on these holiday trips. He remembered one Thanksgiving when she insisted on having the children help in the kitchen, and the meal, when it was finally served, two hours late, bore signs of their overinvolvement: giant hand-torn pieces of celery in the stuffing; a pie with no pastry, as they had shredded it over and over until it seemed best simply to bake the filling in a soufflé dish. Another time, visiting in the summer without him, Penny bought a small wading pool, and her mother's roses were flooded twice when the children experimented with standing on the pool's flimsy walls.

"He made a scene yesterday, too," she said. "Dad told Mom and she told me. She was very upset—you know how rigid she is."

Penny had said this many times, but Bill found his mother-in-law to be quite flexible—and youthful in a way he couldn't recall his own mother ever having been. "It's a small house," he said. "Tight quarters."

"I guess we should have thought of that before we had four children!"

He nearly bumped into her as he reached around her to close the bathroom door. "Please lower your voice."

"Don't you dare be so high and mighty with me!"

"All I said was please lower your voice."

"Yes, but I know what you're thinking, and you didn't want him, either."

"Oh, Penny, my God. Please."

"You can't agree with me?"

"This is hardly the—"

"Do I have to remind you of the foundation?"

At first he had no idea what she meant. Then he remembered the three R's he'd carved into the wet concrete. Eight years after that, when Penny was overwhelmed by James's birth and he wanted to soothe her, he told her that when they were first married he'd truly been with her in thinking that the right number was three; and that alongside her secret sketches, her childhood drawings of two boys and a girl, he had his own secret physical proof in the form of a daydream etched into hardening concrete. It struck him as dangerous that she remembered this—something she could use against James if she wanted to.

"Penny," he said. "You must never—"

"Oh, don't worry. Your secret is safe. But he's a problem, and it's not fair to leave it all on me."

"He's an active ten-year-old."

"You didn't say anything to him?"

Bill wanted to sit down with his older children and talk to them about the picture they'd assembled, to ask what they remembered about the trip to Michigan and to answer any questions. He was also hungry. But he didn't move. He looked at his wife, just yards away from the room where, on Thanksgiving night, for the first time in months, they had made love. He recalled the early years of their marriage, when their bed had served as a treatment room for the ills his separate daytime life inflicted on their relationship; how he'd soothed her with the calm, steady attention, the gentle strokes he recommended for colicky babies. And how, with her emotional hunger sated, a wilder hunger took hold of them both.

"What?" she said. "Is that an unreasonable question?"

"I was thinking," he said, "about the other night." He tilted his head in the direction of the bedroom.

Penny's mouth tightened, and he wished he hadn't spoken; they made love rarely and had a tacit agreement not to talk about it—the activity or the infrequency. He thought of James, the way he'd swum down the sidewalk, his chaotic curiosity stilled only through action. "I'll talk to him," he said. "I'll make a point of it."

They left Sacramento at midmorning on Sunday and arrived in San Francisco just as the fog was lifting. Everyone was hungry, and Bill got off the freeway so they could stop for lunch. Ryan, who rarely asked for anything, said he had heard from Sierra about a place called the Magic Pan, in Ghirardelli Square, and because that meant sundaes at the Chocolate Factory might be a possibility afterward, the others agreed. The Magic Pan was a crepe restaurant, which called to mind something small and dainty, so each of the Blairs was surprised to be served a giant lacy half-moon oozing creamy chicken or crab with cheese sauce.

Robert was not an adventurous eater, and he sliced his open and watched suspiciously as the filling spilled out. Rebecca ate five quick bites and felt a little sick. James scraped and rolled and scraped and rolled until his crepe was free of all but a thin coating of sauce, and he chewed it quickly, saying it wasn't bad if you just ate the crunchy parts.

Ryan fell in love. He ate slowly, arranging each forkful to contain a stamp-size piece of crepe and a single sauce-coated piece of meat, the combination of which struck him as almost magically balanced between crisp and soft, dry and creamy. He understood why the place was called the Magic Pan and imagined telling Sierra about it in the morning, and how maybe they could come back together, maybe toward the end of the school year, when their time at Sand Hill Day was running out. They would be attending the same high school, but it was so big that Ryan wasn't certain he would be able to find her at recess and lunch. At this thought a tear seeped from his eye, and he stuck out his tongue and caught it, pleased when the extra salt made the food in his mouth even more perfectly savory.

Bill didn't care for the food, but he smiled encouragingly at the children. "Crepes," he said, "are particular to a certain region of France called Brittany. That's where Mont Saint-Michel is. Do any of you know about Mont Saint-Michel?"

"It's a fortress on an island," Robert said. "When the tide comes in, you can't get to it. Then the tide goes out and a natural bridge comes up again."

"There's actually a road," Bill said. "But that's the general idea."

"Have you been there, Dad?" James said.

"He hasn't been to Europe," Rebecca said. "Only Korea. And Japan."

"Let's go someday," Bill said. "Shall we?"

"Mom, what do you think?" Ryan said. "Would you like to go to France? To Paris?"

Penny looked around the table. She once harbored a deep wish to go to Paris, just as she once wanted nothing more than to sit with her family on the porch of her husband's childhood home. The jigsaw puzzle, its old photograph transformed into a warning about the danger of desire, had upset her more than she'd expected, and her response to Ryan was brief and bitter. "I'd rather go nowhere. Then I'd never be disappointed."

For the next several minutes, everyone was silent. Forks scraped over plates, milk was sipped. Bill asked for the check and paid with two fifty-dollar bills.

James still wanted the Chocolate Factory, but he was overruled and they got back into the car. Bill made his way to Van Ness. "There's city hall," he said as they passed the back of the giant domed building. He wondered if there might be a memorial inside to Congressman Ryan, whose body had arrived in San Francisco a few days earlier. Bill had seen footage of Mayor Moscone weeping at the funeral.

"It's beautiful," Ryan said.

"The front is better," Robert said, "if you like that grandiose sort of thing."

Back in Portola Valley, Penny disappeared immediately, and the children settled into their rooms, happy to spread out. All except Robert, who drove to Gina's without calling. He couldn't wait to see her. Parked out front, he waited for a moment, looking at her house. It was incredible that he'd known her for less than three months.

When he knocked, she came to the door and spoke to him through the screen. Her mother had a headache, so Robert couldn't come in. "Can you come out?" he said, disappointed by her expression, which conveyed a not altogether happy surprise at the sight of him.

She hesitated before disappearing briefly and then reappearing with a pair of tennis shoes dangling from her fingers.

"How was Sacramento?" she said as she joined him on the porch. "Did you miss me?"

Robert had expected to have a lot to say, but now that they were together, now that he was finally looking at her soft, kissable mouth, he was stupid and tongue-tied. She was still barefoot, and this struck him as a bad sign: if she wanted to spend time with him, wouldn't she have put on her shoes?

"I missed you," she said.

"I'm sure."

"I did."

He shrugged and then stood there.

"What's the matter?" she said. "Why are you being so weird?"

"I'm not."

"I'll be the judge of that!" she responded playfully, but he quickly dismissed the playfulness as an attempt to deny the terrible awkwardness that had sprouted between them.

"My grandfather," he said, "is very sick."

Gina's face grew serious, her small brown eyes narrowing.

"He has congestive heart failure," he added.

"Your mom must be upset."

"She doesn't give a shit."

"Robert, I'm sure that's not true!"

"In case you haven't noticed, she doesn't care about anyone but herself."

Gina sat on a low wall at the side of the porch. Absently, she brushed off the bottoms of her feet and put her shoes on. Leaning forward, she put her forearms on her knees like a boxer resting in his corner between rounds.

"You have noticed, haven't you?" he said.

"Maybe we should just talk at school tomorrow."

He stepped off the porch and headed for the car. He tried not to stomp, but he could feel himself emitting upset and knew he looked ridiculous. If he had called her over the weekend, this never would have happened.

At home, the afternoon was condensing into a typical Sunday evening, and after dinner he holed up in his room and began what he knew would be about seven hours of homework. He couldn't stop thinking about the terrible scene on Gina's porch, returning again and again to the truth of the statement he'd made about his mother. She didn't care about anyone but herself. He was tired of pretending she was normal. He decided he'd prefer an out-and-out broken home like Gina's over the sham that was his family. Then he thought about Gina's father and realized that she had never once complained about him, though Robert knew she didn't like him. Robert, in making such a true statement about his mother, had brought honesty into their relationship. He spoke the truth while Gina spooled out lies. She was just a junior and a full year younger than he, so maybe she wasn't ready to be genuine, but he was.

If he hadn't been so overwhelmed by homework he might have

stayed in his room and nursed this idea, held it close until it was ready for the world, perhaps even discovered it was only half-formed and would not survive for long. Instead, doomed to be up until one or two in the morning, he decided to hell with it and went out to the living room.

His siblings were sitting with his father, all quiet with books or their thoughts, even James. "Where's Mom?" he said.

"Where do you think?" Rebecca said.

"After dinner?"

No one responded. It wasn't unheard of for Penny to go back to the shed after dinner. Sometimes she didn't come back until everyone was in bed.

"I wanted to tell you," Robert went on, "that I'm going to break up with Gina tomorrow."

His father looked up. Rebecca frowned, conveying doubt rather than disapproval. Ryan was stretched out on the couch, and he laid his book facedown on his lap. James shouted "You can't do that!" and ran from the room.

"What happened, Rob?" Bill said.

"She's just too young for me. She's immature."

"Immature," his father repeated.

"I don't really have time for a girlfriend. It's senior year—I'm so busy. I have college applications."

"You're almost finished with your college applications," Rebecca said.

"People say fall semester senior year is the most important time of high school. Kids get ahead of themselves and think they're finished, but they aren't. You have to be careful not to get sidetracked."

"Did something happen?" his father said.

"I don't see what the big deal is," Robert said. "It's not like I was going to marry her."

James had disappeared into the bedroom hallway, just out of the others' sight. He came back and said, "Then *I* will!"

"James," Robert said.

"You can't break up with her! I love her!"

"James," Bill said, holding out an arm. "Come here."

"Everyone does this!" James cried.

"Does what?" Rebecca said.

"Breaks up."

Bill had been wondering when this would happen. When he tried to talk to Penny about the message she was giving the children, she brushed him off or began a recitation of grievances both old and new. "Come here, honey," he said, and James joined him on the couch.

"In the past," Bill said, "when we've talked about your mother and the shed, we've focused more on why she needs time alone for her projects. But I know you must be wondering what's going on between the two of us. James, is that what you're wondering?"

"I'm not wondering anything," James said.

"I am," Rebecca said.

"No one's going anywhere," Bill said. "Or at least nowhere else—nowhere farther."

"She can go wherever she wants," Robert said. "As far as I'm concerned."

"Mom or Gina?" Rebecca asked him.

"Very funny. Gina's not going anywhere, *I* am. To college."

"Any second now."

Robert glared at her. "Are you on the rag?"

"Rob," their father cautioned.

"It makes women irritable," Robert said. "You told me that yourself."

"Maybe Gina was," Rebecca said. "Did you think of that this afternoon? When you had your fight?"

"We didn't have a fight," Robert said. "How many times do I have to tell you guys? Maybe I won't break up with her after all, I don't even know for sure."

"Don't break up with her," Ryan said. "You love her."

Robert returned to his room, but his homework was more daunting than ever. He went to the telephone. Gina answered on the first ring, and he said, "Yes, if you're still wondering." It was important to him that he not have to explain himself: that she understand he meant yes he missed her without his having to say so.

"Oh, good," she said. "Though I never doubted it."

Relief flooded him. He was a fool and had come close to losing her. What would his life be without her? Dry, dull, dead. He said, "I wish you were here."

Back in the living room, Bill and the three younger children were quiet again, James burrowed into Bill's side as if they needed each other for warmth. Bill was thinking about his family, his first family: his parents and sister when he was a child in Michigan. Thanksgiving always brought the past back to him, as it was contrived to do. In Michigan, the holiday had elevated the ordinary formality of a Sunday dinner into an affair of state. Both sets of relatives came for the day, his mother's farm family and his father's townsfolk. The occasion was as tightly orchestrated as a military maneuver. Even the conversation was orchestrated, with groups and subgroups forming and re-forming around observations about the weather. In the Thanksgivings of Bill's memory, there was always snow on the ground, and he and his sister, along with their two much older cousins, twin boys named Gilbert and Lester, sat at the parlor window and watched as the shadows on the snow darkened in the falling light. Bill's father said grace from the head of the table, and if he couldn't stop himself, Bill carefully opened his eyes to see if anyone else might be opening theirs. Once, his maternal grandmother was watching him, and the look she gave him would have shamed a stone. Penny's indifference to religion had been a relief to him, enabling him to avoid what had seemed the inevitability of raising his children in the church. Now the horror at Jonestown made him wonder about the cost of keeping his family out of organized religion—out of religion altogether, yes, but more important out of organized religion, the practice of it, the activity of belonging to a congregation. It seemed to him that Jonestown must confound his children all the more because they had no experience of worship. James had said Jim Jones forced his followers to live in shacks. To teach him and the others that the people had gone willingly, voluntarily, seemed to Bill a task beyond his capabilities as a parent.

"Dad," Rebecca said. "You said no one's going anywhere. Are you sure about that?"

"Yes," he said, though he wasn't.

"Did she actually say it?" Rebecca was sitting very straight at the front edge of her chair, her dark hair pulled away from her face in a ponytail so tight that Bill thought it must hurt.

He hesitated. Ryan's book was open, but Bill could tell he was listening. James was listening, too.

"I wish you weren't worried," he said at last, knowing the words to be inadequate, though no more so than he felt.

At ten o'clock, with all the children in bed except Robert, Bill drank a glass of milk in the empty kitchen, found a flashlight, and went outside. It felt as if it had been dark for days, but it was only November 26 and the nights would get longer before they began to get shorter. He made his way down the driveway to the spur. At the shed, he knocked.

"What?" she said as she opened the door. She took in his serious look and said, "What is it? Is someone sick?"

"What are you doing?"

"Working."

"No, here. What are you doing here? Away from your family."

She hesitated. "Not far away."

"No more," he said. "No more of this. From now on, you stay in the house after dinner."

She stared off to the side, and for a moment she had the wistful look that had captivated him twenty years earlier. He'd staked a lot on the idea that he could make that look go away but had not counted on what might replace it.

"All right," she said.

"All right?"

"Yes."

He waited to see what else she might say. When nothing was forthcoming, he thanked her and made his way back up the hill, wondering if it was in his character always to ask for too little. Was it in hers always to ask for too much? He said good night to Robert and went to bed. He lay awake, watching the clock, and then fell into a light sleep during which he dreamed that he was awake, waiting. When he woke in the morning he could hear her in the kitchen, and though her side of the bed was lightly disturbed, he wasn't sure she'd been there.

Breakfast was generally chaotic but never more so than after a vacation. The children were up and down from the table constantly, running back to their rooms for pencils, homework, books. Most mornings, once everyone was gone, Penny sat with coffee for an hour or more, absorbing the tranquility of the empty house, but today she went straight to her studio. If she had to give up working in the evening she wanted to get every second she could out of the daytime. Once she was there, though, she felt paralyzed, wondering what she'd promised and why he'd objected—why now?

The Sacramento trip must have galvanized him—their unexpected coming together on Thanksgiving night. She thought back: the room overheated, the poor quality of the mattress angling them both toward the middle. She lay on her side facing away from him while he lay on his back. She waited for him to fall asleep, but after several minutes he rolled closer and rested his fingertips on her hip. The last time had been early summer, and as she was thinking regretfully about how much she once loved this, he pushed her hair aside and touched the back of her neck. She could smell his erection. The kids were nearby, her parents right across the hall. She pushed her hips back, then pulled her nightgown to her waist and pushed closer. She felt heat and arousal, uncertain which was his and which was hers.

"Turn around," he murmured, but she stayed as she was, reaching between her legs for him.

"Not like that," he said, pulling away and rolling onto his back again.

She turned and faced him. She could tell that he wanted her, but not the whole of her—not the part of her that mattered most, her soul, her essence.

He touched her waist. She touched his cheek, his lips. He sighed, and she slid her leg over his. Fondling his nipple, feeling his hand on her thigh—what in years past had been a single system became two systems, the things she was doing to him and the things he was doing to her, the two of them like trains on parallel tracks as they arrived at their separate destinations.

She lay next to him, not even their hands touching. After a moment she felt his toes brush hers. He said, "Let's go back."

"I can't."

"You won't."

"I can't," she said, and she rolled away from him and grabbed a tissue to dry herself.

Monday morning, and sunlight angled through her studio window. Her worktable ran along one wall, its surface littered with sketches and pencils and glazes and pastes and glues. Most mornings she began by clearing space, the task itself a warm-up for whatever she would do in the hours that followed, which in recent weeks had been collage. She liked how finite each board was, finite and yet receptive, limited and yet capacious. She used nine-by-eleven card stock, black or cream, and she set the finished collages on a narrow shelf she'd had the contractor install around the perimeter of the room, two feet below the ceiling.

But she wanted a third dimension. Out of nowhere she remembered balsa wood—a thin, lightweight wood the boys had used to make airplanes and boats. Maybe she'd think of something to do with that? She hurried up to the house and searched Robert's room, his desk drawers, his bureau. Nothing. Ryan and James's room was far messier and she took a deep breath before entering. She went through their drawers before turning to the closet, which was big and dark and littered with games and cars and trucks and puzzles and even a bin of chunky building blocks no one had touched in years. She found Ryan's badger and James's dog. Finally she came across a small tugboat that she thought had been made of balsa wood, but none of the wood itself.

That was okay, though. It was better, because she'd have to buy some, and who knew what else she might find at the craft store? There was a new store she'd heard about in the city, and she decided to go later in the week; she could take a look at some of the galleries on Geary while she was there. *This* was the life she wanted—not the life of that foolish girl in front of her husband's childhood home, that girl holding a fourth baby. Who had four babies? "Think how much we love the three we have," Bill said when, newly and accidentally pregnant with James, she wept and wept. "I'll die," she said, and he smiled an indulgent smile that chilled her. They'd always agreed on three, but in those days before *Roe* v. *Wade* she'd been unable to bring up the possibility of "taking care of it," too afraid of what he'd say, the law-abiding citizen, the moralist. That he was a doctor who almost certainly could have found someone to help—well, that had just made it all the more impossible to mention. The night shortly after James's birth, when he told her about what he'd done while building the shed: for a time it had made her feel better, but that was long ago.

She returned to the kitchen. In the old days she'd worked in the mud pantry all morning long, inconceivable now that she had her studio. The mud pantry was tiny, cramped. Where formerly she kept bags of clay there were now jars of bulk granola and dried beans—the groceries of a family not quite hers, though you couldn't fault her for trying. Her children preferred Frosted Flakes and Chef Boyardee, and Bill, who ought to care about such things, insisted it wasn't a big deal if they ate junk from time to time, not in the grand scheme of things it wasn't. But she wanted the children to eat what she thought they should eat. She wanted them to *want* to eat the right foods—not to complain, when she served dried fruit for dessert, that they were being mistreated.

This had happened the night before. After a weekend of eating her parents' diet, all the more galling in light of how bad it was for her father, she'd put out a plate of dried apples and walnuts, and the children had laughed at her, even Ryan and especially Robert, who at dinnertime had been more down at the mouth than he'd been in Sacramento, which was saying a lot.

Tonight she would serve the kind of dinner she wanted to serve, which meant she should drive down to the store now, before it got busy at lunchtime.

On the car radio she heard "shot and killed" and "city hall" and

"Jim Jones," and she switched it off. The memory of James on Saturday, climbing onto the dining room chair and shouting, "Welcome to Jamestown!" What kind of maniac streak did he possess? And what kind of violent streak, if she was to believe her mother about Friday afternoon? James beating on Ryan—that could not happen again. She would have to crack down on James if Bill refused.

Making her way through the grocery store, she gathered spinach, mushrooms, brown rice, unsalted crackers, wheat germ. In the bulk-food aisle, she shoveled pumpkin seeds into one plastic bag and raw almonds into another. She found unfiltered apple juice, cloudy as an old aquarium, and yogurt made from the milk of goats.

She kept the radio off as she drove home. At the house, she unpacked the groceries and hurried to her studio, where she had pots to glaze and a pair of collages to finish.

Just before three she heard the sound of Ryan's carpool, and a little after that the sound of James's. It was a blessing that Sand Hill Day dismissed early, so that Ryan was always home when James arrived. Her mother had admonished her about being absent when the kids got home from school, but really the kids preferred each other, and Ryan was as motherly as she was, if not more so. He would make James a snack, ask James about his day. Robert and Rebecca usually got a ride from a neighbor girl whose parents had bought her a car, and they would walk up from the road in a little while.

Time got away from her, and it was pitch dark by the time she made her way up to the house, late to embark on the healthy dinner she'd planned. Instead of the spinach and brown rice casserole she'd imagined, she decided she would cook each one simply and separately. Chop the mushrooms and throw them in a salad. She used the kitchen door to enter the house, surprised to see all four kids in the room together, sitting around the table. She glanced at her watch, thinking it must be later than she'd realized, but it was only a little past six, an hour earlier than their usual dinnertime. Bill wouldn't arrive for another twenty to thirty minutes.

"Mom," Rebecca said, getting to her feet as Penny entered the room.

They looked grim, all of them. Ryan's friend Sierra was there, too, sharing Ryan's chair with him, her cheek resting between his shoulder blades.

"Goodness," Penny said. "You all look like someone died."

In the sudden quiet, the stove clock ticked audibly. Rebecca and Robert had argued, during the car ride from school and periodically since arriving home, about how their mother might have reacted—might be reacting—to what had happened. Rebecca contended she'd be upset—she imagined her mother in tears, was convinced that was why Penny hadn't come up yet. Robert believed Penny wouldn't—didn't—care and was in the shed because she was still working. Neither considered the possibility that she didn't know.

"Who died?" Penny said. "Oh, my God. Not Grandpa. Oh, don't tell me, don't tell me this happened the day after we left!"

Sierra looked up. She had an ordinary small nose and an ordinary bow-shaped upper lip and an ordinary high hairline, but her features, especially her clear green eyes, were arranged in such a way as to make her extraordinarily lovely. Perhaps it was the sweep of her jawline or the openness of the space between her eyebrows, but she was a thirteen-year-old who turned heads, a child so pretty that the word itself seemed to need a new definition.

"Assassination," James sang. "Assassina-aytion is making me wait, it's keeping me wayayayayaytin'."

"James!" Rebecca exclaimed. "Don't."

"What?" Penny said.

"In San Francisco," Robert said. "The mayor and another guy were killed. Shot. You didn't hear?"

"What do you mean?" Penny said. "Leo Ryan was shot. He was a congressman."

"Mom, today," Robert said. "They were shot today."

"It was an assassination," James added proudly.

"No," Penny said. "That can't be right." She recalled the few seconds of radio she'd heard in the morning. "I'm positive. I heard something on the radio, and they mentioned Jim Jones—they were just going over all of that again."

"They thought it was related at first," Rebecca said. "But it wasn't."

Penny pulled a chair away from the table—she pulled it all the way to the wall before she sat down. She shook her head with disbelief. "What is Sierra doing here?" she said at last.

"Staying with me," Ryan said, speaking for the first time since Penny had entered the room.

"I'll be quiet," Sierra said without lifting her head.

"But it's nearly dinnertime."

"Mom," Rebecca said, and Penny didn't persist.

It *was* nearly dinnertime, and she went to the refrigerator. She no longer had the energy to cook anything, let alone something the children would protest, and she sorted through the food that was already there, that had been there since last Wednesday. She took out bread and potatoes and cream cheese and an old head of romaine lettuce. Her mother had insisted she bring home the leftover turkey, and she pulled that out as well, opening the foil to find little other than scraps and a single unappetizing wing. But she found some cranberry sauce and some stuffing and some frozen peas, and she thought that on a night like this simple was better anyway.

Sitting next to Ryan and Sierra, James felt the song coming back. "Rebecca," he whispered.

She'd been watching their mother, and she turned to look at him.

"Assassination," he sang softly.

She shook her head, but her voice, when she spoke, was not the one he was expecting. Gently, she said, "Shhh, it's okay." Then she actually smiled a little and gave him nice eyes and said, "It'll be better when Dad gets home."

"I'm not trying to be mean," he said softly. "What's the word?"

"What word?"

"Instead of 'assassination.' In the song."

"Anticipation," she said. "But I don't like that record anymore."

It was puzzling to James that she was being so nice to him. He said, "Do you still like Carly Simon, though?"

"Not as much. Now I like Stevie Nicks. Want to know something funny? Fleetwood Mac's album is *Rumours* and Carly Simon's, my favorite, was *No Secrets*." She sat back in her chair and waited, and James, who had no idea what he was supposed to say, nodded seriously as if he understood.

Sierra lifted her head. The side of her face that had been pressed against Ryan's back was pink and bore a crease from a wrinkle in his shirt. She was so pretty that Robert almost couldn't look at her. At least she wasn't Ryan's girlfriend.

His own girlfriend had reacted strangely to the news from San Francisco. Happy that they'd recovered from their first fight, he'd found her at lunch and was shocked first when she told him about the murders and even more so when she said, "Well, it's been a while, right? We're probably overdue." Once he found his voice and asked what she meant, she said, as if it were perfectly obvious, "Kennedy in '63, King in '68, another Kennedy in '68. It's been ten years if you don't count Squeaky Fromme and Sara Jane Moore trying for Ford in '75. Which you shouldn't, since they didn't actually get him." Robert nodded to show he knew all about the history but was dumbfounded by . . . what? Her coldness.

He watched his mother now, putting oddball food in bowls. "Wait," he said. "We're having *leftovers*?"

"No complaints," she said. "Next person to complain cooks the whole meal."

The children dispersed to other rooms. Left to themselves, Ryan and Sierra stretched out on his bedroom rug with their fingers laced behind their heads, a pair of stargazers. His right elbow touched her left elbow. At the end of the school day, they had stood in the parking lot and waited for their rides. He had told her first thing in the morning, before the news came, about his crepe at the Magic Pan. In the parking lot he told her the rest, about how he had seen the very building where the shootings had taken place, how he kept thinking about it, the columns, the arches, the giant dome. Somewhere inside that building there were two pools of blood. His ride came first, and Sierra told the mother driving that she was supposed to go home with him. At the Blairs', she called her mother and explained that she and Ryan had work to do together. "Later" was her answer to her mother's question about when she would come home. "This is important."

Sierra reached for his hand and kissed his fingers. "Your hand tastes like dirt."

He rolled onto his side and scooted forward. "Your ear tastes like . . ."

"What?"

"I can't remember what it's called."

He kissed her ear and the part in her hair and the inside of her elbow. She kissed his fingers and his neck. They lay on the floor with the door open, kissing experimentally—not to find out how it was to kiss, what kissing felt like; they would do that and much more over the next few years. No, that first day it was to discover and name all the smells and tastes available in the other, until now unknown despite all the years they'd been friends. The door was open, and the others wandered by, and still they kissed.

Most days Bill tried to leave the clinic by six, but today had been busy with sore throats and influenza, and the terrible news from San Francisco seemed to have slowed his staff, who paused to discuss it and tune in to the news when they got the chance. He was half an hour behind with his last patient, a two-year-old with thrush, and didn't get to his car until after six-thirty.

Driving home, he heard Dianne Feinstein's voice, a replay of her shaky announcement of the shootings. He wondered how his children had heard the news. He'd noticed a trend toward an abrupt and premature dissemination of information at schools, without an attendant plan for monitoring or responding to the students' reactions. Somehow, upon hearing the first reports from Guyana, he'd had the presence of mind to be glad the news was arriving on a weekend, with his children at home.

He parked next to the station wagon and stood for a moment in the cold air, thinking about how he might help the children. Penny was in the kitchen, her back to the doorway. "I'm home," he called, but she didn't turn around. At breakfast, neither of them had mentioned his evening visit to the shed.

He went to his bedroom closet, where he took off his coat and tie.

Rebecca and James appeared in the doorway. "Oh," he said at the sight of them, and heat swept into his face.

Rebecca said, "Dad, are you crying?"

He shook his head and held open his arms. James came running, but Rebecca stood where she was. He wrapped his arms around James and stroked his head.

"What?" Rebecca said. He hadn't turned on the bedroom light, so she was silhouetted against the bright hallway behind her. She was fifteen years old and nearly five-eight.

"Happy to see both of you."

James pulled back and looked up at him. "Dad, did you hear? Two guys were killed in the city."

"I did." Bill looked across the room at Rebecca. "You found out at school?"

She nodded. "It's not related to Guyana. They thought it was, but it's not."

"Yes, I heard that."

At dinner, the six of them took their usual places and Sierra sat on a chair brought in from the mud pantry—a chair that in recent months had been used mainly by Gina. Ryan pulled it so close it touched his own chair, and throughout the meal he held her hand as he ate, avoiding the foods on his plate that would have required him to drop her hand so he could use a knife.

James spent his talking time describing his newfound affection for Fleetwood Mac, Rebecca's current favorite band. He'd made a study of the album cover and spoke passionately, if not entirely convincingly, about how much he liked the picture of the bearded man with the ponytail holding out his hand for the blond lady.

Ryan said he wanted Sierra to stay as late as possible. After that he fell silent.

"I wonder," Bill said, "if you're remembering that we drove past city hall yesterday. After the Magic Pan. Did you tell Sierra about the Magic Pan?"

Sierra looked at Bill with her pond-green eyes. "He told me everything."

No one spoke. Robert didn't like the fact that she was sitting in Gina's chair. He wished it had occurred to him to bring Gina home—but what if she'd started up again about it being time for an assassination?

"I don't know if I want to take my turn," Rebecca said. "I kind of do and I kind of don't. I had a normal day. Normal except *that*—but that's sort of 'How did you like the play, Mrs. Lincoln?' I had a pop quiz in chemistry. I tutored lower-level math at lunch."

"You don't have to say 'lower-level,'" Robert said. "Obviously it's lower-level. You couldn't exactly tutor your own level."

Rebecca hesitated. In fact, she could and sometimes did tutor her own level. She decided against saying so. "Mrs. Emory said something interesting in English. She said Harvey Milk is more important than Mayor Moscone."

"That is interesting," their father said. "Did she say why?"

"Because he's a homo," James said.

"James," Robert said.

"He is," Rebecca said. "There's nothing wrong with it."

"I didn't say there's anything wrong with it," Robert said. "I'm telling him not to use that word."

"Wait a minute," Penny said. She was tired of the conversation, tired of being in the kitchen—tired, period. She wanted to get back to her studio but then remembered, with abrupt dread, Bill knocking on the door last night.

"What?" said Rebecca, who technically still had the floor.

Penny set down her fork, rattled. She strove to remember the conversation. "Can you really say one person is more important than another?"

"I imagine," Bill said, "she meant more important historically."

"She did," Rebecca said. "She said Mayor Moscone was just a mayor, but Harvey Milk was a homosexual supervisor."

James burst out laughing. "Who did he supervise? 'I'm going to make sure you do a good job being a homosexual!'"

"James," his father said a little sternly. "Supervisor is a job in city government."

Embarrassed, James fell back on the tactics of an earlier time and blew a wet raspberry at the table.

"Never mind," Rebecca said. "I'm finished."

"Are you sure?" her father said. "Robert?"

"Oh, that's right," Ryan said suddenly, looking up at Robert. "Did you break up with Gina?"

Irritation washed through Robert: he had forgotten his ill-advised announcement of the night before. What could he have been thinking, telling his family he was considering breaking up with Gina? Now he would have to worry that one of them—James—would tell her. He was glad he hadn't invited her to dinner. "Do you mind?" he asked Ryan.

"So you didn't break up with her?"

"No."

"Wait, you were going to break up with Gina?" Penny said.

"This might not be dinner-table conversation," Bill said.

James smirked. "Why, because it's about lovey-dovey stuff?"

"It's about private stuff."

"Not so private he didn't tell Ryan about it," Penny said.

"He told all of us," Rebecca said. "Last night. Except you. You were in the shed."

"I was working!" Penny said. "And it's not 'the shed.' It's my *studio*. No one," she went on, "seems to realize how hard it was for me to see my father so sick. Not even you," she added, looking at Bill. "And you know just how sick he is!"

"How sick is he?" Robert said.

"No sicker than a month ago," Bill said. "We just know a little more about it now."

James said, "What do we know?"

"Blood tells stories. So does urine. When someone like Grandpa feels tired, we can look at his blood and urine for hints as to what might be going on."

"But I thought he was tired because of his congested heart failure," James said.

"Congestive," Robert said.

"He is," Bill said, "so that makes it harder to recognize additional issues. A few weeks ago, Grandpa found out his kidneys aren't doing their job very well. Remember how your kidneys filter out waste products? When the kidneys aren't working, the waste stays in your blood, and that makes you feel sick. Sicker."

"I don't want Grandpa to die," James said. He thought about the noise he'd made Friday afternoon, pounding on Ryan and screaming, and for an instant he saw himself falling into line: a soldier stepping back into the march, hup-two-three-four. But this vision was no match for all the distress and confusion inside him, and he leaped from his chair and rushed at Ryan again, fists flying. "You said he'd be okay," he shouted. "You said, you said."

Penny screamed, Sierra tried to shield Ryan with her body, and Bill got up and wrapped his arms so tightly around James that James couldn't move.

"Shhhh," Bill said, his lips at James's ear. "Shhh shhh."

"Unbelievable!" Penny shouted. "James, go to your room!"

"The boy is upset," Bill said. Arms still wrapped tight, he crouched behind James, whose considerable strength was now devoted to backward kicks against his father's shins.

"No no no no no," James cried. "No!"

Bill braced himself, lifted James from the floor, and carried him out of the kitchen.

"Well, I think this meal is over," Penny said. "Dishes into the dishwasher, please." She carried her plate to the sink. Surveying the open containers on the counter, the dirty spoons and condiment jars, the empty milk and the crumb-encrusted half-stick of butter, she put her face in her hands and began to cry.

"Your mom," Sierra said softly.

Ryan held her hand tighter.

"What should we do?"

He led the way to the sink and patted Penny's shoulder; after a moment Sierra joined in. Penny shook her head and cried harder. "Never mind," she sobbed. "I'll do the dishes. You guys go, okay?"

They headed to the living room, followed by Robert and Rebecca. "Sierra," Rebecca said, "your mom should probably come pick you up."

"Half an hour," Ryan said.

He lay on the couch with his head in Sierra's lap. James had attacked him twice in four days, and though he couldn't have put it into words, Ryan believed James had chosen him because he wouldn't fight back. The upset Ryan felt now was not defensive but protective. As Sierra stroked his hair, he fell into a waking dream in which he was Congressman Ryan and James had shot him, and he was Mayor Moscone and James had shot him, and he was Harvey Milk and James had shot him, and in each of the three scenarios he rose up from the fallen and bloody body, himself again, and embraced James, who dropped his gun and wept. Ryan wrapped James in a tight embrace that squeezed the violence out of him.

Down the hall, Bill and James were sitting on James's bed. James had calmed down, and they were paging through a picture book of California, looking at places they might go once they began bicycling together. A two-lane highway in the Sierra foothills caught James's eye, golden fields on both sides, the road itself dipping behind hills and then rising into view again. "I want to go here," he said.

"It's very pretty."

"If I don't do anything wrong can we go for my birthday?"

Bill hesitated. It was so much harder with your own child: he wanted to discourage bad behavior, but he also wanted to provide an out, a refuge from total failure—a point of view James could adopt about himself if or when he did something wrong. Yet James couldn't be allowed to hurt Ryan; less for Ryan's sake than for his own.

"You know why I think you were mad?" Bill said.

"Why?"

"Because you're worried about Grandpa."

James considered this. "Maybe I was mad at Grandpa's kidneys."

"That's a good way to look at it."

"And his heart."

They looked down at the picture in the book.

"Can we?" James said.

"Sure."

"I'm glad Robert didn't break up with Gina."

"I am, too."

"Ryan and Sierra were kissing."

Bill took this in, surprised and yet unsurprised. Ryan had loved Sierra since they met. "They're very close. Did it make you uncomfortable?"

James picked up his pillow and hugged it, pressing his face against it and saying, "Oooh, I love you. Kiss-kiss-mmm-mmm-mmmm. Dad, who do you think will do it first, Robert and Gina or Ryan and Sierra?"

Bill took a deep breath. He had always answered his children's questions about sex as simply as he could and with close attention to how much they might really want to know. But until now the subject had been abstract. "I think you're wondering about sex," he said. "You're curious and your body is starting to change, and it's very natural."

"No," James said. "I'm wondering about fucking." He grinned and began chanting, "Robert and Gina sittin' in a tree. Eff You See Kay Eye Enn Gee."

"That's not a good word," Bill said. "I don't want you to say that word."

"Sorry."

"It's not a bad thing—it's a good thing. It's just a bad word."

James was silent for a moment. "I don't get how boys do it."

"Do what?"

"Eff You See Kay. Together."

Bill hesitated. "Any two people can make love."

"I'm probably not going to get married. I might be a bicycle racer. Can we still go to that place? In the book?"

The book lay open in Bill's lap. The hills were so golden he could almost smell them. "We'll make a point of it."

Robert lay on his bed, more and more bothered by Gina's having said the country was overdue for an assassination. She hadn't even said "the country." She'd said "we." She'd made it very personal, as if the two of them were the ones who were overdue. And "overdue"—that made it sound like a library book, which seemed awfully glib to Robert. Unserious. Here was something he hadn't properly considered until now: in addition to being less mature than he was, and less honest, she was also less serious. Was she really the right girl for him? Maybe not.

In another part of his mind, a small dark region governed by small dark motives, he saw that the only way to make sure James didn't tell her he'd been thinking about breaking up with her was to break up with her.

And in another region, bright with artificial light, he told himself that he didn't want to put her on the spot about sex—which, being a young man, he would inevitably end up doing—and so the noble, the kind, really the loving thing to do was to end it before things got that far. To protect her.

He noticed that one of his desk drawers was slightly open, and because of the drawer's contents he knew he had not left it that way himself. Who had been in his desk? He opened the drawer farther and grabbed the pack of cards that was not actually a pack of cards but a container for three foil-wrapped condoms. They were still there. He dumped them out and rehid them in the top drawer of his dresser, in the toe of a sock. He did need to break up with Gina. No matter how much he'd practiced putting condoms on, and he'd practiced plenty, he just couldn't imagine how you did that in front of a girl.

A little later, the doorbell interrupted Ryan and Sierra, lying on the couch wrapped in each other's arms. The room was generally lit by three lamps, two on tables and one on the floor, but once the others had left, Ryan had extinguished two, leaving himself and Sierra in the near dark.

"I think it's my mom," Sierra said.

"Probably," Ryan agreed.

Neither moved. They knew Sierra would have to go home and they didn't want to part until the last possible moment.

The doorbell rang again, followed by a knock.

"Where is everyone?" Rebecca said, appearing from the bedroom hallway and heading for the door. "You guys don't hear that?"

"We do," Ryan said.

Sierra's mother was on the doorstep, hugging herself against the cold. She resembled most of the Sand Hill Day mothers, with her unstyled hair and artless attire, a baggy tweed sweater and desert boots on her feet. But with her high forehead and small nose and bow-shaped upper lip, she was clearly Sierra's mother, though age had transformed Sierra's disarming prettiness into a somehow ordinary beauty.

"I'm sorry," Rebecca said. "Come in, you must be freezing."

The woman peered past Rebecca into the living room. Rebecca looked, too, and realized that from this angle, lying in the dark, Ryan and Sierra could be viewed as a little too cozy for eighth grade: Ryan on his back and Sierra more or less on top of him, their legs like crossed pairs of scissors.

"Hi, Mommy," Sierra said.

"Hi, baby." The woman stepped inside and said to Rebecca, "Sierra asked if she could spend the night, but I don't think so, do you?"

"Oh, my gosh," Rebecca said. "I'm not the mother. You know our mother, right? Penny?"

The woman laughed. "Of course. I know who you are, you're the amazing Rebecca. And I'm Janice."

"Mommy, don't embarrass her," Sierra said. "Or me."

Rebecca hesitated. "Did you want me to get my parents?"

"No need, no need. I'll just scoop these two up and take them back to our house."

Now Rebecca felt her eyes go wide.

"Oh, honey, I'm sorry," Janice said. "I was kidding. Baby, come on," she called to Sierra. "You two lovebirds will see each other tomorrow." She turned back to Rebecca and said, "I've been watching these two for years, cheering them on."

Sierra disentangled herself from Ryan and they both stood. Ryan tucked his hair behind his ears and took Sierra's hand. He whispered something into her ear and they came to the door. He looked radiant. When they were gone and the door was closed, he sat down on the entry hall floor and clutched his knees to his chest. Rebecca knelt next to him.

"This day," he said, "has been terrible and wonderful."

She was about to hug him but thought he might not want her to. Robert had had a girlfriend for almost three months, but until today she hadn't truly believed anyone in her family would ever love someone outside it.

But Ryan would—he already did. And he would be loved in return, for six years. Despite the forces of puberty, he and Sierra would grow to resemble each other—his hair growing longer, hers cut shorter; his clothing becoming a little feminine, hers a little masculine—so that when the end came, as it would when they were nineteen years old, they would feel as if they were dividing a single being with only one copy of each character trait.

Robert would break up with Gina on the day after George Moscone and Harvey Milk were shot, and he wouldn't date another girl until his sophomore year at the University of Michigan. She was from New York, and she told him after a couple of weeks that he was too nice for her. Next he tried to woo a midwesterner who told him after three dates that he was too caustic for her. The following year he developed an infatuation with a lesbian that kept him distracted and miserable for months. At last, still encumbered by his virginity on the night of his twenty-first birthday, he went to a bar on State Street with the sole intention of correcting this once and for all. He struck up a conversation with an older woman (it turned out she was thirty) who had no eyebrows and wore a head scarf. After a couple of drinks she confided that she had alopecia and was totally bald. After a couple more drinks he confided his problem to her. She invited him to her apartment, and they began a relationship that lasted until he left Michigan for medical school sixteen months later.

On the night George Moscone and Harvey Milk were shot, Penny washed the dishes and then went down to her studio. She knew she was failing to honor her word to Bill, but the circumstances were extraordinary and seemed to justify a postponement, and she was still there when the sun came up.

She served breakfast to Bill and the kids and then, once they were all gone, she drove to a furniture store in San Mateo and bought what was called, incorrectly for her purposes, a daybed. And from then on she slept in her studio, though no one but she ever called it that.

7

RYAN

She had such pretty skin. I looked at her and smelled her and touched her and didn't want to do anything else. Her mouth was sweet and rosy. I would rest my face against her body and feel full of love, more than I ever had before. This girl. People tell each other "You're mine" or "You belong to me." There are songs. I didn't feel she belonged to me. I felt she was part of me.

This is science—genetics—but it is also emotion. Mothers say it all the time. For fathers I think it can be too much, like looking at the sun or into the face of God if you believed in God.

She was born on August 7, 2002. About a week before, I had felt Marielle's cervix start to soften, and a few days after that my fingertip found an opening. Then one morning the opening seemed to have widened. Marielle had been uncomfortable, up with contractions in the middle of the night, and we called our doula. No, she said, it didn't sound like labor had really started. The contractions were irregular and too far apart. She urged us to go for a walk, as a change of scene or a way to move things along. We drove to the coast, to the small sheltered beach where San Gregorio Creek empties into the ocean.

It was deserted, socked in with fog. I wrapped a blanket around Marielle's shoulders and we made our way along the wet sand line. Ropes of seaweed lay in our path, smelling salty-sour. Gulls circled overhead.

Marielle was five-nine to my five-eight and she was sturdy, with beautiful broad shoulders and a small upturned nose. Pregnant, she was so much larger than I that we laughed whenever we saw our reflections in a shopwindow or the mirrored lobby of our OB's office. *La Géante,* she called herself. But she was still graceful, and as she moved across the sand I imagined a great ship gliding over the ocean.

"Love," she said, "you're too quiet, what are you thinking? Don't be frightened. It happens every day. Every minute."

I reached for her hand and squeezed it. I was scared about the pain. She wanted an intervention-free birth, and she liked to stick with a plan once she'd made it. I had asked my father to reassure her that the baby would not be harmed if she accepted pain relief. "I think she knows that," he said. "Don't you?"

"I'm okay," I told her now. "I'm excited."

A troubled look came over her face, and she turned away and vomited onto the sand. She heaved a second time and then a third, so violently she nearly lost her balance.

"Oh, my God," I said. "Are you all right, love?"

"I think so. I think I am."

"Maybe we should sit down."

"I'd never get up again. Let's go back to the car."

We took a diagonal toward the parking lot, leaving the wet sand. She held one hand on her belly and the other on my arm. As we reached the asphalt, a contraction gripped her, and my heart galloped. We were entering something unfathomable. We got into the car and began the climb up the mountain. A few minutes later she gasped.

"I should pull over."

"No!"

She timed them herself: steady, four minutes apart. She moaned as each began but was quiet as they continued. She vomited again in the hospital parking garage and again waiting for the elevator. "Sorry," I said to the people behind us. "We're sorry."

By the time she was checked it was too late for pain relief. In all the years I'd known her she had kept her hair very short, with little pieces hanging over her forehead and in front of her ears like the bristles of small paintbrushes curling as they dried. These were damp now, and once the nurse was gone I wiped her face with a cloth.

"Do you want to feel?" she said.

"Your cervix?" At home, the two of us lying in bed, it had been easy for me to snap on a glove and slide my fingers into her vagina—just an extension of our closeness. But her body seemed different on the sanitized paper liner of the labor bed. "What if I hurt something?"

"You won't."

"Do you want me to?"

"*Oui,*" she said, inhaling hard so that the syllable sounded even more French than usual.

I pulled on a glove. With her feet in stirrups and her back elevated, her vagina seemed very shallow, and my latex-covered fingertips found her cervix instantly. I could hardly believe it was the same thing I'd touched hours earlier. It felt a little like one of the rubber rings that came with the mason jars we bought for making jam one summer.

I washed my hands again and took a steadying breath. My phone vibrated in my back pocket. We wanted the birth to be private, but I'd called my father to alert him, and he'd called Robert and Rebecca. I turned off the phone and put it in Marielle's overnight bag.

She gripped my hand so tightly I could hardly pull my fingers apart after she let go. She labored in that room for less than two hours, but it felt like two days. Then she delivered our daughter with just four pushes.

A nurse told me that I cried out at the moment Katya was born, but I don't remember that. The earliest photo shows me calm at Marielle's side, eyes on the baby.

We spent two nights in the hospital and then stayed at the big house with my father for a week, happy to have our meals prepared for us. Rebecca told me later that no one expected us to go back to the shed. They all thought we'd get used to the house and eventually it would be our father who moved, to an apartment somewhere or even Rebecca's guest room. But we loved the shed and when we got back there, in the middle of August, we were so happy. I had two more weeks until school started, and we gave ourselves over to newborn-baby rhythms, slept when Katya slept, the three of us living life from our Murphy bed. The rough plank walls were hung with my students' paintings, special pieces they'd made for me, and postcards from art museums around the world. We liked pictures you could breathe in, landscapes and seascapes, blues and greens, and we had images of farmland and forest and ocean by first- and second-graders and by Titian and Monet.

The shed was surrounded by trees, so it was cool and dark, and there were days when we didn't go outside. Other days we carried Katya up to the big house or put her in her car seat and drove to a pretty outdoor place, a park or café, for an hour in the sun. Marielle wanted bright, clean tastes, and I flavored herbal tea with spearmint leaves and sliced lemon and served it to her iced as she nursed. One morning she asked for something sweet, and I drove down to Webb Ranch and bought half a dozen containers of raspberries and blackberries; while she and Katya slept, I baked a pie with a lattice crust. Marielle woke first and I arranged some pillows so she could sit up and then brought the pie over and held it close as she pulled off sticks of golden pastry and dipped them in the steaming purple fruit.

In those first weeks, Katya made noises like a mewing kitten as she emerged from sleep. When she nursed she sounded like something smaller and less feline, though we couldn't think what it was. Her hair was thick and black and after a bath dried in a soft Mohawk.

The night before school prep started, I couldn't stand the thought of leaving, but once we were in our next phase it was okay. When I got home each afternoon Marielle handed Katya to me or I lay down next to her, and we found our way back together.

I didn't get scared until my father's pneumonia. He began coughing on a Thursday evening and by Monday he was in the hospital on IV antibiotics. It wasn't Katya's immediate health that concerned me, the time she'd spent in his company before his symptoms began. It was what she'd face in the months and years and decades to come. Somehow I had not thought about this. She was going to get sick. Coughs, colds, fevers, worse. She was five months old and it was not if, it was when. In bed the morning after my father's admission to the hospital, I began to cry. With the heel of her hand, Marielle pushed my tears away, up toward my ear. A little trickled in and I shivered.

It came upon me at odd times. I had her in a baby swing at Peers Park in Palo Alto, green and shady on a day in early May. She was about nine months old. I was pushing her gently and saying, "Higher, higher," and suddenly I could hardly stay upright, I was so distressed by how dangerous it was to be alive.

Another time, after she'd started walking, we were all at the zoo and I lost sight of her briefly. She wasn't far away, a few yards, but for a second or two I had to look for her. That was all: I had to look for her. I hadn't thought about all the times when I wouldn't know where she was.

And then there was the night James met her, when she was seventeen months old, just after our father died. James was in Chile when he heard, and he had to make his way home, flying from Santiago to Panama City to Houston to San Francisco. He'd been away so long I was nervous about seeing him, not knowing what he'd be like.

His flight landed very late. Robert and Rebecca went to pick him up at the airport while Marielle and I waited at the house. We'd put Katya to sleep in one of the bedrooms, but at the sound of the car doors she started crying, and I went to check on her. She was in the collapsible crib my father had bought for grandchild naps, half asleep but alert enough that she heard me and lifted her head. When she saw me she pushed herself onto her knees and raised her arms.

"Get you out."

"Little baby, it's nighttime."

"Out."

I lifted her and her head went straight to my shoulder. I hummed a little and tried to put her down again, but she shook her head and I knew she needed to be held for a while. I carried her to the living room, James becoming audible as we got closer. He was talking fast.

"This guy in first class, had to be a drug lord, multiple diamond rings, a maroon leather jacket—"

"Maybe he just had bad taste." That was Robert.

"No, he was definitely a drug lord."

I reached the living room and saw James before he saw me. His hair was matted and he wore an old motorcycle jacket over a faded T-shirt. He had bloodshot eyes and dry, cracked lips. He'd been traveling for twenty-six hours and had to be exhausted. But he looked aged, too, as if he'd lived through more time than I had since we were last together. He'd left in the summer of 2002, shortly before Katya was born, with a thousand dollars and a tense look on his face. We heard from him irregularly via email. Once or twice he called our father and asked for a loan. After these calls our father always seemed sad, and Robert speculated that he was disappointed in James. I thought he missed him.

"Hey," I said.

He looked up, and all at once I wished I'd left Katya in the crib.

"Fucking fuck!" he cried as he crossed the room to us.

"This is your niece."

"Kind of figured."

"It's amazing to see you, J."

He hadn't shaved in several days, and up close he looked even more tired. Holding out his arms, he said, "Will she come to me?"

Katya buried her face against my chest, and I stroked her head. "She's a little sleepy now." I signaled to Marielle to come get her, and then I wrapped my arms around James. He felt thinner than he looked, and he smelled bad, like old cooking oil and unwashed hair. In the days since my father's death I'd cried so much I was surprised there was more in me, but there was. I cried, he didn't. "Let go," he said at last, barely audible, and I stepped away.

Later, back in the shed with Katya and Marielle sleeping inches away from me, I recalled the look on his face when he first caught sight of Katya. It made me uneasy. I remembered being five or six years old and following him around the house as he pointed at things and said, "Want!" Then I thought of the yearning Katya might inspire when she was older, and I was terror-struck again.

After our father's funeral, James stayed home for two or three months and then moved back to Eugene, where he'd lived briefly in the early nineties. He sounded pretty good when we talked, so I wasn't prepared for how unhappy he seemed when he showed up. It wasn't just the way he went after Robert. There was something sad in his eyes. Even his hands looked sad, the way he held them as he sat, one index finger curled around the other.

I told Marielle I thought it was love troubles. He'd had love complications in the past, or relationship complications, but not love troubles.

Her name was Celia, and as soon as I saw her picture I understood. Faces fit with other faces. Sometimes it's a match and sometimes it's a contrast. Theirs was a match. They both had dark eyes and good chins. Their earlobes were the same, long and unattached. They both had strands of wavy hair framing their faces.

Late one afternoon he showed me picture after picture. We were on Rebecca's couch, sitting opposite the large painting of the land. I loved being there with him and the painting, and I held his computer on my lap and put my feet on the coffee table and sank into the photographs.

They first met in some kind of group, so there were a lot of pictures of her with other people. James liked to take candids and I got to see her unposed, maybe unaware of the camera. Talking to another woman, she leaned forward and held her fingertips to her throat. She had small, plump hands with dimples at the knuckles. In a couple pictures she sat cross-legged on the floor with her children draped over her like shawls and seemed to glow with happiness.

He said he didn't fall in love right away, but he was drawn to her. She was kind to people. She had a way of listening that made you want to keep talking. He talked and talked and told her he didn't usually tell people so much about himself. She said, "I hear that a lot."

We came to a photo of the two of them sitting on a picnic bench in front of a table piled with food. Her hands were together in her lap, one on top of the other, and her head was turned in his direction. He was looking at her, but she didn't seem to be looking at anything—more looking at nothing because she was listening so carefully.

"That was last spring," he said.

"She already loved you."

He tipped his head back against the couch and stared at the ceiling. I put my hand on his, and he let me keep it there for a moment before pulling away to scratch his jaw.

There was a picture of her alone, a close-up of her face and torso. She wore a long, droopy white sweater that flared out at the bottom. The sleeves covered her hands and flared out, too. She was like a cluster of closed white lilies held upside down.

Another one I liked showed her lying on a bed, her head propped in her hand. She wore a bathrobe and her feet were bare.

"Oh, you shouldn't see that," James said, reaching for the computer.

I had seen pictures of him with other women, but this was different. Celia was different. Marielle thought so, too, and she hadn't even seen these pictures. We'd talked about it as we were falling asleep the night before, hoping it would work out for him.

"You'll love her," James said.

"Of course I will."

"No, I mean you'll really love her. We'll have you guys for a visit once we get settled. *If* we get settled. Selling the house will be huge for me."

I looked across the room at the painting. On that autumn afternoon Rebecca and Walt's living room had a milky light that seemed to bounce off the walls and hover over the painting like a fine mist. There was a thing I did sometimes, blinking the house into place in the painting and then blinking it out again, but I couldn't do it now.

"Am I terrible?" he said. "Do you hate me?"

I loved the house, but I knew we couldn't hold on to it forever, just as I knew that Marielle and Katya and I couldn't live in the shed forever. My dad's death had started the clock ticking. I said, "It's been three years since Dad died. Almost three years. It's probably time."

"No, not selling the house," he said. "Do you hate me about that? I'm sorry, I know it's not what you want."

"No, it's okay. Really, it's got to happen eventually. You mean Celia?"

"Yeah. Am I terrible?"

"Of course not. It's complicated, and obviously her kids have to be protected, but can love be terrible? I don't think so."

"You're such a simpleton," he said, but he closed the computer and put both palms on it and seemed peaceful.

Living in the shed had changed for us after the Vincents rented the big house. With my father up there, the shed had been like a suite that we occupied in a large shared house that included a lot of land in addition to two separate structures. Once he was gone, our space shrank to the shed and the spur off the driveway. Then Susanna started practice babysitting for us—playing with Katya for half an hour here, an hour there—and we got friendlier with them. They invited us to dinner and while the girls were in another room told us they were worried about Daphne. She had trouble making friends, she didn't like school, she was terrified of squirrels. "You know that thing 'failure to thrive'?" Lewis said. "It's like that, only mental."

"It's not only mental," Lisa said. "She has allergies, she burns after five minutes in the sun."

"I didn't mean it's *only* mental," Lewis said. "It's both. She's like the boy in the bubble. You remember the boy in the bubble? His immune system didn't work, so everything affected him? Everything affects her."

A few days after James showed me the pictures of Celia, I arrived home to find a fire truck parked at the foot of the driveway. I raced down the spur to the shed, dropped my bike, and ran inside, but no one was there. I ran up to the big house, where two EMTs stood at the base of the steps, talking to Marielle. Katya was in her arms and I was worried she'd been hurt, but when she saw me, she wiggled to the ground and ran to greet me. She was wearing a pair of overalls that had originally belonged to Robert's boys, but Marielle had sewn flowers and butterflies on them, and as she got closer I saw big new daisy patches on the knees.

"Daddy."

"Look at you," I said. "Look at those daisies." I hugged her but kept my eyes on Marielle.

"It's okay now," she called.

Holding Katya's hand, I joined Marielle and the EMTs. Daphne had gotten stuck inside an end table and Lisa had called 911. The EMTs had tried a number of things before finally turning the table on its side. From there they had helped Daphne get one foot free, and after that, the rest was relatively easy. Daphne was upset but not hurt physically.

"Lewis?" I asked Marielle.

"In Chicago."

"I guess this is like a cat getting stuck in a tree," I said to the EMTs. "Or do people really call for that?"

"I never had a cat," one of them said.

"I had a cat on a roof," the other said, "but it was hurt."

They said goodbye and headed down the driveway. I looked at Marielle and shook my head. "Oh, dear." Dusk was falling fast, and as I glanced up at the house the kitchen lights went on. This illuminated the Halloween silhouettes Lisa had put in the windows, arched black cats and witches with pointy hats. It was a couple days after the holiday, and it wasn't like her to have left them up. Something was wrong in there. "Should we go check on them?" I said.

Marielle squeezed my hand. "They need to recover." She put her arm around me and we started down the driveway.

Katya ran ahead and I said, lowering my voice, "That must've been awful."

"It was. Poor Lisa. The firemen kept telling her not to worry, but she was *bouleversée*."

"And Daphne?"

"Screaming when we first got there, but she was pretty meek by the end."

We were almost at the spur where Katya was waiting, and with a look we agreed to finish the conversation after she was in bed.

Dinner was leftover chicken stew, and once Katya was bathed and in her pajamas the three of us sat on the love seat and worked on a story we'd begun a few evenings earlier about a small bear whom we called the Katya bear. In the past Katya always wanted a book, but lately she'd started asking if she could "be the story," so we had several small Katya-like animals enjoying adventures of one kind or another.

"Tell what she learned," Katya instructed Marielle. "Tell about how she saw the other bear be stuck."

"She learned that some places are smaller than they look."

"But why?"

"Because you can't always tell what something is like from the outside."

"Like omelets?"

I smiled at Marielle; Katya had recently discovered that inside an omelet you might find something other than cheese, something dismaying like spinach.

"Kind of like that," I said.

"*Why* the other bear got stuck? Why her mama didn't tell her not to go?"

"I think the mama bear must not have known what her little bear was doing."

Katya sat in silence for a moment, taking in this troubling idea. "Well, what about . . . what about . . . what about the Katya rabbit?"

"The Katya rabbit is sleeping now," Marielle said, "and it's time for that in our house also."

It had been only a few months since we'd put a bed in the side room for her, and I imagined tonight would be one of the nights when she asked to sleep with us. Instead she slid off the love seat and bowed her head for Marielle's kiss and then followed me into the other room. It was tiny, with just enough space for the small bed we'd created with cinder blocks and plywood and custom-cut foam rubber; a regular twin wouldn't fit. We'd been thinking we'd have another three or four years, but now it seemed we'd be gone before she outgrew the room.

I tucked her in and sang a song or two. "I'm sleeping," she said as I finished. "See my eyes?"

"They're closed tight."

"I'm squeezing them."

"I see that."

"I'll squeeze them all night, okay?"

"Okay, baby."

A little later, Marielle finished with the dishes and joined me on the love seat, her hands still damp as she took my face and kissed me. We sat together, one of her legs draped over one of mine.

I said, "We may be hearing more about that other little bear."

"Poor little bear. Lisa told me she wouldn't go to school yesterday. She went today but only lasted till lunchtime. Too bad they wouldn't let her go with you."

I had suggested Sand Hill Day when the Vincents first talked about taking Daphne out of the local elementary, but like a lot of people, they thought we were old-fashioned because we didn't have a computer lab. This was initially a matter of funding, not principle, but as other schools adopted more computer-based learning, we recognized that we wanted to keep our students' eyes in the classroom.

"We're not for everyone," I said.

"Maybe you should offer again, for next year. You could get her in, *non*?"

Like every private school on the Peninsula, we had more applications than openings, but unlike at most other schools, our admissions process occupied the entire staff, and many children were admitted because of an outside relationship with one teacher or another. As Tom, our director, often said, it wasn't fair, but it was true. He didn't mean true in the sense of factual. He meant true in the sense of faithful to who we were. We worked hard to be the community we wanted to be.

I said, "I think so."

"They should take her to therapy, that's what they should do."

"I like it when you're opinionated. It's very alluring. Very French."

"Ach, that did it."

She was referring to a joke of ours about what did and didn't turn her on. Usually I could put my thumb on her nipple and move it around a little and she'd get aroused. Other times she was slow to light, like a fire with damp kindling. And then there were occasions like now, when a scrap of conversation got her going and I had to catch up with her.

"Really?" I said.

"Yes, but is our child even asleep?"

I climbed over her and went to the door. I opened it a crack, enough to see Katya's head on her pillow. Her eyes were no longer squeezed tight, just softly closed.

"She is."

Getting ready for the night was a little complicated, but we had it down to a science. We'd attached these caps called Magic Sliders to the legs of the love seat, and when we were ready for bed it was easy to slide it out of the way so we could open the Murphy bed. The love seat temporarily blocked access to the bathroom, but you could climb over it.

"It'll be okay," Marielle said.

I knew she meant leaving the shed, and I nodded. It would be. Sad but okay. We'd been here almost seven years. I remembered the first time she saw it, about a week after we met: I was living in the big house with my father, and I brought her over to meet him. Penny had been in Taos for several years, but the shed was still full of her stuff, and I showed it to Marielle not with any idea that we might live there together but because she was curious. "Tell me about her," she said as we stood on the threshold and looked in at the worktable and the narrow bed. "She must have been very sad, no?" I said no, I didn't think so.

And I didn't. Thinking of Penny now, I recalled a summer afternoon toward the end of high school when I needed to ask her something. The door to the shed was open, but she wasn't there: it was empty, her bed neatly made, her worktable cluttered with papers and paints and glues. The extra room was empty, too, and so was the bathroom. I turned around and there she was, coming from the driveway. She was wearing blue espadrilles. I said, "Were you up at the house? I don't know how I could've missed you." And she said, "Oh, no, when it's this beautiful out I can't stay inside and work all day. I went for a stroll. Too bad you didn't come down sooner, we could've gone together." All those years when we tried so hard to keep her with us: she hadn't wanted to go that far away.

"You're thinking about your mother," Marielle said.

I smiled, loving the way she understood me.

"I can't believe James hasn't talked to her since Robert and Jen's wedding. Do you think he really didn't speak to her at our wedding? The whole weekend?"

"It's possible," I said. James had stayed with Robert and Jen that weekend, the house overflowing with Marielle's family.

"Maybe you should help him call her."

"That's a good idea."

"Come here," she said, and I walked into her arms.

Sand Hill Day School was located on Cañada Road, on land formerly used for grazing cattle. It was made up of a series of low-slung dark brown buildings connected by covered walkways. The idea was that in the rain you would be able to go from building to building without getting wet, but unfortunately this wasn't true. Because of the way the buildings were sited, even the lightest rainfall was blown sideways, and a quick walk during a downpour guaranteed a drenching.

For this reason we kept dozens of plastic ponchos near the classroom doors. The ponchos were color-coded so the students didn't have to bother opening one and looking for a size tag, they just reached for the right color: red for the big kids, green for the in-betweeners, blue for the little guys. In October or November, whenever the first storm of the season hit us, we taught the new children how to pull on a blue poncho and duck their heads and go. Every Sand Hill Day student got this lesson, which was how the phrase "grab a blue" entered our lexicon as a metaphor. It meant something like "get ready" but without any admonishment, more with encouragement and confidence. When we told a student to grab a blue, we were telling her that we knew she already possessed the skills to tackle the challenge at hand. We were saying: "You can do this."

It seemed to me that Daphne didn't know how to grab a blue. It rained the day after Lisa called the EMTs, and once my students left I shook out the wet ponchos and thought maybe Marielle was right and I should bring it up with the Vincents again, Sand Hill Day as a possible alternative.

As I headed to our four o'clock staff meeting, I got a call from Marielle, unusual for the busy end of my day.

"Sorry, love, but it's Daphne again."

"Oh, no. What?"

"She came down here. By herself. The babysitter didn't even realize she'd left the house. I don't know what to do. She's acting strange, and I can't reach Lisa."

"Strange how? Did you try Lewis?"

"Apparently he's on an airplane. She's in Katya's bed and won't get out."

"What's she saying?"

"She won't talk."

I told my colleagues I had to leave and went to the bikeport. The rain had stopped, the clouds had cleared, and it was colder. Off to the west the sky was a quiet, fading blue, with streaks of salmon above the hilltops.

By the time I got home, Lisa's silver sedan was parked just past the turnoff for the spur. The main room of the shed was crowded, with Marielle, Susanna, and an older teenage girl all standing at the door to the side room.

Lisa leaned over Katya's bed. "Please stop, please stop," she was saying to Daphne. "Please, please, please." Then she turned and saw me. "What should I do? Lewis is out of town. What should I do?"

Daphne lay on her side with her knees drawn up and held close to her chest. She was making a noise I couldn't decipher, not quite speech but close. I leaned down. "Daphne, honey, what's the matter? Don't you feel well?" The sound she was making turned into the word "no," but it was more of a chant or a hum, like a yoga teacher saying "Om" at the end of class.

"'No' what, Daphne? Can you help me understand?"

She clutched her knees tighter and shook her head.

I went back into the main room and Lisa followed me. "What should I do? What should I do?" She began to weep, and Marielle led her outside. Susanna sat down with Katya, and the two of them began coloring together. Only the teenage girl and I remained standing in the room.

"Are you okay?" I asked her.

"I went to the bathroom. I wasn't ignoring her."

On some level I knew the situation was critical only because everyone was so worried, not because of Daphne's behavior. But I still felt anxious.

"Ryan," Susanna said from the floor.

I looked over at her.

"Just tell her she has to leave."

Katya came over, and I lifted her and held her on my hip. Lisa came back inside. Her blond eyebrows looked especially pale because of how red her face was.

I said, "What do you want to do, Lisa? Can she just stay here until she's ready to go? She will be eventually, you know. Sooner or later. We can give her a snack and bring her up to the house."

"No." Lisa shook her head vehemently. "I can't let that happen. That's not okay."

"Why?"

"I don't know. It's just not."

"Let's step outside," I said. "All of us."

I waited for everyone to go and then carried Katya out. Deep in the woods as we were, it seemed evening would begin any second.

"I think there are two possibilities," I told Lisa. "You leave her here and go up to the house and wait, or I carry her up to the house. Actually, no, I can't do that, I don't want to do that. The thing is, I don't think everyone waiting here is a good idea." I looked at Marielle. "What do you think, love?"

"Leave her," she said to Lisa. "At least for a bit. Lewis's flight lands soon, *non*? Go. You'll be happier calling him from home. The other girls can stay if you like."

The babysitter looked uneasy. "I kind of have to get home? Soon?"

"I'll drive you," Marielle said. "Are you close? Katya, do you want to go for a ride?"

At last everyone had something to do. Lisa and Susanna headed up the spur, Marielle knelt on the backseat of the Jetta buckling Katya into her car seat, the babysitter settled herself in the front seat, and I went back inside.

I moved around the main room, wanting to let Daphne know that someone was nearby but not about to confront her again. After a few minutes I heard a noise and turned around. There she was: cheeks flushed, like a child just awakened from a fever. She said, "Where is everyone?"

"Your mom went back up to the house. How are you doing?"

"Fine." She shrugged. "I was tired."

"Would you like something to drink?"

She went over to the love seat. She wore a denim skirt and her legs were bare, with red patches behind the knees that looked like eczema. Sitting down, she crossed her arms tightly over her chest and stared straight ahead.

I filled a mug with water and took it to her.

"Actually, I just want to go home."

She kept a distance of several feet between us as we walked. At the driveway she said she would go the rest of the way by herself, but I said I wanted to go with her. It was almost dark.

The house came into view and she stopped. "My mom's here?"

"Yes."

"What about my babysitter?"

"Marielle and Katya drove her home."

"And my sister?"

"Here, as far as I know."

Daphne stared at the house. "I'm not ready to go in."

"Okay."

"Where's my dad?"

"On his way home from Chicago. I think Chicago."

"It'll take about a year."

"What's that?"

"Crashing the house down and building a big one. Okay, I'm ready now."

We climbed the steps, my mind lagging as I thought about what she'd just said. No wonder she'd had such a hard week. Not only was she dealing with whatever tension her parents had about the house, she was also probably worried about where she was going to live during the construction, if it happened.

We'd reached the top step, and Daphne looked at me expectantly. I knocked.

There were footsteps, and Lisa swept open the door. Relief flooded her face, as if she had not been sure Daphne would survive. I realized I should have called her to say we were on our way.

"Oh, my God. Daphne. Ryan. Come in, come in," she urged, beckoning me forward with one hand while with the other she pulled Daphne close.

I hadn't been inside the house in months—not since an afternoon in late summer when Susanna asked if she could babysit at home rather than at the shed so she and Katya could play with her Barbies.

Susanna appeared from the bedroom hallway. I waved at her and she waved back. She stared at her sister. After a long moment she turned and headed away.

"What am I going to do with you?" Lisa said to Daphne.

I saw some form of heartbreak pass across Daphne's face, and I turned away and stared into the living room. Something about it was different. I tried to remember it from the summer, and of course it was nighttime, and fall, and the curtains were drawn across the windows, but that didn't seem to be it. Was there a new couch? Then I got it. An end table was gone. The end table. In its place was a floor lamp with too much space around its base, and indentations in the rug where the table legs had been. I felt sick with pity for Daphne, and I said I had to get home and hurried out. At the top of the steps, I waited for my heartbeat to slow down.

It started raining again the next day, and it was still raining Sunday morning. Katya had slept in the Murphy bed with Marielle and me, and she and I stayed under the covers while Marielle got up and made our café au lait—or, in Katya's case, just plain lait. We got a call from Mémé and Pépé, our names for Marielle's parents. They were a big part of our lives: we visited them every summer and they spent a week in California every January. In contrast, Katya had met Penny only twice, and she had no memory of either occasion. We'd shown her photos of herself in Penny's arms, but they seemed to confuse her. She understood the idea of grandparents—Mémé was Mama's mama and Pépé was Mama's daddy—but she couldn't make sense of a grandmother she didn't know.

It was different with my father. She claimed to remember him, but I thought it more likely that she just wanted to remember him because we all talked about him so much, and Sammy and Luke remembered him, and we lived down the hill from his house. I'd wanted her to have the house as a tie to him; I'd wanted that for all three of his grandchildren.

Late in the afternoon we headed to Robert and Jen's house for an early dinner. Much of the ground floor was taken up by a giant family-room-and-kitchen combination, with couches and easy chairs at one end and a long reclaimed pine table in the middle and, at the other end, a kitchen outfitted with a six-burner stove, an island with a prep sink and a heavy-duty stand mixer, and a massive wood-fired oven. As soon as we arrived, Katya raced through the kitchen and dove onto the couch where Sammy and Luke were watching cartoons.

"Katya, no," Luke cried, "don't, you're not allowed," and Jen quickly apologized and said she'd turn it off, and Marielle explained for the tenth or twentieth time that it was fine with us, TV at other people's houses.

"You're not going to be able to do it, you know," Robert said, twisting off the cap of a beer.

"What's that?" I said.

"The TV thing. You're going to have to get one."

"To put where?" Marielle said, our usual response to comments like this, but then she glanced my way, and all at once it occurred to me: if we moved we would no longer have space constraints to explain our not having a TV. We would no longer have space constraints to keep us from buying bags upon bags of groceries at a time, inevitably resulting in waste. We would no longer have space constraints to keep us from accumulating toys and games and puzzles at the high-speed rate of most parents we knew, who didn't seem to notice that the more their kids had, the more they wanted. We would no longer have space constraints to help us live the way we wanted to live.

I said, "Well, it looks like we're going to get the chance to rethink a lot of things."

"I don't get it!" Robert exclaimed. "Why aren't you more pissed off?"

"I'm just not."

Jen called for the boys to turn off the TV anyway, and Robert asked me to give him a hand getting wood for the oven, which Jen was going to use for homemade pizzas. The garage was very tidy, with Jen's minivan on one side and Robert's Saab on the other and the family's four bicycles parked in a careful line, each with the forward wheel turned to the right.

"You're your father's son," I said.

He rolled his eyes. "What, the garage? Jen keeps it like this, not me. In fact, I've been thinking lately that I'm my mother's son."

"Rob, are you okay?"

"How could I possibly be okay? Our idiot brother shows up out of the blue mooning over some woman and we're supposed to drop everything and sell our house?" He sighed. "Sorry, I didn't mean to bite your head off. Can you imagine what Dad would say about all of this, though? Adultery with kids involved? He'd be appalled."

I wasn't so sure. "He'd be concerned," I said, "but I think he'd also be curious. He'd want to know what James loves about her."

Robert shook his head impatiently. "Aren't you the good little hagiographer. Dad was plenty moralistic."

"For himself. Not so much for other people."

"You think he didn't give Penny massive shit for abandoning the family? Not that she didn't deserve it. And do *not* say he pushed her away."

"I never said that. I said maybe she *felt* he pushed her away. Rebecca thinks—"

"Rebecca thinks it's complicated!" Robert said. "What does Rebecca not think is complicated? Ask her name and she'll equivocate. Come on, let's deal with the wood."

Back in the house, Rebecca and Walt and James had arrived. James was with the kids—all three of them talking at once, clamoring for his attention—while Rebecca, Walt, and Marielle stood in the kitchen with Jen.

"Daddy," Katya called.

I waved at her. "Hi, baby."

"What do you see?"

"I see a girl with her two cousins and her uncle, sitting inside on a rainy day."

Katya got up from the couch she'd been sharing with Luke and climbed under a square wooden end table. "Now look. Now what do you see?"

I glanced at Marielle, who was also watching. "I see a girl under a table."

"But who do you see? Who am I being?"

"Who are you being?"

"You have to guess."

"Are you being Katya hiding?"

"I'm not hiding. You can see me. Who am I being *like*?"

"You're being like Daphne," Marielle said. "Aren't you?"

"But I'm not stuck. I can come out if I want. Should I come out?"

"If you want," I said. "You're okay under there. You're safe."

"What's going on?" Robert said.

I realized that everyone was watching now. "The Vincents' younger daughter," I said, explaining what had happened.

"Really?" Jen said with a frown.

"The EMTs had to turn the table over," Marielle said. "If that hadn't worked they were going to take it apart."

"And then on Friday," I said, "she came down to the shed and got into Katya's bed. And wouldn't leave."

"Are you talking about that kid?" James called. He made his way to where we were all standing. "Vince's daughter? The little one?"

I nodded. Glancing over my shoulder, I motioned for everyone to gather closer so the kids wouldn't be able to hear us. I said, "I kept wishing I could consult you, Rebecca. She was just lying in Katya's bed, saying no over and over again."

"Rebecca and I saw this," James said. He looked over at her. "Don't you remember? She got under a table in the living room and her mom was *pissed*. You don't remember?"

"No, I do," Rebecca said.

I turned to Rebecca. "Wait, you guys saw the same thing? With the table?"

"We saw something," Rebecca said.

"When? What did you think she was doing?"

"Maybe Wednesday? I thought she was . . . saying something. Without words. But I wouldn't want to speculate."

"Speculate," Robert said. "This is interesting."

"But not appropriate."

"She's not your patient, is she?"

"I'm not comfortable with it."

"Exercising good boundaries?"

"Good sense," Walt said.

Rebecca's expression didn't change, but I thought she must love it, the way he came to her aid. I liked the word "helpmeet" as a synonym for spouse or partner. It sounded Shakespearean, but I'd used it in conversation with a Sand Hill Day parent a month or so earlier and learned it was a biblical term. People on the religious right used it to justify the idea that women should serve their husbands. Too bad, because to me it described so nicely what marriage was about, though going in both directions. Walt was a good helpmeet for Rebecca. Though Robert found him boring, I saw a man who only appeared colorless but whose blood was a deep, rich red.

"We felt bad for her," Marielle said. "Well, for both of them. Daphne and Lisa. When she got into Katya's bed . . ."

"It was hard," I said.

"But you did just the right thing, love. He sent everyone away and just waited for her to get up."

"And she did, eventually. And oh, I forgot to tell you this, love. I walked her up to the house, and right before we went inside, kind of out of nowhere she said it would take a year to build a new house. To 'crash it down and build a big one,' that's what she said. Obviously they've been talking about it in front of her. That's got to be adding to her stress."

"It's sure adding to mine," Robert said.

"Robert!" Jen exclaimed. "Can you please not do this tonight?"

"What do you think the problem is?" Marielle said, turning to Rebecca. "Susanna's fine, it's not the parents."

"It's never the parents," Jen said. "It's how they come into the world."

"Yes, but their temperament dictates how parents are with them," Rebecca said. "A feedback system develops from birth onward. You could argue that it starts *before* birth. The baby influences the parent who influences the baby who influences the parent . . . The Vincents could function one way with Susanna and completely differently with Daphne. Think about it. No two siblings have the same parents. My father was not the same person as Robert's father. My mother was not the same person as Ryan's mother."

"And God knows she wasn't the same as mine!" James said. "Hardy-har, let's all laugh now."

"You didn't get the best of her," Rebecca said. "I think we can agree on that."

"But you're saying I got what I deserved. Being such a problem child."

"I'm not saying that at all. Maternal ambivalence is always—"

"Kidding!" James said. "Jesus, let's tank this topic."

I asked the kids if they wanted to help me set the table, and they raced over. Sammy carefully and deliberately put a fork and knife on each napkin, and Luke followed after him and just as carefully and deliberately turned each fork upside down or sideways, anything to undo his brother's work. Sammy got mad, and while I distracted Luke with a story about a mountain lion our school custodian had seen early one morning, Sammy went around one more time and corrected them. He was so like his father.

After we ate, the kids went to Sammy's room and the adults took over the couches and easy chairs. The rain had tapered off, and it was dark out. Marielle and I sat close together on one couch, while Rebecca and Walt shared the other. Robert, Jen, and James were all in armchairs.

I closed my eyes and listened to a conversation about fish oil turn into an argument between Robert and James. There had been a news report linking higher levels of a certain omega-3 fatty acid to a reduced risk of Alzheimer's, and James said maybe now people would start taking supplements, as he'd recently begun doing. Robert said there was a difference between cause and correlation and asked James if he knew that the study had been funded in part by a company that manufactured fish oil supplements. James countered that fish oil had also been shown to aid heart health, that people who regularly ate fish had healthier hearts than people who didn't, and Robert asked James if he was sure it was the fish. "Think about it," Robert said. "Say I eat a lot of fish and my heart is healthy. Is that because of the fish, per se? Or is it because by eating fish I'm avoiding red meat?"

"I can't believe I'm related to someone who says 'per se.'"

"I can't believe I'm related to someone who's planning to break up a family."

No one spoke, and I became aware of the dishwasher sloshing at the other end of the room. I said, "Please, you guys." Then my eyes were burning. "Why do you have to do this?"

"I think 'have to' is a good way to put it," Rebecca said.

"Hear that, James?" Robert said. "We're acting under a compulsion."

Marielle reached for my hand, and I let my head fall to her shoulder. I wished we were back home at the shed, the three of us. It was our cocoon—our tiny, happy bubble. How would we bear losing it?

Robert and James went back and forth, and I spaced out. I stared across the coffee table at Walt and Rebecca. They never touched in public, but the back of his hand was very near the back of hers, and I wished one or the other of them would extend a finger and close the gap. Marielle always said she thought they had a strong erotic bond. She even used that phrase, "strong erotic bond," though that was probably because it turned me on.

I wished my father had lived to see Rebecca married. He hadn't lived to see James married, either, though this had never seemed like a real possibility until now. Then it occurred to me: James and Celia could have a child together. There could be another Blair in the world. This made me incredibly happy. I looked over at James, and he gave me a strange look back, almost as if he knew what I was thinking. But then he spoke.

"Listen, you guys," he said. "About the house. I have a different idea."

8

THE PIECE

The Blairs got a second phone line when Robert entered high school but a third car only when Ryan began to drive. By then Robert was away at college and Rebecca was a senior. The car was a Honda Accord meant for Bill, who planned to pass down to the kids his '68 Plymouth Valiant with the proviso that they use it only around town, where a breakdown would be manageable. It was a bright February Saturday when he drove home in the new car, forest green with sumptuous leather seats. Everyone admired it. Then Penny said she wasn't really comfortable with the idea of the kids driving the ancient, ailing Valiant; it would make more sense for them to take over her reliable station wagon, the car they most often borrowed. She said to Bill, "I'll drive the Valiant . . . unless of course you don't want *me* taking it on the freeway, either. In which case I guess I could drive the Accord."

So Penny got the new car and Bill kept driving the Valiant, through 1981 and a new transmission; through 1982 and a breakdown on Market Street in San Francisco, the car dead in the middle lane as the traffic light went green and red and green and red and people honked incessantly; through 1983, when, on the very day Ryan graduated from high school, the odometer finally passed 200,000; and all the way up to the January night in 1984 when James drunk-drove Penny's station wagon up the driveway, misjudged the distance to where his father's car was parked, and hit its rear end with so much force that the car leaped forward and slammed into a wall.

Both cars were totaled, but James walked away with some bruised ribs and a forehead laceration that required five stitches—that and a parentally mandated three-month suspension of his brand-new driver's license.

The incident brought him a certain amount of celebrity at Woodside High, and he began to get invited to the parties from which underclassmen like him were usually excluded. At one of these, a few weeks after the accident, a senior girl named Cindy pulled him into a bathroom, kissed him wetly for a few minutes, then stuck her hand down the front of his pants. "Tell me," she said as she stroked him, "is it true you wrecked both your parents' cars in one night?"

"Not exactly," he said, trying not to gasp.

She stopped moving her hand and said, "I heard you wrecked two cars."

"I did. They just weren't exactly my parents' cars anymore."

The bathroom was off the main hallway of the house, and he could hear people yelling and laughing. She started working again. "Are you in a ton of trouble?" she asked hopefully.

For James, losing his license had been nothing compared to the look on his father's face—not right after the collision but later, when the two of them were in the emergency room and James was holding a towel to his forehead. It wasn't even disappointment he saw; it was exhaustion. Of course, it was two o'clock in the morning, but his father's exhaustion looked deep and expansive, an ocean rather than a temporarily flooding river. "I'm sorry," James kept saying, "I'm sorry." His father just shook his head and wouldn't really look at him. In the car going home they were both silent until Bill turned in to the driveway. Penny, asleep in the shed, didn't know yet. Bill braked at the turnoff, and James was afraid he'd be sent to wake his mother. Instead Bill reached over and brushed his fingertips along James's hairline, just above the bandage covering the stitches he'd received. He said, "Do you remember the night of your poison oak? We got home right around this time." He waited, but James didn't respond, and finally he drove the rest of the way up the driveway. There was broken glass everywhere; when the tow trucks were finished in the morning there would be a lot of cleaning up to do. "You don't remember?" Bill said, and James shook his head, although he did.

He wasn't going to tell Cindy any of that, though. He said, "Grounded for life."

She smiled. "Can you sneak out?"

"Our laundry room has a door to the outside, and my dad's room is pretty far away, so you know. It's not really sneaking."

"What about your mom? You have a mom, right? I heard your mom wanted to throw you out."

"I threw her out. She lives in the shed."

"Funny," Cindy said. "You know Tony Misner?"

James shrugged. People were always asking if he knew this person or that person. If he said no, they acted as if something was wrong with him, so he stayed noncommittal. This contributed hugely to his popularity, though he didn't know it. He was about to cream his pants, so he batted her hand away and pushed his jeans to his knees.

"Ew," she said, looking away from his dick. "I don't want to see it."

"Yes, you do."

When they got back to the living room, the crowd had grown even larger and spilled through every opening, including the front door, which had been closed earlier by Michael Greer, the kid whose house it was. Greer had the idea that if everyone stayed inside, the neighbors wouldn't find out about the party. James saw Greer on the kitchen floor and figured the night was winding down. He was supposed to be home at midnight, but that wasn't going to happen. It already hadn't happened.

In the backyard he found the three guys he'd come with, two juniors and a senior named Rufus who'd driven them in his Jeep. "Want to get out of here?" James said.

"I don't know, I think there's more beer," said one of the juniors.

"Did Cindy blow you?" said the other.

This embarrassed James, and he stuffed his hands into his back pockets.

"HJ?" Rufus said. "That's her specialty."

"You guys are wasted," James said.

"I heard she fucked Tony Misner," Rufus continued. "The night before he got sent to boarding school. Kind of a goodbye fuck."

The other guys snickered. "Nothing like a good-luck fuck," one of them said.

They headed for the kitchen, James following. There was a crowd circling something, everyone staring at the floor. James squeezed forward and saw Greer flat on his back with a pee stain on his pants. Someone was kneeling next to him, saying, "Greer, come in, please. Greer, do you read me? Do you read me?"

"Maybe we should go," said Rufus.

"Watch, now he'll puke," said someone else.

James followed the guys to the car. He grabbed shotgun and then told Rufus to stop before they'd gotten ten feet from the curb. Rufus glared at him. "What the fuck? You were the one that wanted to leave."

"I think we should roll him on his side."

"Greer?"

James opened the door and stepped down from the Jeep.

"I'm not waiting," Rufus cautioned.

"People shouldn't inhale barf," James said.

"People shouldn't inhale weed," said one of the juniors, "but we all do it."

The crowd in the kitchen had thinned, five or six people leaning against the counters or sitting at the table. Greer was motionless on the floor, his face flushed and sweaty. You were supposed to remember A-B-C: airway, breath, circulation. James didn't want to stick his hand in Greer's mouth, so he just knelt and tried to roll Greer on his side; he went too far and Greer's face hit the floor. "Nice one, Blair," someone said. "You want to give him a bloody nose?"

James went back outside and tried to figure out who might be heading to Portola Valley. No one. Greer's house was in Redwood City, in a confusing area where most of the streets were named after states. James headed in the direction he thought would take him out to Woodside Road, but after a while he thought maybe he'd gotten turned around. It was February and cold. Every house he passed was completely dark. He wondered if he might find a back door unlocked. He wasn't going to call home, but he could call Rebecca, whose Stanford dorm was only a few miles away. She didn't have a car, but her roommate did.

He made his way up a short driveway to a gate. It creaked really loud and he hurried back to the sidewalk. Some German shepherd would probably kill him. He wished he knew how late it was, but he didn't have a watch, which was unfair: both his brothers had watches from their grandfathers, and he had nothing. Grandpa Greenway's watch wasn't even nice, it was a Timex with a stretchy metal band, but Ryan had inherited it and wore it every day. Robert didn't wear his all the time, and it was actually worth something.

The better treatment his brothers got was a subject rich with the power to enrage him, and as he walked he felt the injustices of his life gather above him as if he were a cartoon character followed around by his own personal rain cloud. There was Robert's silky passage through school and the way his father showered praise on him, which Rebecca should mind more than James did, seeing as she was a better student than Robert and a lot less of a bragger besides. There was Ryan's position as the family pet, like people actually petted him, even now, when he was a college freshman.

But James was pretty sure neither of his brothers had gotten jerked off at a high school party. Cindy was a slut, but that went with the territory. Who else was going to jerk you off? He'd never heard of Tony Misner, but if James got shipped off, as his mother threatened at least once a week, he was going to make sure he got Cindy alone somewhere for a few minutes before he left.

He'd spent half his life listening to Ryan and Sierra moaning. After Robert left for college, Ryan took over Robert's room, and with the closet door open, James heard everything. Oh oh ohhhhh. Almost worse was when she started to sleep over—she wandered around the house in her pajamas with her hair unbrushed, as if she were one of them. James didn't understand why his father allowed it. Neither did his mother. "What are you thinking?" she screamed when she found out, which didn't happen for a few months because she never slept in the house herself. His father said, "What am I thinking? Do you actually care what I'm *thinking*?" And she said, "Is that girl on the pill?" And he said, "I think that's private." And she said, "For God's sake, you're a pediatrician." And he said, "Are you suggesting I don't know about unwanted pregnancies?"

It was the summer before Rebecca started college. She told James that he wasn't old enough to understand that their father was actually watching out for Ryan and Sierra by allowing them to sleep together—otherwise they would do it somewhere else. "If people want to have sex," she said in her most schoolteacherish voice, "they're going to have sex." James was furious that she thought he didn't understand that. He was thirteen and knew plenty. The conversation took place on a cool July night, after Rebecca had picked him up from a movie. They sat in the car, pulled over just before the turnoff for the driveway, for five or ten minutes.

"What do you care?" James said at one point. "You're not even going to be here much longer."

"I'll be two minutes away. Why do you think I chose Stanford?"

"Because Dad paid you."

Rebecca rolled down her window—the car was old enough that you actually rolled it. "Dad didn't pay me."

"Why are you doing that?" James said. "You about to light up?"

"James, it's stuffy. You see people breaking the law everywhere you look."

"Ryan *is* breaking the law."

"But that's just it. He isn't. I'm not—I'm just going to college. Robert just went to college. We don't mean to be leaving you behind."

At that, James got out of the car and ran. She looked for him, driving slowly with the brights on, but he hid in some bushes and at last she yelled out her window that she was giving up, going home. He walked through the front door twenty minutes later, and she had covered for him—told their father there was a mix-up and someone else had picked him up from the movie. Now here he was three years later, wandering around a maze of little streets in Redwood City, and whom would he call if he found a phone? Rebecca.

He walked for another ten minutes, wishing he'd paid attention in school when they talked about using the stars for navigation. At last he turned a corner and saw a commercial road up ahead, and in a few minutes he was at a pay phone.

Rebecca was in her junior year at Stanford, a double major in biology and psychology, the kind of college student who blocked out her study schedule in a Filofax. She designated twenty-minute breaks every three hours because she'd found that to be the best plan for optimal efficiency. On this Friday evening, she had done some reading and then typed up a paper for her Developmental Psychology class. She went to bed at one, and when the phone woke her sometime later, she figured it was her roommate, skipped the greeting, and said, "Just try to be quiet when you get here."

"Rebecca?"

James's voice was unmistakable, the lowest-pitched of her brothers' voices and hoarse from the late hour or drinking or marijuana—from who knew what.

"I'm lost," he said. "Well, not lost, but I don't have a ride home. I'm fucked."

He told her about the party, about his ride leaving ahead of him because he'd gone back inside to make sure a guy didn't asphyxiate his own vomit.

"Aspirate," Rebecca said. "Wait, what are you talking about? Where are you? Dad must be worried, why didn't you call Dad?"

"I didn't want to wake him up!"

"James, he's not asleep. You know he's not."

"Well, what should I do?"

Rebecca was already pulling on jeans, the phone tucked between her chin and her shoulder. She told him to stay where he was and then called her father, who answered on the first ring. "The corner of Woodside Road and Kentucky Street," she said, "but I'll get him—I just wanted you to know he's okay."

"Rebecca," he said, his voice choked with gratitude.

"I know, Dad, it's okay." She paused. "It turns out he was being a Good Samaritan."

As soon as she said this, she knew she shouldn't have. Her father wanted to know what had happened, and what she knew was so much less than what he wanted to know that by the end of the conversation he was saying he'd go for James himself.

"Dad, no, it's much easier for me."

"James said this boy vomited?"

"No, he said he rolled him over just in case."

"So he was unconscious?"

She knew she'd lost by then, but she didn't have the ability to hand over problems to other people. She pretended she was giving in, but once she'd hung up she left her room and went to the lounge, where she found someone willing to lend her a car.

Hurrying through the parking lot, she let herself understand the absurdity of two people going to pick up James, but she also knew she could be useful to her father, just being there.

The roads were all but deserted. Her psych paper was on attachment theory, and as she drove she thought back over what she'd written. From the moment she'd begun her research, she understood that she'd found words for partially formed ideas she'd had most of her life. She believed James's chaotic character reflected an insecure-ambivalent attachment to their neglectful and distracted mother, and that monotropy, the child's need to attach to one main caregiver, meant that despite their father's attempts to be a good substitute, James had suffered maternal deprivation. Rebecca and her brothers had tried to mitigate it by watching out for him, but they hadn't succeeded.

She wondered what John Bowlby and Mary Ainsworth, two of the central psychologists behind attachment theory, would think of Penny. From another psych class Rebecca knew that most people parented the way they had been parented, and she wished she'd been more alert during visits to her grandparents' house, so she could have studied her grandmother's relationship with her mother. Then again, she knew from her father that his mother had believed it wasn't a good idea to hug or hold children, and her father certainly hadn't followed that model.

She slowed down so she could see the street signs. Though she'd told James to wait at the phone booth, she knew he might have chosen to walk, thinking he'd intercept her. She saw a phone booth and slowed, but it was empty. She passed a bar with a "closed" sign in the window, in front of it two men drinking from paper bags. Please don't let that be James, she thought, and then: Please don't let that be what James becomes. He hadn't really sounded drunk, but he'd had time to walk it off. He'd certainly been drunk on the night of the accident. Her father had told her later that James's blood alcohol had measured .09.

She happened to look across the street, four lanes of traffic and a median strip, and there were her father and James, James climbing into the Accord. Leave it to James to have gotten the side of the street wrong! "The south side," he'd said on the phone. "No, the north. No, the south, I'm positive."

She made a U-turn, pulled up abreast of her father, and powered down the window.

"Ah, Rebecca," he said. "Isn't this just like you, coming to help anyway? I want to check on James's friend before we go home."

From the passenger seat James gave Rebecca a furious look.

"I'll follow," Rebecca said, "just in case."

They wound through the streets until James recognized the house. There were some kids out front, two sitting on the hood of a car, three or four on the front lawn with cans of beer.

It was a scene with very different meanings for each of the three Blairs. James felt guilty, as if he'd led a bloodhound back to the foxes, even if his father was a pretty mild bloodhound who had no interest in disturbing the foxes, much less reporting them to the police. Rebecca, who'd never been to high school parties herself, found the sight discomfiting because it was so unfamiliar; she wondered not if she'd missed out but if having skipped this part of adolescent life might compromise her ability to be a good psychiatrist. Empathy was a big part of the work, and she wasn't sure she had it. Sympathy, yes, but she wasn't sure she had empathy.

Bill felt the passage of time. The years of his life as a father had 365 days each, and the days had twenty-four hours, and while he didn't remember all of them, he knew about them; he sensed them. Yet there were times, the present moment among them, when it seemed he'd skipped great chunks of his children's lives and couldn't fathom how they'd gotten so far along without his noticing. With James, the moment a few weeks back of seeing the cars totaled was an obvious one. And somehow this evening, this late hour in front of this strange house: the big-boned teenager in the seat next to him seemed unrelated to the primary James, who was forever five years old in his father's mind, innocent and passionate. Bill supposed that for every child there was a defining age, a fixed reference point in relation to which his parents would always view him; whereas the child's own truest self would always be the present one.

And thus could begin any number of problems.

"Let's see how your friend is doing," he said to James.

"I'll stay here."

"I'd like you to come with me, son. Can you do that?"

"What do you need me for?"

"The folks in there don't know me from Adam."

"They don't know their ass from Adam," James said, but he got out of the car.

Greer was still on the kitchen floor, but someone had set him on his side with pillows front and back so he wouldn't roll. Otherwise, the room was empty.

"Someone was thinking," Bill said, more to himself than to James, but James took it as a rebuke and stifled an objection. It was true that he'd been thinking, but it was also true he hadn't really done shit.

Bill knelt and put his fingers to the boy's neck. His pulse was normal, but his respirations were quick and shallow. "What's his name?" Bill asked, shaking the boy's shoulders and slapping his face lightly. "Son, wake up," he said to the boy. "Wake up. What's his name?" he asked James.

"Greer."

"Greer, it's time to wake up." Bill tried a sternal rub, his knuckles hard against the boy's upper ribs. The boy let out a guttural groan but stayed limp.

Bill got behind the boy, pushed the pillows away, and tried to lift his head and shoulders. Greer's chin flopped to his chest. "Help me," he said to Rebecca, and together they sat Greer up, but Rebecca didn't have the upper-body strength to support half of Greer's weight all the way to the car. "James," Bill said, "step in here, son." On the count of three they lifted Greer, James supporting him under the knees while Bill wrapped his arms around the boy's chest. Once they'd gotten him into the car, Bill took off, leaving Rebecca to drive James home.

At the ER, Bill found a couple of orderlies to bring out a gurney. He didn't take much call anymore, and he wondered if he'd recognize the attending. He hadn't on the night he'd brought James in.

He found the charge nurse and explained the situation. "I'm concerned," he said. "There was alcohol and marijuana and who knows what else. Parents out of town."

He stood by while the boy was given IV normal saline and a catheter to collect urine for a tox screen. The attending was a woman Bill knew slightly, not from medicine but because she lived in Portola Valley, one hill over from the Blairs. She ordered blood tests and a head CT when Bill couldn't say there hadn't been a fall.

"So this is how it works?" she asked Bill. "You move away from call right around the time your teenagers start having crises in the middle of the night?"

He smiled. "That's about the size of it."

Midmorning, Rebecca sat at the kitchen table watching James, his forehead supported by his hand and a plate of half-eaten toast pushed away. She'd slept in her old room, and the only way she could be sure her father had been home at all was a lingering smell of soap in his bathroom. Where had he gone so early on a Saturday morning?

"Dad's too old for this," she told James.

"What did I do?"

"Hmm, that's actually a decent point. You're right."

"I didn't *make* a point. What are you talking about?"

"Sorry, I'm going too fast. When you asked the question 'What did I do?,' I realized you hadn't done anything, so I said, kind of by way of shorthand, that you'd made 'a decent point'—meaning you'd been right to object."

"Blah blah blah. What's that noise? Is someone talking?"

She left the table and got herself more coffee. It was strange to be home; aside from short breaks from school she hadn't lived here since the summer after her freshman year at Stanford, when she'd worked at the lab of her Intro to Psychology professor. The following summer—last summer—she'd worked for a human biology professor at the University of Michigan, a job she got through Robert, who had graduated and was spending one last month with his girlfriend before moving to San Francisco for medical school. Rebecca's whole time in Ann Arbor, she saw Robert exactly twice. It had been a valuable learning experience for her, a lesson about the power of assumption. "Sorry," he said both times. "Are you mad? I'm just really, really busy."

James sighed heavily.

"Honey," she said. "I know it's been hard this year with all of us gone."

"Ryan's here all the time."

"It's not the same."

"How would you know?"

Ryan was a freshman at UC Santa Cruz, back most weekends because Sierra was at home figuring out her next move and working part-time at Sand Hill Day.

"Is it the same?" she said. "What's it like?"

"I wish I could puke," James said. "Or take a huge crap. Have you ever noticed you wake up earlier when you have a hangover?"

"How much did you have to drink?"

"Enough, Rebecca. All right? Enough."

"Alcohol or questions?"

"God, I pity whoever gets you for a shrink." He picked up a heel of toast, bit into it, and tossed the rest back on the plate. "I'm taking a shower," he said. "Really great to see you, thanks for stopping by."

Rebecca watched as he left the kitchen. He had grown five inches in the last year and had the hands of a giant.

She headed down the driveway but stopped at the spur. The shed windows were open, and she could hear the high-pitched whine of her mother's power saw. Penny had gotten rid of her kiln and turned the tiny extra room that had housed it into a woodshop so she'd have a place to make frames for her new work. She was doing assemblages, essentially 3-D collages: she used sleeves from worn-out clothing, sprung mousetraps, plastic hair curlers, even discarded food wrappers (there was always a cellophane egg noodle bag, attached to the wallpaper background with a thumbtack). Basically she was making collections of domestic detritus. Lately she'd been adding broken bits of crockery, an idea that Rebecca believed she had borrowed from a famous artist in New York.

Rebecca knocked and the sound stopped; a moment later Penny opened the door. She was forty-nine but looked older, with her steel-gray braid hanging down her back and an absence of makeup so complete that her face seemed to have been cut out of a sepia photograph. She said, "How funny. I dreamed you were in the house last night, and now here you are."

"I was in the house last night," Rebecca said. "I'm leaving, I just wanted to say hi."

Penny had pushed her goggles onto her forehead, and now she took them off and used the back of her wrist to wipe a lock of hair away from her eyes. "How is it outside? I was about to go up."

"Clear, maybe sixty."

"Where's your father? I thought I heard the car earlier."

"Gone somewhere," Rebecca said, but as she spoke it occurred to her that he'd returned to the hospital to check on Greer.

"Well, I'm going to need the car later. I'd love it if you would talk to him about getting another car. The three of us can't survive with just one."

"The two of you," Rebecca said. "James can't drive."

"Oh, how long will that last?"

Rebecca shrugged, not interested in a conversation about James; he and Penny were in mortal combat these days. She peered into the shed. The twin bed was shoved into a corner, and the room was jammed with assemblages, two and three deep against the walls. On the high shelf just below the ceiling, Rebecca noticed a collage she'd never seen before, strips of different blues that she could just make out were torn from maps. "Is that new?" she said, pointing. "I like it."

Penny looked over her shoulder. "No, I don't do collages anymore—I just moved things around a little for a change of scene. Do you want to come in? We could have some tea."

"I have to get going."

"I got one of those kettles you plug into an outlet and it boils water in a minute or two."

"I really have to get going, I borrowed a car."

Penny tipped her head to the side and looked closely at Rebecca. "You're almost twenty-one. When are you going to forgive me?"

Rebecca was surprised by this, almost too surprised to wonder what Penny was referring to, what particular transgression was on her mind. But wonder she did. There was a long list of possibilities, but there was also the simple fact of Penny's personality. Could someone apologize for that? Could you expect her to?

Then again, Penny hadn't actually apologized. Rebecca had been wondering lately if her mother ever apologized or even felt guilty. According to Freud, there were two sources of guilt: fear of authority and fear of the superego. Rebecca wasn't sure how strong Penny's superego was. Or James's. Her father's was mighty.

"Mothers and daughters," Penny was saying, "can have a very hard time getting along. You may not know this, but Grandma and I really struggled."

"Did you?" Rebecca said, the question itself an effort and perhaps also a token of forgiveness.

"She wanted me to be like her."

"Content?"

"She wasn't content! She sure wasn't content with me."

Despite having wondered about this just the night before, Rebecca found that she didn't want to talk about it. She had a lot of work to do and said goodbye, feeling some guilt herself as she headed for the car and even more as she decided to see if her father was at the hospital.

Penny watched Rebecca walk away, but she was thinking of her mother: not as she'd been in the last years of her life but long ago, the mother of her young childhood. "Penny, *please,*" that mother was always saying. "Come *along.*" And Penny would have to leave her crayons, leave her paste, and do as her mother wished. It was no wonder Penny was so protective of her art; she'd needed to protect it for most of her life. In adolescence she'd hidden her drawings in the back of her closet, her mother was so scornful of her "hobby," as she called it. "Do something useful," she was always saying. Inevitably, Penny gave it up. Art wasn't adult, she told herself. Only romance was adult, and marrying saved her. For a time. Bill began pulling away during Robert's babyhood, and though getting pregnant with Rebecca brought him back for a while, he became even more remote with two children in the house. When she was pregnant with Ryan she felt barely any tenderness from him at all. It had made her so sad. "What's *wrong* with you?" her mother said during one visit to Sacramento when Penny had no energy to take the kids to the park. "I thought this was what you wanted."

No, *this* was, Penny thought as she put her goggles back on and returned to her power saw. This was.

The day was glorious for the middle of February, the temperature heading toward seventy; when Rebecca got back to campus, she changed into running clothes and jogged to the hospital. She paused in front of the entrance. Robert had been denied admission to the medical school, and it troubled her to think she would probably be accepted and probably go.

She took the fire stairs to the pediatric ward and found her father in the corridor, wearing his white coat and badge, as he always did at the hospital even when just stopping in. He thought visitors were comforted by the sight of white coats, and he didn't mind being stopped with questions, especially simple ones about directions or visiting hours. "It's part of the job," he always said, "to allay anxiety. When we can, we should."

"Is that Greer's room?" Rebecca said as she joined him. "Is he okay?"

"He will be."

"Is he still passed out?"

"Rebecca, you know I can't say. What brought you here? Just checking?"

"On you."

"Well, I should have expected nothing less." He pulled her close and kissed her forehead.

Through an open door Rebecca saw the bottom portions of two beds, and two pairs of feet draped with sheets. "Are his parents in there?"

"Walk with me," Bill said. "Let's get some fresh air."

They walked back to her dorm, where Bill kissed her forehead again. The temptation to take advantage of her maturity was powerful. He could think of nothing her point of view wouldn't likely illuminate, and her competence in virtually everything she undertook meant her help was always helpful. How soothing it had been to hear her voice on the phone last night, telling him where James was. Bill didn't know if he could have kept calm had the call come from James himself, over an hour past his curfew and just weeks after the nightmare of the accident. Bill had been waiting up that night, too, and the sound of the cars colliding had shaken him deeply. Opening the front door and seeing the wreckage: he hadn't felt that combination of horror and dread since his first days in the navy.

He drove home, trying to decide if he'd say anything to Penny about where he'd been and why, given that it would have to include at least a little about what James had been up to. He'd last seen her at dinner the evening before, a typically gloomy fifteen minutes of the two of them plus James spread out at the formerly crowded kitchen table. The tradition of everyone taking a turn to talk about his day had been abandoned when Ryan left for Santa Cruz. It probably would have been abandoned earlier if not for Sierra, who had participated eagerly whenever she was present.

Penny was on her way up the driveway before he'd gotten out of the car, and he decided to keep quiet. "Morning," he said. "Or I guess I should say 'Afternoon.'"

"Where have you been?" she said. "I can't be stranded here all day. It's absurd for two adults to share a car."

"It's quite common, actually. Are you going somewhere?"

"I thought I would."

"That's fine, that's fine. What's James doing?"

"I haven't seen him. What makes you think he's up? It's not even one yet."

Bill shrugged and went up the steps. Rebecca had said James was heading for the shower when she left, but his bedroom door was closed, and when Bill knocked gently and pushed it open, he found the room dark and stuffy, with James facedown on his bed, asleep. Penny was in the master bedroom, opening and closing drawers. Bill didn't like to think of himself as avoiding her, but if he came up with a legitimate reason to do so, he used it. This sometimes involved checking on things, and now he left the house and headed for the garage, where he checked on plant food and fertilizer, thinking it might not be a bad idea to spend a few hours in the yard tomorrow. The family bicycles were neatly parked in the rack he'd bought to keep them organized, and on a whim he wheeled his and then James's out to the driveway, where he pumped air into the softening tires and used a rag to clean the gears. While he was working Penny got into the car and drove away, which coincided nicely with his running out of things to do outside.

He returned to James's room and sat on the edge of the bed. It was still the room of little boys, with baseball quilts and desks so small that a few books and puzzles rendered them all but useless for homework.

James groaned and lifted his head a few inches.

"Good afternoon," Bill said.

"What time is it?"

"Two something."

James groaned again and buried his face in his pillow. "Maybe I'll just skip it."

"What's that, son?"

"The day."

Bill opened the curtain. Bright light spilled into the room. "That's a lot to skip."

James rolled onto his back. "Don't give me any crap about life being precious."

"Check."

"Is it nice out?"

"Very. Good day for a bike ride. I actually just pumped our tires."

They hadn't taken a bike ride together in years, not since an accident that sidelined Bill when James was twelve. They had ridden up Page Mill Road and were heading along Skyline when a squirrel darted in front of them. Bill braked, lost his balance, and hit the ground, all before James knew anything was amiss. He was riding behind his father, and then his father was lying on the shoulder of the road, gasping in pain. James had no idea what to do. He thought—this went through his mind—that maybe if he moved slowly enough, someone would come along to help before he'd gotten to his father. He put down his kickstand very deliberately and then carefully turned his forward wheel to balance the bike. "James," his father said when at last he'd gotten there and knelt down. "It's okay. Don't be scared."

What happened after that? James turned thirteen, Ryan turned sixteen, Bill bought the Accord. The bicycles stayed in the garage. James occasionally sat in his closet, held his old stuffed dog in his lap, and listened to Ryan and Sierra in Robert's bed. It excited him when they stopped talking—he knew they were getting down to business. Sometimes as he listened to their groans and sighs he stroked the dog, and sometimes he stroked himself. That summer he told his father he was no longer interested in father-son bike rides. "You're a teenager," Bill said in his kind, understanding way, and James—proving the point?—said, "And you're a genius."

Now, with the possibility of a ride hovering between them, James rested the back of his forearm over his eyes. "It's too bright in here."

"Your pupils are adjusting."

"Where's Mom?"

"I believe she's doing some errands in service to an art project."

James snorted.

"What?"

"'In service to.' It's like the art orders her around. Do this, do that."

"Very commanding, that art."

"It's a fucking five-star general."

"James."

"You started it."

This was true, and it silenced Bill.

"I'd rather go by myself if I'm going."

"That's fine."

"Actually, who am I kidding, I'm not going anywhere."

Bill patted James's shoulder and left the room. They came together a little later in the kitchen, where Bill made sandwiches and they ate without talking.

They heard the Accord climbing the driveway, and in a moment Penny was in the kitchen, shopping bags in hand. She'd been in Menlo Park, at the decorators' shop that sometimes supplied her with scraps of wallpaper for her assemblages. She looked different—her cheeks a little pink, eyes bright.

She said, "Guess who I ran into?"

In the parking lot she'd spotted Mary Lawson, wife of Bill's old friend and colleague Harold Lawson. It had been a few years since they'd met, but something made Penny call hello, and Mary was warmer than Penny remembered, asking after each of the kids by name. She had grocery bags full of club soda and tonic, and when she saw Penny notice them, she said she was having a small birthday party for her husband the following evening.

"She invited us," Penny told Bill. "Six o'clock at her mother's."

"Robert's coming down for dinner."

"I really want to go. She said any and all of us."

"You don't think she was just being polite?"

"What if she was? Her mother's an art collector, you know." Mary's parents had begun buying in the early sixties, and after her husband's death Phyllis Grant had become even more active, collecting pieces by nationally known artists as well as up-and-comers in the Bay Area. Penny thought there was a real possibility that Mrs. Grant would be interested in her work. "Please," she said. "I can't go without you, and it could really help my career."

"You don't have a career," James said.

"James," Bill said.

"No, he's right. I don't have a career. That's the problem. That's why we need to go to the party."

Bill took the lunch plates to the sink and began washing up. "Quite the artist, your wife," a colleague had said to him a month or so earlier, and Bill had smiled wryly, even gratefully, before realizing the other man was speaking with admiration. He was referring to Penny's annual Christmas card, that year a series of green strokes on midnight-blue paper, with flecks of gold and silver. It was lovely, Bill thought, but was there any more to it than that? She tinkered, she played, but was she an artist? With the children he tried to conceal his doubt, but he knew he'd done a poor job concealing it from her. The thing was, it had all started so—what was the word?—amateurishly. Innocently. A young mother crayoning with her children. The years when Robert and Rebecca were elementary-age and Ryan and James were still at home: he could recall the difference in her on certain days, an ease, a temporary disappearance of the troubled look with which she most often greeted him when he came in from work. And alongside the children's pictures on those days there'd be one or two created by an adult hand. She'd be relaxed, languid, almost post-orgasmic.

"Please?" she said. "Robert will understand."

"You know I don't like to go back on my word."

She sighed and turned to James. "You're not even dressed. Have you done your chores?"

In order to get a reaction, James once told a teacher that his mother made him clean the entire house, top to bottom, every weekend, but in reality she asked only that he keep his room and the children's bathroom tidy and in any case cared more that he obey her than that the work be done.

He nodded.

"Well, you better have," she said, gathering her bags. "I'm going to talk to Robert," she told Bill as she left. "I'll call him."

Because when else might she meet an art collector? As she headed down the driveway she thought again—she'd been thinking about this a lot lately—of how the inequities of the patriarchy extended through every realm. Male artists got far more attention and gallery representation than female artists, especially female artists working in a purely feminine idiom, as she did. All of this had become clearer to her after she encountered the work of Judy Chicago. With *The Dinner Party,* Judy had said women mattered, women's lives mattered, women's bodies mattered and were beautiful. If Penny was entirely honest with herself, she would have to admit that on first consideration the giant ceramic vaginas at the center of *The Dinner Party* had made her a little uncomfortable, but she understood now that was the point. What was disturbing was powerful.

Her own work was not disturbing, at least not in the same way. It disturbed assumptions. It said the tossed-away artifacts of daily life could illuminate life. Surprisingly, Robert seemed quite interested in what she was doing. When he drove down from the city, he always asked what she was working on, and he was the reason she'd started using cellophane egg noodle bags. One morning she had a pile of things on the kitchen counter and he walked in, saw what was actually a piece of garbage on the floor, and said, "Here, don't forget this." "Very funny," she said, but she took it anyway, and now those homely bags were integral to what she was doing.

Robert might have been surprised to discover that his mother found him supportive, but he would not have minded, not in the way he might have at an earlier age, when it seemed that to be in favor of her was to oppose the rest of the family and therefore himself. He didn't think much about what she did in the shed, but he had adopted a bemused attitude, and he often stopped in to see her latest efforts.

But this was never his reason for going to Portola Valley. More and more, he had something on his mind that he wanted to discuss with his father. On the Sunday of the Lawson party he had something particularly pressing, and when his mother called that morning to ask if they could reschedule, he said he'd come down anyway and meet his parents at the party.

It was dusk when he arrived at the Atherton mansion. There were four or five cars parked ahead of him along the driveway, but the Accord wasn't among them, and he sat and waited and remembered the bright April afternoon when he'd last been at this house. The woman who'd spoken to him that day had seemed so much older than he, but he guessed now that she'd been in her early twenties and that the age difference between them had been no greater than the one between him and Julie Anne, the woman he'd left in Michigan.

Like a mildly uncomfortable physical state that ebbs from consciousness in the face of more immediate concerns only to reassert itself later with extra force, his yearning for Julie Anne emerged from behind the mundane problems of the day, and he began to ache for her. Medical school left him no time for any kind of social life, but somehow it offered plenty of opportunity for loneliness.

His parents were suddenly at his window. He got out of the car, hugged his father, and kissed his mother on the cheek, a son-to-mother greeting he'd seen in an old movie and decided to adopt for himself. Penny always laughed when he did this, which he took to mean that she approved or at least didn't mind.

The Lawsons and their guests were in a large white living room—painted white but also full of white furniture, white vases, calla lilies. White silk drapes hung in front of eight-foot windows. In contrast, the art on the walls was bold and dramatic and included what Penny recognized as a Franz Kline.

She had worn a simple navy silk blouse and matching slacks, and she felt good about her choice, which blended well with what the other women in the room were wearing.

But there weren't many of them. Nor men—just five or six other couples in all. Bill felt awkward and murmured to Robert as they were offered drinks that they'd stay thirty or forty minutes and head home. Then Harold Lawson came over with a great, wide smile, and Bill felt a pang over not having seen his old friend in so long. The truth was, people didn't have parties the way they used to. Bill and Penny had abandoned their annual party a few years earlier.

Bill occasionally saw Harold at medical staff meetings, but somehow seeing him out of the work context enabled or forced him to see how much Harold had aged. He was significantly Bill's senior and must be approaching seventy. Mrs. Grant, his mother-in-law, appeared to be in her nineties.

Mary Lawson steered Penny to an empty spot on a sofa, and as Penny settled back she let herself study Phyllis Grant. Tiny and extravagantly wrinkled, she wore an expression of dazed curiosity that it took Penny several moments to chalk up to a long-ago face-lift. She was seated in a high-backed chair on the far side of the room, dressed in a pink tracksuit and bright white Keds.

"Wouldn't consider another outfit," Mary said, pushing a dish of cashews closer to Penny. Mary was tiny but smooth-skinned, with the neck of a woman in her thirties. "Do you still have your mother?"

"She passed a couple years ago," Penny said, then immediately wished she could take it back and say "died" rather than "passed." She didn't want to be someone who would say "passed." That was someone who'd say "down there" rather than "vagina," and no artist influenced by Judy Chicago should do that.

Another woman, seated next to Penny, began to talk about her mother, and Penny let her mind drift to the question of what kind of opening statement she should make to Mrs. Grant. She would have to circle the group to get to her, and as she was working out her route, Harold Lawson came over.

"You must be so proud of Robert," he said, lowering himself onto the arm of the sofa. "And how nice that he's back in California. But I hear you're down to one child at home now. What are you doing with yourself?"

"Oh, I was never one of those women."

Harold's eyes widened slightly, and he ran his hand over the smooth dome of his head.

"I mean," she went on, "it was never all I did. Your mother-in-law is looking well."

"Isn't she?"

They sat in silence. The conversational possibilities seemed to have been exhausted, but apparently Harold was too polite to leave. At last Penny mumbled something and got to her feet. Someone had just vacated a white silk ottoman next to Mrs. Grant's chair, and Penny made a beeline for it. Once she was settled she smiled and introduced herself, and Mrs. Grant smiled and said nothing.

"My husband," Penny said, "is a pediatrician. That's him over there, see? Standing with our son. We met Harold and Mary when we first moved here from the city in 1964."

Mrs. Grant continued to smile.

"Your granddaughter is older than our children. Mary says she just got engaged?"

Nothing from Mrs. Grant, so Penny explained that Robert was in his first year of medical school, and then moved on to Rebecca and Ryan. "And our youngest," she said, "is in high school. I was just telling Harold, I have all this time on my hands these days."

Still Mrs. Grant said nothing, and Penny began to think she must be deaf. "I love this room," she added, louder.

Now Mrs. Grant leaned forward. She patted Penny's knee and said, "You're a good girl."

"I'm sorry?"

"No, I'm sorry. I never should have told him. I'm truly sorry, dear."

Penny felt someone's eyes on her and looked up. Mary was mouthing something and shaking her head.

Penny turned her palms upward and shrugged slightly.

Not all there, Mary mouthed, pointing at her head.

Penny hesitated and then rose and crossed the room again.

"She's gone," Mary said. "Did she say she was sorry? She thinks all women are me and all men are my father, who by the way died during the Ford administration. For the last two years she's been apologizing for something that happened in 1953."

"Oh, dear," Penny said. "I was going on and on."

"Sorry, she's purely ornamental at this point."

"I was going to ask her," Penny said, and then she paused. "I was going to ask her if she might want to take a look at a piece of mine."

"Oh," Mary said. And then, with an entirely different and comprehending tone, "Ohhh."

Penny looked around the room and wondered what she should say next. She caught Bill's eye and watched unhappily as he whispered something to Robert and the two of them headed over. She could tell they were ready to leave.

"Really?" she said. "But I'm so enjoying myself." She cast a desperate glance at Mary, who seemed to be eyeing another conversation.

"Well," Bill said, "we have two cars. I'll catch a ride with Robert and you can come when you're ready."

And so Robert and Bill left by themselves, Robert wondering a little at his father leaving his mother when she obviously wanted him to stay. His car was a limping old Nissan he'd bought from a guy heading for a residency in New York, and he apologized to Bill about the stale-air-freshener smell and greasy seat belts. Julie Anne had always said he cared more about neatness than cleanliness, and now that he was truly living alone for the first time in his life, he had to acknowledge that this was true.

He cleared his throat, ready to tell his father what was on his mind. Suddenly he wasn't sure he wanted to and substituted that old standby, his long-term career goals. "I definitely want to do primary care," he said, "but children or adults? Pediatrics or internal medicine? I really can't decide. I feel like I'd probably be okay at either."

He waited for his father to say, as he generally did, that Robert would be *good* at either, good at anything, but Bill shifted in his seat and looked at him.

"Which would you enjoy?"

The question took Robert by surprise, and he was embarrassed that he'd never wondered. Which would he enjoy? He had no idea. "How do you know?"

Bill smiled. "I guess you don't, son. The whole thing is a leap, isn't it? Thinking you'll be able to do it at all? I remember my grandfather's waiting room, I'd sometimes be there when I was quite young, left to sit with the folks waiting for him. This was 1932, 1933—before I started school."

"What do you mean 'left'? By whom?"

"My mother. She suffered from headaches—migraines, I suppose, though she just called them headaches, or 'sick headaches' more often. On her bad days we would go to his office and he'd give her ergotamine and put her in a dark room for an hour. I'd sit and wait for her. He came into the waiting room to greet each patient, so I'd see him every fifteen or twenty minutes. He was always a very powerful figure to me, but I don't think it was because he was my grandfather—it was because of how the people in that room viewed him."

"With awe?"

"With hope. With need."

Robert considered. He knew all too well what his father meant about the difficulty of believing he'd be able to do it at all. His hands on another person's body. That was the problem. How did you acquire the skill? The nerve? That he'd finally become intimate with a woman made it all the more difficult to imagine. Hands meeting skin: the purpose was pleasure.

He looked at his father. "You always say children deserve care," he said. "Like pediatrics would be more noble."

"It may be less noble," Bill said. "It may be cowardly. Children get better. I'm shielded from a lot of pain."

"A guy I know was talking about that. Saying you can't make it in medicine if you feel too much."

"Hmm," Bill said.

"What?"

"I'd say the opposite is true. You can't make it if you feel too little."

"But you're always talking about your colleagues who could as easily be diagnosing and fixing machines as humans."

"I am?"

Robert knew his father liked to think of himself as generous-minded, and evidence to the contrary sometimes disturbed him. Robert could recall few instances of his father being truly upset, and they all revolved around unkind statements he'd made and then regretted. Once, when Robert was home from Michigan on a break, his father came in from work in an uncharacteristically tense mood and brooded for a few hours until, sitting down with Robert while the other kids did their homework, he confessed that he'd spoken harshly to a medical student who was rotating at his office. The student, whose role was to watch and learn, had not only interrupted a mother describing her child's illness, he'd been dismissive—rude, in Bill's view. Bill told Robert about this without preamble, without the headline that he viewed himself as the party at fault. He simply narrated it, step by step—"and then I said," "and then the mother said," "and then the student said"—and as Robert listened, he thought the whole point was to caution him against crossing any lines during medical training. It was only when Bill arrived at the end of the story and explained that he'd scolded the young man after the visit that Robert realized the upset coming from his father had been generated not by anger but by remorse.

"I just mean," Robert said, "it seems like there are plenty of successful doctors who don't—who aren't emotionally invested."

Bill was silent for a moment. "I guess we'd have to back up and define successful," he said at last.

They'd arrived at a row of businesses that included a gas station, and Robert pulled in and stopped at the first pump, then thought of his father's long-ago instruction always to pull forward in case someone came in behind you and advanced a few yards. While the gas pumped he washed the windshield and then the windows, taking time to rub clean each of the side mirrors. His father looked very serious. He'd been the only man wearing a necktie at the party, and Robert wondered at the conservatism that seemed to define him. Not political—it was a moral conservatism, a personal conservatism. In many ways he stood with his heels dug into the hard ground of an earlier time. This was something Robert thought he might discuss with Rebecca someday when they were both home. Which would happen soon, for Ryan's birthday.

He got back in the car and they rode along in silence. On Robert's mind was a pain he'd developed in his groin, most likely a strained muscle (this was all but certain), but just when he thought it was gone it would come back, nagging at him with its diffuseness, its resistance to description. Was it throbbing? Stabbing? Piercing? Shooting? Cramping? Gnawing? At different times each of these words was right. It was nothing, he was sure. But—but!—groin pain was on the differential for testicular cancer. He was absolutely, completely positive he didn't have testicular cancer—he had medical student's disease, it was so obvious, defined as unwarranted anxiety about one's own health—but there was a small voice that every now and then spoke up and said, *Boy, will you feel terrible if you do have testicular cancer and could have discovered it early.*

He also was experiencing a persistent cough that was a nuisance, nothing more, but he had to acknowledge that a persistent cough could be a symptom of something very serious.

On the other hand, there was no way he had two terrible diseases, which somehow reduced the likelihood that he had one.

Soon they were home and he hadn't said a thing about his health.

James lay on the couch watching TV. "Robbo," he said, barely looking up. "What's the matter, no lives to save?"

"Fuck you, too," Robert said, but low enough so that their father couldn't hear him.

"Mom?"

"Still at the party."

A throw pillow lay next to James, and without looking at Robert he tossed it aside, making space. Robert looked into the kitchen, saw his father at the table reading, and joined James.

"Good weekend?"

"Very funny."

Robert took a closer look at his brother. His hair lay helter-skelter on his scalp, unwashed, uncombed. He looked as if he hadn't been out all day.

"What happened?"

"Nice try."

"James, whatever it was, I didn't get the report."

"A kid at a party passed out and Dad took him to the hospital."

Slowly, the story came out. It made sense to Robert that James had turned to Rebecca, since she was close by while Robert was nearly an hour away, especially when you considered how hard parking was in his Inner Sunset neighborhood and how often he had to leave his car blocks away from his apartment. Still, he didn't like the idea of Rebecca getting to help, especially with something medical.

Their father came out of the kitchen. "I think," he said, "that I might go to bed."

Robert glanced at his watch. It wasn't even eight o'clock.

"I had a late night Friday night. I'm more tired today than yesterday—like a toddler."

"What do you mean?"

"Oh, children tend to show the effects of a late night a day or two afterward." He raised a hand in farewell and headed for his room, leaving James and Robert looking after him.

"It's not my fault he's tired," James muttered. "It was his choice."

"You're so self-centered," Robert said, though he was thinking his father's early bedtime meant there'd be no discussion tonight about his worries.

James headed for the bedroom hallway. Robert tried to make sense of James's TV show for maybe thirty seconds, then turned it off. He'd last talked to Julie Anne Wednesday evening, a phone call that hadn't gone well. It had been close to midnight in Ann Arbor, and she'd been asleep. She said, "It's okay, I had to get up to answer the phone," but without a trace of humor.

He headed for his father's room. Bill's legs were under the covers, but he was sitting up holding a magazine, though the magazine,

Robert noticed, was closed. "Son," Bill said. "I'm sorry to be such an old man."

"Hey, I hadn't thought of that."

"What?"

"Geriatrics."

"Come have a seat. Now that I'm actually here, I'm not quite so sleepy."

Robert sat near his father's knees. He didn't know when he'd last seen his father in bed. It had been many years. "James told me why you were up late Friday night."

"He hasn't left the house all weekend."

"You grounded him?"

"No, I'm thinking he grounded himself."

"Didn't see that coming."

"It's hard to be the youngest. He's got two more years at home after this."

"Assuming he goes to college."

"He'll go somewhere—it doesn't have to be college. I worry sometimes that I didn't let you kids know how many different good paths there are in life."

"What, we don't have to be doctors?" This was the moment for Robert to bring up his groin pain, which he could do lightly, in the context of how school was going—what a joke, huh? But he didn't. He looked away, and when he looked at his father again, Bill had opened the magazine and was smoothing the pages. Robert got to his feet. He said he should be getting back, and he leaned down and kissed his father's forehead and headed for the door.

Bill heard the front door closing, Robert's car starting, the engine noise on the driveway. He could feel the imprint of Robert's lips. It made him think of the last time he saw his own father, on a frigid day in 1962. His father was in the hospital, if not at death's door then halfway up the front walk wondering where the doorbell was. He had the raspy voice of a cigar smoker and the belly of a man who'd lived on a steady diet of butter, cream, and eggs for seven decades. He was only seventy-two, but an old seventy-two, with hypertension, emphysema, and, emergently, an MI. When Bill arrived, having rented a car at Detroit Metro straight off the red-eye from San Francisco, his mother and sister leaped to their feet as if he'd brought with him something far more powerful than love. "I want you to talk to the doctor," his mother said. He stayed for thirty-six hours, as long as he could be away from his medical practice and his pregnant wife and his twenty-month-old son, and when it was time to go, his father summoned a bland expression and wished him a safe trip. His mother said, "Tell Penny it's obvious she's doing a good job taking care of you," and his father, as if praising the financial practices of someone he'd known for a long time, said, "Yes, you always had sound judgment." Bill said, "You were a good model." By then he was at the door, and it would have required a giant shift in his basic life orientation to return to his father's side and kiss his forehead, though he'd wished ever since that he'd done so.

He woke less than an hour later when Penny came in the front door. He was still sitting up with his bedside light on, and he quickly switched it off and moved under the covers. He heard her calling for James, and he thought he heard James's voice, and hers, but he was asleep again before he could be sure.

Had he stayed awake and listened, he would have heard Penny scolding James for the mess he'd left in the kitchen—not because of the mess, which was minor, but because she'd failed to advance the cause of her career at the Lawson party, and James was a handy target. James said Penny blamed him for everything, and she said that if the shoe fit he should wear it. He grabbed a shoe off the floor and lobbed it, and it struck her—though only because she'd lowered her head into its flight path. They looked at each other in astonished silence. She let out a sound that was both laugh and shriek, and he stepped into his closet and slammed the door. She knocked, and he told her to fuck off. She knocked harder, and he jerked the door open. She lunged at him with both hands up, and he dove to the floor and hit his head hard against the metal leg of his bed. He lay there moaning and writhing in pain, and she fell to her knees and said, "It's me, it's me, it's always been me, it's me, it's me."

Neither spoke of the incident ever again. For a brief period, James would believe she'd been confessing her guilt, her feelings of responsibility for all the pain he might have felt or might feel as represented by the pain of hitting his head, but this would be too much for him and he would retreat to the more obvious interpretation of maternal self-importance and cement the entire episode to the other pieces of grudge that together formed his rocklike objection to her, which would stay in place for decades.

At dinner the next evening, James had a lump on his forehead and a scowl for his father, whose Friday-night heroics had brought James the wrong kind of attention at school—not the outlaw admiration he'd gotten for wrecking two cars but a sort of sainthood by association that made people talk about him but not to him. Greer came up to him at lunch and said with resentful embarrassment that his parents wanted to thank James's father, and James imagined a terrible future in which he was the guy other people's parents encouraged them to befriend. He left the dinner table as quickly as he could.

Penny had spent the day prowling the house for items to use in her next assemblage, and she felt the restless exhaustion of having worked without really working. Her failure with Phyllis Grant had put her exactly where she'd been Saturday morning, before her stop at the decorators' shop, though she felt as if she'd been moved backward in life, unfairly.

"I could use some help, you know," she said to Bill once the two of them were alone in the kitchen, and for a moment he thought she meant with the dishes, which was confusing because he was already doing them.

"What can I do?" he said once he understood.

"Ask around? There must be lots of people in the medical community who know people in the art world."

"I'm not sure I have the opportunity," he said, and she lifted her palms beseechingly.

"Make it. You have to make the opportunity."

"What happened at the party?"

"If something had happened at the party, do you think I'd be talking to you?"

Bill turned off the water, methodically wiped his hands on a kitchen towel, and turned to face her.

"That's not what I meant."

"Where do we go from here, Penny?"

"We don't go anywhere. I go to my studio, as I do every evening."

"That's my point."

"You don't even want me here. Think about it. All you care about is the kids."

Bill sighed. They'd been married for twenty-five years, and there was little about their current situation that had not been true for a long time. Nonetheless, the past several months had brought him anguish of a new order. Ryan was gone, his kindness was gone, and Sierra was gone, too. Together with the two of them and James, Bill had felt some peace, the safety of numbers.

In a few days everyone would be home for Ryan's birthday, and Bill thought about the last time they'd all been together, over Christmas, when even Robert spent a few nights at home. For the previous few years, Ryan and Sierra had occupied Robert's room, but now that he had returned from Michigan and lived close enough to come home fairly frequently, it was not quite so obvious who should sleep where, and in the end Robert got his old room, Bill shared with James, and Ryan and Sierra took the master bedroom. Falling asleep in Ryan's old twin bed, knowing his children were all under one roof, Bill had the familiar and much mourned feeling that all was right with the world. And in the morning, up early and not wanting to wake Ryan and Sierra, he showered in the children's bathroom for the first time in his life and decided he could make do with anything, any small corner of the house, if only his children would stay there with him.

Penny saw this and almost pitied him. He was so dependent: as she'd once been on him. What she wanted now was much less than what she wanted originally. Just a little help, a gesture of support. A phone call or two. He had to know people who cared about art. She wasn't asking for a handout; she just wanted a chance. An opening. She was ready for the next step.

She had not let go of the idea several days later, on the evening of Ryan's birthday celebration. Everyone was in the living room after cake, chatting idly about playing a game or possibly going to a movie, the conversation itself the only activity they needed, though the occasion necessitated that they contemplate doing something more. Penny came in from the kitchen and said, looking first at Bill and then at the rest of them, "Have you asked yourself, has anyone asked himself or herself, what it would mean if I began selling my art?"

Sunk deep in an armchair, James plonked his bare feet on the coffee table, belched loudly, and said, "What about 'itself'?"

Penny ignored him and focused on Bill. "I'm not getting the support I need. That's not unusual for a woman artist, of course, but I've asked and you've essentially said no."

"What kind of support do you need?" James said. And then, seized by righteousness, he leaped to his feet and shouted, "What more do you want from him? God!" He crossed the room and took a small watercolor of hers from a shelf where it leaned, unframed, against a row of books. It was a picture she'd done years earlier, of the front of the house in the late afternoon, with the low sun reflected in the narrow panes of glass that flanked the front door. "You think someone would pay for this?"

"James," Rebecca said.

James looked around the room, at the smug, aloof faces of his family, none of whom understood what life was like for him, how boring and pointless, and he held up the watercolor and ripped it in half.

"No!" Penny cried.

Robert felt a twinge in his upper thigh, the first pain he'd felt in several days. Rebecca looked at her father and imagined leading him to a quiet white room that she understood, thanks to an emerging ability to think about what she was thinking, to be a combination of heaven and a mental hospital where someone might go for a nice long rest. Ryan thought ahead to the moment when he and Sierra would be in bed together and he would rest his head on her shoulder and his middle finger on her clitoris and they could begin to return to each other. Sierra felt Ryan press his thigh against hers, and she pressed back and wondered what it meant that she loved the Blairs more than she loved her own mother. Bill knew it was up to him to speak, but he was pinned to his chair by a combination of denial and astonishment and couldn't say a word.

"That," Penny said, "was a favorite piece of mine."

"Piece," James said scornfully.

"That's what artists call their work."

"James," Rebecca said. "Do you think maybe—"

"Piece of shit," James said.

Penny touched her fingertips to her throat. She said, "Does no one in this family have a single thing to say to James?"

Everyone stayed silent, and James was seized by an idea, only half-formed and therefore all the more powerful, that she was excluding him yet again. "Fuck you!" he cried.

Sierra climbed over Ryan and went to Penny's side. "We can tape it," she said. "Really, it'll be okay. We'll tape it from the back, it won't even show. Here, James, you didn't mean it. Do you have any of that clear tape in your studio, Penny? I'll bet you do."

"Why did you do that?" Robert asked James.

"Because that's the kind of person I am!" James shouted, and he flipped the two watercolor halves into the air, a gesture that should have given him a feeling of power but that backfired because they were so lightweight that their descent to the floor was drifting and leisurely. Furious, he bolted out of the living room, grabbed the Accord keys as he passed the table where they were kept, and yanked open the front door.

"He's not allowed to drive," Penny cried, and Ryan ran after him and somehow made it down the pitch-dark steps to the driveway in time to position himself between James and the car. For a moment they wrestled, James trying to shove Ryan out of the way while Ryan planted his feet and bent his knees and pressed against the car door with all his weight. James looked over his shoulder, saw his father and Robert and Rebecca coming, and with a murderous yell threw the keys as high into the air as he could and took off at a run. He ran down the driveway, past the turnoff for the shed, and all the way to the road. There, fury pulsing through him, he yelled again.

Bill hurried back into the house to search for flashlights while

Sierra tried to tape the watercolor and Penny hoped she wouldn't succeed. Penny was incensed and yet also somehow pleased by what James had done, for in crossing this line he had more or less demanded a strong reaction, and she had one in mind.

In 1957, around the same time Bill began bringing Penny to picnic at the Portola Valley property, a group of Benedictine monks from Hungary was founding a small boarding school for boys less than a mile away. By the 1980s, the Priory, as it was known, enrolled day students as well and had developed a reputation as a good place to send a boy who for one reason or another was in danger of going astray. Assisted by lay teachers, the monks, in their flowing black robes, taught according to Benedictine principles and every June graduated a group of fine-looking young men whose photograph appeared on the front page of the local newspaper. Penny had always liked the idea of the school, not for the Christian values but because the students, when she saw them around the village in their button-down shirts, struck her as the kind of kids who would treat their mothers with deference and respect.

"No," Bill told her on the phone the next morning, pulled from an exam of a five-year-old with second-degree burns. "And please don't tell my staff it's an emergency when it isn't."

"No," he told her that evening at dinner, the two of them alone at the table because James had refused to join them—with the certain knowledge, Bill figured, that once Penny was out of the house, his father would heat up the leftovers.

"No," he said when she flipped the bedroom light on at midnight and announced that she couldn't sleep, she was so worried—this was a new word—about James.

"Woodside High is so big," she said, standing at the foot of the bed and glaring at him. "And his friends! It seems like a very bad place for him. I really think he would benefit."

"Benefit."

"From the structure. He'd have to do chores around the dormitory, he'd have to live with other kids again."

"He wouldn't *live* there."

"Of course he'd live there! That would be the whole point! For all I care, he can live there and keep going to Woodside High."

"I don't think the monks would go for that," Bill said, and that one tiny slip into "yes but" logic cost him another twenty-four hours of argument until finally she gave up on trying to convince him and called the Priory herself to set up an appointment.

Ryan, back in Santa Cruz but very worried about what was happening at home, spent hours each evening on the phone with Sierra, not talking about James but rather, because of James, extending the already significant amount of time they spent on the phone together.

"If you came here," Ryan told her one evening, about an hour into a long, meandering conversation, "we could take a love-poetry class together."

Sierra had already told him a hundred times that she didn't want to go to college, but she went along with the fantasy because they always went along with each other's fantasies. "They really have that?" she said. "A love-poetry class?"

"I'm not sure, but I bet they might. I met this woman at the Arboretum and she recited a poem to me."

"I believe that."

"I wish I could see your face right now. Are you smiling amused or smiling charmed?"

"I'm smiling loving."

"Don't you think it would be nice if James had someone to smile like that at him?"

"He's young," Sierra said, because that was what Bill always said and she trusted Bill to understand James.

"But don't you think?"

"Of course. He will someday."

"Oh," Ryan said.

"What?"

"I'm thinking about you. What you'll do someday."

"Please don't. Not tonight."

And so he didn't—bring up what they both knew, that Sierra's days at home were numbered. Soon, neither of them knew when, she would come up with a goal for herself and be gone. Yet despite the dread he felt, or maybe because of it, Ryan saw the force that was going to carry her away as external. He and Sierra were like two golden leaves lying under a tree, knowing there was a big wind on its way. The Ryan leaf would be tossed up in the air, flipped over once or twice, and then deposited in the exact same place, while the Sierra leaf would be blown out of sight.

"You met a woman?" Sierra said.

"In the Australian area. At the banksia, you know what I mean, with the crazy yellow flowers that sort of look like toilet brushes? They probably weren't in bloom last time we went, I'll show you next weekend. She's a volunteer at the Arboretum, she teaches in the English Department. I'm standing there and she walks up to me and says, 'A morning glory satisfies me more than a book' or something like that. I said, you know, 'Hi, nice to meet you,' and she said that was something Walt Whitman said, and did I know his poem about a child asking what grass is. And then she recited it—it was very long."

"What grass is?" Sierra said.

"Grass, not grass. Ha, I didn't even think of that."

"James would have."

"I'm not sure."

"No, he would have. I asked him."

"You asked him . . ."

"If he's smoking. Weed. He is."

Ryan was silent.

"*We* did at sixteen."

"We were seventeen. And that was different. We were together."

"Are you really surprised?"

"No, I guess not. I just want him to be good."

"Good like a good boy?"

"Good like happy."

"She won't make him go."

"I hope not."

"She can't."

"You mean my dad won't go along with it."

"Right."

The appointment at the Priory was set for Friday afternoon. James sat in the kitchen and waited for his parents: his mother because she was the one taking him and his father because he had the car.

Penny came in first, breathing hard because she'd had to hurry up the hill from her studio. Her clothes were old and paint-stained, and there was a faint band of sawdust at her hairline. "I'm still mad about the watercolor," she said, "but I just want you to know, this is not a punishment. It's for your own good."

"Said the prison guard as he slammed the door of the cell."

"I know I can't convince you, so I won't bother trying."

"It was pretty old."

"What?"

"The watercolor."

"You are perverse," she said. "Does it not occur to you that a remark like that only makes me angrier?"

"But you said it's not a punishment."

She left him sitting there and went to wash up and change. While she was gone, Bill arrived, ten minutes behind schedule and rattled by his tardiness, which had begun with a mother hailing him in the parking lot as he got into his car. "I meant to ask you," she said, her feverish toddler balanced on her hip and resting his flushed cheek on her shoulder, "if you have any thoughts on apple juice." Which Bill did, and which he communicated as succinctly as he could, the main point being that if she was worrying about apple juice, then everything that was actually in her control would most likely be fine; but it set him back several minutes and aggravated him enough that once he was in the car he replayed the scene in his mind and instead of reassuring her, he told her that she ought to get her child home and into bed rather than worry about protecting him from the knowledge that there was sugar in the world and it tasted good.

It bothered him even to imagine talking like that.

"Mom said I'm a pervert," James said once Penny was back in the kitchen and Bill was handing her the car keys.

"Oh, I did not," Penny said.

"She did," James said. "I'm not complaining, I'm just saying. I doubt they'll want a pervert at the Priory."

"James," Bill said, "it's just a visit. It might be interesting. Haven't you always wondered what goes on back there?"

"Haven't *you*?"

Bill hesitated.

"I mean, it's really nice of you to bring the *car* home and everything, but I notice you aren't going with us."

"Do you want me to?"

"What do I care?"

And so they all went, the three of them silent under a bright blue sky, passing stands of daffodils and tiny, poisonous lilies of the valley. The school was set way back from the road, at the base of a hill dotted thickly with pine trees. They didn't see a single person as they made their way to the office.

Surprisingly to James, it wasn't a black-robed monk who greeted them but a barrel-chested middle-aged man wearing a striped necktie, named Mr. Calhoun. After politely welcoming them into his office, he talked about the Benedictine principles on which the school had been founded. "We're looking," he said, "for the best in every young man who comes to us," and he gave James a smile full of manufactured warmth.

James slouched in his chair. On the walls were black-and-white photographs of the monks before the school was built, and it occurred to him that he didn't know the difference between a monk and a priest. Obviously priests weren't allowed to get laid, but what about monks?

After about twenty minutes, Mr. Calhoun led them around the campus, which was exactly as small and shady and devoid of people as Woodside High School was huge and exposed to the sun and crowded. Penny matched her stride to Mr. Calhoun's while Bill and James walked behind them. At the dormitory James saw a pair of boys playing Ping-Pong and pictured himself standing at one end of the table and slamming the ball at his opponent, who in James's imagination turned into Robert and crouched with his forearms hiding his face.

Mr. Calhoun described the eleventh-grade curriculum and said transfer students did very well thanks to the Priory's excellent academic advising. Arriving at the chapel, he mentioned that mass was celebrated every morning but that the boys were not required to attend. The entire school came together in chapel once a week and on certain special occasions. Spiritual guidance was always available by appointment.

James wanted to see where the monks lived, but Mr. Calhoun said their area was private, and James found himself wondering again about the sex lives of monks. Now that he was thinking about it, he remembered that priests weren't even allowed to jerk off. Monks, either? What about the students? Asking this question was the kind of thing he once did all the time, but now that he was older he often caught himself partway through a statement or action only to realize that continuing might mean undesirable consequences. Typically, this happened too late to abort the whole thing but too early to proceed without feeling guilty or stupid. This annoyed him greatly. If he was going to realize something was a bad idea, he wanted to realize it *beforehand.* He had confided this to Rebecca once, and she had remarked that since he knew how often he did the wrong thing (she'd said something a little nicer than this, he couldn't remember what), he should always *stop and think first.* "Always when?" he asked, and she said, "Always always. Before you do or say anything." Which was so useless that he disregarded it completely. It was like saying he should stop and think before he breathed.

Mr. Calhoun gave them a large packet of papers before they left. "We'll look forward to hearing from you," he said, and then he put a hand on James's shoulder and added, "Good luck to you, son."

Walking to the car, James felt a ferocious sense of doom. He didn't want to go to this school, but suddenly he didn't want to stay where he was, either. He wondered what would happen if he dropped out of school and worked at a gas station. He'd always sort of enjoyed the smell of motor oil, and it would drive everyone in his family crazy.

"Well," Penny said, "I thought that was very interesting. James, wouldn't you like to live in a dorm? Don't you think that would be fun? Then you'd be just like Rebecca and the boys."

"Robert doesn't live in a dorm," James said.

"Well, he did," Penny said. "He used to. Remember how much fun he had?"

James snorted. Whenever Robert had come home from Michigan, he'd spent all his time complaining about college life, especially the lack of privacy, which James found funny since that was the one thing he refused to give anyone else.

They drove toward home and Penny said idly that she had nothing in the house for dinner. "Now that it's just the three of us, I actually sometimes forget to go shopping."

Bill said, "The good news is that no one ever forgets to eat."

"That's not true. I sometimes realize at three or four in the afternoon that I haven't eaten all day."

"That's what I mean. You remember because you get hungry."

James stared out the window. He was supposed to be at detention, and he figured touring the Priory was better than that. It had gotten to the point where he owed detention for cutting detention, and in the last month or so, pretty much since the car accident, he'd been intercepting letters about his delinquency from the vice principal.

"Dad?" he said.

"Yes?"

"What religion are monks?"

"Why, they're Catholic," Bill said. "I'm sorry. You didn't know that?"

"No, I did. I just wanted to make sure." James hesitated. "So monks are priests?"

"Not exactly. Monks aren't ordained. They don't celebrate mass."

"Celebrate. Ha."

"That's what it's called, James," Penny said, glancing over her shoulder. "It's very sacred."

"I'm not sure," Bill said, "that the word 'sacred' can be qualified. I think something either is sacred or it isn't."

"You sound like Rebecca," James said.

"Rebecca sounds like your father," Penny snapped. "I don't know why everyone always says it the other way."

James stared out the window and resolved to keep quiet. They approached the turn for home, and when his father kept on driving he didn't even voice a pro forma objection to being dragged to the grocery store. The only way to avoid being restless was to be very, very tired, and he leaned his head against the door. "Everyone else has a religion," he muttered, but so quietly that neither parent heard him.

By the time they got back home it was dusk, and James was realizing he didn't know where the parties were this weekend. Someone had said something about a bonfire on the beach, but without knowing whether it was tonight or tomorrow, let alone which beach, he might as well know nothing.

At the top of the driveway was Sierra's old green VW Beetle.

"Ryan must be here," Bill said, and though James was pleased by the idea and the distraction it represented, he said, as dully as he could, "Whoop-dee-do."

The three of them carried the grocery bags up to the house. Ryan and Sierra were in the kitchen, holding hands across the table and sipping from mugs of the heavily scented cinnamon tea she bought in bulk at a health food restaurant in Palo Alto. Ryan wore an old Sand Hill Day T-shirt that had been Sierra's originally; it was so small on him that the front image was distorted, the school's famous tiny green sprout growing from a terra-cotta pot stretched to look like a shallow pink pie pan.

"James," they both said, getting to their feet.

"Studly shirt," James said.

"How was it?" Ryan said. "I didn't want to hear by phone, so I had Sierra drive down to get me."

"Well, I was driving down anyway," she said. "But we both

wanted to find out as soon as possible, so we turned right around and drove back."

"You act as if I took him to look at a prison," Penny said. "It's a school."

"No, no, not at all," Sierra said, "we're just really curious. Was it nice?" With her right hand she reached over her head and drew the hair away from her left temple, a habitual gesture of hers that James found sexy, the way it caught her bare elbow pointing at the ceiling for a moment.

"It was very nice," Penny said.

"It *was* very nice," James said. "Very. I saw some righteous-looking playing fields. But I could never go there."

"Why not?" Ryan said.

"Well, because of something Mom said earlier. She said I'm a pervert and it's true, so I could never go there because Catholics aren't allowed to jerk off."

Ryan took in his mother's outrage, his father's consternation, and Sierra's pink-faced amusement, a look he knew could give way at any moment to helpless laughter. "We're taking you out, James," he said, exercising an option he and Sierra had discussed. "That's the real reason we came. It's a brotherly kidnapping. Not going to tell you where we're going, you just have to come with us and be ready for an adventure."

"How much are they paying you?" James said, but he let Ryan point him to his room and into warmer clothes and back to the kitchen to say goodbye and into the front seat of Sierra's car, all without a sarcastic or disparaging comment.

Penny and Bill were left in the kitchen. "What was that?" she said, but all Bill could think was how sorry he was to face the evening without any kids in the house, and he delivered an edict: "He's not going to that school. I won't have it."

Sierra drove and Ryan sat behind her, and in the passenger seat James felt captive and commanding by turn, though when they reached Alpine Road and headed not in the obvious direction, toward Palo Alto and Menlo Park and every likely restaurant, but instead in the direction of the Priory, he felt himself plunging deeper into captivity and pressed his feet into the floor of the Beetle to slow things down.

But they passed the Priory and kept going. Sierra made a sharp left into Woodside, and James realized they were going to her house. She and her mother lived on the edge of an estate on the thickly forested Mountain Home Road, in a so-called carriage house that once was an actual carriage house and had a trough out back to prove it.

Their landlord was just nosing his Jaguar out of the driveway when Sierra, Ryan, and James pulled in.

"Evening," he said to Sierra, leaning through his open window.

"Happy Friday," she said. "Have you ever met Ryan's little brother?"

James sat forward and raised his hand in a gesture meant to bridge the gap between a wave and a salute. Unfortunately, it ended up looking a lot like a Heil Hitler, and from the backseat Ryan whispered a cautioning "James."

"What?" James said, turning around. He was aware of Sierra playing with the Beetle's pedals—gas, clutch, gas, clutch—and the forward and backward movement of the car had the rhythmic feel of sex. Ryan shook his head and waved at the landlord, and Sierra pulled forward and parked.

"Are we *going here* going here?" James said. "Or just stopping by?"

"Just stopping by. I need to get something."

A rickety outside staircase went up to the second level, where she and her mother lived. James watched as she jogged up the stairs and disappeared through the door.

"So tell me about the Priory," Ryan said.

"Nerds in ties."

"Not robes?"

"Monks in robes, nerds in ties."

"That was weird on my birthday," Ryan said. "With the watercolor."

"You mean the 'piece'?"

"James."

"Look, I'm sorry, okay?"

"She won't make you go, James. She can't."

James shrugged, and Ryan leaned forward and put his hand on James's shoulder. Tears swam in front of James's eyes, and he stared straight ahead and tried not to blink.

"Remember how we used to talk at night?" Ryan said. "Sometimes when I'm almost asleep I forget I'm not at home, and I start talking to my roommate like he's you. One night I was sort of already asleep and dreaming, and I said to him, 'Do you have Dog?'"

James had met Ryan's roommate only once, a guy from Malibu who was such a surfer he was like a cliché of himself. He even had a surfer name, Brett. "Little bro!" he said to James when Ryan introduced them. James hated him.

"That doesn't even make sense," he told Ryan. "You stopped sleeping in our room about ten years ago."

"Three."

"But who's counting."

Ryan was still leaning forward, and he gave James's shoulder a squeeze and said, "I love you, J." At which point James did the only thing he could think of doing, which was to get out of the car and climb the stairs after Sierra. There was only so much of Ryan he could deal with. Besides, he had to take a leak.

Sierra had left the door ajar, and he could hear her and her mom talking.

". . . driving literally all afternoon," her mom was saying in a peeved voice.

Sierra said, "Where's my Chinese jar? I've got forty dollars in there and I need it."

"And you'll drive back down there tomorrow, I suppose. And then home again, when, Sunday? And back down there Tuesday or Wednesday?"

"It's an hour," Sierra said. "And we're trying to take James out tonight, so if you don't mind." There was a silence, and James held his breath, afraid she'd open the door and see him standing there. He wanted to hear more.

"I could make something," her mom said. "I could make minestrone."

"That takes hours. Anyway, we want to take him out. He's so lost. Ryan's afraid of what he'll do."

"Like what?"

"Oh, here it is," Sierra said. "What's it doing here?"

"Or you could have a glass of wine with me."

"Mommy, we're underage. I'm going now, okay?"

Not wanting to be discovered, James rapped on the door and pushed it open. He'd been to Sierra's only once and had forgotten how cluttered it was, and froufrou, two couches and two armchairs all covered with flowers, and several small dim lamps casting the only light, which in each case was filtered by a piece of colored gauze. Sierra and her mom shared the single bedroom, which he saw through an open door: twin beds separated by a nightstand. The walls in the living room were covered with photographs of Sierra: some serious black-and-white shots from when she was around ten or twelve, and dozens of bright color pictures from every other time in her life. Looking at pictures of her, you thought you'd never really known how pretty she was—and then you looked at her and realized that of course you'd known. She had velvet skin and cascading blond hair, and if she'd been paid to model the gray T-shirt and torn jeans she was wearing, no stylist or makeup artist could have made her look better. She could easily be a model. Some weirdo had stopped her on the street in San Francisco to tell her that very thing.

"Sorry," she said when she saw him. "I'm coming."

"Can I go to the bathroom?"

"No, James, that's not allowed."

"Come *in,*" her mom said. Her hair was long like Sierra's but more gray than blond. She was decent-looking herself, way better-looking than his mom. "James, it's so good to see you. Why did Ryan stay in the car, we could've all had some hummus."

The bathroom was small and damp and perfumey, and there was nothing in the medicine cabinet except Midol and melatonin, that and a million different loofahs and herbal foot creams and natural oatmeal soaps. It occurred to James that Rebecca had never kept a lot of girlish stuff around, and for a moment he wished she were with them, but she was always so busy.

The sink had a curtain around it instead of a cabinet, and after he pissed he squatted and pulled aside one panel. Sitting behind the pipes was a leather case that looked like a miniature trunk, with hardware on the corners and a brass lock with the key sticking out. He slid the box out and opened it. Inside he found a snarl of jewelry, fine gold chains with knots so tiny it would take a magnifying glass to untangle them. Hanging from each chain was a charm—a pearl, a black-and-white Minnie Mouse head, a small gold cross.

The whole mess of necklaces was in a tray that lifted out, and in the large undivided space underneath James found a leather book full of loopy cursive. He flipped through the pages and caught phrases like "my heart is so full today" and "Sierra is as majestic as her name" and "I love my house, I love my job, I love my daughter." He closed the book and tossed it back into the box. *The lady doth protest too much,* he thought, and then he wished he hadn't thought it because it made him think of Rebecca again; it was what she used to say when their mother pretended she'd really like to stay in the house after dinner but felt duty-bound to return to the shed to do some more work.

He took out the clump of chains, clenched the cross in his fist, and yanked as hard as he could, but all that happened was a tiny rope burn where the chains had slid across his palm. He opened the medicine cabinet again, grabbed a pair of nail scissors, and easily snipped the chain in two. From there it was simple to slip the cross off, and he shoved it in his pocket, closed the box, and returned it to its place behind the pipes.

Flushing the toilet, he opened the door and found Sierra standing right there.

"Everything okay?"

He gave her a mild smile and the shrug he used at school when he didn't want to admit he didn't know the answer to a question.

"James, what's your favorite band these days?" Sierra's mom said. "Do you like Hall and Oates? I love 'One on One,' I was just going to play it."

She was in front of the stereo, holding a record by its edges. Once when she was at the Blairs' for dinner, years ago, James had joined in a conversation she and Rebecca were having about music, and ever since then, whenever she saw him, she brought up some song or other.

"Kind of," he said, though in fact he hated Hall and Oates.

"I love 'Sara Smile.'"

"That's because it reminds you of Sierra."

Sierra's mom blushed and smiled. "James, that's so touching. You're really sweet."

"Mommy, stop it," Sierra said. "We're leaving. See you I don't know."

"See *you* I don't know," her mom said, sticking out her lower lip in a pretend pout that James knew she really meant.

"Mommy."

James waved and left. On the stairs he remembered Rebecca talking about Sierra's mom's musical taste. "She likes Air Supply," Rebecca had said. "How embarrassing is that?" Then she'd sung, "'I'm back on my feet and eager to be what you wanted.' I mean, no offense, but how messed up is that?" And it confused James, because he didn't understand why it was messed up. What was wrong with being eager to be what someone wanted? He still didn't get it.

Ryan reclined in the back of the Beetle, his feet propped between the two front seats. When he saw James, he straightened up and smiled. "Did you see Janice?"

"Saw and heard. And smelled."

"Oh, it's kind of strong in there, isn't it? Incense, right? I almost don't notice it anymore."

It was dark now, and when Sierra returned they took back roads to a large county park that climbed the Woodside hills. A light mist had floated over from the ocean, and James felt his face grow cool and damp. Sierra and Ryan pulled on sweatshirts and got headlamps out of a box in the trunk, plus backpacks stuffed with blankets. They walked without talking, James curious but unwilling to ask what was going on because he knew it would be revealed *in the fullness of time*. That was some other fucking quote. He imagined it was Shakespeare, since every quote seemed to be Shakespeare.

Just ahead of James, Ryan walked with a purposefulness that belied the second thoughts he was having about the evening's plan. Sierra had stopped at home not for money but for the mushrooms she'd bought earlier in the week, and he was uneasy about the prospect of actually doing them. It would be their first time, and Ryan didn't even love getting stoned all that much. But he didn't want to disappoint her, and he thought that the more fun they had together, the longer she'd put off doing whatever it was she was going to decide she wanted to do.

They began climbing a narrow trail, slowing to stay within the light cast by their lamps. They made their way up a series of switchbacks, Ryan in the lead, then Sierra, then James. Redwoods soared fifty feet above them and higher.

Ryan and Sierra murmured back and forth, or murmured to the degree that you could successfully murmur while hiking single-file. It was their habit to talk about their memories of the last time they'd done whatever they were doing, and he reminded her of a recent hike they'd taken near Santa Cruz, at a state park that was full of amazing redwoods.

"Why do you guys hike?" James said. "You should bike. You can see more."

"We could all bike," Ryan said. He turned around, and the light from his headlamp shone into James's eyes.

"Ow, watch it."

"I could get my bike back in shape, and Sierra could use Rebecca's."

"You're quite the scoutmaster," James said.

"What I said in the car?" Ryan told him. "About loving you? That's what's making me suggest this stuff."

He began thinking that James's mood might not make for a very good trip. He had heard that mushrooms could amplify whatever feelings you were having. He also thought it might not be the best idea to do this in the dark—in case any of them ended up freaking out. But Sierra wanted to do it, and he couldn't bear to disappoint her.

At a meadow, they spread out one blanket and wrapped themselves in the others. They had bottles of ginger ale to wash down the mushrooms, and Ryan had brought apples and a large bag of Oriental snack mix in case they got hungry. As he and Sierra unpacked everything, James said that if all they'd wanted was a nighttime picnic, they could've saved time and just gone down to the tree house. He'd begun to enjoy himself, though, and they all knew he was complaining in order to protect his reputation as a malcontent.

"Wait, don't eat yet," Sierra said as he reached for an apple.

"You may be wondering," Ryan intoned, "why we've brought you here. We have something very special in mind for you, young man. It's not something we'd offer just anyone."

"What are you doing?" Sierra said, lightly swatting him. She leaned toward James and said, "Guess what? We have shrooms."

Immediately, James felt dread. Shrooms—he'd never done them. Never dropped acid. Never done any hallucinogen at all. He didn't want to be a pussy, but as bored as he was, he didn't feel like spending eight hours tripping. Visiting the Priory had been enough weirdness to last him a week. But he couldn't say so, and he nodded enthusiastically.

"You know," Ryan said, "just because we have them doesn't mean we have to do them. We could just hang out here and then go home." He paused. "Or to a movie or something."

"But I want to do them," Sierra said.

He reached over and put his hand on her leg. "Then we'll do them. But first I have to pee."

"Me, too," James said.

They walked across the meadow, following some code of decorum that required they go as far away from Sierra as they would have if it had been light out. The moon was low and less than half-full. James thought of the night of Greer's party and was gripped by remorse over what he'd put his father through. Then he thought of how nasty he'd been to his father since then, and he punched his thigh and cried, "Fuck."

"What?" Ryan said.

"Nothing."

James's fist had come in contact with the gold cross, a small spiky thing under the denim, and he pressed on it until the points of the cross dug through the lining of his pocket and into his leg.

"Listen, J?" Ryan said. "I'm not going to do the mushrooms. It's good to have someone with you in case anything happens."

"What could happen?"

"I don't know."

"What are you going to do?"

"Just watch you guys. Take care of you."

James stared at Ryan. It was rare for them to stand so close, and he was more aware than usual of the difference in their sizes. Ryan was four inches shorter than he was and fifty pounds lighter. And he had a worried look on his face.

"The only thing?" he continued. "I'm not going to tell her I'm not doing it."

"That's fucked up."

"It's the least fucked-up thing I can think of. If I tell her, then she won't do it, either, and she really wants to."

"So *I'm* supposed to pretend you did it?"

"If you will."

When they returned, Sierra had already set out the mushrooms on a white cloth—a cluster of long, slender stems with caps that looked like flattened moths. There were five or six of them, dried and papery, though when James lifted one to his nose, he nearly gagged from the pungent smell. He asked how many they were each supposed to eat.

"We start with one," she said. "Then we wait an hour, and if we want it to get more intense we eat another."

"Is it going to be gross?"

"That's what the ginger ale is for. Here goes," she said, and she lifted a mushroom and bit off its cap. She chewed for a moment and cried, "Ewww! It's disgusting!"

"Spit it out," Ryan said, cupping his hand in front of her chin.

But she shook her head and chewed vigorously. Quickly, she folded the stem into her mouth and ate it, too. "The ginger ale, the ginger ale," she said, waving her open hand at Ryan. He seized the bottle and tried to twist off the cap, but it wouldn't budge. "No way!" she cried.

"Bottle opener," Ryan said, thrusting the bottle at James and getting to his knees. He grabbed his backpack and said, "Please, please, please."

"Ryan!" Sierra cried.

Ryan unzipped the main compartment, groped around in the emptiness, and then unzipped the front pocket and felt the paper towels he knew were the only things in there.

"Forget it, I'll eat something," she said, and she bit into an apple.

James put down the ginger ale bottle and brought the mushroom to his nose again. Again he nearly gagged. "Walk around a little," he said to Sierra. "It'll help, I swear."

She stood up, retched, and ate more of the apple. Ryan held her.

"I'm not getting sick yet," she said quickly. "It's just the taste."

James had forgotten—if he'd ever known—that mushrooms

made you sick. He slipped the mushroom into his pocket while she wasn't looking. Then he put his hand to his mouth and made chewing motions. "It's not that bad," he said, swallowing air.

She shuddered and took a last bite of the apple. "I'm better," she said. "I just didn't think it would be so nasty."

Ryan turned her gently and pointed to the edge of the meadow. "James is right," he said. "Walk over and back. You'll feel better."

"I already do."

"But even more," he said. "You'll feel good."

She shrugged and took off, walking normally for a few paces and then beginning to skip. She knew this was silly, obviously not the drug, but she felt like doing it. When she reached the edge of the meadow, she turned around and couldn't see Ryan and James.

"Hellooooo," she called.

"Hellooooo," she heard back, but she couldn't tell which of them had spoken.

"Hellooooo," she called again.

"Hellooooo," she heard.

For the last six months, since Ryan had left for Santa Cruz, she had felt an agitation under the skin that sometimes woke her in the middle of the night and almost always found her in the sinkhole of four p.m. On the days she worked at Sand Hill Day, four was the hour when the teachers finished tidying the classrooms and sat together in the Big Room for tea and review. She had imagined she'd enjoy these sessions, but she found them excruciating in the way they forced her to imagine the incessant sensitivity the same teachers had felt in relation to her needs when she was a student there.

Sex helped with the agitation, and so did driving: when she got out of the car in Santa Cruz, she felt a welcome deadness in her legs and shoulders that was almost as good as the Valium she once tried. Being with her mother made the agitation worse.

She began skipping again, straight back to Ryan and James. She'd heard the first hour or so could be kind of scary, and she thought that if she got her body into a playful state, perhaps her mind would follow.

"Baby," Ryan said, opening his arms for her.

"Did you eat yours?"

"Pretty bad. But I had some apple."

"How are we going to get that bottle open? We've got to have something to drink."

"Baby, don't worry. We'll figure it out. We're just at the beginning."

And so they were—or she was, the unwitting soloist in their psilocybin adventure. James knew she was the only one, whereas Ryan believed both she and James had partaken until about two hours in, by which point Sierra had vomited, complained that she was freezing, wept over the problem of the ginger ale, giggled madly about the idea of James going to the Priory ("the *Priory,*" "the *Priory,*" she kept saying between shrieks of laughter), and finally begged Ryan to massage her shoulders. At last, she took her blanket to the edge of the meadow and lay on her back looking at the trees.

"You didn't do it, did you?" Ryan said to James.

"What do you mean?"

"I can tell."

"Neither did you."

"But I told you. You didn't tell me."

James shrugged. "I didn't feel like it. Let's walk around."

They walked without talking, Ryan thinking the whole thing had been a mistake and James recalling a story a friend had told him about babysitting his older sister while she was on an acid trip. James's friend had said the main thing was that it was incredibly boring, but James hadn't understood this until now. He had imagined that the person tripping would be describing hallucinations so intense it would be almost as if the person hearing about it were tripping, too. But if Sierra had started hallucinating, she hadn't said anything. At one point she had become incredibly drowsy and stopped talking, and it wouldn't have surprised him to discover her asleep.

"Sorry she was laughing about the Priory," Ryan said.

James pressed his fingertips to the outline of the cross in his pocket.

"But it's not like you want to go there anyway."

They'd strolled across the meadow and back, and James flopped onto the blanket and lay on his back. It was almost midnight and very cold. Ryan gathered a couple of apples and the Oriental snack mix and went to Sierra. She looked into his eyes and smiled, but she didn't say anything. "Hey, baby," he said. He sat down and felt in the bag for some of the wasabi peas she liked. "Hungry?"

She didn't speak. After what felt like a long time, she lifted her hand and passed it over the length of her face, closing her eyes in the process as if she were both the mortician and the deceased. "Lie with me," she said, her voice deep and faraway.

He lay down next to her.

"Did you ever realize," she said wonderingly, "that the branches of trees are threads in a tapestry?"

"Huh," he said. "Tell me more."

She was silent for a long time, and he wondered if she'd fallen asleep or passed into a hallucination from which he wouldn't be able to retrieve her. He twisted around and tried to make out James through the dark, but he couldn't.

"It's warp and woof," she said. "Like yin and yang."

"Opposites," he said, relieved that he could follow some logic.

"Threads," she said, "are the paint of a tapestry. Trees are the threads of the forest."

"There's also wax and wane," he said. "Hey, where'd the moon go?"

"Lie down with me."

"I am."

"Lie on top of me."

"I don't know," he said. "James—"

"Don't you feel so beautiful?"

"You're the beautiful one."

"No, I'm not beautiful, I feel beautiful. My feelings are beautiful. Are yours? The trees are threads. The world is a loom. Lie on top of me. This could be the best sex we've ever had."

"We don't rank it, do we?"

"I'm not even sure I feel my skin anymore. Please?"

He slid his hand under her shirt and stroked her belly. "Baby, James is right over there."

"He won't mind."

Ryan knew he had put James through some awkward times because of the thinness of the wall between Robert's room and the room where James slept alone. "I can't," he said.

"Hooomp," she whimpered.

"We didn't think of this. I wish we'd talked about it."

"Just touch me."

He unbuttoned her jeans and slipped his hand down until his fingertips reached the silky band of her panties. He paused there and then continued until he got to her pubic hair.

"Please," she said.

His middle finger found her spot. When they had to name it, they called it her spot, never her clit. "Clit" sounded rude.

"I'm going to come so fast," she said. "Or maybe I won't. Maybe I just think I will."

"Don't mind me," James called. In the moonlight he'd been able to see Ryan's progress, from sitting to lying to fondling. Or he thought he could, which amounted to the same thing.

Ryan kissed Sierra's cheek and stood up. "Be right back," he said, and he crossed to where James was now sitting cross-legged, holding an apple by its stem and banging the fruit lightly against his mouth.

"Is this going to take five more hours?" James said. "It's after midnight. I'm starving."

"I don't know if we can move her."

"She didn't break her neck."

Ryan went to get Sierra while James folded the blankets. He wished he'd stayed home; he would've found something to do eventually, or he could've watched TV with his dad, big-time fun for a Friday night. He thought of Mr. Calhoun, the man at the Priory, saying they were looking for the best in every young man who went there. If he went, if he wore the dorky shirt and tie, might he become a young man in whom the best could be found? He imagined seeing his family only on holidays: he'd show up and everyone would be incredibly impressed by how mature he was—so impressed, and he'd be so mature, there'd be no need to talk about it.

"Don't you feel amazing?" Sierra said, surging toward James with her arms out. "Everything is so beautiful. You're so beautiful."

"I'm a guy."

"You're a beautiful guy. You have a beautiful animal inside you."

James exchanged a glance with Ryan.

"'Thank you,'" Ryan said. "Right, James? 'Thank you, Sierra.'"

It was slow going down from the meadow. "Look at the trees," Sierra kept saying, stopping and gazing around. "They're actually threads. There's a secret tapestry covering the world."

When they got to the car it was almost two a.m. James and Ryan were both exhausted. Ryan urged Sierra into the backseat and got behind the wheel. As they drove past the Priory, James said, "I think I'll go there."

"Ha."

"No, really. They find the best in every young man."

"The best in you isn't lost, J."

They drove on, the Beetle's headlights illuminating the empty road. Ryan glanced into the backseat; Sierra was staring vacantly out the window and didn't notice him. On the driveway he tried to be extra gentle with the gears to keep the sound low. He parked next to the Accord and cut the engine. "Phew," he said softly.

James slid his hand into his pocket and pulled out the cross. He tossed it onto the dashboard and said, "I stole that."

Ryan looked surprised. "At the Priory?"

James considered correcting him but didn't. They sat side by side, Ryan looking at the evidence of James's bad character, James nearly holding his breath, he was so nervous about what Ryan would say. He was expecting to be yelled at, but Ryan never did that.

"James," Ryan said softly. "It's okay. You can take it back."

"You don't think I'll burn in hell?"

"We don't believe in hell. That's the beauty."

There was a gasp from the backseat. They both turned around, and Sierra was smiling rapturously. She clapped her hands together three times and then leaned forward and rested her forearms on their seat backs. "That's why he stopped me," she said. "That's why."

Ryan didn't say anything, but James felt him tense up.

"Martin Degenhart." She dug in her back pocket and withdrew a worn leather wallet from which she took a business card that had been fondled so much its edges were soft. She held out the card. "It's the difference between beauty and beautiful. He stopped me because of beauty."

Ryan looked at his lap.

"It's not being a beautiful girl," she said. "It's being a girl who has beauty. The trees are threads. They have beauty."

James couldn't take any more, and he grabbed the cross and got out of the car. The night had gotten clearer, the moon brighter. *Father, guide me,* he thought. But he wasn't sure if he meant his dad or God, and he felt like an idiot and kicked at the gravel.

Ryan and Sierra were out of the car, too. They all started toward the laundry room, but after a few paces Sierra stopped and said, "There's the oak tree."

Each of them looked at the thick twisting branches, heavy ink brushstrokes on charcoal canvas. "I love that tree," she said. "And if you think about it, Martin Degenhart is a funny name. He's famous. I told you that, right, baby? That he's famous?"

"Aren't you coming down a little?" Ryan said. "I am. James, are you?"

Sierra held up her arms and began to goose-step, like a child doing Frankenstein. "Degen Martinhart. That's what his name should be. His hair is so straight. He takes pictures for *Vogue*."

"Let's not talk about him right now," Ryan said. "I think we should go inside."

And to his surprise and relief, she dropped her arms and let him take her hand. The hidden key was exactly where it was supposed to be, and he slid it quietly into the lock and opened the laundry room door.

"Where are we going?" Sierra said, but she said it in a whisper, and Ryan thought she *might* be coming down—she was making more sense of the world, or just making more sense.

He opened the door to Robert's room and turned on the light, and there, asleep in his childhood bed, was Robert.

What followed was five minutes of hushed confusion, with Robert quick to awaken but slow to figure out where he was and why Ryan had come into his room, and James taking on the very new job of reminding everyone else to be quiet so they wouldn't wake their father. Earlier in the evening, Robert had driven down from the city on the spur of the moment, a single decision that had delivered effective treatment for two separate cases of loneliness. He and Bill had spent the evening talking about his career plans, and he'd had the opportunity to slip into the conversation a humorous remark about his stubborn case of medical student's disease. In five minutes, his father had put his mind at ease on both the groin pain and the cough.

Finally Ryan and Sierra settled in Rebecca's room. Sierra was dazed and a little nervous again, and she jerked involuntarily each time a floorboard creaked in another room or the toilet flushed. She didn't want sex anymore, and she didn't want to go to sleep, so they lay awake together, Ryan drifting and bringing himself back, and drifting and bringing himself back, over and over. He watched the numerals on Rebecca's clock flip toward morning. At one point Sierra whispered that she was "egg smooth," and he saw a giant egg hovering above him in the dark. He blinked and it was still there, and he wondered what it had been like for her, up in the meadow hallucinating. He was going to have to tell her he hadn't eaten his mushroom, but he wondered if he had to tell her about James. She wouldn't like the idea of having been the only one.

Early in the morning Bill rose and found all three children's bedrooms occupied. He knew Rebecca always got up first thing Saturday morning to start her laundry, so he called and said, "Everyone's here. Let me come get you. We'll have a big breakfast." Waiting for him in front of her dorm, she looked like an out-of-place adult among the few bleary late-adolescents who were up early on a weekend morning. Or up very, very late on a Friday night.

There were a few exceptions. "See that girl?" Rebecca said, taking her seat in the Accord and leaning over to kiss her father.

A young Indian woman walked purposefully along the sidewalk, a Stanford sweatshirt half covering a pale yellow sari.

"She got a Rhodes Scholarship. She's going to study astrophysics."

"I guess it's true what they say about the early bird."

"She's the early airplane."

They headed home past the Stanford driving range and along the shaded road that ran between Hole 7 and Hole 9 of the golf course. They passed runners sweating in the cool March air. Rebecca had spent the evening with a psychology grad student named Ben, and as she sat beside her father she thought she should trust her instincts more and say no when people asked her out. Ben was a guy she'd sort of known for a couple of years—he'd been a TA in her first psych class, though not her TA—and late in the afternoon he'd approached her in the library and invited her to go with him to First Friday, a monthly psychology department gathering for faculty members, graduate students, and undergraduate majors. Rebecca had agreed because the last time she'd gone, in December, she'd gotten involved in a very interesting conversation about cross-fostered rhesus monkeys and what happened when an anxious baby was raised by a calm mother and vice versa. This time Ben kept trying to steer her to his dissertation adviser, a musty senior professor whose research was about memory or learning, she wasn't sure which—either she didn't remember or she'd never learned, ha ha. She was polite to Ben, but it had gotten tiring, slipping away and then seeing him approach yct again from across the room. "I keep losing you," he said, and she thought: No, I keep trying to lose you.

Robert was in the kitchen when they arrived. The three of them got to work, one cracking eggs, another halving oranges for juice, the third pulling apart bacon slices and laying them in a frying pan.

"Isn't this great?" Bill said. "It's only been a week or so since we were together for Ryan's birthday."

"And Robert's is coming up," Rebecca said. "And then mine in April."

"When I was a kid," Robert said, "it really bugged me that our birthdays weren't in the right order. I thought mine should've been in January, Rebecca's in February, Ryan's in March, and James's in April."

"Imagine James," Rebecca said, "if he'd had the last birthday on top of everything else." She paused and looked at Bill. "So what happened at the Priory?"

"Bit of a bust. I'll let James tell you about it. Or better yet, don't ask."

"Why?"

"It's water under the bridge. By the time your mother went down to the shed last night, she'd forgotten about it and was talking about a new piece she's working on."

The truth was that Bill wished he hadn't allowed the Priory thing to go so far. He should've stopped Penny before she ever called to set up the appointment, and failing that he should have told James he didn't have to go with her. Accompanying them had been a form of acquiescence, even collusion.

"Should I go tell her about breakfast?" Robert said.

"Certainly."

"That's funny," Rebecca said. "I thought Robert was asking if he should go tell her *now,* but you answered as if he'd asked whether we should tell her *at all.*"

"Did I?" Bill said, feeling caught out and trying to conceal his guilt behind a veneer of curiosity.

"That's what 'certainly' sounds like," Rebecca said. "If you'd said, 'Sure, go ahead,' it would've sounded more like, 'Yeah, now's a good time.'"

"Remember," Robert said, "how we tried to think of ways to get her to do stuff with us?"

"Oh, my God!" Rebecca exclaimed. "I haven't thought of that in so long." She turned to Bill. "We had a crusade. We brainstormed things we thought she'd like and wrote them down. I'll bet I still have the piece of paper somewhere."

"Was bacon on the list?" Bill said, but he was distinctly uncomfortable and busied himself at the juicer, pressing hard on each orange half as, behind him, Robert and Rebecca exchanged uneasy glances. For the first time—though hardly the last; she would puzzle over this for years, until the question itself became the story—Rebecca wondered if her mother's protracted withdrawal from the family could be seen as a response to some behavior or attitude in her father. *It was an equal and opposite reaction,* she imagined explaining to someone, and then she tried to remember if there was a concept in physics that meant *You started it.*

Robert felt bad, too, and he struggled for something to say. "Have you both realized," he began, uncertain where he was going, "that in a few years," and then it came to him, "if the three of us are waiting somewhere together, whoever comes to get us will say, 'Dr. Blair, Dr. Blair, and Dr. Blair'?"

"Hey, you're right," Rebecca said, and Bill looked over his shoulder and said, "That's pretty nifty," and all three of them began to feel better.

Bill said he'd wake the kids and suggested Rebecca start cooking the bacon and Robert head for the shed.

It was gorgeous out, and Robert went down the driveway slowly, thinking both that he should get back to the city to study and that he would very much like to spend the whole day in Portola Valley, maybe the whole weekend, especially if he could convince Rebecca to stick around for a while.

"Mom," he called as he passed his car, parked at the shed last night because he'd looked in on her when he first arrived. "Yoo-hoo."

She came out and waved. "Perfect timing!" She was wearing the same clothes she'd had on the night before and looked as if she hadn't slept: hair still in its braid but wild and mussed around her face.

"We're making breakfast," he said, but as soon as the words were out he was close enough to see into the shed, and he stopped short. Behind her, leaning against her worktable, was a new assemblage. He gaped at it. "No way."

She looked over her shoulder and then faced him again. "I need your help. It's too heavy to carry, I want you to drive it up."

"You've got to be kidding."

"What?"

"James will—"

"Oh, don't be silly, he won't care. Can you give me a hand? I think I've made a real breakthrough, I want everyone to see it."

By then Bill was back in the kitchen with Rebecca, and James was in the shower, but Ryan and Sierra were moving slowly, Ryan sitting naked at Rebecca's desk while Sierra lay naked on the sheets and tried to explain what she'd learned on her trip and why Ryan shouldn't be sad about her decision to call Martin Degenhart and tell him she was ready for the plane ticket to New York that he'd offered her. "I won't be gone that long," she said. "And if I don't go, I'll be like the planted seed that never sprouted."

"You figured it out," he said.

"What?"

"That I didn't eat my mushroom."

"No, baby, no, I just need to do this. Look at you at Santa Cruz. I—Wait, you didn't eat your mushroom?" Slowly, she sat up and looked at him. Her breasts were sweet and full, her nipples with the same flat, satiny smoothness and deep rose color as her mouth.

He shook his head. "I wanted to take care of you."

"Oh, my God, Ryan. Now I *really* have to go."

"That doesn't make sense."

"I thought you were getting it last night, I thought you were *with* me. Beauty is different from—"

"I was. You feel beauty instead of you are beautiful. I do get it. You think that guy—"

"Martin—"

"—stopped you because of something in you, not just your looks."

"That's sort of it," she said. "But Ryan, you lied."

"It was dark up there. James was in a weird mood. You won't be the unsprouted seed, I promise. You are sprouted."

"I'll come back. Or you'll come with me. You can meet me there this summer."

"You're talking about *now*?" He began to cry, and after a moment so did she. They lay down together and salted each other's skin. Sierra had been approached by Martin Degenhart on a Tuesday in October, and while she listened politely to a straight-haired stranger in a leather jacket tell her he could make her famous, Ryan sat innocently in a lecture hall at UC Santa Cruz with no idea that sixty miles away an assault was being launched against his life.

"Guys," Rebecca said from the hallway, knocking lightly. "Are you coming?"

There was no way for them to pull apart and get dressed, not until they'd made love, and so they began, their fingertips and palms and lips and tongues traveling routes so familiar that the ground had scarcely to be touched before the destinations were reached. Sierra was in a state of exquisite sensitivity, and she came three, four, five times, until the hallucinations of the night before seemed never to have stopped and the tapestry of trees that had revealed itself to her in the meadow draped over her again like a heavy and gorgeous blanket.

Ryan left her sleeping. He went into the bathroom and was washing his face when James appeared in the open doorway. "What's the matter?" James said.

Ryan looked in the mirror. His eyes were red, and despite the washing his face looked blotchy. "Nothing. Sierra might go to New York."

"Change is cool," James said. "I'm going to the Priory."

"Come on."

"No, really."

They made their way toward the kitchen. The front door was open, and their mother was standing just outside with Robert and Rebecca.

"What are they doing?" James said.

"Boys," their father said, coming out of the kitchen. "I just put biscuits in the oven. Where's Sierra?"

Rebecca spun around and held up her hand. "Stop."

But James wasn't going to be ordered around, and Ryan and Bill kept pace with him, and in a moment they were all looking at Penny's new assemblage, larger than any she'd ever done, a four-by-six-foot open box with a cellophane egg noodle bag thumbtacked at the top, an ancient nursing brassiere dangling nearby, a bent wire hanger suspended from a teacup hook, a crumpled cookbook page held in place by a safety pin, a plastic Halloween witch's mask hanging from an elastic thread, and a handful of Christmas tree tinsel clumped around a rusty nail. There was more, much more, but the thing that had everyone's attention was at the center of the piece, held in place by four poultry trussing needles. It was Dog.

"Mom," Ryan gasped.

James barked out a laugh, but his face was burning.

"It's okay," Ryan said to Penny. "Just take him out and give him back."

"It's not like I care," James said.

"Of course you care," Ryan said. "He's your dog."

Bill was dumbfounded, but at last he found his voice. "Penny, this is outrageous. It's beyond the pale. What were you thinking?"

She stared at him for a long moment. "You want to know what I was thinking? Do you kids believe he really wants to know what I was thinking?"

No one had a response. Robert felt guilty about having helped her get the piece up to the house, and the guilt made him angry, and the anger made him wish he'd stayed in San Francisco or even in Michigan with Julie Anne—in some place that felt like home. Rebecca remembered that "beyond the pale" referred to the part of Ireland that was beyond the area controlled by the English, and then, almost but not quite aware that she was intentionally distracting herself, she distracted herself further by wondering if the nursing bra was one her mother had actually worn and saved or if she'd bought it at Goodwill. Ryan looked at the thumbtacks and imagined a picture of Sierra on the cover of a magazine and how thousands and thousands of copies of that picture could end up pinned to the walls of thousands and thousands of men.

James came closest to thinking about his mother's question and its obvious answer. Instead, he noticed a tear in her shirt that exposed the vulnerable skin of her underarm, and he recognized a kind of rigidity in his father's posture, and in order to resist going where these observations would take him, he made a decision. Summoning a tone of great injury, he shouted, "I'm out of here," and he took off at a run.

9

JAMES

I was born at the Stanford Hospital on January 6, 1968, the same day Dr. Norman Shumway reported to a crowd of waiting journalists that he had transplanted a heart into the ailing body of one Michael Kasperak, the first such surgery in America. The hospital had the air of a carnival, and in the maternity ward my mom's obstetrician had to call three times for someone to come suction meconium from my tiny lungs. To me this says everything—not the medically historic significance of my birth date but the fact that I was born with my mouth full of shit.

Thirty-seven years later, I was born again. I don't mean I accepted Jesus Christ as my lord and savior. I mean I arrived at last among my people.

I was at a low point when I found them, a part-time cashier at a Costco in Eugene, Oregon, making ends meet only because of my share of the rent we were collecting on the Portola Valley house. I lived across the Willamette River from Eugene, in working-class Springfield, in a four-unit apartment complex that backed onto the parking lot of a multiscreen movie theater. My roommate was so quiet and reclusive that all I really knew about him I learned on the day he interviewed me, when he said certain scents gave him migraines so I'd have to use his brand of shaving cream and deodorant if I wanted to live there.

I spent my free time watching Three Stooges DVDs on my dad's old laptop. Dating seemed like too much work, but a U of O dance professor had flirted with me in a café, and we had sex from time to time. One evening we were on her porch and her neighbors walked by, a middle-aged couple carrying matching water bottles in pouches at their waists. We chatted, and maybe because I was in a bad mood anyway I started in on a spiel I'd been developing about the isolation of modern life. Where had I gotten this? I didn't know. I'd been spouting it for a while, long enough that even I found it boring.

"I mean," I said to the dance professor and her neighbors, "how well do you guys know each other? You live on the same block and this is only the second or third time you've talked, am I right? I wish there was a club I could join that would give me a bunch of people I could call if my power went out. Or I got sick. And they would have to help."

"I have half a dozen people like that," the dance professor said. "They're called friends."

"But friends can bail. They're allowed to be busy."

"You're talking," the husband said, "about an intentional community. We know people in one, right here in town. They're looking for new members. Do you want to talk to them?"

I kept myself from snickering. I imagined a bunch of earnest people with a mission statement, having three-hour meetings to talk about how often and where they should have their three-hour meetings. "Thanks, but I think I'll pass."

"Why?" the dance professor said. "Call and find out about it. It's not like you've got anything else going on in your life."

Nothing like hearing the truth to shake a guy up.

They called themselves the Barn, twenty-six people spread over seven households dotted around Eugene. The idea had originated with two couples, the Smith-Berkoffs and the Rankin-O'Sullivans, who'd met when their children were in preschool together. They wanted a community and decided to make one. Getting dinner on the table seven nights a week was at the top of everyone's stress list, so each Tuesday and Thursday one household made enough dinner to feed the entire Barn, and the other households sent someone to pick up the food. Next, a monthly workday rotated from household to household, when everyone would pitch in on a big project. And finally, the whole group got together on the first Sunday of each month for a meeting and potluck.

I was invited to a gathering at Amazon Park. It was July, and there were blankets spread under trees, kids swarming a play structure, adults chatting. I liked the way subgroups formed and re-formed, by age, gender, hobbies, pieces of common history. I talked to two guys who shared my passion for Neil Young, a woman who'd grown up in Palo Alto. "This is James," people kept saying. "He's interested in us."

That evening I logged on to the Barnboard with my guest password and found a list of the members. In addition to the Smith-Berkoffs (Marie, Dan, two kids) and the Rankin-O'Sullivans (Sarah, Greg, three kids, and a live-in grandfather), there were the Lees (Priscilla, Mike, no kids), the Batchelors (Terri, Tom, three kids), the Komarovs (Margo, single mother with two kids), the Norton-Fieldings (Celia, David, two kids), and the Kinsellas (Beth, Stan, no kids).

"So I guess I'd be the Blair?" I typed, and within minutes I'd gotten four responses, from "Whatever you want" to "Wouldn't you just be James?" to "Let's see what happens organically" to my favorite, from Celia Norton, "You already are."

"So I'm in?" I asked Dan Berkoff on the phone a couple days later.

"Why not?"

"I don't know, don't you want to do a background check?"

"You like us, we like you. What we're doing is pretty simple. If it doesn't work, we vote you out."

It was like falling in love, but with a whole crowd rather than a single person. Everyone was so open and welcoming. I found out that the group had been inspired by Dan Berkoff's childhood memory of growing up Jewish in suburban New York. Within his synagogue, groups of families helped each other with religious observation and other aspects of Jewish life. The Barn had the same idea, minus the religious observation and the word "Jewish": a group to help each other with life.

If the official activities were the monthly meetings and the workdays and the twice-weekly dinners, the community's true life sprang from postings on the Barnboard. "Does anyone have a good recipe for tamales?" "We're going to feed the ducks and have two extra seats, anyone want to get rid of a kid for a couple hours?" "Starting clothing drive for Katrina victims, care to help?" I jumped right in. I didn't have much to offer in the way of recipes to share or equipment to lend, but I had a lot of time and got an enthusiastic response whenever I said I was going to such-and-such a store and did anyone need anything. I participated in as many threads of conversation as I could, even posting one- or two-word responses so I would get notified when there were further comments. Not that I really needed to get notified, since I was checking the board every hour to see what was new.

The first workday happened about three weeks after I joined, a daylong project digging out and replanting the Kinsellas' backyard. By dinnertime I was completely wiped and felt better than I had in a long time. "Feels good, doesn't it?" Tom Batchelor said. I twisted from side to side, stretching my back. "Yeah," I said, "in that oh-hello-muscles-I-forgot-about way." "No, this," he said, sweeping his hand to indicate the group. "I mean this."

I really didn't know how to cook, so for my first dinner I used my employee discount to buy bags of salad and pans of Costco enchiladas. I knew this was pathetic and was a little worried I'd get a discontinue notice, like the phone company turning off your service: *Due to incompetence we are hereby terminating our agreement with JAMES BLAIR to participate in the organization known as THE BARN.* Instead, people started inviting me to come watch how they did it—to learn how to cook for a crowd, someone said, kindly skipping over the more basic fact. "What do you normally eat?" Marie Smith asked as she showed me how to make tomato sauce with actual tomatoes. She was asking how I'd gotten by in life. By the skin of my teeth was the answer.

Being six-four, I was asked to clear off the top shelf, get the ball out of the tree, hang the new light fixture. "You're so handy," Terri Batchelor said one workday as I painted her kitchen ceiling without a ladder. I figured she meant tall. "Isn't James great?" people said to each other. "You're a great addition, James."

I was used to disappointing people, so all of this was pretty new, and I wasn't surprised a few weeks later when it seemed the other shoe was about to drop. "Can I be honest about something?" Margo Komarov said to me one afternoon as I stood at a picnic table slicing watermelon. I was gearing up to make a joke out of whatever came next, but she smiled and said, "I wasn't sure about you at first, but I'm so glad they voted me down."

Twenty-five hours a week I still worked at Costco. Still hated it, but it bothered me less. My boss was an asshole, but even that didn't bother me much. Most Mondays I worked one to seven, leaving my mornings open, and in late September I answered a post from Sarah Rankin looking for someone to drive her dad to physical therapy. From then on, I was his chauffeur, this cool grandpa from Seattle who'd ruptured his Achilles doing a half Ironman. He was maybe five-seven and all muscle, though the injury had sidelined him and he complained about how fast he was losing tone. The physical therapy office was on the other side of town, so we had some time in the car together. "Don't get old, James," he told me one morning. "Are you exercising? Can't do anything about your genes, so get your butt moving." He was seventy-five, the age my dad was when he died, but he seemed younger, more like sixtysomething. Back at the house that day, he showed me photos from his two dozen triathlons and then directed me to make us a vegetable smoothie while he sat at the kitchen table with his foot propped up. "Another thing?" he said. "Don't let your wife die. Get a wife—and then don't let her die."

That kind of talk usually bummed me out, but there was something about hearing it in a happy house: it made me optimistic. Not about finding a wife but because he'd said it. He couldn't tell I was someone you didn't say that to, someone who had no future. Maybe I did.

When the weather changed, the monthly meetings moved indoors. In November we met at the Smith-Berkoffs' house, and suddenly the kids dominated. They were everywhere, and even when they were out of sight they were still in mind.

"Notice how the girls sit and the boys run? I didn't truly believe in gender differences until I had kids."

"She's having trouble with the baby." "Nursing trouble?" "No, she loves him more. She thinks the other two know."

"They met with the teacher, and it turns out the twins aren't *being* bullied, they're bullying."

I moseyed around, picking up bits of conversation and wondering how I'd feel about the whole thing after six months indoors. Rain hammered at the windows. It was four o'clock in the afternoon and the sky was the color of wet concrete.

Stan Kinsella joined me at the fireplace. He and his wife were the oldest couple—midfifties—and didn't have kids. "Lots of small fry," he said. "Hope you're not overwhelmed."

"No, no. I have a niece and two nephews."

"Beth and I debated about this. Did such a kid-oriented group make sense for us. But our only other option was a group of folks in their sixties and seventies, sort of an ad hoc retirement community. Their bylaws included mandatory advance directives."

"You had options?"

"This is where we're all headed. Or should be. No one goes to church anymore, so we have to make our own congregations. You know what 'congregate' means? It's from the Latin. 'Greg' means herd. 'Con' means with. We're with our herd."

"Huh," I said. "One thing that really got me after 9/11 was Bush saying we should all go to church. 'Go to your churches and temples and mosques—go and pray.' Something like that. It pissed me off so much."

"Like you didn't count?"

"Like I didn't care."

Stan nodded. "If something like that happened again, I'd want to be with these people."

I thought of my life at the time of the attacks, how bad it sucked. I was living in Santa Rosa, washing dishes at a lousy restaurant and fucking the bartender. I didn't like her very much, and she alternated between scorn and indifference toward me. There was a lot of stuff in the media about people drawing together and being kinder and whatnot, but things between this woman and me went downhill. I finally just walked off the job—punched my time card one last time and drove away. When I arrived at my pit of an apartment, I realized I hadn't even taken off my apron.

Across the room, ten-year-old Rosie Rankin-O'Sullivan caught my eye and stuck out her tongue at me. I put my fingers in my ears and crossed my eyes. She lolled her head sideways and let her tongue hang out the side of her mouth. I reached my arms behind my neck and simultaneously wiggled my right earlobe with my left fingers and my left earlobe with my right fingers. This made her laugh.

Later, she tracked me down in the kitchen with two younger kids in tow. She directed me to "do that thing again," and when I reached behind my head for my earlobes, they all squealed.

"How long are your arms?"

"How do you do that?"

"I want to try, I want to try!"

This led to a discussion of proportion and flexibility, and finally to a step-by-step demonstration that attracted so much kid attention we had to move to another room. "Look, everyone!" Rosie called. "Look what the Blair can do!" A little later, I was lying on my back on the rug and four or five children were pulling and bending my limbs, and from the doorway tiny, dark-eyed Celia Norton smiled at me.

Half a dozen weeks went by. Rebecca offered me a plane ticket so I could go home for Christmas, but I didn't want to use any vacation days. Plus I knew at least half the Barn would be gathering. "What will you do instead?" Rebecca said, and because I hadn't told any of my siblings about the Barn, afraid they'd mock me or disapprove, I said I was going to work, prepping the store for the huge sale starting December 26. In fact, I went to a feast at the Batchelors', and it turned out to be the happiest Christmas I'd had in a long time.

"You seem to be getting the hang of this," Celia said one Thursday in January when I stopped at her house for my dinner basket. We didn't always see the cook when we picked up, but she happened to be on her porch, gathering her mail.

"Guess I am."

"You're a natural."

"Oh, that's funny. For a sec I thought you said *You're unnatural.*"

She smiled. "No, you're very natural. *And* you're a natural."

"Phew, I like to be more than one thing."

"Oh, you're definitely that," she said, blushing slightly. "No question."

Another time, on a workday, she was boxing books in the corner of a cramped living room, and I asked if I could help her. "It's kind of crowded back here," she said, and I said, "I can stand it if you can."

We started chatting every time the Barn met. Harmless, I thought. Light. I was attracted to her, but that was fine, that was just being alive. I hadn't seen the dance professor in a while and I had to have someone to think about.

In March we were able to have our monthly meeting outside. We gathered at Alton Baker Park, everyone happy to be in the thin spring sunlight. We spread tarps on the ground to protect the blankets, and our butts, from moisture. I ended up sitting with a small group of women, Celia and two others. They were the young moms: among them they had seven children under the age of seven. One was nursing an infant. We all watched as Celia's husband, David Fielding, tried to run a soccer game for a bunch of kids. The kids didn't want to play by the rules, and he was having a tough time keeping them focused.

"You know what I've noticed about you?" Celia said to me after the other women had wandered away.

"What's that?"

"You can't sit still."

I was surprised—actually kind of flattered—but tried to hide it. "ADD, no doubt, but even my pediatrician dad didn't think of it back then."

"What would happen if you just sat here for half an hour?"

"No problem. If you'll sit with me, I won't even be tempted to get up."

"Did you fidget when you were little?"

"I was a perpetual motion machine. With a snotty nose. Youngest of four."

"Yeah, you already told me that."

"I did?"

"A couple weeks ago. You have two brothers and one sister. You don't remember?"

"No, but that doesn't mean anything."

"James, slow down."

I hadn't been aware I was talking fast. It was because of her. She was small but voluptuous, with a heart-shaped face and a sweet chin. She wore a gold chain around her neck with a seagull hanging from it, which already didn't seem like her even though I hardly knew her. "Sorry," I said. "I'll try."

"No harm done. It's not for me, it's for you."

"You're sort of healer-ish."

"Actually, I'm not."

At that point there were shouts from the soccer game; Theo, her older son, was jumping up and down in front of one of the goals. David waved his hand back and forth over his head, and when he saw that Celia was watching he pointed at Theo and stuck his thumb in the air.

She said, "Ah, thank God."

"Competitive?"

"You can't imagine. And I'm not talking about my son."

"James," shouted one of the other men from the field. "Come join us."

"The moment of truth," Celia said.

"Oh, I'm not going."

"But you want to."

"No, I don't."

"You don't feel all coiled and ready to spring?"

I did, but not in the direction of the soccer game. In my mind she and I were rolling around naked together. Charming guy that I was, I might have said so to a different woman. I wanted her to tell me a secret and I tried to think of a question that would prompt one.

"So how about you? I'll bet you were never a perpetual motion machine with a snotty nose."

"What makes you say that?"

I let myself look at her body before I answered. What I mean is, I let myself look at her body in such an obvious way that she couldn't miss the fact that I was looking at her body. It wasn't that I couldn't resist being the asshole I knew myself to be; it was more, it felt like the honorable thing to do. To admit my attraction. When I met her gaze again she gave me a sorrowful smile.

"I just have a hunch," I said. "I'll bet you were calm and quiet."

"Not really. I cried a lot."

"Cried like you threw a fit? I did that."

"No, cried in fear. Or relief. I spent a lot of time in fear or relief."

"What were you afraid of?"

"Crying."

I sighed and lay back on the ground. She was too lovely to bear. The blanket was thin, and a rock dug between my shoulder blades. I scooted sideways and found a smooth spot. More cheers from the soccer field, and she turned to look. She had a mole high up on her neck, right at the corner of her jawbone. I wondered what it would feel like against my tongue.

"Twenty-three more minutes," she said.

"Piece of cake."

Joe Rankin, the triathlete grandpa, graduated from physical therapy, and we started biking together on Monday mornings. He kicked my ass in every way, but I couldn't deny it felt good to be riding. I used an old bike that belonged to his son-in-law, who'd recently gotten a beautiful new two-thousand-dollar Cannondale. We cruised around the hills south of town. One Saturday we got a whole group of Barners to go out with us, and afterward, sitting on the Rankin-O'Sullivans' front porch, we talked about doing a longer ride sometime, maybe to a campsite where we could spend the night. I thought this sounded great, and Priscilla Lee, the group's most avid cyclist, said that if I would start polling people on possible dates she would help me figure out a good destination. On our next workday, Celia's husband told me he'd heard about the idea and would like to be on the list, and as he talked I saw her out of the corner of my eye, standing by herself watching us.

I was becoming a regular at the Rankin-O'Sullivans' dinner table. In addition to Rosie, they had twin eight-year-old boys who missed no opportunity to replay the limb-twisting game. One evening as I lay on the living room rug letting my muscles and joints recover, Sarah asked where I'd lived before Eugene. Normally I didn't talk much about the endless moving I'd done since I dropped out of college, but I ended up spilling my whole long, pathetic story.

"After my dad died I counted the addresses he had for me. Thirty-one. And there were some places I lived where I didn't send an address because I knew I'd be moving on too soon. Thirty-one addresses, probably twenty different zip codes. A couple dozen phone numbers."

"Listen," Joe said. "How will you ever get married when you move around all the time?"

"That's sexist, Grandpa," one of the twins said. "Women can move."

"He could marry Margo," the other twin said. "Then instead of the Komarovs and the Blair we'd have the Komarov-Blairs."

Rosie threw a pillow at her brother. "That is totally stupid. He doesn't even like her. He likes Celia."

There was a silence, and I felt Sarah Rankin's gaze grow pointed. Hot with shame, I lay as still as I could. Evenings lately, I'd been too restless to watch movies and also embarrassed that my taste ran so consistently to the stupid. I'd started surfing the Web, bouncing from Monster.com (maybe I could get a different job) to Craigslist .org (maybe I could find a better apartment) to REI.com (I want shit) to Walmart.com (I'm poor) to Dictionary.com (does "congregate" really mean "with the herd"?). That last had taken me down a path that led to "egregious," which in my mind meant "really, really bad; unforgivable" but had the same root as "congregate" and began life with the value-neutral meaning "outside the herd." I didn't want that and knew I had to watch myself with Celia.

At work I was given a promotion. This was only the third promotion of my life and I debated calling Rebecca. I went so far as to bring up her number on my phone, but there was something pitiful about calling with good news, almost more pitiful than calling with bad news.

The Barn was excited for me. At our April meeting there was a homemade sheet cake with "Congratulations to the Blair" written on it in shaky blue icing. I could see the hand of a Barn child or two in the huge volume of colored sprinkles covering the cake.

"I can't thank you guys enough," I said. "I don't want to go all gooey on you, but you opened your arms and—"

"Group hug!" shouted Adam Smith-Berkoff, the lone teenager in the group.

"Adam!" his mom said.

We were sitting in a jagged circle on the grass at University Park, kids sprawled in front of their parents, the younger ones with little bags of crackers to keep them occupied.

"It was a win-win," someone said.

"We love your energy."

"And your employee discount."

Smiles all around: I'd purchased a huge supply of biodegradable plates and cups and utensils.

"Any other business?" Greg O'Sullivan said. He was running the meeting that day. We traded off, household by household.

"Actually, I have one thing," David Fielding said. "Weren't we talking about a group bike ride some weekend? We should probably choose a date if we want it to happen."

"Oh, sorry, my bad," I said. "I was going to do that. I saw a really cool bike at a shop on East Thirteenth—dream on, right? But no, sorry, I'll definitely get to it."

He gave me a tight smile. "The road to hell is paved with good intentions. I don't know if you ever read our bylaws, but we're big on follow-through."

Fuck you, too, I thought, but it didn't really bother me. "I'll post something tonight," I said.

It was time to eat, and as people started getting up from the circle, I saw a tense-looking exchange between David and Celia. Then she put her hand on his shoulder, and I thought maybe I'd read it wrong, maybe it hadn't been tense. Maybe, long married, they simply didn't smile at each other all that much. But then she unfolded her legs and began to stand, and I realized she was just using him for stability.

"Sorry about my husband," she said to me a little later. We were bussing the same picnic table.

"No worries."

"He doesn't have the best social skills."

"Really, no worries. You've got enough for two."

She smiled and touched my arm, then drew her hand back and

said, "Did you know that across cultures the elbow is the most neutral place to touch another person?"

"I didn't know that."

"Well, it is," she said. "It's very neutral."

It would've been nice to think there was still nothing to any of this, just a promise of friendship if either of us had the time or desire to pursue it. But my heart pounded when I saw her, and she stared at me across rooms and lawns, and there wasn't nothing to it at all.

"You know what I love about the Barn," Sarah Rankin said to me one night in her kitchen when I was helping with the dishes. "It's how much respect we all have for each other's families. We're connected but we're also distinct entities that come first, ahead of the community."

Got it, Chief, I thought.

And I avoided Celia. A few times she approached me with a comment or question and I was maybe a little curt. I emailed the dance professor and we started up again, a relationship that was more booty call than anything else, mostly her calling me. She was in her forties and knew what she wanted, which was sometimes sex and sometimes a foot rub and a mug of chamomile tea.

The last Thursday in April it was my turn to do dinner baskets. I'd become really good at cooking strips of chicken for fajitas, and I got discounted tortillas at work, so once every two months that was dinner for the Barn. I felt guilty making people come to my apartment in Springfield, so I used the Kinsellas' house as the pickup point for my meals. I generally waited through the pickup period to ensure there'd be nothing left behind on the Kinsellas' porch (which had happened the first couple of times and which I knew only because Sarah Rankin told me about it; she was a little like Rebecca, but with long, frizzy hair and three kids). The first five baskets went fast, and then I sat with the final two, the

Lees' and the Norton-Fieldings', for about half an hour. It wasn't unusual for there to be a few stragglers, but when Priscilla Lee showed up at six-thirty and took their basket and there was just the one left, I began to wonder what I'd do if no one came. The Norton-Fieldings lived fairly close by, and I argued with myself about the wisdom of running their basket over to their house so I could be finished with the whole thing and on my way. It wasn't really much of an argument.

"You came," Celia said, answering the door in the kind of sweatpants women wear, tight on the hips and thighs and flared at the cuff. Hers had a seagull on one thigh, and I thought I'd never asked her about her seagull necklace and also that I was in deep, wondering about her seagull necklace.

I held up the basket. "Home delivery."

She looked upset. "I wasn't sure if you would. I thought so but I wasn't sure."

"What's going on?"

We were on opposite sides of a screen door, and she pushed it open. "Please come in."

"I just wanted to drop this."

"Come in."

I entered the house. It was a small, boxy place with just two bedrooms. I could tell no one else was there. "Where is everyone?"

She'd taken the basket from me and set it on a table. When she turned around her eyes were wet.

"What's wrong?"

She shook her head and put her face in her hands.

"What?" I said, stepping close and taking hold of her shoulders. She sobbed and pressed her forehead to my shirtfront.

"Celia?" It was the closest we'd ever stood and I realized just how small she was, probably not even five feet tall.

"They'll be here in five minutes," she said. "Three. When can you come back?"

The following Monday morning, the first of May, I cancel my bike ride with Joe. Celia closes the blinds and we fuck so fast and hard she gets rug burns on her back. "He won't even notice, he hardly looks at me." Glasses of limeade on her back step, an awkward foot between us, a terrible mistake we know we'll repeat.

The May meeting six days after that, so carefully not looking at each other that it would be totally obvious to anyone watching.

A phone call from the Safeway parking lot, late at night. "I said we were out of milk. Hope he doesn't look in the fridge." She shifts to a memory from girlhood, a man who looked at her funny, how little David cares about her stories. "That's how he is. He's been like that from the beginning."

I arrange a Wednesday morning off, and she comes to my place, her look of dismay at the grim building, the slatted chain-link fence that divides our garbage area from the movie theater parking lot.

Another phone call and I'm describing my mom and her warm, maternal personality, ha ha. I've done so plenty of times before, but it was always comedy. Now it's completely different. "That's sad," Celia says, and I say, "Yeah, I guess it is," and fuck if I don't get all teary.

Another workday, painting again but this time a house exterior, a bogus errand for a half-dozen paintbrushes with her kids in the backseat acting as our beards. The older one, Theo: "Why did the Blair come with us?" "I need help," she says with her eyes on the rearview mirror. "The Blair is a good helper."

A Tuesday evening, arriving just ahead of me to pick up dinner baskets at the Batchelors', her boys beg to go inside. We sit in wicker chairs on opposite sides of the porch and stare at each other. "How turned on are you?" she says in a low voice. "I'm dying."

Over and over again we say: "We can't do this." "We have to stop."

We don't. We can't.

A Friday night at the Rankin-O'Sullivans', Sarah asks about that bike ride thing, did I ever poll people? "Sorry," I say, "I'm a loser." "James," she says. "You can just say, 'No, I haven't done it yet. I've been busy.'" A pause. "You have been busy, right? Something's different. I've been wondering."

Celia and I take turns arguing for a halt. "No one knows. I'm positive no one knows." "But how much longer can that last?"

The fantasy of being in love gives way to the clobbering reality. She wants to be with me. I want to be with her. I've never felt this way about anyone. She weeps over the possibility of hurting her kids.

Late June, she tells David she's going to Portland for the night, one of her best friends from college is passing through. "Dawn," she tells him. "You don't remember Dawn?" There is no Dawn. It's too much lie, she frets. We meet at a hotel on the coast. The little bottle of lotion is runny and smells of lavender, but it's my first time massaging her shoulders, and she says I am an amazingly gentle and kind person, and I have to cancel out the thought that she has me confused with someone else. I'm supposed to be on my way by seven a.m., but I call in sick.

"You had a crush on Sierra, didn't you?" The phone again: she's at home in the middle of the morning, I'm on break. "Not really," I say. "I don't know. Yes." "Your dad shouldn't have let her sleep over." "Whatever. They were really serious." "No, not because it was wrong. It took Ryan away from you." And I can hardly speak, I suddenly miss him so much. Why do I never call him? I remember being six, seven, eight years old and home after school with him, before Robert and Rebecca returned, our mom down in the shed. He'd make me a snack and spread a beach towel on the living room rug so we could picnic in front of the TV. Our favorite was *The Doctors,* which was about "the brotherhood of healing," as the announcer always said. "Can we be a brotherhood of healing?" I asked him once, and he said he thought so but we would ask Dad to be sure.

Celia's dad is a doctor, too. A plastic surgeon. We talk about how different that is from pediatrics. He's sixty-five and has had a little work done himself. He promised her a tummy tuck for her fortieth birthday, three years off. "Oh, that's awful," I say. "Isn't it?" she says. "Isn't it totally? No one else gets that."

There's no monthly meeting in July. Too many people will be away. This is the first time they've skipped one. We've. A thread starts on the Barnboard. "This is sad." "No, it's life." "But maybe it's the thin end of the wedge." "The nose of the camel is in the tent."

"People," David writes. "Relax."

Her younger boy is Cesar. He develops a cough in the middle of July, three days before the family is due to go to the San Juan Islands with David's parents. Then he spikes a fever. The pediatrician says it's probably okay to go, though if the fever lingers he will need to be checked. The island is a twenty-minute boat ride from the nearest medical care, farther from a chest X-ray. Celia decides to stay home with him. I stop by daily with food and DVDs for him and wine for her. We haven't been alone together at her house since the first time, at the beginning of May. We've had sex at my apartment three times and once each at the coastal hotel and a Days Inn just off I-5. We've kissed in my car and made each other come and either laughed or cried at the awkwardness, depending on our mood. Mostly we've talked on the phone.

Cesar lies on the couch coughing, dozing, asking for mango sorbet. She tells me he's not sleeping much because of the cough. He cries from exhaustion and exhausts himself crying. I leave, return. So does the fever. Sunday night it's 102.5 and she calls the doctor. No, he isn't blue around the lips. No, his breathing doesn't seem labored. He vomited once, but that was after he ate a big bowl of macaroni and cheese. "Call again in the morning," the doctor says, but once Celia has hung up I think of my dad saying the important thing a doctor needs to ask himself is *Does this child seem sick?* I look at the limp little boy on the couch and tell Celia we should take him to the ER.

He has pneumonia. It doesn't escape me that in the last year of his life my dad had pneumonia and I wasn't there for him. Cesar is admitted to the hospital for IV antibiotics, and Celia weeps. She doesn't want to wake everyone at the island house and so doesn't call. She curls up in a chair at Cesar's bedside and tries to sleep while I drive to her house for her toothbrush and a change of clothes. She wanted me to post the news on the Barnboard, and I'm all set to do that from their family computer when I decide it really shouldn't come from me. Back at the hospital I arrive at Cesar's room just as a nurse is coming out. "Ah, there you are," she says. "Your wife's asleep. Your little boy will feel better in just a few hours."

After this things change. Everything is more serious, what we feel for each other, how urgently we need to be together and how urgently we need to stop. The Barn praises me for being so helpful when David was away, and he makes a point of thanking me on the next workday. The two of us are helping Margo Komarov assemble an IKEA bunk bed for her kids. "It was really lucky," he says, looking at me across an expanse of white melamine, "that you were there so late on a Sunday night."

"Dropping off orange juice," I say. It's the truth and also the thing Celia and I agreed we would say. "I had to work late." Also true. My shift that day ended at nine p.m.

"Well, thanks again. She never would've gone to the ER on her own."

"My dad was a pediatrician. I'm not smart enough to be a doctor, but I managed to learn a thing or two."

"I think you're plenty smart," he says. "You have this dumbass act going on, but I think you know exactly what you're doing."

Celia and I spend hours trying to figure out what he meant. School starts up again and we have more time. Cesar is now in preschool five mornings a week. I rearrange my work schedule to start most days at noon. "Good thing I'm having an affair," she says one morning as we sit together in my car. "Otherwise I'd be thinking about going back to work, and I'm really not ready for that."

Financially, she is entirely dependent on David. Financially, I am a joke. There's no way she can leave him.

Naked, she is an endless series of curves, the slope of her hips, the inward arc of her waist, her small, round ass. When I put my finger inside her, the first dip is like reaching into honey. She laughs when I say this and then tells me not to stop, to shower her with sexy talk, she's never gotten any from David. I've said plenty to women but never meant it. "Perfect match," she says, and then she's crying again.

We go a week without any contact. It's impossible. The whole thing is impossible. "What would we do?" she asks when we see each other again. We're at my apartment, another Monday morning. Still dressed. Holding each other like old people. "Find a way," I say. "We'd find a way. I know you don't want to go back to work, but . . ." "I was joking," she says. "Of course I would go back to work." "Kids go through it," I say. "They survive," she agrees.

September winds down. There's a big rainstorm, early this year.

Four days. The sky stays a dull gray, even when the rain stops for a few hours. Our October meeting happens early, on the first of the month. October has five Sundays this year. July did, too, and so did January. We call these long months. We go an extra week between monthly meetings when this happens.

The parks are wet, so we gather at the Smith-Berkoffs' house. Same place as last November, when I first saw her looking at me. It makes no sense that a woman was looking at me and now this. I don't recognize myself. It's weird. It's awesome.

The first half hour is milling, and then we sit in our circle. We added a ninth family, a lesbian couple with a baby, and now we are thirty. The older kids stay upstairs, but still it's crowded. Terri Batchelor leads. She announces news that isn't really news: the Kinsellas will be dropping out. Stan says they're glad they got to be part of something so special. The thing is, they feel the difference between themselves and the families with kids. Mike and Priscilla Lee say they understand but are in for the long haul. "However," Mike says, and he tells us they've been feeling that the dinner baskets aren't really fair. This is something we've talked about, how the smaller households give more than they get. Mike says maybe the households with two or fewer people should make dinner baskets less frequently than the households with three or more people. Margo Komarov says she thinks the cutoff should be three, not two. Melissa and Kat, the new couple, say that would make them uncomfortable, they're three but want to take their turn as often as anyone else. Margo says it's different because she's one adult with two kids, whereas Melissa and Kat are two adults with one kid.

We're all a little cranky by the end of the meeting. Food is laid out and people fill their plates and scatter. I take only salad and don't eat much of it; I'm not hungry these days. Celia and I have stopped talking at Barn events, but after a while she sits next to me on the stairs, where a moment ago the Rankin-O'Sullivan twins were telling me about the mountain bikes they got for their birthday.

"We'd lose this," she says.

"I know."

"The boys love it. I love it, even when it's like today."

"Me, too."

A couple weeks go by and then one day, out of the blue, she asks me to leave town. I don't want to, and we have our first fight. I have vacation days, she points out. Sick days. It'll do us good to spend some time apart, to figure things out.

I say it won't do me good, it'll do me terrible. Finally, still pissed, I say okay. I tell my boss I have a family emergency and post a message on the Barnboard saying the same thing. "What?" people write. "What is it, can we help?" I say no, it's personal.

I'm betraying the Barn by lying. I'm afraid I will lose it regardless—with her or without.

Portola Valley was childhood and then it was failure. Typically I landed at home between bad ideas and good ones, the bad always what had just happened, the good where I'd go next. I'd be there for a few days, two weeks. In the house with my dad. Then off I'd go again.

Until 9/11. I went home and stayed for eight months. From the safety and comfort of my childhood bedroom I launched offensives against my entire family, arguing with my dad, insulting Robert, mocking Rebecca, teasing Ryan about the fuckfest he and Marielle were conducting in the shed. All kinds of things set me off. People in favor of bombing Afghanistan, people against it. Someone being rude, someone else being overly polite. Oh, after you. No, no, after you.

I spent everything I had on a plane ticket to Peru and stayed in South America for a year and a half, keeping a roof (or sometimes a tent) over my head by teaching English as a foreign language. I managed to pick up enough work and to be decent enough at it to stay solvent, but I couldn't seem to get comfortable.

There were Internet cafés everywhere, but during one stretch I couldn't get online for a week or so, and a long string of emails awaited me. My dad had had a stroke, and over the course of a dozen messages my siblings updated me on his condition. The final one was from him, subject line "Don't worry, I'm OK," but it was too late for me not to worry. Three minutes of speed-reading bad news at a café in central Arequipa is not good for a guy with chronic traveler's diarrhea, and I spent the next few days in agony. When I reached him I was holding a borrowed satellite phone on a tiny twin bed in a grimy hostel, knees drawn to my chest because my belly hurt less that way. "You don't sound so good yourself," he said, and damn if I didn't spill a hot tear or two.

He was okay, apparently this was true. But each time I talked to him after that—and there were exactly three of them, three more times in my life that I spoke with my dad—he sounded weaker. "How are you?" he said the last time. It was Christmas Eve, and I knew the family would gather soon to hang stockings and eat candy off the roof of the homemade gingerbread house we were given each year by his former nurse.

"Lonely as fuck," I said.

"Oh, honey, maybe it's time for you to come home."

I was in a phone booth, and I looked through the smudged glass at the throngs of people doing their final Christmas Eve errands, couples arm in arm, families gathering before church. I said, "Hey, I should get going, but merry Christmas, okay?" And he was dead eight days later, his own gut acting up.

When I left Eugene to give Celia space, I knew going home would remind me of all those other times I went home in trouble or in desperate grief, but where else could I go? I didn't want to spend any money, not with the possibility that I'd need every penny and then some to make a life with her.

I was in a foul mood and did nothing to hide it. Hell, I made the most of it, I'm not proud to say. I was an asshole, especially to Robert, though he sort of seemed to enjoy it.

Celia and I talked—while Theo and Cesar were at school, or in the middle of the night, Celia taking her phone into the garage so David wouldn't hear her. We forgave each other for the stupid fight. I came up with the idea of selling the Portola Valley house, but I didn't say anything to her about it, not wanting to get her hopes up until it was settled. We had short conversations about Barn news, long conversations about all kinds of things. On Halloween night we somehow got onto our youthful misadventures, and I told her about the time I broke my arm trying to scale the fence around a neighbor's swimming pool. She told me about a weekend when she and a friend shoplifted twenty-seven packs of gum from eleven different drugstores in order to get wrappers for a chain they were making. "You shoplifted?" I said, and she told me that the following summer she stole a necklace on a dare. "My seagull necklace," she said. "I've never been so scared in my life." I said, "I always wondered about that necklace," and she said, "You mean why I wear it every day? It's to remind myself that I can be brave. I know it's not exactly the most ethical reminder, but . . ." "No," I said, "I wondered why you wore a seagull. I was afraid maybe it had something to do with Jonathan Livingston Seagull." And she laughed and said, "It had something to do with what was right in front of me when the saleswoman turned around."

Her seagull story reminded me of the gold cross I stole on the evening Ryan and I watched Sierra tripping on mushrooms. I'd told Celia about that night, but not about the morning that followed, when I saw my childhood toy stuck in my mom's artwork. I described this to Celia now, and she was horrified.

"That's so violent. What a thing to do. And why on earth would she put a stuffed animal in her artwork?"

I explained how my mom jumped from sand candles to ceramics to collages and then finally settled on these ridiculous collections of household junk.

"I can't imagine," Celia said, "how she could've thought that was okay. Her child's security toy?"

"Well, she never would've used Ryan's badger. His love for that thing was epic."

"But she could take yours?"

"She hated me."

"James."

"I'm pretty sure she wished I'd never been born."

"I don't know, sweetheart. Some people just aren't cut out for motherhood."

"She'd have been fine with three kids. Or a different fourth kid. I was the straw that broke the camel's back."

It was after midnight. I was at Robert's, having spent the evening trick-or-treating with Sammy and Luke. Celia had been going all day: Halloween parades at both boys' schools, two separate trips to get the right candles for the pumpkins, a hurried dinner, and an evening of trick-or-treating. We talked a little more, me alone in the dark in the family room, Celia in her car with a brand-new bottle of Pepto-Bismol in its Walgreens bag in case David came out of the house wondering where she'd gone.

"You must be so tired," I said.

"Of being apart from you. This is going to happen."

"You mean us?"

"Of course."

Excitement buzzed through me, but at thirty-eight I finally had the self-control to be a little cautious. "You mean you've decided?"

"Yes."

"So I should come back?"

"Can you give me a few more days? David's parents are coming for the weekend. If you're here I'll need to see you."

My heart was racing now. "Are you positive? Is this for real?"

"For absolutely real."

I went to Luke's room, where I was supposed to sleep, but there was no way. I was elated but also really nervous, because as far as selling the house went: it was time. Was I going to do this or not? Offer some financial stability to Celia or not? I had to call my mom, and maybe if the choice was between calling her or being eaten alive by rodents I'd choose the call—but it would be close.

I hadn't told Celia what happened after I saw my dog in my mom's artwork, but I thought about it as I lay in Luke's little bed: how I took off running and kept going until I was on the hill above the Priory. By the time I stopped I was embarrassed about acting like a hurt little boy, and I couldn't go back. The night before, with Ryan and Sierra, I'd felt twinges of misery, and now they took over. I was sixteen and alone and worthless. At sixteen you don't think that, though—you just feel it. I felt it deeply.

I ended up staying at the Priory for three days, hiding in the woods from early morning until sundown, stealing food from the cafeteria, sleeping on the dorm room floor of a guy whose friendship I bought with some weed I happened to have in my pocket. Crazed with worry, my family called all my friends and ultimately the police; it still kills me to think about it, even after all these years. When I finally went home, my dad could hardly look at me. "Give it time," Rebecca said, and she was right as usual, but I sometimes thought he was never the same with me after that. And I wasn't the same with my mom. On the surface I was the identical pain in the ass, I'm sure, but I had started to be done with her.

I tossed and turned all night, and by the time I heard the household getting up for the day, I was in the hands of full-on dread. Thank God I had Sammy and Luke to hang out with over breakfast: Robert alone and I'd have snapped. They dumped their Halloween loot on the dining table and I helped them sort out the stuff they didn't like and then bought it from them for five cents apiece. "What are you doing?" Robert said. "They don't need money." I told him to mind his own beeswax, which got a big laugh. It was time for Jen to take the boys to school and she offered to drop me at Rebecca's afterward. In the car, Sammy asked if I could come down for Halloween again next year, and Luke said that if I did, I should dress up, too. "We can go as the Three Stooges," I said, and they begged me to promise I'd be there. "And for Christmas!" Sammy said. "And forever!" Luke cried.

Back at Rebecca's, I thought that Theo and Cesar would really like Sammy and Luke and vice versa. I imagined a big family trip to Sea Ranch, all four of us Blairs with our spouses and families, and how I would organize races on the beach, with silly prizes for the winners. Celia would enjoy it; she loved the coast and I was sure she'd get along well with Jen and Marielle. In fact, with her fancy Los Angeles upbringing, she would fit right in to Silicon Valley.

Then I had my lightbulb moment. Why sell the house? Why not bring Celia and her kids to California to live in it? Rent it ourselves? We'd have so much space: the boys would each have a room, and we'd have a guest room on top of that. And the land! Theo and Cesar could tromp up and down the hills. They could play in the tree house!

Days went by and I got more and more excited about my new plan. Then on Sunday we were all at Robert and Jen's, sitting around after pizza with the kids off playing, and I laid it out. Forget selling; I knew none of them wanted to sell. I had a better idea. Celia and the kids and I would rent the house.

There was a terrible silence for a second, and then all hell broke loose, my siblings interrupting and talking over each other.

"Wait, our house?"

"I don't understand, how can you—"

"Let him explain."

"Is *this* why we went back there the other night?"

"That is the most fucking ridiculous—"

"Rob, be quiet."

"Don't tell me to be quiet, it's—"

"I think this is a reflection of how much you—"

"Don't psychoanalyze him, you're just humoring him."

And on and on until I held up my hand and said, "You guys, Jesus. Wait. Why is it ridiculous?"

"Because first of all," Robert said angrily, "you could never afford it. The Vincents pay us eight thousand dollars a month. And second—"

"I wouldn't have to pay myself, so it would be less than that."

"And second—assuming Celia would even get custody, which is not a sure thing at all—you can't move children away from their father! It's morally bankrupt!"

This pissed me off hugely, and I said, "Fine, I'm a force of evil."

"I didn't say that."

"You didn't have to. I know what you're all thinking. 'Children deserve care.'"

"Well, they do," Robert said. "And it's not just Celia's kids. What Ryan was saying earlier—there's Daphne to consider, too. If she's stressed about having to live somewhere else while they build a new house, imagine how she'd feel if they had to move permanently!"

"Robert," I said. "Oh, my God, you are so full of shit, you couldn't care less about that kid."

Robert looked affronted. "It could have an effect on her."

"So either way I ruin her life."

He turned to Rebecca. "Don't I have a point?"

Rebecca shook her head slowly. "Trauma isn't the content, trauma is the effect. Divorce isn't traumatic, but some kids are traumatized. The same is true of moving, or having your house rebuilt, or whatever. Change. Daphne's behavior is concerning, but—"

"Fine!" Robert cried. "Never mind about Daphne! Never mind about *children*." He glared at me. "What happened? It's not like I want to encourage you, but . . . Why haven't you called Penny?"

What was I supposed to say? That I hadn't called her because I was a wimp, because I was afraid? Afraid of what? Instead I said, "I did call her. She's changed her mind—doesn't want to sell." And with that I walked away.

I slipped into Robert's office. What mattered was me and Celia; the rest we'd figure out. I had to get back to Eugene. If there was an early-morning bus, I could be there by late tomorrow night.

I jiggled the mouse to wake Robert's computer, and the first thing that appeared was his calendar: November 2006. I peered at the grid, and the entire month contained the same event every day: "More of the same." I couldn't believe it. I imagined him hiding from Jen and the boys, killing time by typing that phrase over and over again.

I felt it before I knew why, a sense of uneasiness. Something was wrong. Then I realized: it was the first Sunday of the month. I was missing the monthly Barn meeting. How had I lost track? When had I stopped checking the Barnboard? I remembered being in Rebecca's guest room the first few nights and logging on every hour or so, just to see what I was missing. When had I last looked?

I logged on.

Subject: James

Monday, October 30, 7:53 p.m., posted by Sarah Rankin:

"It's been over a week, has anyone heard anything?"

Monday, October 30, 8:08 p.m., posted by Terri Batchelor:

"Was it a medical thing? One of his siblings?"

Monday, October 30, 9:13 p.m., posted by Marie Smith:

"Maybe a parent."

Tuesday, October 31, 8:17 a.m., posted by Sarah Rankin:

"That would have to be his mom. His dad died almost three years ago."

Tuesday, October 31, 10:43 a.m., posted by Terri Batchelor:

"He's not close to his mom."

Tuesday, October 31, 10:44 a.m., posted by Terri Batchelor:

"Still, I guess you'd go back if she got sick. James, are you reading this? We miss you!"

Tuesday, October 31, 11:10 p.m., posted by Adam Smith-Berkoff:

"You guys sound like a bunch of moms. Oh, right, that's what you are."

Tuesday, October 31, 11:12 p.m., posted by Marie Smith:

"Adam, go to bed."

Wednesday, November 1, 7:03 a.m., posted by Dan Berkoff:

"Has anyone emailed him?"

Wednesday, November 1, 7:14 a.m., posted by Joe Rankin:

"Leave it alone. He'll get in touch when he's ready."

Wednesday, November 1, 8:33 a.m., posted by Sarah Rankin:

"Dad, people are concerned."

Friday, November 3, 8:44 p.m., posted by Mike Lee:

"HAS anyone emailed him?"

Saturday, November 4, 11:33 a.m., posted by Sarah Rankin:

"Celia, have you heard from him at all?"

After that the thread stopped. Because David's parents were visiting, I hadn't talked with Celia in days. I hoped Sarah's question hadn't caused any trouble. The Barn meeting was at Melissa and Kat's, a place I'd never seen. This bothered me a lot, that I couldn't picture it.

I still hadn't told any of my siblings about the Barn. I didn't want them asking about it, talking about it. I could just imagine Robert telling everyone I'd joined a commune. Or Rebecca saying: *James has found a substitute family*. And who would believe that a bunch of strangers liked having me around? That I contributed to something, added value? That had never been my reputation.

I read a thread about a planned workday at the Lees': they wanted help installing new carpet. Deep in the thread someone said they hoped I'd be back in time because I was always undaunted by a new task. I remembered how I'd led the charge when the Kinsellas wanted to insulate their garage. "How hard can it be?" I'd said, and I'd researched insulation methods and reported back on what I learned.

I started a Google search of DIY carpeting. It looked like a lot of work. I thought it would be best if the strongest among us formed teams and traded off shifts through a weekend. We'd need work gloves and utility knives, which I could buy discounted. We'd need to figure out how to get rid of the old carpeting, a fancy white kind; Celia had said once you could tell there were no kids at the Lees' from the moment you walked in. I imagined asking her if she thought they wanted to replace their carpet so they could have a baby.

I reread some more old threads. One about how we might streamline the monthly meetings by using the Barnboard to express opinions in advance of getting together. Another about the process by which we decided on new members. I'd been active in both discussions. It was funny to me that I'd once assumed this kind of thing would bore me.

Finally, I went to the Greyhound site. It turned out there was a bus at one a.m.—even better.

In the family room Ryan was holding Katya, and Walt was helping Rebecca into her coat. "Oh, good, there you are," she said. "Ready to go?"

"Back to Eugene. I'm going to catch a bus tonight."

They all looked at each other, and Robert said, "We know you didn't call her."

"Rob!" Jen exclaimed.

I glanced from face to face. "What the fuck?"

"We called Penny," Rebecca said. "We talked to her."

"What?"

Ryan transferred Katya to Marielle and came over to me. "I'm sorry, it's my fault, it was my idea."

"I made the call," Robert said. "I take responsibility."

"We all talked to her," Rebecca said.

I started laughing. It was too perfect—I should've wanted to kill them, but I owed them. I said, "Jesus fucking Christ, you guys, you saved me a lot of trouble. This is unbelievable. You screwed yourselves over but did me a huge favor. She must be so happy, she's finally getting her way. One of you will have to call Vince, though, 'cause I'm leaving tonight. I've got to get back or I'll lose my job. And my mind."

Even as I was saying this I knew it was textbook James—breeze in, breeze out—and somehow it occurred to me to be glad my dad wasn't there to see how little I'd changed. It took all I had, but I said, "Shit, you guys, I'm sorry. I know you didn't want this. But isn't selling really the best thing? You said it yourself, Ryan, it's got to happen eventually."

"Actually," Rebecca said, "she won't agree to selling until she sees you."

The road to Taos climbed through a vast high desert with mountains constantly in sight. As the elevation changed it seemed that the sky changed, too, the color leeching away little by little. Rafts of cloud covered the sun and then floated away. I'd lived in Tucson one spring, drawn by rumors about the girls and the weed, but I'd hardly left the city and had never been anywhere else in the southwest. It looked exactly as I expected it to, but much bigger.

About a mile after I'd driven through town, I left the main road and headed toward the mountains. A few minutes later I arrived at a big barnlike structure fronted by a parking lot one car shy of empty. By the time I'd gotten out of the car, my mom was standing at the entrance, an angular, leathery old woman in silver-tipped cowboy boots. But she also looked like the Mom I remembered, with the same air of perturbation.

"Well, this is certainly strange," she said by way of greeting.

By way of response I said nothing.

She led me into a large, bright studio with giant square windows and a ceiling two stories high. Along one wall were long tables made of plywood and sawhorses, each holding dozens of spools of wire, from yo-yo size on up. The wire was steel and copper, bare and insulated. The biggest spools were the size of hubcaps, holding heavy cable. Scattered on other tables and on the floor were dozens of sculptures made of these wires, ranging in size from something you might put on a shelf in your living room to giant structures suitable for a sculpture garden or the lobby of an office building.

"That's a lot of wire," I said.

"Go ahead, take a look."

I was tired and overwhelmed by the weirdness of having spent eight hours traveling to see my estranged mother, whose last words to me, spoken eleven years earlier, had been "It's now or never, James. Are you going to get your life together or not?" At which point I'd walked out of Robert and Jen's post-wedding brunch and hitchhiked to Humboldt County, where a buddy of mine had grown a particularly excellent batch of weed.

"Maybe in a minute," I said now.

She smiled. "Not what you expected, right? Believe it or not, this whole thing started with clothespin dolls. You know those old-fashioned wooden clothespins, with tiny faces painted on the ends and scraps of fabric glued on for a dress? I bought a box of them at a yard sale. I wrapped them with twenty-four-gauge wire, and it was thrilling, instead of being inert they were entrapped. After that I started using the wire on its own and combining different wires." She picked up a small piece. "Take a look. Have you seen the article about me in *Southwest Art*? They said I'd become 'both more playful and more profound.' Have you seen it?"

I said, "I've been traveling for eight hours. Do you think maybe I could have a glass of water?"

She set the sculpture down. "Sorry." In a corner of the studio were two chairs and a small table, and just beyond them a foot-deep steel sink with a paint-spattered tap. She filled a smudged glass with water and brought it to me, not quite smiling but without her old irritated expression.

"So," she said.

"So," I said. "What is it you want from me?"

A look of surprise passed over her face. She fingered the collar of her shirt and then slid her hand to her throat, where she wore a slim silver necklace punctuated every inch or so by a chunk of turquoise. Her fingers found the center stone and rubbed it. I recognized this—both the necklace and the gesture—from Ryan and Marielle's wedding. I'd made my dad very unhappy that weekend, refusing to talk to her.

She dropped her hand. "I don't want anything *from* you. I just wanted to see you. It's been a long time."

"Well, here I am."

"Here you are. Overnight. I had no idea you'd come so fast. Why are you in such a hurry to sell the house?"

"I need the money."

"You're living in Oregon?"

Out the great windows, the sun sat on the horizon. A sign facing the road had listed Penny Greenway Blair along with three other names. I said, "Who else works here?"

"Other artists. They mostly quit around three. Rebecca said Eugene?"

"She's a smart one, that Rebecca. She usually knows what she's talking about."

"If you're going to do this," she said, "I might as well get back to work!"

I left the studio. It was cold out, and I hurried to my rental car. I pulled my phone out of my pocket to check the time and saw that I'd received a text from Ryan. "R says u should b there by now. Good luck."

R says. He meant Rebecca, of course, but oh, how it had always bothered me, the three R's and me left out. I started the car and turned on the heater. I wasn't about to leave without securing my mom's agreement on the house, but I wasn't going right back into the studio, either. For the past fifteen years Taos had *been* my mom to me, of no interest and vaguely offensive, and as I sat in the parking lot and felt the mountains behind me, rising dark and abrupt from the desert, I knew I couldn't see it clearly, though I understood it was beautiful. When I told Celia about South America and how restless I'd been there, how indifferent to the place, she said, "We'll go together someday and it'll be different because you'll be different." Maybe that would be true of Taos, too. I couldn't wait to see her.

R says. How hard would it have been to come up with another R? I could have been Roger, Randolph, Ralph. Imagining wishing you'd been named Ralph!

"We really liked James," my dad always said when I raised the R issue, and when I was little he would follow this statement with a recitation of the A. A. Milne rhyme "Disobedience," which I loved, especially the ending.

James James
Said to his Mother,
"Mother," he said, said he;
"You must never go down
to the end of the town
if you don't go down with me."

I was easily distracted, and this usually worked. "Say it again," I'd cry, "say it again!" At three or four years old I believed I could take great care of my mother. I wondered where the end of the town was and asked her every time we went out. "Is this the end of the town? Is this?" There were a couple years when she and I were alone together for hours every day. We spent a lot of time in the car. This was before car seats, and I had the vast backseat all to myself. I pretended to be a dog and scampered around barking or sat on my hind legs with my tongue hanging out the window.

Once she left me in a store. I was carrying on about something and after we'd faced off for several minutes she turned and walked away. When she didn't come back I began racing up and down the aisles screaming and looking for her. I attracted the attention of the store manager, who lured me to his office with a promise of candy. He sat me down in his desk chair with a handful of jelly beans and announced over the loudspeaker that there was a lost little boy waiting to be claimed. I always remembered that phrase: "waiting to be claimed." I hoped she would come faster than anyone else who might want me.

But she didn't come fast. It was a full ten minutes before she came back. That phrase stuck with me, too: "a full ten minutes," spoken by the manager. She told him I needed to learn my lesson, and for years afterward the whole concept of lessons, and therefore school, upset me.

"She made a mistake," my dad said repeatedly over the next few days. "Everyone makes mistakes."

I looked out across the New Mexico desert. In just a few minutes the sun had flattened completely, and now it sank below the horizon. I went back into the studio.

"I'm sorry," she said.

"Whatever."

"No, I am. I am. We got off on the wrong foot. I did. And now I'm stuck—you don't want to tell me about your life, and if I tell you about mine I'm just like old times, completely selfish."

I shrugged, unwilling to take the bait.

"I guess we can talk about everyone else. What's Walt like?"

"Nice enough guy. A little stiff."

"She told me they didn't have a real wedding."

"They didn't. Or at least she told me the same thing."

"I would have gone."

Just before I'd gotten out of the car at the San Francisco airport that morning, Rebecca had said, "Leaving the house out of it, don't you think it's good that you're getting this done?" I said, "You make it sound like a necessary step before some inevitable future event can happen." And she said, "Well, some things in life *are* inevitable."

"I don't know what you want," I said to my mom now, "but so help me, if you're secretly dying and wanted me to come so you could—"

She smiled. "I've never been better. A little creaky in the mornings, but I'm the picture of health. I walk, you know. Five miles a day. Let's go out to dinner. Honestly, that's all I want. Just time to talk. Rebecca said you aren't spending the night?"

Rebecca had made my travel arrangements: reserved the car, bought the plane tickets. I'd flown from San Francisco to Phoenix to Albuquerque, and the next day I'd fly from Albuquerque to Salt

Lake City to Eugene. She'd also given me five hundred dollars. "This is really costing you," I said, and she said, "The money's the least of it. I'm also going to have to spend hours in my analysis talking about what I'm trying to do. Or undo."

"I have an early flight," I told my mom.

"Do you have anything warmer to wear? It'll be below freezing tonight."

"I'll be fine," I said.

It was the off-season and the restaurant was only half-full, of people she said were mostly locals. The proprietor knew her, and she waved at one or two groups as we were shown to our table. We talked about Taos and how much it had changed in the eighteen years since she first visited. She asked about Sammy and Luke and Katya, and I told her a few stories from my two weeks in Portola Valley. As time passed, the hard edges and lines in her face seemed to soften. I asked if working with heavy-gauge wire was difficult, and she laughed and held out her hands. She had cuts and scars all over the backs of her fingers, and calluses on her palms.

"No more egg noodle bags, huh?"

"You know, it's funny. I did those assemblages for years. Then when I got here and learned how to make them smaller and they started to sell—well, I got tired of them. Wire talks back. I have a dialogue with it. Broken teacups don't have a lot to say. Why are you smiling?"

"If your wire is talking to you, you might want to call Rebecca. They may have a pill for that."

She smiled. "I'm so glad you're here."

Midway through our meal, two older men stopped at our table to chat with my mom, and she invited them to join us. They were a couple, transplants from Boston, one a painter and the other a retired CPA. I felt like an idiot deflecting their questions, so I began talking about Eugene. I even made a reference to the Barn, and the men asked me to explain.

"Wait," the CPA said. "What's to stop someone from taking advantage? He's happy to have everyone come work in his backyard, but somehow he's always busy when the work is elsewhere?"

The painter said, "Ignore him, he's airing his issues." His name was Todd; the CPA was Carver. "So is it all families?"

"Except me."

"You're single?"

"Guilty."

"Wait," Carver said, turning to my mom. "Is this your youngest? The one who . . . travels a lot?"

"I guess my reputation precedes me."

"What could I have told them?" she said. "I know nothing."

"You've heard about the doctors and the teacher?" I said. "I'm the other one."

We'd moved on to dessert, and the men ordered drinks. Carver told us he was flying to Boston the next day for a funeral. Not someone close—his ex-wife's second husband.

"He's just going to support her," Todd said.

"I'm a classic caretaker," Carver told me. "My ex-wife is very needy. Horrible to be married to her, not to mention the obvious, but we're great friends now, except when she drives me crazy."

I thought of Celia and David and whether they might be great friends one day. They weren't great friends now, but maybe that wasn't a good predictor. Would I want them to be?

"Did you hear what happened at Benjamin's opening?" Todd asked my mom. "Benjamin came up and said to me, 'Would you like to meet Carol Fishman? She's letting me bring a few people over to say hello.'"

My mom laughed, and Todd rolled his eyes.

"I don't get it," I said.

"It was a put-down," she told me.

"A one-up," Carver said. "Unintentional." He explained that Carol Fishman was a locally famous sculptor whose work was sold in one of Santa Fe's most exclusive galleries. "The thing is, Todd already knows Carol. Quite well. He introduced her to her dealer."

"I still don't get it."

"Benjamin thought he was extending this *largesse* to me," Todd said. "That he was doing me a big favor. It demonstrated his perception of me as lowly and striving."

"And made you *feel* lowly and striving," Carver said. "It was a narcissistic blow."

"I've recovered," Todd said. "Barely."

"You're very strong," my mom said.

"Wait," I said. "What's a narcissistic blow?" They all looked at me and I felt stupid, the little kid who knows nothing. "I guess I shouldn't be so ignorant, having a shrink for a sister."

"It's a wound," Carver said. "An assault to your self-esteem. Something that makes you feel bad about yourself."

"So what's something that makes you feel good about yourself?" I said. "A narcissistic blow job?"

Carver and Todd laughed, and my mom gave me such a warm, fond smile that I felt a lurch of affection for her.

But somehow that made me think about what a bitch she'd always been. Completely selfish, as she'd said back at her studio. Worse, though. Cold. Hateful. "She's changed a lot," Ryan told me right after my dad died. "She's gotten mellow." "So mellow," Robert said, "that she didn't even feel the need to come to her husband's funeral." This was maybe two weeks after the service, a week after we spread the ashes. We were all at the house, where we kept gathering for dinners. We never ate at Robert's, never at Rebecca's. Obviously never at Ryan's. Every day, one of them showed up with groceries at around six and began cooking. I was the only one sleeping there and the only one never to cook. On that particular evening, Marielle and Katya had stayed at the shed and Jen had fed the boys early and taken them home. It was only us Blairs. We were in the living room, looking through photo albums.

"She *couldn't* come to the funeral," Rebecca said.

"Because she was getting ready for a show? Please."

"Emotionally. She couldn't manage it."

"That's what I mean," Ryan said. "She's mellowed."

"Wines mellow," Robert said. "Then they turn into vinegar."

"She's less defended," Rebecca said.

I was only half listening, focused instead on the albums and what a little ham I was in every picture, striking a silly pose or making a face. The rest of the family was of a piece, even my mom with her distracted or sour look, and then there was James: blond, big-boned, bursting. I was the kid who entered your house at a run and knocked over the crystal vase on the sideboard without a backward glance. If you left an important document out, I found a Magic Marker and scribbled all over it. If I wanted a Popsicle, I took the last one, left the empty box in the freezer, and ran off without closing the door. A misfit if a misfit had no idea he was a misfit.

But I knew. I knew.

"You know," I said to my mom, looking from her to Carver and Todd and back, "thanks to you, my whole childhood was a narcissistic blow."

She began to cough. "Oh," she gasped, "oh," and she reached for her water. "Sorry, wrong pipe." She pressed her napkin to her lips and hurried from the table.

"Oh, dear," Carver said.

"Families," Todd said.

"We're very fond of your mother," Carver said.

"I'm glad someone is."

She was gone for a long time. Carver and Todd worked to keep a conversation going, but as soon as she returned they said it was time to call it a night. She signaled for the check. It was after eight, and I was beyond exhausted. The airport in Albuquerque was two hours away, and I was torn. Should I make the drive tonight so I could sleep in, or find a place to stay in Taos and set an alarm for five a.m.?

"I'm not upset by what you said," she told me once we'd settled in her car. "I had a good time tonight. Thanks for coming."

"You're not upset but you're also not sorry."

"Oh, I'm sorry. For all the good that'll do you."

"You're not exactly saying it."

"I'm sorry about my . . . distraction."

"Your distraction? You despised me!"

She looked at me through the dark. "James. I didn't despise you."

"Let's not talk anymore."

We made our way to the main road, and she turned in the direction of her studio. I realized I didn't even know where she lived.

I said, "So you'll sell the house?"

"Of course. Nothing's changed, I want my own place, just like three years ago. I didn't realize you were in such a hurry when I told Rebecca I wanted to see you first."

We continued in silence. In under twenty-four hours I'd be in Eugene, settling back in, counting the minutes until I could see Celia. Talking to her on the phone from the airport in Phoenix, I'd felt enveloped with relief that the last six months, the deception, would soon be over. I knew it would be hard on Theo and Cesar, but what Rebecca had said about trauma had stuck with me. Celia and I would watch them carefully and get them help if they needed it.

We pulled into the parking lot and my mom cut the engine. "It hasn't been so awful, has it?" she said. "You're good company. You're very funny."

"It hasn't been so awful."

"That was all I wanted. For it to be not so awful."

"Lofty goals," I said, and she smiled. "Show me your stuff," I said impulsively. "Before I take off."

"Really?"

"Really."

The studio was very cold, and she turned on the lights but didn't bother with the thermostat, saying it would take too long for the place to heat up. She had an electric kettle, and she turned it on, for mugs of tea that would warm our hands while she showed me around.

"At first," she said, "it was really about the wire. I did things like this, pretty small-scale but occasionally bigger and more complex." She was walking me from one small sculpture to the next, basically loose balls of wire twisted in different ways.

"They kind of look like Brillo pads," I said. "Maybe you didn't get as far away from your old stuff as you thought."

She smiled. "Then a couple years ago I started moving away from pure abstraction. Here's a piece I made last winter."

It was a small wire swing set with delicate wire people, the three-dimensional equivalent of stick figures. Triangles on legs, they were obviously women. In place of a head each was topped by a tiny plastic television set the size of a sugar cube, its screen occupied by an image of a woman's face.

"Whoa, this is weird," I said. "Did you make this little TV set? It's so perfect."

"Dollhouse furniture. I did a series of these and they sold so fast."

"I kind of love it."

She looked pleased. Her hair was shoulder-length and completely gray, and because of the light fixture hanging from the high ceiling, I could see how much it had thinned. “Look,” she said, “this is what happens when they get bigger.” She led me to a large piece with a central braided trunk resting on three heavy-gauge wire feet, and a canopy that looked like a giant bird’s nest. I stared up into the canopy: there were hundreds of figures like the ones in the small sculpture, wire women with tiny television heads. Each screen displayed the face of a woman from another age, with a stiff hairdo and dark lipstick and an intense look of pleasure or pain.

The kettle whistled, and she poured water into hand-thrown mugs. I thought of her ceramics and how fascinated I’d been by the kiln she got when I was in first grade. Whenever I was home alone with her I wanted her to take me to the shed, and she said only if I stayed quiet and didn’t touch anything—neither of which was remotely possible.

“I’m not sure how you’ll feel about this,” she said, “but I’m working on something new. I haven’t even decided if I like it myself.”

She led me to a table that was scattered with tiny television sets, dozens of them, most with tiny black-and-white photographs glued to their screens. Here was Rebecca’s sixth-grade school picture, the first in which she wore glasses and as far as I knew the only picture of her in existence that had made her cry. There was Ryan standing in his crib; my mom had cropped out everything but his face, but I knew the photograph so well that I could see the crib. Robert gazed dolefully from a missing piano in one and smiled up from an absent bathtub in another. The table was heaped with photos, familiar shots from our family albums but smaller and in black and white, many with their fingernail-size faces already cut out. Beyond the pictures was a row of little wire stick figures, still headless.

“So they’re going to go like this?” I said, sliding a TV with a picture of Ryan to a wire boy.

"I didn't do you yet," she said. "I didn't know how you'd feel. Actually, what am I saying, I did. If you don't like it, I won't use it. I may not use these at all. People like the women. They want the facial expressions explained, though, and they want titles."

"Mom."

She opened a covered Tupperware, took out another tiny TV, and laid it on the table. There I was at about age four, squeezing my eyes shut and smiling a huge fake smile. I knew the photo: just outside the cropping I was holding Dog. It was a picture I'd always disliked, my face moonlike and empty.

"Well," I said, "you definitely get points for courage."

"Does it bother you?"

"No, it's fine. But I should probably hit the road."

"James, really, I won't use it if you don't want me to. It was stupid, what I did with your dog. Heartless. I've always felt really bad about it."

I sighed.

"I'm not asking you to forgive me," she said, "I'm just telling you. Should I throw this away?"

"I don't care," I said. And I didn't. I slid the cube over to the others, so that my little moon face was in a crowd of images of my siblings. I couldn't imagine the patience she would need to make the things, cutting out the tiny faces, gluing them to the TVs. It would take a kind of concentration I'd never had in my life.

"Your group sounds wonderful," she said. "The Barn. Why is it called the Barn?"

"I guess because there's room for a lot of us."

"You know what I was thinking at the restaurant? You finally got your Jamestown."

"Oh, my God. What a thing to remember."

"Didn't Rebecca?"

"I didn't tell her about the Barn. Didn't tell any of them."

I thought she was going to say something about how strange it was to be receiving a confidence from me, but instead she shook her head and said, "My God, those years. You were such a little maniac."

"Guilty."

"That's what you said when Carver asked if you were single."

"I guess I did. Thing is, I'm about to be unsingle. But first I'm going to be a home-wrecker."

And then, exhausted and freezing, I told her the whole story of me and Celia. I told her more than I'd told any of my siblings—more than I'd told all of them combined. She nodded every now and then but stayed silent.

"Everyone in Portola Valley is appalled," I concluded. "Robert in particular. You know what Dad always said. 'Children deserve care.'"

She gave me a thin smile. "Yes, he always had firm notions about that. It was like he was on a mission. A crusade."

I thought of our crusade, wondered how she'd react to hearing about it. *We wanted you with us.* We had, for a time.

I said, "Well, it's not wrong."

"What about adults? They don't deserve care? Clearly I didn't."

Toward the end of Ryan and Marielle's wedding weekend, I tracked my dad down in the garage and found him alone, just sitting there on a small wooden bench. He asked if I would reconsider my refusal to talk to my mom, and I told him I didn't understand why he cared. "You're not talking to her that much, either," I said, and he told me it was different; she didn't *want* to talk to him: "She'd still be living here if she did."

I looked at her, curious now. "Wasn't the whole thing mutual?"

"I don't follow you."

"Didn't he deserve your care?"

"You don't understand. He was a doctor, it was a one-way street."

"Robert's a doctor, and I think Jen—"

"He was a certain *kind* of doctor. And when we met, I was so young."

"Twenty-two."

"But I was really younger than that. And he was older than twenty-eight."

"Because of the war."

"Who knows? Whatever the reason, he didn't want care from me. He wanted babies."

I was too tired to pursue it any further and said I had to go. There was a little bathroom tucked into one corner of the studio, barely big enough to house a toilet, and I went in for a pit stop before I hit the road.

"You're so worried about Celia's children," my mom said when I came out. "What about the Barn?"

"I'm sorry?"

"Aren't you worried about what will happen to the Barn when you and Celia get together?"

"We're going to lose it. We know that. We've talked about it."

"No, not what'll happen to you, what'll happen to *it.* Aren't you afraid you'll ruin it?"

"How would we ruin it?"

Her fingers went to her throat, and she found the piece of turquoise. She said, "Isn't that what we have in common, you and I? That we ruin things?"

10

THE HOUSE

The excavator came on a Thursday in late July, making its slow, noisy way up the driveway at 7:50 a.m., ten minutes prior to the official start time. The Blair children—Sammy, Luke, and Katya—had been promised the opportunity to watch the giant yellow machine at work and were disappointed when they arrived too late to see the first blows it delivered to the house where their fathers had grown up. By the time they got there, the huge bucketlike thing at the end of the enormous mechanical arm was bashing the part of the roof that covered the kitchen. Standing safely back in their protective goggles, they debated whether it was clawing like a giant hand or biting like a giant mouth.

Ryan hadn't wanted Katya to be there, but she was determined to do whatever her cousins did, and Marielle had convinced him it wasn't the same as watching the destruction of her own little house, scheduled for a few days hence.

The excavation contractor walked over and stood with Ryan and the kids. He was strongly built, with Popeye arms. "You don't want to film it?" he said. "It's pretty fun to watch speeded up."

The boys pleaded with Ryan. Couldn't they run home and get their dad's video camera? Couldn't Ryan, while they stayed and watched?

"You know the best kind of movie?" Ryan said.

"If you say memory, I'm going to be really mad," Sammy said.

"Got me."

"Let's call my mom. She'll bring it."

"Let's not bother her," Ryan said. "She's pretty tired these days."

Jen was eight months pregnant, surprisingly happy to be expecting another baby but embarrassed to have wound up in this situation by accident. It was a birth-control failure of a type you really couldn't tell other people, so she was saying it was caused by a switch from condoms to the minipill, which had to be taken at the exact same time every day, a task well within Jen's abilities, but no one was going to subject the story to that much scrutiny.

In fact, the pregnancy had resulted from a failure of the failure method. For a long time Robert couldn't stay hard, and so when they fooled around they were really only just fooling—until suddenly one night.

"Friends of the Vincents?" the contractor asked, and Ryan said yes, pretty much.

By midmorning it was clear to the three kids that the entire house would come down and also that it would take some time and not get any more entertaining as the minutes ticked by. But Ryan was reluctant to leave. He kept fearing a new gash would reveal something that shouldn't be destroyed, like a room that had somehow survived the final emptying of the house and still contained furniture and lamps and clothes—even people. He wanted to be there so he could signal to the operator that he should stop.

Finally they all waved goodbye—to the contractor and the machine operator and the house and the big oak tree—and got into his car and drove to the beach. They spent the next few hours building a phenomenal sand castle, using a huge supply of empty plastic containers that Ryan had borrowed from Sand Hill Day. When they were finished—all four of them wet and cold and hungry—they sat on a piece of driftwood and made up a song about the sand castle and its inhabitants. Then they drove down the coast to the town of Pescadero, where they each ate a large bowl of artichoke soup and a slice of olallieberry pie.

"I just have sand in my eyes," Ryan said when they wanted to know what was wrong. "And wind."

"Wind can't stay in your eyes," Luke said.

"You wouldn't think so, would you?"

But it did stay in his eyes—something did—and a few days later he called Rebecca and said he wanted to get together. "Just us," he said, "if that's okay."

They met for breakfast at the same café where they'd sat with Robert and James just before Halloween, almost a year earlier. It had been a long time since the two of them had been alone together, and for a while they talked about how long. Ryan thought he remembered a quick upbeat conversation over coffee during some recent Christmas, probably 2005 because it wasn't last year and he didn't think it was 2004, the first Christmas without Bill. Rebecca thought it was 2003, just before Bill's GI emergency, and that they'd been alone together since then, just after Bill died, the two of them out for a walk on a cold January morning. She remembered a mist hanging in the trees, making the neighbors' houses seem ghostly.

She said, "I guess the thing is, it's been a long time."

"Do you remember the last time you were alone with Dad?"

"Besides at the hospital? Probably a few days before that Christmas. I did his shopping for him and took the gifts up so he could see them before they were wrapped."

"You don't hold it, though," Ryan said.

"Hold it?"

"As a thing."

"No, I guess not. You hold yours?"

Ryan put his face in his hands.

"Honey."

His last time alone with Bill had been on the day after Katya's first birthday—almost five months before Bill's death. Ryan clung to this because it wasn't enough. The family had had dinner at the big house, with the requisite cake for Katya to palm into her mouth, and Ryan had gone up the next morning to fetch some things he'd left behind. Bill was at the kitchen table, dressed in his summer uniform of an ironed shirt and crisp chinos. Ryan sat with him. They talked about Katya; that was what they always talked about. "Glorious" was the word Bill used. Ryan felt so full and proud, he didn't realize until later in the day that he'd forgotten to thank his father for hosting. His father didn't want to be thanked—he'd said so many times, said "It's your house, too" to all four of them, over and over—but still, Ryan wished he'd thanked him. More, he wished he'd said something to him about the kind of father he'd been, and how much that was guiding the kind of father Ryan was trying to be. Next time we're alone together, he thought as he fell asleep that night, I'll tell him, but it never happened—Marielle and Katya were always with him, or else Rebecca was there, or Robert and Jen and the boys. Sitting with Robert and Rebecca in the waiting room while Bill was in surgery, all Ryan could think was that he was going to make the time, create time alone with his father as soon as he was home from the hospital, so he could say all the things he wanted to say. What made this so painful to remember was that Ryan wasn't the kind of person who had trouble telling people what he felt about them. He told his students every day how much he valued them, appreciated them, learned from them. He'd told his father, throughout his life, what he felt. Nothing was a mystery, nothing a secret. He just wished for a better last time alone together.

"Do you think there's something wrong with me?" he asked Rebecca. "I get so sad. Do you think I need therapy?"

"What would therapy look like?"

"Sitting in your office talking to you."

She gave him her quiet, sympathetic smile, and he started to feel a little better. Rebecca at forty-four had a wisdom he associated with the elderly. Sometimes, picturing her, he gave her more gray hairs than she had in life.

"Are you really worried?" she said.

He shook his head.

"Adjustment disorder."

"What?"

"That's the diagnosis I'd give you. You're under stress, not surprising given the huge change in your life."

"You mean the shed."

"And the house," she said. "The house, too. And Dad."

"That was almost four years ago."

"Exactly. Not long at all."

"You still haven't been up to look at the demolition?"

"No."

She'd spent a good deal of time thinking about it, what it would mean if she went and what it would mean if she didn't, aware all the while that she was trying to protect herself from being pierced—this was the word she settled on—by grief. "And what's so bad about that?" her analyst asked her. "It's painful," she said, and her analyst said, "No, not what's so bad about being pierced by grief. What's so bad about avoiding it?"

Two children in Rebecca's care had died in recent months. The boy with leukemia, and a girl who was killed in a car accident along with her entire family. These were two very different kinds of death, Rebecca explained to Walt a few days after her coffee with Ryan.

"Expected versus unexpected?"

She said she meant something different having to do with her relationship with each child: how death had been in the background all along with the boy, whereas it wasn't part of the landscape with the girl.

"I'm not sure I see the difference," Walt said, "between that dichotomy and the one expressed by expected versus unexpected."

She tried again, saying she probably never would have treated the boy if he hadn't had the illness that ultimately killed him, whereas her treatment of the girl had come about because of a sleep phobia, and the girl's physical health—her life—had never been in question. "Now do you see the difference?"

Walt said he didn't, but that didn't mean there wasn't one. He said he wanted to hear more and patted the space next to him on the couch, urging her to join him. She had a feeling that if she moved, she would lose her train of thought. "With the boy I had a part to play in his death, whereas with the girl it was much more, I don't know, innocent."

"Innocent like the opposite of guilty? You were supposed to save him?"

"Like the opposite of corrupt."

"Death is corrupt?"

"I'm not sure."

Walt patted the couch cushion again, and now she sat next to him. He'd turned sixty a month earlier; she had married an old man. "Is that good or bad?" she imagined her analyst saying, and she smiled at how she used the introjected figure of her analyst to challenge herself to think further. "You like to keep me close," her analyst said to that, and Rebecca made an effort to quiet that conversation for the moment.

Staring at the painting, she thought about her father's story of the day he first saw the land. It was September, hot and gold, and he had just turned twenty-six. He lay on the ground under the oak tree and looked up between its snaking branches at the bits of startling blue. He wanted to figure out a way to live under that sky without forgetting the other sky, halfway around the world, that for two years had seemed always gray and always to bear down on the land and sea, no matter the season and no matter the weather. Both skies were empty of heaven; both were governed by phenomena that he sometimes understood and that also were beyond comprehension. Lying on his back, he spread his arms wide and his elbow came down on a fallen leaf, dry enough that its spikes bit into his skin. He brushed the offending leaf from his arm. A short-sleeved shirt—that was his answer to Rebecca's question of what he was wearing. She wanted to be able to picture it accurately. White with blue checks. Sitting up, he no longer had to contend with the sky, and that was when he began to imagine children, laughing and shouting. "Not us, though, Dad, right?" Rebecca said. He said, "No, not you. I could say it was you, but I want you to be able to trust me. I want you to know I'll always tell the truth. Of course it wasn't you. But they were children in the abstract, and they helped me."

On a Sunday in August, Robert drove up to take a look at the house, or the absence thereof. He knew the Vincents had offered their contractor a bonus for finishing ahead of schedule, but he was surprised by what he found. The shed was still rubble, awaiting removal, but everything else was utterly changed. The driveway had been widened, and many of the trees that had climbed alongside it were missing. Every trace of the house was gone, and a new foundation was being built, the original footprint vanished and irrelevant. A bulldozer had cleared an area just down the hill from the house, creating a space that would be used for a swimming pool. And the oak tree was gone.

The afternoon was hot and quiet. Robert had offered to bring the boys, but they wanted to stay home with Jen, hoarding her last days before the baby was born. The baby was a girl, to be named Margaret for Bill's mother, but they would call her Greta because this was Silicon Valley in the year 2007, and "Margaret" was traditional without the necessary additional quality of being charming.

From the site of the future swimming pool, Robert could not at first find the remaining bit of trail down to the tree house. Logic said it should be at about the midpoint of the newly denuded and flattened area, but logic apparently misremembered the placement of trees that no longer existed, so Robert decided to bushwhack. Squeezing between shrubs, he found he was only twenty feet up from the tree house, which also seemed altered. The changes were behind him, but the abundant light made the tree house look pitiful, like a treasure trunk of jewels found by moonlight that in daytime reveals itself to be a mere cardboard box containing a cheap trinket or two.

He didn't want it left for the Vincents to find, but he also didn't want to spend the day dismantling it. The nearby fence dividing the property from the lot next door was in a state of repair almost worse than the tree house, with the strands of barbed wire only intermittently in contact with the wooden stakes meant to support them, and the stakes leaning over so drastically they were nearly lying on the ground. The fence, Robert thought, was exhausted. He saw that with very little trouble he could detach the wire from a few stakes, which he could then move ten feet onto his family's former land, creating a property line that would exclude the tree house. It would also cost the Vincents something like twenty square feet of prime real estate in Portola Valley, but what they didn't know wouldn't hurt them.

Not that he would do this. Maybe, with the terrace and pool construction most likely on a slower timetable than the house, it would be a while before anyone found the tree house. Or maybe they already had. It occurred to him that the appraisal of the house—executed back in December during the tumult of the holidays, and finding out Jen was pregnant, and negotiating with the Vincents over a sale price—most likely required the appraiser to walk the perimeter of the property. Wouldn't he have been obliged to report the existence of the tree house?

For all Robert knew, the Vincent girls played here. He wondered if the younger one was still having a hard time, and he thought maybe it would be therapeutic, this tiny retreat from luxury. Which was relative, he knew: he lived in luxury compared with Ryan, who lived in luxury compared with . . . well, no one Robert knew personally. Still, he was hurting no one by seeing the Vincents as exemplars of a new kind of wealth, even if it really wasn't all that new or all that wealthy. Shaking hands with Lewis when they finally agreed on a purchase price, Robert had found himself grateful for the first time in months, maybe years, for his modest primary care medical practice and his modest goal to supply a very nice and yet modest living for his family. People he'd known who'd gone into dermatology, plastic surgery—in some way they lived less satisfying lives because they were closer to true wealth, where distress seemed to collect like dust on the surface of his desk at home, these days rarely used.

Before leaving, he went to look at the remains of the shed. The walls lay in pieces, surrounded by bits of the life they'd contained—a metal handle from a cabinet door, the spigot of the sink installed in 1974. The remodel that had converted the shed from an eight-by-ten box into a twelve-by-sixteen structure with plumbing and electricity had taken several weeks and cost twenty-five hundred dollars, which now seemed like a pretty good deal but at the time had seemed a vast sum, proof that his father loved his mother—which perhaps meant that he, Robert, had been wondering. He spotted a piece of pottery and kicked aside a board, exposing about three quarters of a ceramic bowl that Ryan and Marielle must have missed when they packed. Sections of foundation lay here and there, and he began to explore with his toe, sliding pieces of wall out of the way, turning chunks of concrete upside down. He noticed marks, carvings, in one of the pieces—something etched before the concrete had dried, a design of some kind. He squatted and found a second piece, similarly etched. He lined them up and saw that they fit together. Someone had scratched into the wet concrete a single letter of the alphabet, three times in a row: RRR.

"It's on the foundation," Bill had said to Penny on a January night when James's birth had temporarily put Ryan in Robert's room. Robert, unable to sleep and therefore entering his parents' bedroom at a time when they believed themselves to be alone, had overheard this. "What is?" he said, and, thinking quickly, Bill told him he was talking about a spare key, a fib that caused Robert some trouble on a summer afternoon when he was ten years old.

Robert didn't remember this, but something made him look at his watch and he saw that he should be heading home. Yet he lingered, turning over piece after piece of concrete, increasingly certain that no matter how much he searched he would not find the letter J.

And this helped him. When his daughter was born a week later, he felt, along with great joy, a slight shift in the hovering presence that was his father, who apparently had not planned for James—though, Robert reflected, could anyone have planned for *James*? Regardless, by becoming in this small way less than perfect, the Bill of Robert's imagination also became gentler and more compassionate. Without knowing why or really even noticing, Robert began to breathe more easily.

It helped that Jen was doing exceptionally well. She'd anticipated a difficult delivery, like the ones she'd had with Sammy and Luke, but this one had gone quickly, and she joked that she finally understood the pioneer women who were up making dinner an hour or two after pushing out their babies.

"Not that I want you to send away the pans of lasagna," she said.

"There aren't any more," Robert told her, adding to his mental list of chores for the day the purchase of something easy to serve for dinner.

"People," Jen said with a sigh. "Having a newborn is harder when you've got other kids at home, but that whole 'takes a village' thing just disappears."

"I could send out an email to your friends. 'Jen is furious. She expected better of you.'"

"Actually, that's not a bad idea, though I'd want to rewrite it. 'Jen is so grateful to everyone for continuing with food deliveries while we adjust to life with the new baby.' That would get them moving."

"God, you're good."

"Child's play."

This conversation took place a few days after the baby was born. School had started that morning for Sammy and Luke, and Robert had been surprised to find Lisa Vincent in the parking lot at drop-off. Daphne was in Sammy's class—returning to public school on the recommendation of her therapist. And the Vincents were calling her Laurel now; Robert had gotten an earful from Lisa.

"She said the last school was too small," he reported to Jen. "Socially unworkable, quote unquote."

"Oh," Jen said. "Mean girls."

"Plus the tuition."

"Please."

"No, she actually mentioned it. 'We've got to tighten our belts.' And then she gave me this look like *Thanks to you*."

Jen laughed. The house had sold for so much more than any of them had imagined it would. $3.9 million. After subtracting for several minor repairs and the Realtor's percentage, each of the four Blair children cleared $469,325. Jen didn't trust the stock market, but Robert told her she was being silly and divided his share among a few different mutual funds, which he hoped would do well enough to allow him and Jen to do something different—something great—when he retired. Late in 2008, just twenty months after the close of escrow, his portfolio would lose half its value, but by then his outlook would be so greatly improved that he would tell himself there was plenty of time for his holdings to regain their value—and he would almost believe it.

With her share, Rebecca put $100,000 into a trust for each of her nephews and nieces, made a sizable contribution to her SEP IRA, and invited Walt to go to Europe, a trip she'd wanted to make since high school but had always deferred because of how much time it would take from her work. Vienna and London were the cities she was most eager to see.

Ryan planned to use his share to buy a house. Everyone expected him to do so immediately, to move directly from the shed into whatever new place he and Marielle and Katya would eventually call home, but he was too flummoxed to be able to move quickly. He wanted to be sure that whatever place they bought would be a place that would make them happy for a very long time, so for now they were in a cramped two-bedroom rental in a not great part of Redwood City. Rebecca had a feeling he was exercising some magical thinking, delaying the purchase of a new house so that if somehow the Vincents changed their minds he'd be able to pick up where he'd left off, in the safest, snuggest home a person could ever want. Meanwhile, he and Marielle and Katya were a ten-minute walk from Kmart, where Katya begged to go every few days so she could ride the mechanical spaceship in front of the entrance. Ryan hated Kmart, but he didn't want to give up any opportunities for family togetherness, so he always went along, bracing himself each time the automatic doors whooshed open for an overwhelming blaze of terrible harsh colors and plastic smells.

And then there was James. As he waited through the escrow period for his check to come, he thought about how best to spend his share of the money. His apartment in Springfield was as depressing as ever, and he considered moving across the river to Eugene, maybe even putting a down payment on a small bungalow, but recent history had him a little gunshy about using the money for housing. He decided he had the rest of his life to figure out how to spend the money—or simply to spend it, forget figuring it out—so for now he just bought an amazing bike. Joe Rankin and Greg O'Sullivan helped him choose, during a long afternoon at REI, and it was definitely the most beautiful thing he'd ever owned. He and Joe rode together every Monday morning, and he joined the Rankin-O'Sullivans for dinner every Friday evening. He was still the Blair, still single, but he felt deeply rooted in the Barn and in each Barn family—except Celia's.

Which was to be expected. By the time he arrived in Eugene from Taos, he had decided that he and Celia couldn't be together. That—for real this time—they had to stop. What he hadn't reckoned on was how much she would try to change his mind and how hard it would be for him to resist. He had never been able to exercise self-control, to act for the greater good, but something had enabled this, and the only explanation he could come up with was Celia herself. "Great," she said the second-to-last time they were alone together, sitting on a park bench because he'd refused a more intimate setting. "Because I love you, you can stop loving me."

"Never," he said, and then he couldn't speak.

The last time they were alone together, over coffee at a busy café, she told him she and David were talking about moving to Portland. Not because of James—she hadn't told David about James and wasn't going to—but because they'd agreed that a change would be good for them. Hearing this, James felt the loss of her all over again, but also, disconcertingly, a hint of relief, a little flicker of hope that it might get easier, life without her—that the monthly meetings could be fun again, the workdays uncomplicated, the Barnboard a place to comment on ideas or accept offers of home-grown strawberries rather than a minefield strewn with her name.

But they didn't move, and it wasn't easy. He passed her picking up his dinner basket, he ran into her and Cesar at the library, he helped her and Terri Batchelor show the younger kids how to transfer seedlings into peat pots. He arrived at a method for dealing with it: he said hello, he smiled warmly, he moved on. It was the most difficult thing he'd ever done.

He hardly recognized himself, partly because of his willpower but also partly because of something he'd gotten in Taos that was more like the absence of a thing, the Penny-shaped grievance he'd lugged around for most of his life. Maybe it wasn't entirely gone, but it was fading. He'd gotten an actual thing, too, a small souvenir, pocketed while Penny was out of the studio for a moment. After she made her blunt remark about the two of them ruining things, she seemed to feel a need to make amends and went out to her car to get him some Life Savers for the drive. And while she was gone, he had just enough time to pocket the TV head with his moon face on it. He'd made his own little wire stick figure, and he'd attached the head to the body with Crazy Glue. Finally, he'd fashioned a harness for it and hung it from the handlebars of his new bike. When he sped down a hill, the little figure appeared to be flying.

ACKNOWLEDGMENTS

Many thanks to the following for their thoughtful readings of early drafts of this novel: Sylvia Brownrigg, Harriet Scott Chessman, Ann Cummins, Steve Harris, Jamie Mandelbaum, Lisa Michaels, Cornelia Nixon, Ron Nyren, Angela Pneuman, Sarah Stone, Vendela Vida, Ayelet Waldman, Ted Weinstein, Meg Wolitzer, Steve Willis, and Diana Young. For answering technical questions or pointing me to those who could: Jane Aaron, Sylvie Blumstein, Monica Corman, Bonnie Friedman, Michael Groethe, Sina Khasani, Michelle Oppenheimer, Heidi Pucel, Tania Tour-Sarkissian, and Patti Yanklowitz.

I'm very grateful to everyone at Scribner for their warmth and hard work, especially Kate Lloyd, Kara Watson, and Nan Graham, whose early enthusiasm and keen editorial eye made all the difference. Abiding gratitude to my agent, Geri Thoma.

And for the UK and Commonwealth edition of this book, thank you to everyone at 4th Estate, especially Kishani Widyaratna, Aoife Inman, Ellen Woodley, Alex Gingell, and Patrick Hargadon. Finally, I'm very grateful to Sarah Bowlin, Erin Files, and Vanessa Kerr at Aevitas Creative Management for helping this novel find its way internationally.